The Solian's hand curved around the back of her neck, holding Heloga firmly, bringing his lips to hers. She opened her mouth under his, feeling the slave's growing lust for her, his desire to take her.

When he let go of her and stepped back, he was smiling slightly. Heloga knew that this one understood. Desire would lead to complete surrender with him, or he would take her over and over again until she yielded. Letting herself go in this slave's hands would be excruciatingly demeaning . . . yet she was as eager as a slave to get started.

Heloga sank to her knees in front of him, offering herself to him in front of the rejected slaves. She leaned back her head, jerking open her skinsuit to expose her proud breasts. Heloga wanted to humiliate and debase herself, to cleanse her mind of everything else. When the slave's hand roughly grasped the back of her head, thrusting his hips toward her, her eyes closed in a burst of pleasure. *Yes*, she thought, *use me as you will.*

The other slaves shifted uneasily at first, but the sexual tension flared and burned hotter as she abandoned all restraint. They gathered around closely to watch. Some were touching their genitals and stimulating themselves as if expecting to join in. As they encircled her, Heloga threw herself into the pit of her corrupted pleasure. Later there would be enough time to think about killing them all for participating in her degradation.

SLAVE MASTERS

SUSAN WRIGHT

POCKET STAR BOOKS
New York   London   Toronto   Sydney

This book is a work of fiction. Names, characters, places and incidents are products of the author's imagination or are used fictitiously. Any resemblance to actual events or locales or persons living or dead is entirely coincidental.

An *Original* Publication of POCKET BOOKS

A Pocket Star Book published by
POCKET BOOKS, a division of Simon & Schuster, Inc.
1230 Avenue of the Americas, New York, NY 10020

Copyright © 2004 by Susan Wright

ISBN: 0-7434-5764-1

First Pocket Books printing January 2004

10 9 8 7 6 5 4 3 2 1

POCKET STAR BOOKS and colophon are registered trademarks of Simon & Schuster, Inc.

Cover design and illustration by David Stevenson; photos © Image Source (woman) and © Digital Vision (cables).

Manufactured in the United States of America

For information regarding special discounts for bulk purchases, please contact Simon & Schuster Special Sales at 1-800-456-6798 or business@simonandschuster.com.

*Dedicated to my editors, John Ordover and
Carol Greenburg, for their unfailing support and guidance*

1

Heloga Alpha flicked her finger at two of the male slaves and one of the females. "Those three are not acceptable. I want superior replacements immediately."

The slave handler cringed and apologized profusely. "I am most sorry to have displeased you with our stock, Heloga Alpha. The senior handler personally chose these exceptional Solians to satisfy your—"

"Take them away." Heloga leaned forward and delicately sniffed the air in front of the female slave. "How dare you supply me with a slave that has body odor? And it's been sterilized by my staff! It must be something you fed it."

The Gamma handler was bobbing his head as he cut the three offending slaves out of the four dozen prime specimens. They were supposedly the pick of the slave shipments to Canopus region, but Heloga would offer only the best for her quarterly social event. After all, Canopus was renowned throughout the Domain as the supplier of native Solian pleasure slaves, so Heloga had a reputation to maintain.

It was because of Sol and its endless supply of Solians

that Heloga had fought to gain this post on the distant frontier of the Domain. This region had lacked everything else, except for Solians—the priceless commodity that was being sucked away without the requisite recompense to its regional commander. When Heloga became regional commander, she demanded a significant compensation for over a century. The result was that the best the Domain had to offer flowed into the fledgling Canopus region. And it all was hers to give or withhold!

Kristolas Alpha yawned. "Aren't you almost done?"

Kristolas had been waiting for Heloga at the Estuary, where her party was being produced. She wasn't sure why he had come. Perhaps he wanted a preview of the slaves for the party. Heloga was somewhat irked that he might monopolize a slave tonight because Kristolas should be paying attention to her. Kristolas had been her constant lust partner every six days, for over a standard year. He couldn't possibly dally with slaves on a regular basis, so maybe he thought tonight would be an acceptable exception.

"Are you in a rush?" Heloga countered. She didn't like answering questions.

"I'd like to talk to you, if I may."

Heloga narrowed her eyes at such a polite request. Kristolas was a handsome Alpha with skin nearly as pale as her own. With his confidence and commanding presence, he ruled naturally over others. Except for her, though he subtly tried when they weren't in lust. She had become deft at slapping him down. But whenever she went into lust, she welcomed his domineering way of controlling what happened. A few days ago, during their last lust, he had ordered her to grovel at his feet and beg for sex. She had writhed on the floor in ecstasy, giving up all dignity in her desire for him, confident that no one else would ever know of her debasement.

"Certainly, my dear, feel free to speak." Heloga strolled into the next room as she spoke.

"I wouldn't want to interrupt your inspection."

Heloga let it drop, knowing there was no use in insisting he talk to her. It was one of his small ways of exerting control even though he was lower in rank. It didn't bother her. She had been attracted to Kristolas from the first moment she saw him at the Arts Complex on Canopus Prime. He had been assigned to manage the complex by the Domain regents, and he had lured brilliant artists to stimulate the cultural ascent of her region. Heloga had enjoyed the increasingly sophisticated entertainment more than anything else she had acquired in her years as regional commander. Kristolas's efforts had drawn the most eminent Alphas in their creative fields from the surrounding regions to her own Canopus Prime.

There was only one problem: Kristolas was attracted to Alpha artists. This quarter it was a new singer who had mastered the avant-garde style. Heloga's security had reported seeing Kristolas in several public and private places in the past few days in the company of Olhanna Alpha. Heloga had examined the images of Olhanna and was jealous of her youthful, nut brown beauty. Olhanna was reputed to be a brilliant interpreter of the innovative pastoral melodies. At Kristolas's urging, she had consented to include the distant Canopus in her galactic tour.

Heloga refused to bring up Olhanna with Kristolas. Instead, she continued her rounds of the Estuary facilities, built over a flowing stream that could be seen through the transparent floors. Other floors had low grav for playing and zero grav for dancing and sex. She intended to spend most of her time on the low-grav floor because her outfit would look stunning there.

She paused at a glimpse of the fragmented mirrors partially concealed behind live, hanging vines. Her body-hugging unitard was black, with iridescent lines that called attention to her full bust and slender waist. Her perfect skull formed a smooth arc, but she had to lift her chin slightly to emphasize the curve of her throat. Perhaps it was a trick of the light—there wasn't really a tiny bit of slackness under her jaw. She was devastatingly beautiful. She had never understood why some Alphas preferred to use pleasure slaves for their lust. Solians were short and stumpy with awkward proportions.

"Everything is sublime," Kristolas assured her. "Except the light in the upper grav chamber should be more rosy rather than blue. I could speak to our lighting designer, if you'd like."

"That won't be necessary," she replied with a smile. Heloga passed her hand in front of one of the large spherical serving trays. It was filled with protein-stuffed shells. The temperature was set correctly, keeping the savory morsels warm. The tray floated waist-high for easy access. There were dozens of servers that would constantly circulate among the guests. The cover automatically closed after she removed her hand.

"I wish I could see it tonight," Kristolas added. "When everyone is here."

Heloga stiffened, though she tried not to show it. She glanced at him, knowing how fierce her violet eyes could be when she was angry.

Kristolas held up his hands, trying to smile. "I told

you I couldn't come tonight. It's Olhanna's opening, and I have to be there. Remember, I begged you dec-nights ago to change the date for your party—"

"I won't defer to some itinerant singer! You should have rescheduled the opening. Why didn't you have it last night?"

"The terms of Olhanna's tour were settled a standard year ago. I can't break the contract. I told you that."

Olhanna! Heloga paced over to the flock of small confection servers. Absently she passed her hand in front of one. It held small, round rhoca puffs. She picked one up to taste it, then put it back down untouched. The server closed as she moved on, checking each one but seeing nothing in her rage at Kristolas.

Finally she whirled and hissed under her breath, "How could you? Everyone will know you've chosen her over me!"

"Stop it!" Kristolas exclaimed. He stepped forward to take her arms. "You know how I feel about you—"

"I'll know it when you come tonight." Heloga held herself rigid, refusing to give in. She wouldn't allow him to disrespect her in this way.

She was certain to win her point. After all, who could refuse the senior Alpha of the region?

But before Kristolas could agree, her comm implant chimed urgently. Her Beta assistant, Waanip, would disturb her only with something that required her immediate attention.

Kristolas recognized the slight inattention. "You're getting a comm, aren't you?"

"Yes." Heloga scanned the image that flashed in front of her eyes. Waanip was reporting that two Alphas were waiting in Heloga's reception area. They had a regents authorization chip and insisted that Heloga be recalled immediately.

"I see you're busy," Kristolas told her, giving her a practiced, placating smile. "I have things to do to prepare for tonight's opening."

"Think about your choice," Heloga warned him. "It's not often that a regional commander favors a lower-ranked Alpha with her intimacy."

Kristolas stared at her, his carefree voice going cold. "I will consider that, Regional Commander."

With a slight bow, he turned away.

"Kristolas!" Heloga called out, but he disappeared through the drop tube to the roof. She would have to run after him to stop him, and that wouldn't be dignified. Yet neither was her open declaration that she was using him for stud services.

Furious at herself, she activated her comm and ordered Waanip to treat the Alphas with every courtesy. Heloga personally didn't care if she left them sitting in her office the entire night. But anything was better than thinking about Kristolas. He shouldn't have gone so fast; she could have reeled him in again. He was not an easy man, but that's what made him so endlessly interesting and exciting.

Heloga quickly finished her tour of the Estuary and signed off on the preparations. As she was heading to the drop tube, she caught a glimpse of her face in a mirror and lifted her chin.

By the time Heloga arrived at her office, she knew what she would find. The two Alphas were strategists sent from the Regents Council in Spinca. Spinca's council was the most junior in the Domain, controlling fifteen regions of unruly frontier space. The regents were quick in responding, but it was not surprising that they had sent strategists to assess the situation after Qin, a neighboring territory thought to be technologically inferior, had managed to invade the Domain and destroy a Fleet spacepost.

So Heloga was in the proper frame of mine as the aircar landed on her administrative complex and she took the lift tube down from her roof-top pad. Respect was due these Alphas, since they were the direct representatives of the Regents Council, but Heloga was still senior to them. She did pause to dial her unitard to a rich brown, simulating a Fleet uniform. She had left off wearing brown since becoming regional commander, a planetary post. But she thought it would be smart to emphasize where her authority lay during this interview.

The two strategists stood up to greet her as Waanip introduced them. Winstav Alpha appeared to be an observant, thoughtful man. He was slender and shorter than Heloga so physically she dismissed him. But she gave him a warm smile that lasted a bit longer than usual. It never hurt to exert some charm.

But Felenore, on the other hand, was hopeless. Heloga hesitated in her greeting, wondering if there was some mistake. Felenore looked like a mutant. How else to explain the oddly shaped skull, close-set eyes, and fleshy nose? Heloga's smile froze as she tried to find some attractive feature she could rest her eyes on, but she gave it up as impossible.

"Come this way," she told the strategists.

They followed Heloga into the office, where she settled herself into her imposing chair. Because of their association with the regents, she keyed a bench to appear for each of them. They began the usual dance of explaining who they were, as if expecting her to show surprise or consternation at being investigated by the "best minds" the Domain had to offer.

Heloga looked at Winstav as much as possible. Felenore's asymmetry was increasingly annoying. Her skin was practically orange, no proper shade for an Alpha, and it was marred by bumps on her forehead and cheeks. And that head! It looked as though it had been both stretched and flattened, with divots and pockmarks marring it. No Alpha had the right to look that way. She should get herself altered by competent biotechs rather than show herself like this.

"So we request your cooperation, Regional Commander," Winstav added graciously, as he finished his explanation of how the regents had sent them to investigate the destruction of the spacepost in the Sirius sector. "We are to prepare and implement strategy for the Fleet's response."

"The regents are wise to see the need for strategists." Rather than listening, Heloga had mostly been admiring Winstav's cinnabar-toned skin, accented by an attractive ruddy glow on his cheeks and smooth head. Too bad he wasn't taller or she might actually be attracted to him.

"Our first task is the Qin," Winstav continued. "We must have access to your records and logs on any interactions your commanders have had with the Qin. We will also need the intelligence information that you acquired about the activities on Spacepost T-3 prior to the Qin attack. That includes your reports on Rikev Alpha and the staff of the spacepost."

"You will have complete access," Heloga replied. "InSec has already begun an investigation."

Felenore said flatly, "We need to interrogate Rikev

Alpha first. Before he discovers there's an investigation under way."

"Rikev Alpha is on a mission to Qin," Heloga said airily. "I sent my report to the Regents Council two decnights ago."

Winstav and Felenore exchanged glances. "Your report indicated Rikev Alpha had returned to Regional Headquarters," the ugly woman insisted. "Surely you didn't let him leave?"

Heloga was not about to be browbeaten by these two. "Rikev is on the *Conviction* en route to Qin to render a fatal blow to their industrial and shipping base. He has a great deal of experience dealing with Qin and was required to assist Captain Luddolf."

"Have you received any reports?" Felenore pressed.

"We expect to hear soon." Heloga didn't tell them that the *Conviction* should have reached the outer Qin territories three decnights ago. Perhaps the next Fleet courier would carry good news.

"That is unfortunate," Winstav said thoughtfully. "But we shall probably have to go to Qin regardless. We don't want to alert him."

"You believe Rikev Alpha is a traitor?" Any inquiries into Rikev's character would keep the attention off her, but it wouldn't be appropriate to be too eager. "It would explain a great deal about how the Qin were successful in penetrating our defenses in Sirius. But there is nothing in Rikev's behavior that would indicate such a tendency."

"You leave that to us to decide," Felenore retorted.

Heloga placidly waited, refusing to respond.

"Then we will get started immediately," Winstav declared, glancing apologetically at Heloga. She softened, realizing that he probably had no choice in his partner strategist.

Heloga pressed the comm. "Waanip, bring your data-port."

As her assistant entered the office, Heloga said, "Waa-nip will take you to your lodgings. Authorize any request they have, Waanip."

"By your command, Regional Commander," Waanip acknowledged.

Heloga smiled the strategists out of her office with a distant air, as if she had far more important matters to tend to. Felenore kept staring at her, but Winstav was more polite.

When the door finally shut behind them, Heloga thoughtfully sat down at her desk. The spacepost was her responsibility, so the blame ultimately rested on her. She could have retained Rikev to offer him up as a sacrifice, but that would have been too quick to satisfy these strategists. She intended for Rikev to fix the problem he had caused, then the strategists could have him. Surely he was motivated enough to wreak the vengeance that was needed against the Qin.

Heloga pushed back from her desk. Strategists were easy to deal with. She would smother them in data, then send them down to the destroyed spacepost in Sirius. If they concentrated on Rikev and his staff, they wouldn't be evaluating her performance. From Sirius, it would be natural for the strategists to proceed to Qin where they could help Rikev finish off that little problem for her.

She had more important things to tend to. She needed to return home to prepare for her party. Perhaps a last-moment comm to Kristolas would be able to sway him. . . .

Her desk chimed and Waanip asked, *"Heloga Alpha?"*

"Yes, Waanip?"

"There's an Alpha here to see you. He came on the same liner as the strategists." Waanip lowered her voice, even though she was clearly in the hush cone. *"It's a new Rikev Alpha."*

Heloga stood up as a brand new Rikev entered her office. Like the other Rikev, this Alpha clone had golden skin and dark, impenetrable eyes. It was difficult to tell with Alphas, but she decided he was younger than the first Rikev who had reported to Canopus Regional Headquarters over four decades ago. From the way he swaggered, Heloga thought this Rikev might even be fresh out of training. How interesting . . .

"Rikev Alpha 6J–151." The new Rikev handed over an official datarod then stood very straight, avoiding her eyes as befitting a lower ranked Alpha. "I have been assigned to replace Rikev 5G–177. Upon release by strategists Winstav and Felenore, Rikev 5G–177 will be returned to Genetics Institute on Spinca Prime for evaluation."

Heloga came around her desk to get a closer look at him. Of course, this clone was identical to the last Rikev. However, as a J-series, it was closer to maturation as a clone, which meant it was a successful line. Heloga herself was an S-series. Only the more developed lines could claim the highest posts in the Domain, including regent's status. She remembered from his profile that Rikevs were noted for their leadership ability and incisive, unflinching minds.

"Rikev 5G–177 is on a mission to Qin," Heloga informed him.

The younger Rikev tried to hide his interest. Heloga had always wondered if his habitual reserve was learned or innate. Apparently it was learned. Now she was convinced that this was a less experienced Rikev.

"If he remains assigned to this region, I cannot stay at this post, Regional Commander."

Heloga wanted to laugh at his naive worry. "You won't explode if you meet your clone. That rule simply prevents confusion in the lower ranks."

"The regents may want to reassign me," Rikev insisted.

"Be silent." Heloga didn't raise her voice, but she made it clear he was being impertinent.

Rikev pressed his lips together briefly, obeying her.

Delighted with the turn of events, Heloga returned to her seat. She leaned back and steepled her hands under her chin. "I'm not sure I want a Rikev in my region. The other Rikev failed miserably in his last command."

Rikev frowned. "The 5G's performance is an aberration for our line."

"Do you know what he did?" Heloga asked sweetly.

Rikev was forced to admit, "He allowed his spacepost to be attacked by a Qin warship."

"Spacepost T-3 was utterly destroyed and is now a drifting wreck. Rikev lost his command."

Rikev absorbed the ramifications. It was undeniable that the successes and failures of those in his line reflected on every living Rikev. There were as many as a hundred Rikevs working in various regions while the geneticists narrowed in on the most successful individuals. They would donate the genetic material for the next series of clones.

"I will not fail you, Regional Commander," Rikev said

formally. Now he looked like the man she had come to know—ruthless and coldly competent.

Heloga gazed at him a long moment, letting him think she would send him back in disgrace. The culmination of events in Canopus could be a blow his line might not recover from. Then she sighed and gave the appearance of relenting. "I am not convinced, but I will let you prove your worthiness."

"You have my loyal devotion, Regional Commander."

She smiled at the nicely-turned phrase. "I'll keep you here at Canopus Prime for now, Rikev. You'll be a special adjunct, subject to my orders. I have several tasks that may be ideal for a man of your talents."

"I am at your command, Regional Commander."

Not bad, the boy caught on quick. Now she would have to see what she could do with him. Something exciting . . . and something that would serve her purpose in getting revenge on Kristolas for thinking about abandoning her in front of all Canopus society.

"Rikev, your duties will start this evening."

"Naturally, Regional Commander."

"It's very important to be prepared for every occasion when you are reaching for the upper ranks." She smiled. "I'd like you to act as my escort for a small party I'm giving tonight."

Heloga arrived late to her own party, as usual. She preferred to have admirers gathered around her rather than play to an empty room. She sailed through her guests on the arm of the new and improved Rikev.

She took it as a compliment that every pleasure slave was being used, some by Alphas whose lust luckily coincided with her party. The public sexual displays were the envy of many Alphas who weren't in lust, and they gathered around to watch. There were still plenty of slaves left to serve as personal attendants, kneeling and awaiting to obey any order.

Heloga had been informed on the landing pad that Kristolas had not arrived. She briefly considered leaving in a fit of pique, but it would be common news tomorrow that he had attended Olhanna's opening. There were sure to be raves about Olhanna's performance on the net. Heloga intended for news of her party to be higher in the queue than a mere entertainment review.

As Heloga strolled among the Alpha guests, none of them ventured to say anything about Kristolas's absence. They must have known that she had the best ears on them that InSec could provide and her analyzer would catch even the tiniest derogatory inflection.

She received many compliments on her outfit, a pale purple cloud that swirled around her chest and hips, trailing down her legs. Under the low grav, it clung and shifted in a tantalizing way. The color suited her perfectly, and it caught the eye in ways more static costumes couldn't.

Rikev was the suave sophisticate, as always, despite his perpetual brown Fleet uniform. Heloga had never seen him out of it, and apparently this Rikev was no more flexible. But the fine material and cut served equally as well in a formal atmosphere as it did on the command deck. Rikev's polished gold head gave a touch of innate elegance that many Alphas couldn't match.

She let other Alphas pay attention to her that night, and danced with a select few, including Rikev. It made her point, along with several intimate conversations she held with him. The seeds of doubt were laid. They wondered if she was finished with Kristolas.

Rikev appeared to respond to her flirtations, but only Heloga knew he was playing a part to suit her. He seemed to imply with a glance that their relationship would return to a professional tone once this night was over.

Heloga had different ideas. Kristolas needed a lesson in deprivation, and she had always had a yen for Rikev. This time she would keep him under control. She knew him inside out. He would be a delightful toy to help pass the time, and she would have plenty of uses for him. Plenty of uses . . .

Yet when it was time to go home, and Kristolas still hadn't made a late appearance after the opening, Heloga felt as if the entire evening which she had planned so carefully was a complete disaster.

2

S'jen was at the helm of her deadly new battleship, the *Defiance*. It was several times larger and many times more powerful than the *Fury*, her old warship. Finally, S'jen had the means to strike a blow against the Domain on behalf of every Ωin who had ever lived and died.

Yet S'jen's hands were clenched uselessly in her lap, because the navigational computer was controlling the minute adjustments of the thrusters. The planet Balanc, S'jen's homeworld, lay somewhere in the distance.

"Approaching target on schedule," C'vid said quietly, breaking the hush that had enveloped the command deck.

"Maintaining cruising speed," S'jen acknowledged.

Within the circle of main terminals, the spectral-enhanced imager was filled with twisting, moving rocks, reaching higher than S'jen's head. The light on the jagged edges of the asteroids had the glinting clarity of objects in space. S'jen had worked in this belt for years, mining fuel ore for the Domain masters. To her, the tones and texture of the black-cratered chips of the destroyed protoplanet seemed familiar.

In the imager, next to the curve of the asteroid belt, a small, three-dimensional replica of the *Defiance* flew next to its identical twin, the battleship *Endurance*, commanded by Captain G'kaan.

In S'jen's opinion, G'kaan should not have been chosen to captain the other Qin battleship. The Armada advisors had named G'kaan only because he had arrived in time to finish off the *Conviction*, a Fleet battleship, as it entered Qin territory with deadly intent. But that kill rightly belonged to S'jen's crew for attacking the *Conviction* and disabling it, while armed with only a warship and faith in their ancestors.

This was a new kind of attack for S'jen, one that had been determined by Admiral J'kart in command of their Qin task force. They had avoided the intrasolar slips, coming straight through the system, placing the sun between them and the Fleet installations.

Then Admiral J'kart had ordered their plasma converters off-line so that no telltale energy signatures would be revealed to Domain patrolships. Their Qin battleships were coiling around the asteroid belt on thrusters, a long two-day journey, in order to avoid the scanners on the mining station until the last possible moment. The extraordinarily long loops around the belt were controlled by the navigational computer.

S'jen was fiercely proud that her ship could land the first blow against those who had enslaved her and killed her clan. She felt the ancestral Qin hovering behind her, supporting her in this fight, especially the shades of her father and mother.

"There it is!" B'hom exclaimed, pointing at the imager.

"Scanners indicate our course will intercept a large space structure," C'vid confirmed.

S'jen could have glanced down at the helm to read the data on the navigational scanners. Instead, she watched the imager as a bulbous shape emerged from beyond the scattered edge of the asteroid ring. As the end of the mining station appeared, it abruptly narrowed to a thin linking tube. Other bulbous sections followed, one after the other.

That distinctive shape could never be forgotten. She knew its pitted surface, the sheen of the hull, and the flexible tubes that connected the segments. It brought back vivid memories of her captivity inside—the starving, crying Qin in the barracks, her own lethargy and pain, and a desire to fall into the black well of nothingness rather than endure the degradation of slavery.

As the four bulbous segments of the station appeared in view, her fingers twitched on the firing controls. Her urge to strike out was almost more tempting than she could resist. But they weren't in optimum range yet.

"No scanner probes," C'vid reported evenly. "Spectral scans indicate there's no Fleet patrolship in the area."

B'hom began to smile; his dark gray fur bristled in anticipation. "They're asking for it," he said with a glint of fang.

The admiral glanced at B'hom, silencing him. Admiral J'kart was seated on the raised platform at the front of the command deck, overlooking the main terminals and auxiliary posts around the circular room. He was a hard-edged man with a single-minded focus that reminded S'jen of her own murdered father. But unlike K'torn, an outgoing, larger-than-life character, J'kart was self-contained and aloof. Similar to how she had become in the crucible of the slave trade.

J'kart met her gaze through the semitransparent, tumbling rocks. His triangular face consisted of sharp planes of light and dark. C'vid, her comm corpsman, had early on mentioned J'kart's resemblance to S'jen, though they were different physically. His sparse downy skin was tan, marking him as a descendant of the few Qin clans that had survived the first space migrations from their native planet.

S'jen leaned forward in grim anticipation as they neared the mining station. She had expected to chafe under the admiral's controlling hand, but his attitude so closely mirrored her own that she reveled in his stern adherence to duty. She had responded to his intelligent and decisive manner from their first meeting, while G'kaan had grappled with the admiral throughout their strategic planning back on Armada Central. That was probably why J'kart had chosen the *Defiance* as his flagship rather than the *Endurance*.

This was the dangerous part, when their battleships were fully exposed. Though the Domain Fleet commanders had become complacent over the decades of occupation, the mining station's computers would perform their job. At any moment, they would be detected—

"Scanner probes!" C'vid announced.

"Initiate converter," S'jen ordered. "Shields to maximum."

The warning lights in command flashed orange, alerting everyone on board that battle was engaged. The *Defiance* came alive beneath S'jen as the helm responded to her touch. She engaged evasive maneuvers as her scanners indicated that the weapons arrays of the mining station were moving quickly into action. The *Defiance* was closing to optimum range.

Livid purple laser beams from the mining station

pierced space, barely missing the *Defiance*. S'jen calmly sequenced through her evasive patterns, but her heart was racing at the sight of the mining station. Suddenly she remembered the touch of her mother's hands smoothing her hair as she slept in her comforting lap, and for a few moments she was protected from everything horrible. Her mouth pursed at the memory of the bitter, rubbery food squares they had been forced to eat. Everything she knew and loved had been ripped away by the Domain.

The purple lasers jabbed at her battleship, but their maneuvers were faster than the commanders on the mining station expected. The Domain didn't know Qin had finally constructed battleships.

One laser beam glanced off the hull of the *Defiance*, jolting them in their seats. But the shields on the powerful ship easily deflected the charge.

"Entering optimum range!" C'vid reported.

S'jen had already initiated the weapons. Their fiery red lasers slashed at the mining station. It was a sitting target. S'jen continued her evasive approach without ceasing laser bombardment. The weapons array was her primary target, but the mining station was heavily shielded against attack. The Qin advisors had determined that this odd-looking station could survive even a suicide attack by one of their warships. But the best shields couldn't hold up under a sustained attack by high-capacity laser generators.

The *Endurance* split away and was on its own approach run. Her scanners show that G'kaan's ship was also suffering repeated laser impacts, but his maneuvers were deflecting the energy harmlessly into space. His battleship wasn't getting off as many hits as the *Defiance* because of his approach vector. G'kaan was always too cautious. He had argued for more training time for their crews to become accustomed to the new battleships, but S'jen had agreed with J'kart that they should commence their mission to liberate the occupied colonies immediately upon completion of the test runs. S'jen had spent too long demanding action while Armada corpsmen laughed and enjoyed themselves at Po Alta as their fellow Qin suffered and died on the mining stations and enslaved colony planets.

S'jen's sustained attack paid off as she closed with the mining station. The forward weapons array burst open like a seedpod as the Qin lasers punched a hole through the shields.

S'jen deftly turned the *Defiance*, keeping the body of the mining station between her ship and the aft weapons array on the engineering segment. That was G'kaan's target. Now that they weren't maneuvering to avoid the Fleet lasers, she slowed her battleship and concentrated her fire on the vulnerable inner curve of the forward command segment. That was where the Alpha commanders worked and lived.

Her fingers moved in a blur as instinctively she located the sensitive power nodes and repeatedly struck them dead-on. She couldn't let a stray laser hit the adjoining bulbous segment. That's where the slaves lived along with the overseers who did the Alpha's dirty work.

The station's shields flared and compressed, while prismatic colors revealed the stress of maintaining coverage. The fluctuations were so rapid that her terminal couldn't track them.

"They're opening their missile bays," C'vid announced.

That's what S'jen had been expecting. The mining station must have been caught completely unprepared or they would have already started firing missiles at the Qin battleships.

"Laser emitters on the starboard side are heating up," B'hom called out. "Prepare for automatic shutdown."

"Override!" S'jen snapped.

B'hom hesitated, and for good reason. If the aft laser head blew, it could take the fuel cells with it. That could destroy their own ship.

But B'hom always obeyed her implicitly. Without looking up, she could see him initiating a manual override. Now every laser bolt must count.

S'jen didn't swerve, using each moment that brought them into direct contact with the mining station.

As the *Defiance* swept over the top of the command segment, C'vid's drawn breath warned her. "Shields are falling on the mining station!"

S'jen's lips pulled back, showing her fangs. Each laser beam was calculated with precision to inflict the most damage possible to the power nodes. As the *Defiance* raked by, their laser banks swiveled to maintain their fire on the nodes.

"Hull breach!" C'vid cried. "She's going to blow—"

S'jen ceased firing. "Full power to aft shields!"

The power nodes on the command segment exploded, spewing debris and atmosphere into space. The mining station was knocked from its stable drift and began turning as it skidded away. Just as their strategic advisors had indicated, a direct hit on the forward power nodes caused a cascade failure through the high-energy waveguides. The buffers couldn't handle the surge. An energy spike shot directly into the forward shield generators.

The explosion was spectacular, as the entire command segment disintegrated into billions of tiny particles. The *Defiance* was buffeted by the violently propelled matter and energy.

S'jen's hands fell into her lap as she looked from the unmistakable readings on the terminal to the imager. The mining station was derelict. She distantly noted that the second segment had suffered no serious damage.

Across from her, Admiral J'kart's hands were gripping the top of his terminal and his eyes were burning. Something softened his mouth though it couldn't be called a smile. "Good work, Captain! It was a long time coming."

"Too long, Admiral," S'jen agreed.

G'kaan knew the plan involved destroying the command segment of the mining station, but the blast came earlier than he expected. It threw his battleship out of their attack pattern against the engineering segment.

Leave it to S'jen to obliterate them in one pass! Most captains would be satisfied to beat their opponents, but S'jen smeared them mercilessly into space dust.

G'kaan had already destroyed the aft weapons array on the mining station. Now that the shields were weakened, powered only by secondary generators in the engineering segment, they would soon have the mining station under control.

G'kaan moved his dark hands across the terminal, carefully targeting the aft missile launchers. If the fuel cells or the converter were damaged, the entire station could blow. It was an indication of Admiral J'kart's faith in him that his battleship was assigned to attack the more sensitive segment of the ship. Perhaps J'kart had also relied on S'jen's ruthlessness in quickly eliminating the Fleet commanders from battle.

This was the first time G'kaan had seen a Domain mining station. There was a menacing vastness about it, and details that hadn't been apparent in the simulations J'kart had given them.

It wasn't long before his red lasers penetrated the thickened hull of engineering. By then the aft missile ports were blackened pits offering no threat to the Qin ships. The mining station drifted slowly and harmlessly, trailed long sparkling streamers of atmosphere and debris from various impact sites.

G'kaan stood up. His ops corpsman, L'pash, quickly joined him. Her pretty face was alive with determination. Their job was just beginning.

"Keep a close watch for their patrolships," G'kaan told M'ke at the comm.

"Affirmative, Captain." M'ke was G'kaan's familial advisor, an honored older uncle from the clan of Vinn. M'ke pulled thoughtfully on his sandy chin whiskers at G'kaan's seriousness. The other corpsmen were grinning, showing their fangs, pumped up with unstoppable confidence. But G'kaan was used to being out of synch with his own people.

"You have command," G'kaan formally told his second, R'yeb, as she took the helm from him. One of Lpash's cousins sat down at the ops terminal. They both had the distinct Clan Bos blaze down their delicate noses, pure white hourglasses marking their pale gray, downy skin.

L'pash followed G'kaan down to the hangar deck. There were two compact pinnaces waiting in the bay. Both were brand new, with the most advanced systems available, but they appeared to be well-used, intrasolar runabouts that were nearing the end of their serviceable life. The pinnaces would be useful in their covert operations in the underground slave network they had created inside the Domain.

But this mission was different. There were Domain overseers on that station, and they wouldn't readily surrender since they viewed Qin as expendable work animals.

G'kaan took the helm of the *Pluck*, while his third helmsman K'so took charge of the *Spunk*. The combat teams were already packed into the cargo holds of the pinnaces. They had trained extensively for this mission.

L'pash slipped into the copilot's seat next to G'kaan. They had bonded as they worked together over the years creating an underground slave network inside the Domain. Yet they had grown closer than ever during their recent experiences activating the underground network in Archernar in order to distract the Domain from Qin. G'kaan was pleased that their friendship was developing into a courtship. He had noticed the familiar mating rituals happening among others in his newly expanded crew as lust ever so slowly approached.

G'kaan smoothly lifted the pinnace and departed through the open bay door. Now it was up to R'yeb and M'ke to protect his magnificent new battleship. No patrolship would be a match for the Qin. But G'kaan didn't want any mistakes now that they were committed to their course. The Domain had already sent one battleship to Qin, and it had taken a miracle to stop it. He was not religious enough to rely on the ancestors to beat the Domain in the future, but doubtless S'jen had no trouble with that.

The pinnace responded instantly to his touch, maneuvering away from the battleship. The *Endurance* accelerated to join the *Defiance* in perimeter patrol. They couldn't allow a patrolship to slip past and attempt to destroy the mining station, not when it held nearly ten thousand Qin.

The slave segment was intact, as was the milling segment, where the cesium-rich ore was extracted from the asteroids. The station could still be used to produce valuable fuel. Once the Domain was permanently expelled, an ore processor could be set up, perhaps even in orbit around S'jen's homeworld. That would help revitalize this system. According to their limited surveillance, the major population centers on Balanc had been devastated by the Domain. And this was only one of the four systems being ravaged by the mining stations. It was almost unfortunate that the outer Qin territories had such a rich abundance of cesium in their planetary matter. But likely the Domain would have found another excuse for exploiting Qin.

The milling segment rapidly expanded to fill the monitor. G'kaan aimed for the bay doors where tiny mining pods were gathering in confusion, their normal routine disrupted by the attack. Qin were inside those pods, so he was careful going between them into the bay. Behind him followed K'so in the *Spunk,* and he could see two more pinnaces approaching in the opposite direction from the *Defiance.* S'jen must be at the helm of the first one.

G'kaan slid the *Pluck* through the bay door. He had to pilot through a narrow corridor meant for mining pods. Rows of empty hooks ran along either side of him. According to S'jen's detailed reports, the mining pods were kept in continuous use, with fresh slaves taking over when exhausted Qin returned.

At the front end of the docking bay there was a platform barely large enough for all four pinnaces to land, one by one. Their entrance had the synchronized feel of an intricate dance, and they had perfected the routine in the simulations. Their alternative approach was to enter through the docking bay where transports were loaded with raw ore to carry to interstellar freighters. But that bay would be clogged with the larger transports, so they had chosen the more unorthodox entry.

"Activate your flightsuits," G'kaan ordered, flicking his own controls. The blue haze settled over his skin, giving an icy tinge to everything he saw. The comm link switched on and he could suddenly hear L'pash breathing fast. The combat teams were on a different frequency.

The pinnace settled with hardly a bump. The doors popped open on landing and the combat teams went through in a rush. G'kaan and L'pash held back until the all-clear signal sounded. L'pash passed G'kaan a long handheld laser. She opened the cobalt chamber to check the charge on hers.

As soon as G'kaan stepped out, he heard the screams through his exterior comm. That meant this segment was still pressurized.

The ugly whine of lasers rang almost continuously. The milling segment would be packed with overseers watching the slaves run the dangerous processing line. Radiation leakage was bound to be severe in this area, but their flightsuits were equipped with an enhanced antigrav layer that repelled particles. It was one of the latest developments from the research and development teams at Armada Central.

G'kaan flicked on the holo in his headset, and a

rough scanner map of the mining station floated on his upper left with his location marked by an indicator light. The flashing yellow lights of the combat teams quickly moved through the milling segment.

He couldn't see S'jen, but her command indicator was over to starboard, rapidly going up the far corridor. G'kaan hurried to catch the rear guard of his combat teams moving through the port side. Glancing into one of the bay doors, he finally saw the enemy. Bodies of slain overseers in brown Fleet uniforms littered the industrial floor. J'kart had approved a "scorched ship" policy in the belief that utter destruction would convince the Domain to avoid Qin. In G'kaan's experience, violence led to more violence, but the Armada advisors had supported J'kart's plan.

Yet these fallen people did not look like the deadly enemies he had come to expect. G'kaan thought they looked a lot like Kwort, the hapless Delta who had inadvertently helped the Qin destroy the battleship *Conviction.* G'kaan had spent more time inside the Domain than any other Qin, and he was convinced that the Alphas were their true enemy. The lower ranks were all subjugated to the Alphas in their own ways.

Then he caught sight of a few cowering Qin scattered among the large milling machines that filled the towering space. These were Qin like none he'd ever seen before. They were all eyes, their bodies hardly filling their flaccid coveralls. They were hunched over, timid and scurrying away at the sight of him.

"Stop!" someone yelled. "Down on the floor!"

Every Qin in sight dropped like a stone. Except for one poor stunned soul in front of G'kaan who was rewarded with a convulsing shock.

G'kaan snarled, whirling to confront an alien in a Fleet uniform. She had brilliant blue skin with small fuzzy knobs on her skull. She was scared, her eyes fastened uncomprehendingly on his laser. "Drop that weapon!" she demanded. "And back off!"

A migration instantly responded as Qin appeared around him, moving away from her. The convulsing skeleton near G'kaan was racked with renewed spasms.

The overseer opened her mouth to give another order, and G'kaan shot her in the chest with his laser. Her astonishment was clear. She reached for the blackened crater in her chest, staring at it as if she couldn't believe her eyes. Her mouth moved, but no sound came out. She was dead before she hit the ground.

L'pash clenched his arm behind him. "The combat team is here, Captain. We should go."

G'kaan shook her off, knowing L'pash was right. He couldn't think about it now. He also couldn't afford to be distracted by L'pash. But he admired how brave she was without having a trace of viciousness in her.

One of the Armada combatants switched frequencies. "We'll clean out this compartment, Captain."

"Affirmative," G'kaan agreed.

He glanced back at the cowering Qin, who didn't seem to comprehend what was happening. Then he rapidly made his way to the central locks that led to the slave segment. Thousands of slaves were housed in that segment when they weren't out in the mining pods or working at milling machines.

If the Fleet counterattacked, they would do it here and it would risk every one of the helpless Qin slaves.

S'jen was there before him. Her lips were drawn back, showing her fangs. She was in high blood lust, her laser clenched tightly. She had probably cut a wider swath through the milling segment than the combat teams.

As the locks were opened between the segments, G'kaan found himself gazing at S'jen. There used to be a rare, distinguished beauty in her face. But now it was a death mask. Her flesh was nearly as shrunken as the flesh of that skeletal slave back in the milling segment. She was wasting away in her fanatic fury.

He could hardly believe that this was the same S'jen he had known for most of his adult life. How could this be the woman who had murmured words of love during their extended days of lust? He had joined with her twice, but she had publicly refused him the last time. It had torn his life apart, though they had hardly been partners outside the few days of lust the Qin experienced every four standard years. But the tie between them had been undeniable.

He had seen her passion and fury even in lovemaking. S'jen had always been a rough partner, especially in the initial passionate phases of lust. But once she began to be satisfied by their joining, a softer side emerged. It was one that G'kaan had rarely experienced. But he had seen her eyes linger with longing on his face, and her hand had felt defenseless in his warm grasp. He had yearned to protect that hurt, little girl, and he had loved S'jen more deeply than he had admitted to himself until now. But anger had overridden his former feelings of tenderness.

Now, looking at S'jen, at her determination to kill, he knew that she was more dangerous than any of these poor Fleet fools who simply had the bad luck to be assigned to work on a mining station in Qin.

His hands tightened on his laser, swinging it toward

S'jen. For one wild moment he fought his desire to remove this blight on the honor of Qin. Despite her heroics, S'jen was not what people thought her. She was destruction incarnate.

As S'jen rushed through the door in the midst of the combat teams, G'kaan hoped that someone would end her life right here. But that was not S'jen's fate. She would smash everything in her quest to liberate her people. G'kaan could only follow along in her wake, picking up what pieces he could find.

3

Rose confirmed the report with navigational scanners. "The *Endurance* and the *Defiance* are on close perimeter patrol."

Knowing that the Qin were guarding the area didn't make Ash feel any better. S/he was at the comm watching the scanner displays as hir stomach clenched in fear. Their old freighter, the *Purpose*, was cruising beside the ring of asteroids in Balanc. They had been instructed to wait with five other transports outside the solar system while the Qin battleships attacked the Domain mining station and eliminated the patrolships. After days of waiting, a Qin warship had returned, reporting that the campaign had been successful. Now their transports were en route to the mining station.

But Ash was worried. S/he knew how ruthless the Alphas of the Domain were. S/he had suffered years of abuse as a pleasure slave even though s/he was an expensive rarity—a herme with dual sex characteristics. S/he still looked like a teen-aged boy even though s/he was four decades old, but s/he hadn't truly lived until Rose Rico had liberated them.

Rose grinned at hir from the helm. "Got a problem, Ash?"

Ash couldn't return the smile. "I guess I don't like being this close to a Domain space station."

"Who does?" Rose flashed her dramatic dark eyes, fringed with black lashes. "But the Qin already beat the Fleet patrolships out of this system days ago."

Ash thought that was easy for Rose to say. Rose was born on Earth, but unlike other natives, she had miraculously survived the shock of being abducted into the slave trade. Instead of wasting away, Rose had led a group of Solian slaves and escaped from the Domain to the promised freedom of Qin. The freighter, *Purpose*, was now their home.

"I wish we'd had better luck finding supply runs in Qin," Ash had to say.

Rose laughed. "I wouldn't miss this for the world. We're massacring them!"

Ash thought it would have been better for their inexperienced crew to learn their trade on a steady supply run, as most freighter crews did. But nobody wanted to do business with an amateur crew. Maybe if they'd had more time they could have done some free runs to prove themselves. But they desperately needed supplies for themselves and the two hundred Solians who were now living in the distant Qin colony on Prian. Ash felt personally responsible for the slaves because they hadn't chosen to escape from the Domain and become fugitives. They had been locked in cargo containers on board the *Purpose* until Rose and her crew had arrived safely in Qin. But they weren't slaves anymore, and neither was Ash. S/he rubbed the back of hir neck where the collar had rested for most of hir life. S/he still felt an instinct to obey any command, yet s/he was learning rapidly to think for hirself. S/he had to because s/he was Rose's second-in-command.

When Captain G'kaan offered them an Armada contract to transport Qin slaves from the Fleet mining stations back to their homeworlds, Rose had jumped on it. Some, like Ash, wanted to stay far away from anything concerning the Domain. But they had no other options.

On Ash's terminal, the energy readings spiked, then were blanked out by the interfering asteroids.

"I see it!" Ash examined the readings carefully on the comm scanners. "The mining station should be coming into view soon."

Rose checked her navigation terminal again. "This is it, everybody. Stay sharp!"

Rose leaned forward as if eager to meet the Fleet. Ash figured the irrepressible girl wouldn't mind if there were a few Alphas left in Balanc to kick around. Rose hadn't calmed down a bit since they had helped G'kaan destroy the Fleet battleship, *Conviction*. If anything, she was bolder and more brash than ever.

"It's about time," replied Stub. He was one of the new crew members, who had taken over at ops. He had been among the two hundred slaves in the cargo holds of the *Purpose*. Mote had asked for Stub's help because he had space experience, having served as a pleasure slave for the crew of a huge spaceliner that catered to vacationing Betas in the Antares region.

Another new crew member, Newt, didn't have any particular skills, but Chad had grown attached to her while they were relocating the Solians to Prian. Chad wasn't easy to get along with, but he was better around the sweet-tempered Newt. They were all glad to have her on board.

"Energy emissions are low," Ash said thoughtfully.

"Look!" Rose pointed at the imager.

A three-dimensional image of the mining station faded into view among the asteroids. The station was huge with three bulbous sections. One end was blackened and a connector section was dangling some mangled bulkheads.

"They ripped its head off!" Rose cried out in glee.

Stub whistled in amazement.

Ash checked hir readings to be sure. "The command segment is missing."

"Got 'em in one whack! That was S'jen, you can bet on it," Rose said knowingly.

Stub was laughing along with Rose. But Ash shuddered, knowing the Alphas would be incensed when they saw this.

Another energy reading spiked Ash's comm terminal. "We're being hailed by a Qin warship. We're ordered to get into the queue on the starboard side. They want to start loading Qin right away."

"Looks like it will be a short stay." Rose glanced at the railing that overlooked engineering. The enclosed cargo section lay beyond. "Ash, call Jot up here to replace you. I want you to go down and make sure things run smoothly with the transfer. Mote will need all the help she can get."

At Ash's call, Jot came running, eager to participate in the operation that would rescue slaves from the Domain. Ash was also feeling better now that it was clear the Domain masters weren't lying in wait to pounce on them. S/he was going to have to learn not to panic at every prospect of meeting up with a Fleet patrolship.

As s/he approached, s/he saw Kwort standing at the doorway into the cargo area. He had apparently been watching their approach on the nearby monitor. Even though he was in charge of supervising the bot techs, he twitched as if he'd been caught doing something wrong.

"The mining station got pretty torn up, didn't it?" Ash hoped to put him at ease. Unlike some of the others, s/he had no fear of Kwort even though he was a Delta.

As Ash joined Kwort at the doorway, s/he saw the dark brown circles around his eyes, and the waxy sheen of his ridged, bald head. He seemed sick, as if he hadn't really slept since he came on board. But he summoned the energy to report. "The cargo containers are operating on full recycle mode. They should be able to handle three hundred passengers."

"They're going to be squeezed in there." Ash remembered hir own time in one of those cargo containers with only nine other people. "Fifteen in each is a lot."

In Ash's opinion, Kwort had suffered as much as any slave on the *Purpose*. It was his actions that had resulted in the death of everyone he knew onboard the *Conviction*, included Horc, his lover and superior officer. He was an exile from the Domain because of it.

Ash had urged the Solians to take Kwort on as a crew member. His expertise with bots was undisputed, but his loyalty was questioned. But Kwort had no reason to hurt the Solians. The Qin at Armada Central had practically bullied him into suicide until Ash had mercy on him and brought him on board the *Purpose*. Kwort himself won over the Solians by being as inoffensive and meek as a slave. Like a starving man, he had devoured the extensive bot work that the *Purpose* required. Ash had seen very little of him since.

"Feel that?" Kwort said. "We've docked. They'll open the airlock soon."

Ash stepped into the corridor. Mote was at the airlock along with Chad, preparing to pop the hatch on their side. "Did you get the atmosphere balanced to Qin specifications in the holds?"

"Yes, to within point eight percent." Kwort wearily passed a hand over his ridged head. "Whit's not a bad tech considered he hasn't been trained."

"I feel much better now knowing you're watching over the bots," Ash assured him. "But you're working too hard."

Kwort briefly shook his head.

"You need to get some sleep," Ash insisted quietly.

He didn't meet her eyes. "I see them when I sleep."

Ash wasn't sure what to say.

"Then it feels worse when I wake up." Kwort shuddered as if remembering the fireball that had engulfed the *Conviction* and the crew along with it.

Ash wished s/he could say something to comfort him. "Maybe it's the sort of thing you have to feel really bad about in order to eventually let go. I'll talk to you anytime if you want."

Kwort muttered something, his head so low that s/he couldn't see his face.

The possibility of putting a comforting hand on his arm didn't enter hir mind. Ash didn't touch anyone or willingly let them touch hir.

"Here they come!" Mote called out. She manipulated the controls and the airlock slowly swung up.

A towering Qin corpsman appeared in the airlock, suspiciously checking out the corridor beyond. "This way," the Qin called behind her, urging the others forward.

A much smaller Qin appeared, thin with patchy down. Ash couldn't tell if it was a man or woman. Suddenly s/he knew what others felt when they looked at hir. It was disorienting because gender was the first thing everyone, including hir, was conditioned to see. But this Qin wasn't a herme, Ash was certain. This poor thing had been starved and beaten until gender was undeterminable.

The first shivering, frightened Qin was followed by another, and another. They clung to each other, pushing through the airlock in sick little clots.

Ash wasn't sure what s/he expected—maybe shouts of joy and thankfulness at being rescued. But s/he remembered how hir fellow Solians had reacted to freedom, with most of them still afraid a word could bring them to their knees. A few, like Dab and Jot, had stayed in their berths, waiting for someone to tell them what to do.

These Qin still wore the hated Domain collar around their necks. Without thinking, Ash rubbed the callused skin on hir shoulders. Hir own collar had been removed by S'jen, and that experience had been both disturbing and liberating. Ash had never brought charges against S'jen for kidnapping hir and raping hir mind in order to get information about Rikev. S'jen was able to pinpoint his location because of it, and now Rikev was dead. S/he could hardly believe it, even though s/he had seen the logs of the destruction of the *Conviction.*

It all flashed back too quickly, leaving hir panting in distress. But Kwort didn't notice. He was transfixed by the steady line of starving Qin stumbling down the corridor. Mote and Chad looked similarly stricken at the sight.

"They're almost dead!" he whispered to Ash.

"The Alphas don't care how many slaves they destroy," s/he managed to say. "There's thousands of planets they can subjugate after these people die."

Kwort looked appalled, as well he should. The Qin were beyond skinny; their bones stuck through papery skin that had lost most of its down. Arms and legs were narrower than the joints. Their skulls were huge in comparison, though their cheeks were deeply sunken in and their eyes glassy with fear. The shiny silver collars looked hard and vicious hanging around their spindly necks.

"Were you like this?" Kwort blurted out.

Ash pressed hir lips together. "They keep pleasure slaves hungry to give us the slender proportions Alphas like." S/he thought with satisfaction of hir fellow Solians who had put on weight and glowed with a health and vitality they had never felt before. "But it didn't get this bad."

The Qin continued to shamble by, filing listlessly into the cargo space where the open containers waited for them. A couple of Qin combat teams were in the cargo area coordinating the loading.

"We were tortured in other ways," Ash added, looking at him sideways. "Some Deltas treated me worse than the Alphas did."

Kwort was shaking his head as if he couldn't believe it, but he also couldn't deny it. He had been persecuted by his fellow Delta crew members to the point that he had disabled his own ship while attempting to retaliate. That mistake had ended in the utter destruction of the *Conviction*.

One of the Qin staggered and listed to one side. Ash reached out to catch her.

The Qin looked blearily up and abruptly began to scream.

Ash leaped back as the woman fell and began to thrash on the floor as if she had been shocked by the collar. The other slaves cowered back while the Armada corpsmen rushed forward, threatening Ash.

Ash backed into engineering along with Kwort, overpowered by the menacing Qin corpsmen. "Get out of here! All of you!" they shouted.

Mote and Chad were rushed from the corridor by angry hands. "Hey! We're here to help!" Chad protested.

"Only Qin can help Qin!" someone yelled back. A burly Qin stood with his arms folded in the doorway. With his triangular face and heavy lowered brows, he glared better than any other humanoid Ash had ever seen.

"It's *our* ship!" Mote retorted hotly. Chad was starting to bluster as if ready to shove the Qin out of the way.

Ash took control. "Let the Qin do the loading. Mote and Chad, you wait here until everyone's in the cargo bay, then you can close the airlock."

The Solians faced the Qin warily, but Mote coolly agreed while Chad satisfied himself with glaring back at the Armada corpsman.

Ash was amazed at how quickly s/he had handled that problem. Who would have thought that such a humble herme would be in position of authority? S/he stood taller because of the responsibility. S/he had never imagined what freedom would be like when s/he was a slave—the very idea was preposterous. But somehow s/he had gotten the life s/he would have longed for if s/he had only known it was possible.

S'jen had seen the shock of her fellow Armada corpsmen at the sight of the slaves when they stormed the mining station. What did they expect? Their distress had been childish and simply proved her right. They had refused to listen to her, even though she was the one who knew the tragedy of being a slave.

She had assigned C'vid to log the Qin slaves and the conditions they lived in. C'vid worked nonstop. She knew how important it was to show the Clan Council why they had to fight against the Domain with every breath in their bodies. C'vid had been a slave too, in this very mining station.

When the transports had been fully loaded, leaving half the slaves still on the damaged mining station, S'jen's battleship escorted the first wave back home to Balanc. G'kaan stayed to protect the slaves left behind, since Fleet patrolships moved continuously among the occupied territories.

It took a full day to reach S'jen's homeworld. As they pulled into scanner range, she magnified the planet in the imager. The atmosphere was a rich violet with purple-tinted clouds from the high levels of metal particulates suspended in the air.

B'hom's mouth moved silently, as if he were saying an ancestral prayer.

"We're home!" C'vid cried out, a rare emotion choking her voice.

The planet looked exactly like a holo S'jen had seen as a girl hanging behind her father's desk. For a moment, she was lost in the precious memory she had forgotten. As a child, she had felt a secure sense of wonder about her world and the galaxy . . .

Then she refocused again. "Targeting the orbital facility with missile tubes one through eight."

Admiral J'kart nodded once. If their battleship was

detected, there was too great a risk that the orbital station would fire on the populace below as a way to forestall their attack. S'jen's plan entailed some risk, but it would be effective.

S'jen had the calculations at her fingertips. "Missiles programmed, armed and ready."

"Proceed," J'kart ordered, taking responsibility for the lives that could be lost if any of the missiles hit the planet instead of the Fleet's orbital station.

Despite the complete success of their first mission, the admiral had remained cold and formal. S'jen preferred it that way. She had never appreciated the joyous celebrations of the crew after their warship destroyed a mere freighter. Those victories had been minor. She wouldn't celebrate until every Fleet ship was either destroyed or retreating back to the Domain.

Her plan required that the *Defiance* wait outside the scanner range of the orbital station while the missiles shot forward. It would be far more difficult for them to detect the incoming stealthed missiles. Once the commander of the oribital station did see them and began sending out countermissiles, his crew would likely be too busy to target the colonists on the planet.

A few moments later, S'jen released the second salvo.

S'jen's own simulations had indicated that some Qin would die when they liberated Balanc. She considered it a small price to pay to rid themselves of these tormentors.

By the time the last missile destroyed the orbital facility, S'jen was en route with the *Defiance*. One missile had been driven off course by a Fleet countermissile. It was caught by the gravity pull of the planet and began its dive.

They watched silently. Without current population

maps, they didn't know if the missile was going to hit the colonists below. When the missile impacted, sending a plume into the atmosphere, C'vid and B'hom let out groans of anguish. S'jen didn't blink.

Instead, when they reached the now defenseless planet, S'jen laid waste to the ground facility that housed the Domain overseers. The handful of Qin inside those buildings were martyrs to the ancestors and would bless her in the battle against their oppressors.

When she was through with the lasers, the site was a deep blackened pit.

S'jen took the helm of her pinnace and brought C'vid and B'hom down to their home planet. As the *Wrath* descended, S'jen used the scanners to check both continents. There were only Qin readings, and not many of those.

She performed a high orbital survey of the clan areas for Moch and Treln, C'vid and B'hom's clans. "It looks like there's not many clansmen left," S'jen told them with regret. The Moch islands appeared to be almost completely under water.

As they descended, S'jen altered course to make a high pass over the southern coastline where the Huut, her clan, had lived and prospered. What had once been a home to half a million Huut now contained a few thousand people in small clumps here and there.

It enraged her to the point that she couldn't think about it. She had known that her clan was destroyed. She had known it from the first laser bombardment, which demolished her compound. Huut had stood against the Domain and fought back as hard as they could, so they were decimated.

She brought the pinnace down much farther inland

on the southern continent, landing next to the Domain facility in the heart of the farmlands. The Qin who had served as farmhands were kept in open electrified pens. The slaves were stunned by their arrival, much like the poor sick workers on the mining station. But these Qin had some life in them yet. When they were let out, they saw the pit where the Domain had once ruled from. S'jen was surrounded by grateful Qin while all she could do was mourn the loss.

S'jen went mechanically about her duties after that, detached from everything around her. The slaves from the mining station needed to be ferried from the space transports down to the planet. But there were only a handful of air-to-space ships available. So S'jen assisted with her pinnace, the *Wrath*.

Meanwhile the combat teams led the slaves in breaking into the Domain storehouses. They began distributing food via grav sleds to hundreds of locations where there were life-sign readings. Most of the scatted Qin were hiding and salvaging in the ruins of the extensive compounds. The pilots didn't report seeing anyone.

After a long hard day of shuttling mining slaves down from the interstellar transports, S'jen completed her last scheduled trip. She managed to return to the planet in time for the day's dedication in the main staging area near the farmland warehouses. There were several thousand former slaves from the mining station as well as the farmhands milling about in the landing area. Less than half the mining slaves were left on the transports in orbit.

Since the food was located in the warehouses, a tent city was being created nearby. They had looted the fabrics made in a local factory, formally staffed by Qin slaves. That's when S'jen heard the ugly gossip about

Qin who had become semi-overseers themselves. These Qin had quickly disappeared and they would not receive the death rites that would bind them forever to the ancestors who would forever guide the living.

All the Qin stood together facing the setting sun, separated from each other yet joined in one sprawling mass. They said the words that dedicated the day and their deeds to the ancestors.

S'jen stood on her native soil, sustained by air that had been breathed by her ancestors. She was surrounded by her fellow Qin, who had felt the terror of the Domain as surely as she did. She lifted her bared chest to the dying sun and cut her skin with the knife, offering a sacrifice of her blood to the ancestors.

"In the name of our ancestors," she cried out along with the others. "Clan of Huut!"

But nothing happened. She had to look down to be sure she was bleeding. There was no pain.

She had never felt more alone. The ancestors who had driven her home, even the constant physical presence of her father, was stilled. Perhaps this was peace. Yet she felt nothing but emptiness.

After the ceremony, C'vid found S'jen. Her expression was eager as she pulled a young man behind her. "S'jen! Look who I found!"

The boy was bony and hunched, old despite the fact that he must still be a teenager. A shiny slave collar was around his neck. It would take time for them to organize the removal of everyone's collars.

C'vid added, "This is E'ven . . . Clan of Huut."

S'jen looked more sharply at the young man. "Huut? Are you sure?"

"Yes," E'ven answered for himself. "My father was R'cob of Huut. We lived in the Anterris valley before—" He broke off, turning his head.

S'jen knew that look. He was telling himself not to feel anything. His dark face was grim and he was young to be that hard. She had been about his age when she had escaped from the mining station, taking C'vid and B'hom with her.

She opened her arms and gave him the proper clansman greeting. It felt strange. He clung to her for a moment, while she wanted to pull away. She hadn't been physically close to anyone since the last lust she shared with G'kaan. It was as though she didn't know how to be near anyone anymore.

Uneasy, she kept looking at him. E'ven shuffled his feet in the gravel, equally uncomfortable under her scrutiny. But she could see his resemblance to the dark gray Huut who had lived in Anterris. She had often traveled with her father, and the Anterris valley was one of the main north-south routes on the Huut coastline.

Suddenly she had to see Huut. All day she had remembered images of a place filled with brilliant colors and graceful forms. She recalled faces of people who were family in one way or another, known her whole life. And favorite places like the windowseat she had loved, where she could curl up and look out at the sea.

She had to confront her loss. She knew, because Huut had confronted her in this young man with his emaciated body.

"I'll take you to Huut," she heard herself say. "I'm going there now."

E'ven opened his eyes wide. "They said it would be decnights before we could be shuttled to our homes."

S'jen exchanged a glance with C'vid. "Huut was severely damaged according to our scanner readings."

"All I've ever known of Huut is ruins. And I haven't seen that since I was a boy." E'ven eagerly added, "There are a few others from Huut. Can they come too?"

"Meet us at the *Wrath*. We have to be quick. The sun will be setting soon in Huut."

In all, there were seven Clan Huut members strapped into the back of the pinnace when S'jen returned. She looked at them closely but they were like the rest of the starving slaves. None were from her compound.

She was luckier that C'vid, who had found no other Mochs alive. S'jen had flown C'vid over her island home on one of their returns. Many of the islands were missing, smashed beneath the waves, while others were desert wastelands from shore to shore. C'vid had not said a word about it, but S'jen knew that she was equally dissatisfied with their victory. They had worked for so long to liberate Balanc, and now it was clear their past was gone forever.

S'jen flew the pinnace over familiar mountain ranges and rivers that turned exactly where she expected. Out in the wilderness, things looked surprisingly normal. For a moment, she could almost imagine that she was flying home from an instructional exchange with another clan, and her father would be waiting for her in the evening room.

But that was dangerous, and S'jen forced herself to concentrate on flying the pinnace. C'vid scanned for life signs and transferred an overlay to S'jen's terminal. There was a group of about sixty people living in the hills on the coast, in the middle of the long strip of Huut land. That was the Penakost compound, where she grew up.

The Penakost compound had once been a series of family complexes and graceful terraces sprawling across a cleft in the mountainside along the coast. Now it was hills and landslides of rubble. Gardens had once marched down to the turquoise sea, but now foliage struggled to grow amid the chunks of plascrete. As a child, S'jen had rolled down the steep streets on every wheeled toy known to Qin, graduating to faster and faster equipment until she was known for her daring. Her father had liked that about her, and always encouraged her to greater feats.

S'jen set the *Wrath* down carefully on one of the mounds near the edge of the Penakost compound. Native plants filled the distant hillsides where the plascrete piles stopped.

She realized C'vid was staring at her. S'jen stood up and clenched her hands together in front of her. This wasn't Huut, but it was the only Huut left.

They unloaded the food supplies from the pinnace with the help of a few of the stronger Huut. E'ven pitched in and he seemed to be the healthiest of the former mining slaves.

The land around them was utterly devastated, so she couldn't tell which slope had held her family complex. But she had the same view of the sea, with towering purple clouds filling the horizon. The breeze carried the scent of rain, as it always did in the late summer. But even that was ruined by the stench of burned plastics and decay. After nearly two decades, the place still smelled toxic.

But there were people somewhere close by. The few pitiful remains of Huut.

One of the men called out, "We are Huut! Our fellow Qin liberated us! The mining station was destroyed!"

He kept turning and yelling out. S'jen wasn't sure it would do any good.

C'vid seemed to agree. "They probably think it's a trap."

E'ven shook his head, resting a bony hand on the *Wrath*. "This looks Qin. Fleet ships are angular."

S'jen realized he was right. The grav sleds had been Fleet; that was why no Qin had showed themselves during the food dropoffs. But her pinnace was roughly egg-shaped, as all Qin vessels were.

As if prompted by E'ven's comment, people began to appear in the ruins around them. They were as dirty as the piles of plascrete. Some disappeared when S'jen looked in their direction, as if they were so used to hiding that they couldn't stop. Others stood far away, wanting to believe but frightened after a generation of subjugation by the Domain. These Huut had gone feral in order to survive.

The Qin who were still wearing collars hurried into the ruins to meet their fellow Huut. E'ven scrambled over two tilted slabs to reach another young man. Their first contact was tentative, but soon enough some of the Huut had gathered on the hill, touching the pinnace in wonder.

C'vid was adored when she passed around a dataport that played their battleship's attack on the mining station and the Domain facility in the farmlands. When they saw that nothing was left except a deep empty hole, they were overcome with emotion. The former slaves had had enough time to adjust to their release, and they joined in wholeheartedly.

They exchanged family names but S'jen didn't find any relatives. But she was from this very compound, and the same leaders once ruled them. S'jen named her father K'torn and saw the respect in the elders' eyes.

The mining slaves S'jen had brought home expressed more emotion than she had seen during the entire liberation. But it didn't touch her. If these people were Huut, then she was no longer Huut. She had become something different in her quest for justice.

The sun began to set on S'jen for the second time that day.

"We have to get back to the battleship," S'jen told the Huut. "They need the *Wrath* to bring the other Qin down."

C'vid and S'jen began making preparations to leave, but E'ven seemed unhappy. "Are you coming back?" he asked.

S'jen hadn't expected that question, but C'vid answered for her, "There are many Huut who will be coming home to help you rebuild, E'ven."

"But she's Huut," he said, gesturing at S'jen.

S'jen finally spoke, "I'll return when Qin is free."

They finished their preparations and warned the Huut to stand back. Some carried the food out into the ruins where many of the Qin waited, still too afraid to show themselves.

At the last moment, E'ven ran to the door of the *Wrath*. "Take me with you!"

S'jen shook her head. "We're going into battle, E'ven. It's too dangerous."

"It's not too dangerous for you!" he protested. "I have to help you fight them."

C'vid was shaking her head. "But you're too young to know what you're doing—"

S'jen raised her hand. "I was his age when I dedicated my life to defeating the Domain." She turned to E'ven. "Think about this carefully, E'ven. You can stay here with all honor in serving the Huut. You don't have to die to prove yourself."

E'ven was showing his fangs now. "But you have to take me—isn't it Armada tradition that clan members serve on the same ship together?"

S'jen suddenly felt a fierce pride in him. Maybe he was Huut in the same way she was Huut. She wanted to keep her kinsman close. So she said, "Yes."

4

Rose Rico was sitting idly at the helm, grinning as she counted up the Qin credit they would get for successfully completing their first job for the Armada. The *Purpose* had made two trips transporting the liberated Qin from the Domain mining station to Balanc. It was easy work, and they had the protection of S'jen's battleship during their journeys. Rose could practically sleep the entire way.

Rose didn't spare much thought for the living skeletons in the cargo hold. Their clans would help them. She wished she had some help with those two hundred Solians they had escaped with in the holds of the *Purpose*. While everyone exclaimed over the destruction of the Qin infrastructure on the planet, Rose had taken a glance at the scanner readings. She could have told them the Alphas couldn't care less if they smashed everything in their path.

Now they were parked in formation with the other transports not far away from the mangled mining station that the Qin were in the process of salvaging. For security reasons none of the transports had been briefed on their targets, but from its close proximity in the star charts, Rose had a pretty good idea that the Atalade system would be next. They had been waiting for a while, so Rose had remained on duty expecting to receive their orders at any moment.

Rose was in the middle of a huge yawn when Ash finally leapt into action. "Incoming message from Captain G'kaan," Ash announced.

Rose leaned forward. "It's about time! Put him on the imager."

G'kaan's imposing head and shoulders appeared in the imager. His dark face was somber, as usual. *"Captain, I have a message to deliver from Admiral J'kart."*

"Sure! Shoot."

But he didn't even smile in greeting. *"I'll have to come over in my pinnace. Are you prepared to dock?"*

"A personal visit?" Qin were so paranoid about secrecy.

"I'll be there shortly. G'kaan out."

Without another word, his image disappeared. Stub let out a low whistle. "Who up and died?"

Rose laughed. She had loved Stub's sense of humor from the first moment she met the orange-haired man. He had experience on ships, so he had been adopted into the crew by Mote and Whit. Stub had helped them get to Prian to settle the Solians into the colony while she was rescuing Ash from S'jen. Rose didn't care about the additions to her crew. She figured the more the merrier, as long as it kept them from working double shifts.

"G'kaan looked upset," Ash agreed, looking down at hir terminal. "The battleships are breaking their direct dock."

"He's always that way after he's seen S'jen." Rose

winked at hir, one eye on the imager where the two huge ships slowly eased away from each other. It must have been some conference to bring them together like that.

"Maybe that's it," Ash said doubtfully.

Rose stood up, brushing the crumbs from her late dinner off her skin-hugging, black flightsuit. If her mother could see her now! A space captain with her own ship and devoted crew. In the last message her mother had left before Rose was abducted, Silvia had been furious because she quit that awful job in the greenhouse. Maybe Tijuana was just too small for someone of her talents.

"I'll go down and meet G'kaan at the airlock. Ash, get Chad up here on the double to take over helm. The nav computer is holding position so G'kaan can dock the *Pluck*."

On her way down the stairs, Rose gave a jaunty wave to Mote, who was checking the bots that maintained the communications relays. She looked as happy as Rose felt. Mote was a worrier, so that was a good sign. Rose made it a point never to worry. It wasted valuable time when you could be sleeping or taking action.

Kwort solemnly nodded as Rose passed. He was wearing a brown flightsuit that looked suspiciously like a Fleet uniform. She would have to talk to Ash about that. Rose usually didn't care what anyone wore, but Kwort seemed to be making some kind of statement. If he didn't shape up and get with the program, the *Purpose* would be out one very competent bot tech. But Ash kept insisting that Kwort was worth it, and Rose couldn't refuse Ash anything.

Rose didn't need any help with the airlock. She waited until she got the go-ahead from Ash in command. There was some kind of space custom that the larger, more powerful ship showed its goodwill by opening their lock first. If the battleship had docked with the *Purpose*, Rose would have waited for G'kaan to make the first move. But this was his little pinnace so Rose opened their lock first.

As G'kaan opened his lock, Rose felt a slight rush of air coming out of the pinnace. Qin kept their ships much warmer. Rose strained to see who the copilot was. Not L'pash. Too bad . . . she enjoyed watching G'kaan negotiate the waves created by his women. Rose wasn't too clear whether either relationship had really started or ended.

G'kaan was already striding forward. Standing next to the airlock, he looked down at Rose. He filled the corridor and she smiled up in admiration. A big, black hunk of a man, with brawny shoulders, piercing blue eyes, and a firm jaw. Qin women looked okay with their pointy chins and wide heart-shaped faces, but it tended to make their enormous men look somewhat effeminate.

Rose abruptly realized she was drooling over G'kaan. She would have to get laid soon or her hormones would turn that puny, ridge-headed Kwort sexy. Maybe Stub would be interested in a roll together . . . something to think about later.

"I'm sorry, Rose, I have bad news." She realized G'kaan was furious. "Admiral J'kart has decided that only Qin transports with Qin crews will be allowed to assist on this mission."

"What?" The implications flooded her. "You're cutting us loose?"

"Not me, I fought this decision, Rose."

She flung up her hands. "Why? We did everything right!"

"Yes you did. And J'kart is willing to pay the cancellation fee on your contract."

"That's nothing!" Rose glared at him. "We can barely refuel and resupply with the credit we'll get for Balanc. We were expecting to make enough to help the Solian colony. You know that. You helped arrange everything."

"I agree it's wrong, Rose. I logged a formal protest."

"What good does that ever do?"

G'kaan winced and shrugged. "I'll try anyway."

"Why are we being fired? Is it S'jen?" Maybe that was why he had kept this off the comm channel.

"No, S'jen didn't have anything to do with it, but she agreed with Admiral J'kart."

"On what grounds?"

G'kaan sighed. "It's because you're not Qin."

Rose was confused. "They don't like Solians?"

"Some of the Qin who were being transported to Balanc saw your crew members and that upset them. They thought you were Fleet."

"That's absurd. We don't go near them. Ash made sure of that from the beginning."

G'kaan reached out and took hold of her shoulders. It surprised Rose so much that she stopped being angry and listened to him. "The admiral is a bigoted man, Rose. And so is S'jen. It's something that I've been struggling with my whole life. You see, my mother was Solian."

Rose stared at him, seeing his face in a whole new light. "I didn't know that!"

He shrugged. "It's no secret. Though from the way S'jen acted when she found out, you would have thought I was lying about it every day."

Her mouth opened. "Is that why things went sour between you and S'jen?"

G'kaan looked startled.

Rose lifted her hands to ward him off. "You don't have to answer that."

"It is impossible to have a relationship with a fanatic," he replied flatly.

"Well, you would know." Rose shook her fists in frustration. "This reeks worse than unrecycled air! So that's why those other Qin wouldn't hire us. They didn't like the shape of our faces."

"I've told you it'll be difficult for Solians to be accepted in Qin. I'm sure the colony on Prian won't bother your people, but it could take a long time for them to get used to them."

She rolled her eyes. "Welcome to a hostile galaxy!"

"Rose, when I'm done with this campaign, I'm going back into the Domain. It's more important than ever to distract the Fleet in their own territory. We can work on the slave network, like we agreed."

"Like this contract?" Rose had to ask.

"Your agreement was with Admiral J'kart. Next time, it'll be between you and me, and no one can interfere. My control of that program comes straight from the Armada advisors and the chief commander. T'ment won't second-guess my judgment, I assure you."

"Well, okay. At least that's something. But can't you give us an advance?"

G'kaan considered it, but reluctantly shook his head. "I won't be able to get budget approval until strategy is determined for the next phase. That won't happen until this liberation mission is completed."

"What? Five, maybe six decnights to finish kicking Fleet butt, then they'll consider it? Those folks on Prian could be dead of starvation by then!"

"Qin won't let them starve."

"Oh, no? Well excuse me if I don't rely on your word."

G'kaan winced again. "You have every right to be upset with me and Admiral J'kart. I wish I could change his mind."

Rose relented when she remembered that G'kaan had never let her down before. "We'll figure something out. We always have."

G'kaan seemed relieved. "That's why I chose you to help with the slave network. Whatever you do, return to Armada Central in six decnights."

"Sure." Rose dialed open the airlock again. "You owe us a big one for this."

G'kaan stopped briefly as he went past, looking down at her. "You're an admirable woman, Rose."

For a moment he held her gaze, then nodded gruffly and went through the airlock. Rose started laughing after the airlock shut again. That sounded like a pass! But he was so formal, so proper, it was hard to tell. Not that she wouldn't mind loosening him up. Sometimes the most uptight people were the least inhibited during sex.

Well, well! G'kaan and sex . . . With a pleasant shiver, she headed up to the command deck. She would tell Ash and the crew the bad news, then take the ship to a safe distance away from the mining station in case a Fleet patrolship showed up. They would need to talk before they moved on. Another one of their infamous conclaves.

Then after that, at some point, she would trip Stub before next duty shift. She could really use some good, hard sex right now. Surely Stub wouldn't mind it if she was on top.

Imagine G'kaan making a pass at her!

* * *

Kwort knew he had made a wrong turn in life. It had happened shortly before he arrived on board the battleship *Conviction,* his first duty post in the Fleet. He never should have stopped those Delta bot techs from attacking that Solian girl. The techs had started by beating him up, and ended by ruining his life.

When shift change was finally announced, Kwort was on his way to his berth when Ash stopped him. "Kwort, there's a conclave in a few moments. I wondered if I could make a suggestion?"

Kwort nodded, supposing that s/he would tell him to eat something. Ash had been very solicitous about his health since s/he had brought him on board the *Purpose.*

"Could you change that brown flightsuit?"

Kwort glanced down at himself. He had a few flightsuits, but this one was his favorite. "Why?"

"It bothers some of the crew. It's Fleet brown." Ash smiled gently. "I think everyone would be friendlier without their subconscious fear of a Fleet uniform."

Kwort realized it was true; his flightsuit did look like a Fleet uniform. That was why he liked it, because it reminded him of everything he missed. Including Horc. He had never been romantic with his friend, but he had loved Horc in his own way. Back then, his only problem had been fending off those violent techs Kitarin and Murroom. Now he wished he had ignored them as Horc had suggested.

Instead, he had destroyed his own battleship.

He could never return to the Domain. If he was discovered, he would be mind-stripped and then sent to an experimental lab where they would try to turn him inside out or dye his eyeballs green! He deserved to die but he didn't want to be tortured to death. He thought a lot about taking a one-way walk out the airlock, and even figured out how to disable the safeties to do it.

But Ash had told him he deserved to live, and s/he gave him a berth on the *Purpose* and a job to do.

Kwort felt awful. He hadn't thought about their feelings at all. "You're right. I'll go change."

"I understand," Ash assured him.

Kwort was sure s/he did, but he felt guilty. Just like when he had seen those poor Qin slaves. It had bothered him a lot, and he had stopped thinking so much about the terrible thing he had done and started thinking about the Domain. He had seen slaves before, but not slaves who worked in a processing facility. He had seen for himself how Deltas could be part of the torture and systemic starvation that had happened to those Qin.

Apparently self-flagellation was his new default mode. As Ash went on to the galley, Kwort ducked into his berth to change into a nondescript gray flightsuit. Surveying himself in the mirror, he felt a rising disgust with himself. If nothing else, these Solians had been very kind to him, especially Ash. He wished he hadn't upset them by wearing brown, and he wanted to do something that would make Ash happy.

So he ran down to the storeroom and rifled through the pile of spare flightsuits. He found a few that were small enough for him. One was bright blue with gold chevrons on the sheeves and legs. He remembered how Horc had admired the fancy gold flourishes on Alpha-Captain Luddolf's uniform. Horc would have loved a flightsuit like this one.

Kwort stripped off the gray flightsuit and put on the new one. He couldn't believe the change in himself.

Looking in a mirror in the refresher, he saw his face light up. He had to smile whenever he caught a glimpse of those gold chevrons. For Horc! As if some part of his good friend were still alive.

When the captain made the announcement that there would be a conclave in the galley, Kwort was ready.

Kwort was the last to arrive in the galley. He wasn't sure what a conclave was, but the captain had announced that everyone should attend whether they were on duty or not. He certainly hoped someone had set the automatic scanners to alert them in case of trouble. But he figured they must know what they were doing.

Kwort hesitated on the threshold of the galley. Everyone turned to look at him. Though he was supposedly one of the crew, he asked, "Did you want me here too, Captain?"

She grinned at him. "Sure, some in, Kwort. This concerns everyone."

Ash moved over to give him room. Hir eyes were crinkled and s/he whispered "Nice!" in appreciation of his flightsuit.

For a moment, Kwort almost felt good about himself. But then it was gone.

Kwort counted twelve other people in the galley. The captain stood at the front, next to the transposers. The strangest thing was that there was no recognition of rank. Ash was the second-in-command but s/he sat between him and Newt, the newest members of their crew. Kwort doubted Newt would ever be a competent bot tech. When he had asked about her training and background, she had lisped that she served as a party rent-a-slave for almost a decade. Kwort hadn't been sure what to do with that information, so he tried to forget it.

Now Newt was snuggling next to her lover, Chad. Chad was the biggest Solian in the bunch, but Whit was nearly as tall. Kwort worked with Whit on the bots along with ebony-skinned Dab. Other than Mote, the one with blood-red hair, he barely knew the names of the other crew members.

"Okay, listen up, people!" the captain called out, silencing the quiet cross talk among the crew. When everyone was still, she continued, "Our contract with the Armada has been canceled by Admiral J'kart."

There were expressions of dismay and surprise. Mote called out, "Why? What did we do wrong?"

" They don't like the way we look," Rose said bluntly. "Only Qin need apply."

Kwort expected them to get angry and protest, but they accepted it without complaint. They continually surprised him.

"What are we going to do?" wailed Jot. She was the youngest of the crew, and her almond eyes were shiny with unshed tears.

"It's okay," several people assured her at once. Ash patted her shoulder across the table.

"I'm open for suggestions," the captain said. She propped one foot on a bench. "You got any?"

Kwort marveled at their casual ways. How did they get anything done? But even though he had more responsibility on the *Purpose*, in many ways it was much pleasanter than being in the Domain Fleet. His work was interesting and no one hassled him. He was allowed to go wherever he wanted, whenever he wanted. He had even wandered onto the command deck one day only to be casually greeted by Nip at the helm.

"Maybe Balanc will hire us," Mote suggested.

"They must need a transport between the planet and the mining station," Chad agreed.

The captain shrugged. "It was the Qin from the mining station who complained about us. We can try, but don't count on it."

Nip was nodding. "During third shift, I heard that they weren't going to get the mining station running again for another quarter."

"We can always ask," Ash interposed.

They nodded, looking at each other, and just like that, some kind of consensus had been reached. Kwort was sure this was not the way that Captain Luddolf had run his battleship.

"So that's plan A," the captain agreed. "What's plan B?"

That stumped them for a while longer, and they exchanged ideas until Whit brought up the fact that there was an alien territory beyond the Tomeeda nebula where the Domain had not yet ventured. Mote called up what was in their databanks about the area, but there was sketchy information. The aliens were called "primitive" and had barely begun an expansion using their newly developed grav impellers. It seemed like a place where they could exert some influence, but they had no grav-slip plots to get there. They would have to search out each grav-slip using their short-range scanners. It would take a lot of time.

That sort of exploring wasn't something they seemed interested in doing. Kwort was relieved. He wasn't ready to be an adventurer.

Someone suggested traveling along the border of the Canopus region. There was reportedly a thick swath of settlements outside the Elaspian sector in upper Canopus. But getting there would take five or six decnights. The only other suggestion was to return to Prian, where the Solian colonists were looking to *them* for help.

While they were talking about that, Kwort had another thought. It was definitely risky, and he wasn't sure if he should say anything.

Then again, he was one of the crew. The other bot techs had quickly dubbed him senior tech when they realized he knew bots better than any of them. He had accepted, but it hadn't felt real. Maybe he should have trusted them when they put such faith in him.

Kwort cleared his throat. "I know where you can salvage tons of bots and supplies. And it's not two decnights away."

The others turned to look at him.

"Where?" Ash asked.

"The spacepost in Sirius that the Qin destroyed—"

"The Domain!" Chad shouted. "You must be crazy!"

The others started shouting too. Kwort was almost afraid they would attack him, but he soon realized that some, like Ash and Whit, were trying to get the others to be quiet so they could hear his proposal.

"Go ahead," Ash finally told Kwort.

Chad was simmering on his bench, his arms crossed.

"Spacepost T-3 broke apart, so everyone evacuated," Kwort explained. "Most of the good stuff is probably being stripped off by raiders right now, but it's a huge spacepost with lots of warehouses. The maintenance bots alone would be worth more than the Qin were paying us."

"Us?" Chad retorted. "What makes you a partner?"

"We do," Whit said, standing up to Chad. "Our bots

would be breaking down left and right if Kwort hadn't come in and set us straight."

That made Kwort feel a bit better. Whit was fair even though he made it clear he still didn't trust Kwort.

"We listen to every suggestion in conclave," the captain said flatly, silencing them once again. She turned to Kwort. "It sounds too dangerous. Between raiders and Domain patrolships, we aren't likely to get out alive."

"You want to get caught!" Chad accused Kwort. "Then you can turn us in and be a hero."

"I'd be a lab rat!" Kwort snapped. "You think I want every bone in my body turned to jelly? Or my skull removed for easy access to my brain for neurological experiments?"

"Then why do you want to go back?" Mote asked.

"I don't. Now that you mention it, it's a bad idea." So much for his first attempt to join in. Kwort sat back and refused to speak.

The others kept talking about it for lack of any other alternative. They asked Kwort how many patrolships were in the pocket. "There was one before the spacepost broke apart," he said sullenly. "It could still be there, or it might be on patrol."

"He's trying to trap you," Chad insisted to everyone else.

"I don't care what you do," Kwort retorted. Chad reminded him unpleasantly of Murroom, though he wasn't as hairy or unkempt. "I guess you really don't want me here."

Kwort stood up to leave but Ash stopped him. "It's an interesting idea, Kwort. But you can understand why we're wary about it."

"I do understand. I keep telling you, I have more to lose than you."

"Then why did you suggest it?" Mote pressed.

"I guess I lost my head," Kwort replied roughly. "I'm going to bed."

He shrugged off Ash's hand and stalked from the galley. Suddenly he was angry. At Chad, and at the rest of them for letting that big guy bully them. Maybe it wasn't such a great idea, but they hadn't come up with anything better.

A knock on his door an hour later woke him from an uneasy doze. It was Ash holding a bowl of stew he liked. The smell made him realize he was hungrier than he'd been in a while.

"I thought you'd like to eat," Ash told him.

Kwort accepted the bowl gratefully. "Thanks. I don't know why you're so nice to me."

"You're a fellow refugee."

"Huh? Tell that to Chad." He spooned the stew into his mouth. It tasted fantastic. "Did he convince you to leave me behind on Balanc?"

"That's your choice, Kwort, not his. We're headed there now to see if we can get another contract."

"You really think that's possible?"

"No, and neither does Rose." Ash looked worried. "So we're going to Spacepost T-3."

"No!" Kwort looked up in surprise, his mouth full.

"If you're having doubts, you can stay at Balanc."

Kwort almost said yes. he was starting to feel alive again; why risk suicide? But there was nothing on Balanc for him, either. The Qin would never accept him. As stupid as it was, it was heartwarming that the Solian slaves had allowed him to be part of their crew.

When Kwort had suggested the spacepost, he hadn't really thought it out. Now the danger looked much greater. But what about the rewards? The Solians could get all the cargo they needed to trade for sophisticated tools and supplies for the colony on Prian. They talked about the Solians on Prian a lot.

But there was nothing on the spacepost for him. Only the risk of being caught—

Unless . . . The only way for him to return to the Domain was if he changed his identity. What better place than Spacepost T-3 to find a blank ID chip?

"What's wrong, Kwort?" Ash asked.

"Not wrong," he said slowly. "I was thinking, maybe I can find an ID chip on the spacepost to change my identity. Then I could pass anywhere in the Domain unless I was given a retinal scan."

"Rose says that once G'kaan is finished with this campaign, the *Purpose* will be returning to the Domain to help activate his slave network. That's what convinced everyone to go to the spacepost. It looks like we'll have to get used to traveling inside the Domain. But G'kaan has done it plenty of times and gotten away with it."

Kwort shook his head. "Sounds like I missed quite a conclave."

"One to go down in history," Ash agreed. "Chad is very angry. I'm going to talk to him again."

At that moment, there was a knock on Kwort's door. This was the most visitors he'd had since he arrived on the ship.

It was the captain, and she grinned when she saw Ash already there. "So you're telling him the plan. You shouldn't have left so early, Kwort."

"I didn't want to upset the crew, Captain," Kwort replied stiffly. He wasn't used to talking to captains, even one as informal as this.

The captain rolled her eyes. "If I tried to please people, I'd still be servicing Alphas. Take my advice, Kwort, say what you think."

Surprised, he said, "Aye, Captain."

"It's Rose, Kwort." She glanced at Ash, then back at him. "So are you going to stay on board?"

"I was thinking about it."

"I hope you do," Rose added. "Whit and Mote say we need you, Kwort."

With both of them facing him expectantly, Kwort couldn't think. But he didn't really have a choice except for that long stroll out the airlock. He had made a terrible mistake, but was that going to stop him for the rest of his life?

"I'll stick with you." He grinned, lifting his bowl of stew in acknowledgment. "Here's to a good salvage!"

5

Gandre Li maneuvered her courier ship into the dock of the starport orbiting Canopus Regional Headquarters. The *Solace* fit with plenty of room to spare. It was a dainty courier ship, but more than adequate for the needs of her few crew members.

Gandre hadn't expected to return to Canopus Regional Headquarters, but a message had been relayed from Regional Command ordering her to report immediately. She locked down the helm and let out a sigh. "Okay, we're here as commanded. Now what?"

Jor glanced up. "Incoming comm for you. It's from InSec!"

"InSec?" Usually InSec maintained the utmost secrecy to keep anyone from connecting their department to Gandre Li and the *Solace*. Her covert duties were supposed to remain a secret, even with her crew. "Are you sure it came from InSec?"

"See," Jor told her, sending the text to her terminal. "It has their return code, and it says you're to report to the regional subcommander of InSec for Canopus."

"Hmmm, the subcommander?" The last few times she

had visited InSec at the Canopus Prime starport, she had gone to one of the secondary offices. This would be a high-level conference.

For a heady moment, Gandre Li wondered if she was going to be fired by InSec. Her schedule among the outer sectors had been severely disrupted during the last quarter. Transporting the message about the attack on Spacepost T-3 to Regional Headquarters, then conveying Rikev Alpha from Canopus to Sirius, had used up nearly five decnights. Coming back to Canopus Prime had completely disrupted their schedule again. They had rushed all the way from outer Pyxis to the sector in the heart of the region. Other covert InSec couriers would pick up the slack, but unfortunately Gandre Li had been forced to dump her private contracts for transport and courier services. Her long-term relationships with her few honest vendors had been damaged, perhaps irreparably.

But reality caught up and Gandre Li realized she would never be fired by InSec. Once you were chosen to serve the Domain, you couldn't go back.

She pushed away from her terminal. "You finish securing the ship, then the crew can take leave. I don't know how long we'll be here, so I'll comm you to let you know our departure time."

Jor nodded, but he seemed upset. His dark face practically oozed alarm. "But it's InSec! Why do they want to talk to you?"

Gandre Li caught herself. She hadn't slipped yet about her covert activities for InSec. Her slave, Trace, knew. But that was different. Trace was her partner.

"It must have to do with the disappearance of the *Conviction*." She figured that would be the most likely reason from the crew's point of view. "We were the last ones to see the battleship before it left for Qin."

Jor was still tense. Gandre Li had to remind herself that everyone in the Domain trembled, and rightly so, at the thought of being called to InSec. Perhaps she had become one of them without realizing it.

"Don't make me any more nervous than I am," she added, trying to joke with him.

Jor nodded uncertainly, even though Gandre Li gave him a reassuring wave as she left.

She stopped off at her cabin to tell Trace she was going to InSec. Trace was worried, too, but she tried not to let Gandre Li know. Of course, the sweet girl was as transparent as her white skin with its sprinkling of freckles. Gandre Li loved those freckles because they were reminders of a few happy planetary vacations. With vibrant bronze hair and laughing green eyes, Trace was as perfect as any Solian Gandre Li had seen. And Trace was hers—body, heart, and soul—just as Gandre Li belonged to Trace.

With an extra kiss, Gandre Li settled her crisp white flightsuit and left the *Solace*. She knew her destination and realized that this time she wouldn't have to take a circuitous route as per InSec regulations. This time she didn't have to go to one of the cover-locations on the decks above or below InSec that would take her down to the private offices.

The web-like starport that orbited Canopus Prime was enormous, with one broad side facing down at the large moon. The view of the shifting aurora trailers in the manufactured, ever-changing sky was spectacular, but Gandre Li didn't pause long too long to admire it.

She wished Trace could see the moon, but the docks were on the outer side of the starport for security reasons.

Gandre Li devoutly hoped she wouldn't have to go down to the moon again. Last time, the intensive sterilization and verification procedures had been extremely unpleasant. She had inadvertently talked her way up the chain of command directly to Regional Commander Heloga Alpha, an experience she would never forget. It had also been her first glimpse of the vast interlocking complexes of the headquarters. The moon was filled with administrative staff who ran the Canopus region with its one hundred twenty-five sectors covering two hundred cubic light-years of space.

Walking in the front door of the InSec offices was strange, but the routine was the same, with retinal scans and gene-typing to verify her identity. Gandre Li waited in a reception room for a while, along with assorted other humanoids. They looked far more anxious than she did, and she wondered if she was giving away her familiarity with InSec again.

Finally Gandre Li's name was called and a bot appeared. It floated in front of her, leading her into a spacious office. She didn't have to see the woman's bald head to know she was an Alpha.

The Alpha smiled as Gandre Li entered, and that was enough to unnerve her. "Beta-Captain Gandre Li, I'm Elsanya Alpha, first subcommander of InSec in the Canopus region."

Gandre Li swallowed—and for the first time felt fear. This woman was very high in rank! "Reporting as ordered, First Subcommander."

Elsanya shuffled her dataports, reading a bit from

each one until she found what she wanted. With a quick smile in Gandre's direction, she consulted the dataport. "Ah yes, you're here as part of the Rikev Alpha investigation."

Gandre Li reminded herself not to be fooled by Elsanya's friendliness. Elsanya had the abstracted air of someone who had too much to do, as if she wasn't paying much attention. But Gandre Li knew InSec after all these years. She never underestimated their Alphas. This one had probably risen to her very high post in part because she disarmed people with her affable behavior.

"Yes, last quarter I transported Rikev Alpha to the Sirius sector," Gandre Li confirmed. "He transferred to the battleship *Conviction*."

"A special assignment directly authorized by Heloga Alpha," Elsanya agreed, clicking off the dataport. She looked at Gandre Li for a long moment. "I'll need to ask you some questions about Rikev Alpha."

"Of course." Gandre Li restrained herself from wiping her palms on her flightsuit.

Elsanya added with an apologetic smile, "It will have to be under the uninhibitor."

The only reason Gandre Li didn't hesitate was because she had prepared herself to always, under whatever circumstances, answer that statement with a ready "Of course, I'm here to serve."

The uninhibitor was more invasive than being cleared to go down to Canopus Regional Headquarters. In fact, it was the worst thing InSec had ever done to her. The uninhibitor had a nasty reputation for scrambling people's brains when they were subjected to it.

She was immediately walked by an armed enforcer to

a special room that contained the uninhibitor. She reclined back in a molded chair. The uninhibitor was clamped around her, over her arms, legs, and body, then capping her skull with a tight-fitting carapace.

She wanted to fight to get free as soon as it locked into place. But there was a sting in her wrist and quickly her entire body went numb. She had no way of knowing how she moved as she reacted. Yet her instinctive flight-or-fight response was captured in all its quivering glory on the computer readouts that lined the walls of the small room. Two Beta technicians monitored the activity closely to provide a complete report.

Gandre Li breathed deeply and tried to calm herself. True, she had tricked Rikev so he wouldn't use her slave. That was nothing InSec would be concerned about. As an infraction, it rated about as high as refusing to allow the senior Alpha of the Sirius sector the use of her cabin for the duration of the voyage. Other Alphas might wonder at her stupidity in irritating a senior Alpha. But it was not a punishable offense.

The worst part was that now InSec would know they could use her devotion to Trace as leverage. Gandre Li hoped that was all she lost. Above all else, she had to cover her encounter with Rose and those renegade slaves.

Gandre Li resolved not to think about that again. Ever.

Elsanya Alpha handled the questioning herself. Her attitude was as if they were two friends sitting down for a friendly chat. But one of them couldn't twitch without having it recorded for posterity. The questions were fairly typical and mostly concerned Rikev. Gandre Li tried to recall every detail. Rikev was on her command deck as he watched the spacepost crumple and break in half. He hadn't reacted, as far as she could tell. None of them had dared say a word. Gandre Li offered to upload the logs that had recorded Rikev every time he was on the command deck, and Elsanya accepted graciously.

During their conversation, Elsanya let drop that the *Conviction* was missing. Gandre Li said, "Yes, we heard a rumor while we were in the Procyon sector. Some were even saying the battleship had been destroyed. I could hardly believe it."

"Why?" Elsanya asked.

"Who could beat one of our battleships? And Rikev Alpha seemed . . . invulnerable."

Elsanya ticked something off on her dataport. "You appear to be afraid of Rikev Alpha."

Gandre Li knew that was true. "There was something about him that instilled dread."

"What did he do to make you dread him?" Elsanya asked.

"He was using surveillance on me and my crew. We found remote devices he had planted."

"Why was Rikev Alpha interested in you and your crew?"

Gandre Li knew this was it. "I think it was because he wanted to use my slave during his lust."

She let Elsanya pull the entire story out of her while clearly feeling ashamed to have to admit it. She confessed to making Trace's fever rise so Rikev couldn't use her. It roused a flurry of questioning and Gandre Li was forced to confess jealousy over Trace. It was relentless and terrible as intimate details about their interactions, right down to how often and in what ways they had sex, were wrenched from her. Gandre Li even admitted that

Trace sometimes took a dominant sexual role with her, and that she never forced Trace to do anything she didn't want to.

She tried not to say anything more incriminating while incriminating herself enough to cover for her fear. Elsanya went to consult the readouts while Gandre Li tried to calm down. She had told the absolute truth. There wasn't much else that Elsanya could pump from her. Except for her encounters with Rose.

But Elsanya returned. She grilled Gandre Li on her courier duties and her feelings toward other Alphas she worked for. Gandre Li spilled everything: how she tried not to breathe around Metelaus Alpha because of his awful flowery fragrances; how early in her career she had been ordered to service a high-level, InSec Alpha-commander during his lust; how she regularly resisted Konstankin Alpha's not-so-subtle hints for the same by arranging for Trace to call her while she was reporting in; how she hated being at everyone's beck and call but cherished the enormous freedom she had as a captain of a courier.

Gandre Li told Elsanya everything because she had to. She only hoped that she would be allowed to return to her ship and Trace after they were done.

Takhan Delta had a busy shift activating diagnostic bots for duty while the *Solace* was docked. She had a standard rotating cycle of maintenance for the key operating systems and subsystems. Most of the ship could be shut down while they were in dock, even environmental systems as long as they were on umbilicals to the starport.

This time the bots would do a comprehensive diagnostic of the comm systems, both internal and external;

the navigational system would be self-tested and outfitted with updated slip points downloaded from the vast Canopus database; and she had a team of trouble shooter bots working on the thruster system. The port thruster was receiving three percent less power than the starboard thruster, interfering in docking maneuvers. Takhan also ran the daily bot checks, which she had long ago memorized. She liked it that she was the only one who touched the bots. It seemed that when the others tried to "help," they gummed up everything.

When Takhan returned to her quarters, she was ready to relax and enjoy herself with Jor and Danal. Their room was much more comfortable and spacious now that they had the whole space together with a triple-sized bunk in the corner. Sleeping between the two men she cared about made her life worthwhile. And it created more opportunities for sex since they were always together. Even if only one of them was in lust, they were learning there were plenty of ways to join in and make it fun.

But one look at Jor and Danal was enough to tell her that sex was not on their minds. "What's wrong?"

"Now, don't get excited," Jor assured her. "It may be nothing. Something happened right after we docked. The captain got word—"

"Don't!" Takhan said, waving her hands quickly. She touched her ear and glanced around.

"You don't think . . ." Jor started to say.

Takhan gave him a hard look. They always had to protect themselves from the higher ranks. But since Gandre Li had allowed them to open up the berths and even take over the corridor to make one large room of their own, these two guys had been acting like the captain was their best friend.

"Can we take leave?" she asked.

"Yes, our departure is undetermined." Jor glanced at Danal, who had been silent as usual during their exchange. He nodded, and they packed daypacks while Takhan changed into a fresh green flightsuit with a hood. Hers was grubby even though she did her best to keep the tubes clean. There was a lot of dust and oily grime in space that eluded even the best cleaning bots.

Danal's satiny yellow face was impassive as Jor led the way out of the ship. Takhan had to admire her two men: Jor was as dark as Danal was bright, but Jor was the one with the easy smile. Danal was a Gamma from Froyt but he rarely spoke of his background except to say that he had served on a passenger liner for nearly two decades before signing on with the *Solace*. Jor had been an ops officer in the Fleet and had served out his standard two decades before going freelance. They had worked for several years on the *Solace* before they came together—almost as one—to become a family. Takhan would no more think of having Danal alone as a partner than she would join only with Jor. But with the three of them everything was balanced.

Trace saw them off at the airlock. The Solian was worried about Gandre Li, but Takhan didn't have any assurances to give. If the captain couldn't take care of herself, then they were all in trouble.

Takhan admired the enormous regional starport as they wandered through the levels looking for a place to eat. They enjoyed trying new cuisine, but Jor was the ringleader in their search for variety. Takhan was more focused on the structure of the starport, made with the newest engineering advances and materials. She constantly stopped to look at the bulkheads and design elements. She was an Aborandeen, one of the ancient spacefaring families, so space stations were in her blood. This was the most important starport in the region, so it made sense that it was better than most.

Finally Jor chose a restaurant, probably because they were too hungry to look further. Takhan didn't catch the name, but the food came in crisp tangled bundles that each tasted different: sweet, rich, gamy, tart, and others in various unusual combinations. Takhan enjoyed it immensely, but she didn't let that stop her from finally talking. The open-air restaurant was filled with noise and laughter. Unless someone had a reason to monitor two unknown Gammas and a lowly Delta Aborandeen, they wouldn't be overheard.

"So tell me what happened," Takhan urged them.

Jor explained how the captain received a message ordering her to go to InSec. "But she wasn't surprised. It was like she was expecting it."

"What was it about?"

"She said it was because of the *Conviction*, which makes sense. But who's that blasé about InSec?"

Danal finally spoke up. "Did she ask for a map? The captain always asks for a station map when she has to meet new clients."

"She didn't."

"Maybe she knows where InSec is," Takhan suggested darkly.

Jor admitted, "Last time we were here, she had to go to Admin, not InSec."

Takhan was sure now. "The captain is hiding something. I've seen the cargo that comes in and out of the *Solace*, and it's not enough to support a planetary taxi service! She must have another source of income. Since it's not goods or people, it must be information. And who specializes in information—InSec."

The other two looked at her with respect. Growing up an Aborandeen, she knew merchant shipping inside and out. She would have stayed on her family ship except for one thing. Her parents had been too closely related and her gene chart was filled with lethal recessives. None of the other Aborandeens would accept her in their mating circles on their ships. When she was fully an adult, she realized she would always be excluded from her intimate family, always a hanger-on. So she left and knocked around the Domain on her own. Until she finally found a new family with Jor and Danal. It was a pale reflection of what an Aborandeen mating circle could be, but it was enough for her damaged body.

Now Takhan was concerned for her men's safety. "I've been suspicious about the captain. If she's a spy, then ten to one she's planted an ear on us."

"But we helped her scour the ship looking for bugs left by Rikev Alpha!" Jor reminded her.

"My bots found seventeen inert devices," Takhan agreed. "What if they were hers? Blaming Rikev Alpha makes for a good excuse if we found them. Or she could have dropped a fresh one in our quarters."

When neither of them had anything to say to that, Takhan added, "Let's pool our credit to buy a baffler. We need to be able to talk freely on the *Solace*."

"I wish we could know for certain," Jor insisted. "I don't like being so suspicious."

Danal thoughtfully suggested, "We could ask Trace."

Because it was Danal, who rarely spoke, Takhan didn't snap at him. "What if Trace is spying on us for the captain?" she countered instead.

"Don't say that!" Jor protested. "Trace wouldn't do that to us."

"She's the captain's slave. She has to do whatever she's told," Takhan reminded him.

Jor sighed. "So much for our new viewer! I suppose we're going shopping for a baffler."

"Do you agree?" Takhan asked Danal.

Danal shrugged slightly, finishing off the last tangled ball of tasty stuff. "Agreed."

The three of them had a nice long leave. They bought a baffler barely big enough for all of them; then they went to see some live entertainment and had a zero-g swim in the observation bubble. A nice relaxing jaunt.

When they returned to the *Solace*, the captain was also just returning. They met her in the docking arm. She looked much the worse for wear, and for a moment Takhan thought she had been jumped by port thugs. Her warm peach skin was flushed dark, and she wobbled when she walked.

Jor took one look and called for Trace to come help. As they helped the captain onto the ship and into her bed, she mumbled something about InSec putting her through the uninhibitor.

The others drew back at that, while Trace looked frightened out of her wits. Since Gandre Li had returned, apparently they hadn't found anything incriminating. But the *Solace* wasn't allowed to leave until InSec released them.

Takhan wasn't sure if that proved her point that Gandre Li was a spy, or not. All she knew was that she was going to keep a close eye on the Beta-captain and her slave. No one else in the universe would look out for her. She had to do it herself.

6

Heloga tried to relax as she was visually enhanced for her appearance at the Renewal Festival. This year she would be alone for the three-day festival, and she couldn't help musing on the negative turn of her romance with Kristolas. Despite her best efforts, he had not yet returned to her side.

But Heloga was irritated out of her daydreams of revenge when the Delta face stylist kept fiddling with the skin on her temple. Heloga glanced into the magnifier and saw the texture expanded into a valley of cracks and crevices.

Heloga brushed the specialists away from her and ordered them out. The Delta face stylist didn't meet her eyes.

When they were gone, Heloga examined her face. A network of tiny creases radiated from the outer corners of her eyes. Everything else was the same—her ivory skin was smooth, her violet eyes were startling in their vividness, her lips as moist as a young girl's. But everything was ruined by those fine lines.

How? When? Her face hadn't looked that way yesterday. Or had it? She hadn't paid much attention. For over a decnight, she had screamed and ground her teeth in fury over Kristolas's coldheartedness. She kept imagining him with Olhanna, leaning over her naked body as they joined together in lust, his creamy paleness contrasted with her brown satiny skin. Olhanna's full lips haunted her, knowing that she would tantalize Kristolas with them, making him moan with pleasure. Would Kristolas use the same words and gestures with Olhanna that made Heloga surrender to him? Would Olhanna debase herself as she did? Clearly Kristolas desired to make Olhanna his own, and that drove Heloga mad.

She wondered if she had damaged herself with her excessive emotion. Yet she couldn't restrain herself from poring over reports of Kristolas appearing in public with Olhanna. Images of them smiling and touching each other had appeared twice in the social section on the net. She didn't care that growth and productivity was down in every sector of her region. These things were cyclical, but a man like Kristolas came along once a century.

Kristolas was both strong enough to sexually dominate her and sensitive enough to know when she needed to take the lead. In every way, they were compatible. She finally understood romance, the ideal of two halves coming together to form a whole. She was the best she could be when Kristolas was around. And she longed for him with a physical ache she had never known before.

But the thrilling love Kristolas had given her had been mixed with real agony in their time together. On the occasions when Heloga had felt the need to share lust with another Alpha, Kristolas made it clear he didn't mind variety. She couldn't stand hearing his stories of sexual conquest or the way his women looked at her afterwards, as if they had taken something from her. Perhaps it was because they had been as defiled by Kristolas as she was, so now they knew what she craved.

Yet Heloga especially disliked it when Kristolas was forgetful of his position. The senior Alpha in the region should always be treated with deference. After all, how could one forget rank, even for a moment?

She had given Kristolas everything. Looking at her face, Heloga realized she was paying for it now.

She didn't want to think of what else it could mean. Alphas lived for two centuries and they retained their natural beauty until the end. The first sign of death was a rapid, physical disintegration, especially noticeable in the skin. Heloga had shied away from such things, so her knowledge was scanty.

When Heloga counted up her years, something she hadn't done in many decades, she was unsettled to realize she was 181 years old.

She assured herself the wrinkles were a consequence of excessive emotion over Kristolas's betrayal. They weren't imminent signs of decay. She had at least two more decades of active life . . . but that was no consolation.

Unfortunately, Heloga couldn't cancel her appearance at the Renewal Festival. It was important that her image be broadcast everywhere on Canopus to associate her with the cheap drugs, sex, and food that would flow for three days. This was the annual festival everyone in Canopus looked forward to. People were already gathered in Canopus Round, the enormous plaza that extended almost beyond sight, to watch her drop the flame that would ignite Renewal.

And Kristolas would be there.

So she carefully painted her own face. Tomorrow she would obtain the services of a skilled biotech who specialized in skin repairs. The biotech would insure that her beauty remained unblemished.

Before leaving, she gave orders to the commander of her personal enforcers to eliminate the Delta face stylist. There would be no rumors flowing out of that one's mouth.

Winstav Alpha had never been so bored as during his decnight at Canopus Regional Headquarters. The Renewal Festival, about which he had heard so much, was nothing more than a fancy excuse for sensory excess among the lower ranks. The Alphas shamelessly joined the celebration, exposing the sad dearth of proper entertainment on the frontier.

Fastidiously, Winstav stood on the uppermost circle within the domed space. Only the highest Alphas could enter this level, and from here he had a view of everything. Outside the clear dome were the gathered crowds celebrating, even though Heloga had not yet officially invoked the festival.

"It's offensive," Winstav finally murmured to Felenore.

"I agree, on many counts," she replied. His fellow strategist was wearing a plain khaki coverall. When she was in space, Felenore wore a plain khaki flightsuit. One thing about Felenore, she was consistent even if she wasn't stylish.

"They're actually letting Betas in here." Winstav looked down at the motley crew of aliens who filled the lower half of the dome. "The last thing in this galaxy I need to see is Betas engaging in sex acts!"

"Rustic pleasures." Felenore sniffed.

Winstav was delighted with his fellow strategist, Felenore Alpha. Hardened in the caustic atmosphere of Rigel, Felenore was suspicious, bitter, and ugly enough to scare away sycophants. She suited his mood perfectly. She left him alone, and he left her alone. By the time they had reached Canopus, they were working as a finely meshed team. They had stripped everything from Canopus regional InSec and were united in their quest for the most minor details about Spacepost T-3, Qin activity, and Rikev Alpha himself.

Winstav noticed that Alphas were turning their heads. The singer Olhanna, instantly recognizable by her rich brown skin, was walking up to the top tier. Winstav had recently heard Olhanna in the surprisingly fine amphitheater in the northern quadrant of Canopus. He considered her to be a competent performer. She gained points by carrying herself perfectly, clearly marking her as a galactic rather than one of these provincial plebes. Her simple transparent gown was the newest thing in more fashionable circles, while the people here were still wearing antigrav designs.

At first Winstav thought the Alphas were starstruck over a second-rate singer. But with the instincts of a master strategist, he picked out the pattern in the comments flowing around him. Holding the singer's arm was a male Alpha who was exciting more attention than Olhanna.

Winstav quickly checked his implant database and came up with a match. It was Kristolas Alpha, manager of the Arts Complex and Heloga's constant lust partner.

Then, in front of Winstav's outraged eyes, a petty drama unfolded. It was apparently a highly anticipated confrontation between Heloga and her lover Kristolas, who had jilted her for Olhanna. Heloga had surrounded herself with fawning Alphas and pointedly didn't look in their direction. Kristolas lingered nearby with Olhanna, speaking to everyone who filed by as he ignored the regional commander.

It was messy and quite public. Winstav was accustomed to a refined subtlety in more exclusive circles. The reports would spread from a select few who witnessed such juicy moments. Here, everyone was openly speculating on whether Heloga hoped that Kristolas would come running to her side. They were comparing Heloga with Olhanna in an unconscionably open way.

It simply showed how far Winstav had fallen.

He was an exile. He had raged against his fate for so long that it burned as part of his very being. Winstav, the best strategist in the Domain, had been sent into exile because his last partner strategist had insisted on recommending a disastrous course of action against the Kund. It didn't matter that Winstav had recorded a dissenting opinion; he was condemned along with his fellow strategist when the plan failed.

His deportation had been a long process as the regents transferred him from region to region, always farther out and farther away from the center of action, where crucial decisions were made. He had seen the marvels of Rigel and had feasted with regents while being lauded for his achievements . . . now he was stuck in this stagnant pond in the distant reaches of space. He scorned the entertainment on Canopus, smirked at the foolishness of the regional commander and her cronies, and despaired of ever getting back to where he truly belonged.

"Felenore," he said, "let's get ourselves a battleship."

She raised one brow, turning her ruddy face toward him. "Now?"

"Now."

Felenore followed him as Winstav strolled to the other side of the dome where Heloga Alpha had set up her court. She stood in the center of one arched nook surrounded by her favorites.

Winstav nodded greeting to Rikev Alpha. He and Felenore had already interviewed the new Rikev on their way to Canopus. It had helped Winstav get a better understanding of the Rikev 5G who had been in command of the spacepost. Rikevs had a particularly acute determination to succeed. This Rikev appeared to be blandly playing Heloga's game while keeping his distance.

Winstav went right up to Heloga without waiting for her to gesture him over. He had watched a few of her favorites do the same, and intended to take advantage of her lack of protocol.

It threw her off balance a bit, but she smiled thinly at him. Her eyes slid off Felenore, as usual. He had already noted Heloga's preoccupation with appearances. Today she wore a great deal of face paint that made her lips and eyes look heavy. Her antigrav gown seemed frumpy and dated.

"Happy Renewal Festival," Heloga said graciously. The Alpha she had been talking to hesitated, and turned to see who had interrupted.

Winstav nodded his head to Heloga without returning the salutation. "We've received no word from you on our requisition order, Regional Commander."

Heloga's smile stiffened as she waved away the other

Alpha. When he had withdrawn, she replied, "There are many things to consider, Winstav. A battleship will have to be recalled, and ship schedules shifted."

As she took a breath, Winstav interjected, "The *Persuasion* is in this system. We could leave for Starbase C-4 in Archernar tomorrow to interview Rikev Alpha's former staff."

"Out of the question." Heloga was acutely aware of everyone watching her, but she could hardly maintain her pleasant expression. "That would leave Canopus Headquarters unprotected. In light of the recent Qin attack, that would be reckless."

"You've known we needed a battleship since we arrived," Winstav reminded her.

"I did not expect it to be this soon. Your request will have to wait until after the festival."

Winstav shrugged, glancing at Felenore. "Our investigation here is complete. If we have to wait, we'll write a preliminary report and send it to the regents now. However, I would prefer to get more information about Rikev from his subordinates at Starbase C-4 and about the Qin situation. A report at this point would mainly concern you, Heloga Alpha."

There was a long silence as she stood very still. Winstav enjoyed it. She was trapped by the curious eyes watching her, and couldn't show that she was angry.

"You can have the *Persuasion*," Heloga finally agreed.

Winstav whipped out his dataport with the order already completed. "This is the recall order and transfer of command for the *Persuasion*."

"You've thought of everything, haven't you?" She sourly took the dataport and entered her official authorization code.

"That's why the regents chose us," Winstav replied smoothly, returning the dataport to his pocket.

As they left Heloga standing alone, Felenore murmured, "Quite efficient."

"Too easy," Winstav muttered. Now that it was over, he felt let down. He had no adversary here worthy of his talents. Perhaps the Qin would prove to be a more interesting challenge. But according to his analysis, the attack on Spacepost T-3 had been an aberration for the Qin.

Winstav turned to see how Heloga was dealing with the fact that he had bested her. But Heloga kept glancing at Kristolas and Olhanna, who were chatting under a nearby arch. They touched each other, stroking arms and leaning in close, making it clear that they were intimate with one another. Heloga could hardly hide her rage at the sight, yet she almost seemed to be in a pre-lust phase. Clearly she had lost control over her lover, and was preoccupied by that rather than the serious problems in her region.

That's when it hit Winstav. He held Heloga's fate in his hands. He could exploit this opportunity and manipulate the Qin situation to make her look very bad indeed, so bad that the regents might even consider appointing a new regional commander in Canopus. He had a good relationship with one person on the short list, Pirosha Alpha, a Fleet commander in Spinca. What if he could spin the information so Pirosha's military talents were needed in Canopus? She would be very grateful for the promotion and could be inclined to assist him in returning from exile.

It was certainly something worth thinking about. Perhaps there was a way he could make this assignment work to his advantage after all.

7

━━━⟋⟍⟋⟍⟋⟍━━━

Chad was at the helm when the *Purpose* approached the planet Balanc. He was glad he was in command so he could cut Rose out of the negotiations with the Qin.

"It's time for an expert," Chad told Jot, his comm officer.

"What are you going to do?" Jot asked with a worried expression.

"There are always other options. The tough part is figuring out what they are."

Chad had gotten close to Jot over the past few decnights as he commanded third shift. She was young like Rose, but Jot didn't try to boss people around. She was a delicate girl with a sweet face and black almond-shaped eyes. Her long dark hair was always silky clean. Chad felt protective toward the girl.

He felt responsible for everyone on board the *Purpose*. He was certain their current mess was Rose's fault. She was the one who had tried to negotiate contracts with civilian Qin merchants, and she was the one who lost their contract with the Armada. If *he* was captain of the *Purpose*, things would be different.

But the other Solians were mesmerized by Rose's

double-talk. What was freedom? Chad didn't like being a slave, but at least when he had been majordomo in his master's house, he was respected and happy. That was the life, as far as he was concerned. But when he lost that, he had become increasingly bitter as he was kicked around the slave trade, passed from master to master until he hardly knew what region he was in.

One thing was sure: He could lead these Solians better than a teenaged girl like Rose. He had run his master's enclave, and he had done it well. But Rose resisted his advice, even after she put him in command of third shift. When it came to making decisions that affected the entire crew, Rose never consulted with him as she did with Ash. Chad liked Ash, but s/he was basically a passive person. S/he had offered no resistance to Rose's wild scheme to go back to Sirius to salvage from the spacepost.

On the way to Balanc, Chad had made his plans. He couldn't talk to Newt about it. She was upset by his arguments with the crew about returning to the Domain, so she cried and stayed in her berth. He had liked Newt from the first moment he saw her, but it sometimes it took effort to be around her. Still, he could sympathize with her confusion and fear—they all felt that. They didn't know what would happen next, and that was exhausting everyone.

Now he tried to explain to Jot. "Rose is too highstrung to handle these Qin. I can take care of them."

Jot looked hopeful. "You can get us a new contract?"

"I used to negotiate our household contracts back on Spinca."

Jot's mouth formed a small "o."

"You don't want to go back to the Domain, do you?"

Chad pressed. Jot quickly shook her head. "Then leave it to me."

Jot still looked upset, but she concentrated on her terminal as the purple planet of Balanc quickly grew in the imager. This was their third trip to the planet, but this time they didn't have any slaves to off-load.

The Qin didn't know they were coming. Chad was prepared when Jot finally announced, "I'm receiving a challenge."

Chad requested the text. It said, *"Identify yourself immediately."*

Jot quickly added, "There's a Qin warship on a parabolic intercept course. Its shields are at maximum."

Chad held his course and sent back a message identifying them, along with the fact that they had recently transported the Qin slaves from the mining station to Balanc.

"We're getting a visual," Jot said nervously.

"Put it on the imager," Chad ordered.

A Qin appeared, facing Chad. It was an older woman, and it took a few distressing moments for Chad to realize she was an aging breeder. Her triangular face was heavy in the jowls, and skin was loose on her neck and hands. Her heavy body spoke of repeated childbearing, which repulsed Chad. He hadn't seen a child since he had left the creche. But the Qin organized themselves in family units.

The woman spoke in a deep firm voice, *"I am Captain M'ha. What is your business here?"*

Chad snapped back into diplomat's mode. "The *Purpose* is here to assist you, Captain M'ha."

"The Armada sent you? Why?"

"We decided to return to Balanc. We know you could use another transport right now."

M'ha was openly suspicious now. *"Who are you?"*

Jot shifted uneasily in her seat, and Chad was glad Rose wasn't here or she would ruin it. "I'm Chad, in command of the *Purpose*."

"Where's your captain?"

"She's off duty right now." He smiled blandly. "We have large cargo holds capable of—"

"Can you carry unprocessed fuel ore?" M'ha demanded.

Chad hesitated. "Our holds aren't shielded."

"Then you can't?"

Chad admitted, "No, but we can transport food, consumer goods, supplies, people—"

"We don't need that kind of transport," M'ha said flatly. *"People and supplies are being carried by grav sleds on the planet."*

Chad held on to his friendly smile. "Perhaps we should ask the commander in charge of this system?"

"Who do you think is in charge around here, boy?" Now M'ha looked angry. That was the aggressive reaction Rose usually provoked.

Chad quickly backtracked. "Good, so you're in command—"

"That's what I said."

Thinking fast, Chad offered, "The battleships will liberate your neighboring systems any day now. You'll be needing a cargo transport to reconnect with the outer colonies."

Captain M'ha shook her head. *"No, Balanc doesn't have anything to trade, and won't for a some time. The other colonies won't have anything to trade either."*

Chad wasn't about to give up. "We'd like permission to orbit Balanc. It may be you'll find you have a need for us yet."

"No, you have to move along. We can't have a trans-

port ship sitting in orbit luring raiders in. We've got enough problems without having to look out for you."

Chad felt a sinking feeling. He had to do something or the Solians would charge boldly into the Domain to steal from that ill-fated spacepost and get themselves captured. He felt a chill on his sweaty skin at the thought of returning to the Domain. He couldn't do it. He would kill himself first.

"Is that all?" Captain M'ha asked.

"No." Maybe he could still convince the rest of the crew to abandon Rose's plan. Chad didn't care what they did, as long as they didn't return to the Domain.

"What do you want?" M'ha asked impatiently.

"We were slaves," Chad admitted. "But we escaped."

"I heard about that," M'ha said noncommittally.

"Our ship doesn't have a contract," Chad said honestly, "and our crew is desperate to help a Solian colony we left behind on Prian. They're thinking about going into the Domain to salvage." M'ha's eyes narrowed in skepticism. Chad hurried to assure her. "I agree with you, it's crazy. But they're desperate. Are you sure there's nothing we can do to help your people?"

"We don't need an interstellar transport."

This Qin was implacable. Jot seemed horrified that he had confessed everything to this stranger. Desperate, Chad offered, "I'm a pilot, I can fly one of those grav sleds of yours."

At that, M'ha perked up her head. *"You can fly a sled?"*

Chad knew it couldn't be any harder than flying the *Purpose.* "Sure. We all have skills. Some of us are trained bot techs, comm operators . . ."

M'ha was nodding. *"We could use skilled pilots and bot techs right now. How many of you are there?"*

"I'll have to let you know," Chad stalled. "I'll contact you shortly. Chad out."

M'ha nodded, then cut the channel. Chad sighed and leaned back in his chair.

Jot's slender fingers were trembling on her terminal. "You're leaving the ship?"

"I doubt it. I've just found a bargaining chip that I can use to force Rose to chose a safer option."

Jot looked confused, but she didn't argue. Still, she was the weakest one in the bunch. Chad knew he would have to convince people like Whit, Mote, and Shard. If they were on his side, then he could take control of the *Purpose*.

Chad sent an announcement through the internal comm requesting everyone to come to the command deck. He wasn't about to run a meeting in the galley. He would speak to them at the helm of the ship. They would see he was fit to lead them.

As they crowded onto the command deck, Rose appeared. She had wild dark hair and was defiantly sultry in spite of her youth. There was a vitality about her that was unmistakable, even when she was bleary-eyed. "What's wrong?"

"I called you all here because we have to decide *now*." Newt tried to sidle close to Chad, but he waved her off.

Rose yawned, opening her mouth wide. "Decide what?"

Chad leaned back in his chair, looking them each in the eye. Jot was cowering behind her terminal, but Whit and Mote were watching him carefully. Ash was right behind them, along with Shard who was languidly stretching. It appeared he had interrupted Shard and Nip. They both had that tousled, sex-charged expression he knew so well.

"We have to decide what to do. It's not safe to go into the Domain."

"You're loco!" Rose snapped. "You woke me up for this? We already voted. You were there. You lost, remember?"

"But we have other options now," Chad told them.

There were exclamations as everyone tried to ask at once what he meant. Even the ridge-headed Delta eased up the steps and stood in the door as if he wasn't sure he should come onto the command deck.

"We don't have to go back," Chad insisted. "There's other ways we can earn credit."

"Did you get another contract?" Rose demanded.

Chad couldn't let her seize control. "It's a way we can live without risking slavery again." That caught their attention. "These people need help down on Balanc. They need skilled bot techs and pilots. We can earn credit at the same time for the Prian colony. Isn't that better than risking everything on the word of a Delta?"

Everyone turned to look at Kwort, who seemed taken aback. "All I said is the spacepost has tons of stuff to salvage!"

"Stop harassing Kwort," Rose told Chad. "He's one of the crew just like you and Newt are."

Whit was shaking his head. "You're saying we should abandon the *Purpose* and go live on Balanc?"

"I have a better idea," Chad drawled, seeing rejection in too many faces. "If enough of us refuse to go back to the Domain, then we'll have to choose another option, like trying to get a Qin contract or going up to the Elaspian sector—"

Mote interrupted, "We don't have time to do that. The colonists need our help."

Chad flung up his arms. "They're fine on Prian! They can gather their own food, and they have shelter. Why should we endanger our lives to give the colonists luxuries?"

It was Shard, desirable sexy Shard, who shook her head. "Those Solians are in trouble, Chad. They need medical supplies and energy sources to take care of themselves."

"Everyone suffers!" Chad insisted. "We've suffered. We'll find another way without risking everything."

Rose stepped forward as smoothly as if she had timed it. "Go down to Balanc, Chad. Anyone who doesn't like the risk should go with him. Because being on the *Purpose* is risky. None of us are safe anywhere, but I'd rather be under my own steam than rely on the charity of the Qin."

"I'm not going back to the Domain!" Chad retorted.

They stared at each other hotly before Rose flashed her easy smile. "Sorry to see you go! Who's with Chad?"

Newt burst into tears and put her hands over her face. Chad wanted to snap at her to get some spine. She was weakening his position. Maybe it swayed the others. Maybe they had already made up their minds. No one spoke.

"Jot," Chad said quietly. "You can't stay on board. You know how dangerous it is."

Jot's thin lips were compressed and there was a worry line between her eyes. But she spoke up firmly enough, "I want to stay."

Chad looked around at Mote and Whit, but they were on Shard's side. Clay and Dab were glaring at him for suggesting they leave. Ash looked upset, and suddenly Chad realized that his strongest ally on the ship hadn't said one word during his plea. But Ash would never leave Rose, not after Rose had rescued hir from S'jen. He should have known that.

"You'll be slaves again!" Chad exclaimed, but they wouldn't listen. He had lost them.

It took more than a decnight to reach the Domain, and every light-year weighed heavily on Ash. S/he missed Chad, and s/he dreaded that he had been right and they were charging back into slavery. S/he had championed Kwort and brought him into the crew. If they were caught, would it be hir fault?

It didn't help that Ash was in command when the *Purpose* neared the Reticulum-Perspokesor slip, which led into the pocket containing Spacepost T-3. S/he could hardly hold still as the grav slip neared. There could be a Fleet patrolship on the other side of that slip stopping everyone who entered the pocket. Other than Kund, Ash didn't know of anyone who had dared to attack the Domain. Wouldn't the Fleet post guards at every slip?

A small whimper escaped hir.

"Is something wrong?" Jot asked.

Ash had to swallow before s/he could answer. "No."

Jot kept eyeing hir until Ash finally admitted, "I'm wondering if I should call Rose for this slip."

Jot glanced down at the grid at the bottom of the imager that showed the estimated location of their target. It was on the other side of the Reticulum-Perspokesor slip.

"Do you want me to call her?" Jot asked.

Ash took a deep breath. Rose spent too much time on the command deck. She was probably sleeping in her berth or was having sex with Stub. Either one would be good for her. What if s/he called Rose to the command deck and nothing happened?

"I'm being jumpy," Ash admitted. S/he knew that Rose, on the other hand, had been remarkably light-hearted since they had left Qin. Rose had kept up the spirits of the others, and was apparently relieved Chad had left. They were too much alike, stubborn and willful. But it felt wrong as Ash had watched Chad go through the airlock after Newt onto the space-to-ground trans-port. They were the only two who left the *Purpose*.

That's why Ash was in command of the third shift. S/he wasn't comfortable with that role, but s/he had done it before on their escape from the Domain. Ash tried to hide hir shaking every time their scanners picked up a cargo transport or yacht. Once they had seen a massive starliner. Twice their long distance scanners had picked up patrolships, but Kwort's alteration in their ship's designation number had passed the test.

They stripped the Fleet beacons that floated in each pocket and pored over the public-access data. As they went deeper into Sirius, they got up-to-date bulletins about safe routes, trade advisories, and health warnings.

Rose had plotted the slips taking them along a little-used route in a roundabout approach to the pocket that held the spacepost. If there was a patrolship in the slip guarding the wreck, the captain would be especially watchful toward Qin. Ash wouldn't be surprised if InSec knew what had happened to the *Conviction*. The Alphas seemed to know everything.

Ash added, "It's too bad this old ship wasn't retrofit-ted with missiles."

Now Jot was nervous and unhappy. Ash knew s/he

was a terrible leader. If s/he could just pull them through this slip without running into a patrolship, s/he would tell Rose to train Whit or Mote to take over third shift. They would be much better at the job.

As the slip neared, the blinking red indicator grew larger. The red shine reflected on Jot's girlish face and on hir own hands on the terminal. Neither said a word but they were breathing too loud. Ash wished s/he could say something reassuring to Jot, but hir fear of what could be on the other side was too strong.

"Here it comes," Jot whispered.

On the final approach, Ash was caught up in the soothing routine of slip entry; reducing speed, setting the angle of glide with the thrusters after reconfirming with close-range scanners the exact location of the slip mouth. S/he was good at this part. Detail was hir specialty. If only s/he had been born in a different arm of the galaxy than the one controlled by the Domain.

Jot squinted her eyes shut as the red indicator flared and covered the entire imager. The *Purpose* entered the slip and was instantly whisked four light-years away. For a moment everything shifted together. Ash's eyes were bedazzled by multicolored stars while it felt as if s/he was flipped upside down.

Ash tried to see the navigational scanner as they emerged from the slip, arriving just outside the gravity well of the Perspokesor system. There was a dramatic view of the Perspokesor spiral nebula on the imager.

"The scanners!" Ash cried out to Jot, who was rubbing her forehead because of the slip shock.

It took a few moments for Ash to realize there was nothing on the navigational scanner. But there could be a ship hiding in the lee . . .

"I'm not reading anything," Jot finally reported, having put the scanners through the various procedures they had established to separate random galactic noise from actual objects in space. No ship appeared out of the lee.

"Can you pick up T-3?" Ash asked. Hir own navigational scanners couldn't locate it in the space nearby.

"No." Jot activated the schematic they had developed of this grav pocket. Kwort had given them an estimated location of the spacepost. "It's way out of range. We won't get there for at least another fourteen hours."

Ash flexed hir shoulders, feeling at a loss. S/he had expected a patrolship to be waiting for them, as if they knew a batch of runaway slaves were returning to the scene of the crime. Of course that was silly, but paranoia wasn't supposed to be rational.

But Kwort was right—space was endless. And the Fleet had a lot more important things to worry about than a few wayward slaves.

Ash realized s/he was setting a bad example for the rest of the crew. After Rose took over command for first shift, Ash went straight to Shard and asked for help. Shard was their sex queen extraordinaire, and she knew a million ways to enhance or alter physical responses.

Ash wasn't looking for sex. For hir, sex was rape or abuse. Ash had never engaged in consensual sex, and s/he wasn't sure s/he was capable of it. But none of the other Solians seemed to have trouble being intimate with each other. The crew was a revolving set of couples, triads, and quads. At any time there were likely to be sex games going on in the party room, formerly the captain's cabin. But Ash only watched, never joining in. The others were sympathetic and didn't push hir, but they must have thought s/he was strange.

When Shard heard what Ash needed, she went straight to the transposer in the galley and programmed it to dispense a hot liquid. She made Ash drink it right there.

"What is it?" Ash wrinkled hir nose at the minty smell that couldn't mask a bitter taste.

Shard winked at hir. "That's my surefire sleep cure."

Ash hesitated, the cup half-empty. "I don't want to be unconscious if anything happens."

"Don't worry, sweetheart, I'll wake you if we get a knock on the door. I *promise.*" Shard gave Ash a confidential smile. "I'm off duty and I don't have anyone to do."

Ash grinned back and finished the drink. "I hope it works."

"You look like you could fall asleep right here," Shard assured hir. "Let me help you back to your berth."

Maybe it was working that fast, because Ash didn't mind it when Shard put her arm around hir, supporting hir shoulders. S/he usually couldn't bear to be touched. But Shard was so easy, so giving and relaxed, that it was impossible to reject her. Ash had almost stopped seeing how beautiful Shard was—a product of genetic enhancement that combined Solian and alien DNA to produce a miracle of femininity. Holding on to Shard's waist, Ash could feel how small it was, how tempting the flare of her hips and the warm globe of her breast against hir flat chest.

Ash felt a stirring in hir genitals that s/he hadn't felt in years, a desire to hold and penetrate . . .

"You're feeling good," Shard purred in pleasure.

Ash was almost jolted out of hir warm fuzzy feelings

of quasi-lust, but Shard knew what she was doing. She didn't press a millimeter. Instead, she let Ash shamelessly rub against her as they walked back to hir berth. S/he had visions of sinking into warm flesh, burying hirself inside of Shard, and letting her stroke pleasure into hir willing body.

Shard helped Ash into the bunk and pulled the covers over hir. Ash felt the warm wetness of Shard's lips on hir forehead, a lingering kiss that told hir how much s/he was loved.

"I'll watch over you," Shard whispered.

Ash breathed deep of her scent, that of a ripe and sensual woman, as s/he drifted off to sleep.

Needless to say, Ash felt marvelous when s/he woke many hours later. When s/he returned to command, Rose had taken the helm from Nip and was controlling their final approach to the spacepost.

"Any sign of ships?" Ash asked.

"Nope," Rose replied cheerfully. "What a sight, huh?"

Ash was shaking hir head at the imager. "It didn't look like that the last time I saw it."

S/he had seen Spacepost T-3 once before from a malfunctioning lifepod. The spacepost had been relatively intact and magnificent despite S'jen's attack. It was the place where Ash had lived for almost a standard year under hir master, Rikev Alpha.

Now the spacepost was crumpled and torn in half. The towering central column was in two jagged pieces connected only by a strip of hull that was bent over backward. The massive landing discs at either end were crushed against each other with their hull plating and bulkheads tangled together.

"What made it break in half?" Ash asked.

Stub shrugged. "I think it was the damage to the processing unit. It's all ripped up."

"It looks like S'jen's work to me," Rose put in wryly.

Ash agreed, though she didn't say so.

"It's moving faster than I expected," Rose added. "I'm going to take us into that wedge."

"Why so close to the other landing disc?" Ash asked. "What if everything shifts and it crushes our ship?"

"We can hide in the crimp and shut down our systems so scanners won't pick us up. But we'll be running passive scans to spot anyone before they get close enough to see us."

Ash nodded slowly. So s/he wasn't the only one hyperaware of the need to stay away from the Fleet. "Makes sense to me."

Rose grinned as she input commands on her terminal. "I'm taking her in."

Ash shivered as the curve of the spacepost grew bigger in the imager, rising over their heads. S/he almost wanted to go to the portal to see it with hir own eyes. But s/he would get a close-up view soon enough. Soon s/he would be walking around that spacepost, trying not to remember hir past life as a slave.

8

Kwort nervously fiddled with his cartridge belt. He had practiced with vacuum environments in Fleet training simulations, but this would be his first walk in real space. It was scary, exactly what he had hoped to do when he joined the Fleet. But the highlight of his former Fleet career had been the last time he came to Spacepost T-3 with Horc.

Kwort was surprised when he was chosen to be one of the advance team. But Rose and Ash decided they needed their best bot tech. Whit had insisted on coming to keep an eye on Kwort, probably because he felt responsible for standing up for Kwort against Chad. Kwort didn't care; he wasn't about to do something stupid like try to attract the Fleet's attention.

"Are you ready?" the captain demanded as she strode up the corridor.

Kwort instinctively went to attention. But the captain didn't even pause to inspect them or give orders. He was wearing a bright green flightsuit with a new Qin cartridge belt they had wrangled because of the broken Armada contract.

"Did you check the seal?" she asked Kwort.

"Uh, negative." He pulled a bot unit out of his pouch and placed it on the crack around the airlock seal. When he activated the unit, two microscopic bots zipped inside the bot hatch to check the leakage factor on the airlock. "It will take a few moments, Captain Rose."

"Stop calling me that," the captain ordered. "It's one or the other, not both."

"Uh . . . yes, Rose," he stuttered, then corrected himself, "Captain!"

Rose rolled her eyes and laughed in Ash's direction. Kwort thought it was very unorthodox.

Before long the lights flashed on the bot unit. Kwort inserted it into his dataport and read the results. "It's not good, Captain. There is a thirty-two percent non-contact rate."

Ash suggested, "We could try another airlock. This one must have been damaged."

Rose shook her head. "This is the best hiding spot on the place. What's the downside, Kwort?"

He blinked. "There's a fail-safe so that if the seal breaks, a temporary forcefield slows the leakage rate. There's enough time to shut the airlock if someone stays right here."

"We'll be wearing flightsuits anyway," Whit pointed out.

Kwort felt compelled to add, "We could also lose our lock on the spacepost. If that happens, the *Purpose* will drift away."

Ash raised hir brows. "That's a bigger problem."

"Someone has to stay on board running scans anyway," Rose pointed out. "Everyone's had the training, so they should be able to handle the helm as well."

"You want Jot trying to redock the *Purpose?*" Whit asked.

"Okay, we'll leave a couple people on board," Rose decided.

Kwort thought he had missed something. "You still want to use this airlock?"

"You got it," Rose said.

"Why not?" Whit agreed while Ash nodded.

He sure wasn't in the Fleet anymore. He couldn't imagine an Alpha taking such a chance.

"Suit up!" Rose called out. "Activate your grav boots."

They only had four sets of grav boots, which was why the advance team was limited to four people. The grav boots were normally used for emergency hull repair work. Their priority was to find more boots inside the spacepost so everyone else could suit up and help with the salvage.

Kwort lifted the safety latch on his cartridge belt, thumbing the control. A light blue haze sprang up around him. His hand was coated in a fine energy field and there was a faint hum in his ears. When he looked up, Ash, Whit, and Rose had turned into bluish aliens.

"Comm check," Rose said.

The others answered, with Kwort last. The comm was slung around his neck, and it sounded like he was in a tiny closet. He felt a mounting excitement as Rose opened the airlock. An alarming hissing sound came through the external comm.

"What are you waiting for?" Rose demanded.

Kwort went inside while Rose stayed to close the airlock. Ash and Whit came after him, pushing him forward to operate the decompression controls. That was fine with Kwort. At least he knew how to decompress an airlock without killing anyone.

Their blue forcefields brightened as crystalline clear vacuum replaced the air. Kwort carefully popped open the inner lock when there was no difference in the pressure. Ash, Rose, and Whit stepped through after him. Their flightsuits gave off enough ambient light for them to see.

They were in the lower landing disc of the huge spacepost. Kwort had come through an airlock much like this last time. Back then, the corridors had looked like every other space station with bluish gray bulkheads and off-white paneling.

Now the walls were ripped open, sliced through during the explosive decompression. Nearby, an industrial plant of some kind had reinforced cross-beams bent around it. When they reached the central lift tube, the other half of the landing disc was gone. A twisted mass of wreckage filled half the disc.

"What a mess!" Kwort exclaimed.

"Roughed up the place up a bit, didn't it?" the captain tossed out.

"I'll say," Whit agreed hollowly through the comm.

"What a mess," Kwort repeated, unable to think of anything more coherent to say.

"Salvage isn't going to be easy in the landing discs," Ash said in a worried voice. "How do we get up to the main station?"

As they circled the central lift tube, it was clearly smashed beyond use.

Kwort gestured up. "There's secondary airlocks that must lead to the terminal above."

"How are we going to get up there?" Ash asked. "The stairs are ripped away."

Kwort showed them. "Like this." He lifted one foot

and placed it on a wall that was relatively intact. With a slight hitch, he shifted his other foot from the floor onto the wall. He started to walk up the wall, jutting out perpendicularly over their heads. "It's easy."

He walked around a bit getting used to the disorientation. There were metal tags and spears standing up where decorative and support elements had been torn away by the decompression. He examined a piece of plasteel that had melted under the strain, pulling out like frozen taffy.

The other three started clumping up to the airlock. It was closed, useless against the vacuum on either side. Kwort got busy with his bots and had it ready to pop in record time. He had always wanted to blow a real airlock.

He set off the bots and was shocked when a puff of atmosphere slammed open the lock. He didn't expect pressure to be on the other side.

But it quickly dissipated, and the others stepped through into a round transfer terminal. He had forgotten that a layer of atmosphere was maintained between the landing disc and the spacepost itself in case a section suffered a rupture.

Kwort decided not to trust the lift tube since it was mangled down below. At the top of an intact set of stairs was another secondary airlock. This time Kwort took the precaution of checking the pressure. Vacuum, as he expected. He got the bots going again, and this lock blew with no trouble. He didn't bother to say anything. The others didn't realize his earlier mistake. He was lucky there hadn't been more atmosphere in the terminal or it could have caused a dangerous explosion. Trial and error was probably why Fleet officers had to work their way up to posts with responsibility. Kwort resolved to follow precedure from now on.

The last time Kwort had stepped into the atrium of the spacepost, the towering cylinder had made him dizzy as he leaned back to see all the way up. He had liked the cylindrical spacepost better than the cubical, mazelike starbases or the webbed starports.

Now the tall cylinder was cut off halfway. Stars twinkled in the mouth of the jagged hole. A towering spire stuck up on one side, a remnant of the link that had once joined it to the rest of the spacepost.

The balconies and terraces that encircled the atrium were in shambles with metal railings twisted and wall panels torn away. But it appeared that the rooms were intact behind the bulkheads, which had been designed to withstand vacuum in case the cylinder was breached.

"All right, folks," Rose said sharply. "Let's see what's left."

Kwort urged them to stay clipped together in twos with the fine line from their cartridge belt playing out or retracting depending on how far apart they were. It was basic space-walking rules. After seeing that gaping hole at the top, everyone appreciated the need for safety measures.

Kwort was linked to Whit. They separated from Rose and Ash to look for things on their priority list, especially grav boots and technical devices they could trade. They were hoping to find stashes in warehouses and abandoned shops. When they found a large stock-pile, they marked it with bright orange glow sticks. As they came across bots and loose salvageable items, they tied them together and floated them along behind. Mostly on

the lower levels they found empty warehouses where
raiders had gotten there before them.

Kwort and Whit were the first to find grav boots, in the
processor maintenance station. They raced back with their
loot and passed it among the crew. Rose and Ash returned to the ship with two large bundles of salvage they
had picked up. Ash hooked up with Mote while Rose took
Shard, Nip took Stub, leaving Jot and Dab behind watching the scanners. They suited up and went back out for
more. The pitiful pile they had accumulated in one cargo
container showed how labor intensive salvage would be.

With four teams and one independent stringer at the airlock terminal to shuttle stuff into the ship, they started to
cover more ground. Kwort stayed tied to Whit. Though
they had worked together on the bots, nothing had
made Whit comfortable with him.

But the excitement of salvage was irresistible. Kwort
felt as though he were back with Horc, deep in the thrill
of rummaging through the spacepost for riches far beyond his means. Whit seemed to appreciate the fact that
Kwort knew the rough layout of the place and where
likely stores could be found.

Kwort and Whit were the first to approach the edge
of the cylinder where the two halves had been split
apart. Kwort was determined to get into the upper half
of the spacepost, because that was where the Alphas and
Betas had lived.

There were stress fractures in the plasteel that had
bent over backward, something Kwort thought was
physically impossible. They carefully made their way to
the rough edge where the spacepost was still joined.
Kwort stretched out one leg and stepped all the way

around. He kept an eye out for the sharp edges of the bulkheads that had been severed all around him.

As Kwort expected, in the upper half they found storerooms for the administrative offices. When they came across a supply of dataports—thousands of them—they called through the comm link and got the others to join them. That much bulk material made the salvage effort worth it. They strapped the dataports into large nets that floated in the vacuum, then spread out so they could pass the bundles by shoving them gently from one end of the cylinder to the other. After that the cargo containers began to fill faster.

Rose and Shard were sending down bundles of dataports from the storeroom while Whit grabbed them before they drifted out of the spacepost. He passed each bundle to Kwort who carefully handed them around the bend to Nip. Nip caught hold and turned to pass them on to his partner Stub. Mote and Ash were at the other end of the cylinder waiting to grab the bundles. They passed them to Dab who floated them back to the *Purpose* and piled them in the airlock for Clay. Clay had the toughest job inside the ship. He couldn't keep up with loading the dataports on grav sleds, so Dab started tying the bundles in the corridor outside the airlock.

Things were going along fine, when it happened.

Kwort passed a bundle around the bend and was turning away when he heard a muffled cry. Nip was slowly falling backward flailing his arms. It was a natural reaction in vacuum. He had lost his balance and only had his boots to hold him down.

One of Nip's arms flung out and struck a jagged bulkhead.

A spray of red drops burst against the inside of his blue forcefield, staining it dark purple. Nip let out a ragged roar of pain and began to flail, jerking his grav boots off the station. Kwort grabbed Nip's arm instinctively, keeping him from floating away while trying to stop the flow of blood.

Nip choked off his screams, but his eyes went wide with shock and panic.

"You'll be okay!" Kwort wasn't sure if that was true but Nip needed to hear it.

Everyone came flying and there was chaos. Kwort was afraid he and Nip would be pushed into the sharp bulkheads and curling layers of hull plating around them. But Whit took care of it, towing them gently into the upper cylinder and anchoring them to the wall. Nip passed out during the move, and for a moment, Kwort thought he was dead.

"We have to get him back to the ship!" Mote cried through the comm.

"No, he needs a biobed," Kwort protested. He could feel the gaping wound.

Rose looked angry. "We don't have a biobed."

Whit was helping Kwort hold Nip. "His arm is almost cut off!" Whit exclaimed.

Kwort tried not to look but he could feel the mass of muscle and the sharp ends of bone under his hands. At least Nip's forcefield had held, surrounding the razor-sharp bulkhead as it sliced into him, keeping vacuum from penetrating. Otherwise they would be dealing with a decompression death rather than a life-threatening injury.

"There must be a biobed on the spacepost," Kwort insisted.

"What about power?" Mote asked.

"Get one of those mini-converters we found. I can use that to power it."

They rushed to do as he said, with some returning over the bend to fetch a miniconverter while others hurried off in search of a biobed. Kwort and Whit held onto Nip. Kwort only hoped he could activate a biobed in time to save him.

It was a nightmare. Nip regained consciousness and began screaming and thrashing around. So much blood was lost that his entire forcefield was stained purple. They had to hold him down.

Kwort finally got to take his hands out of Nip's severed biceps while Dab stepped up to plug the gash with her own hands. Kwort felt sick at the blossoming of red under the forcefield. Dab pressed her dark hands against Nip's slippery arm.

Rose and Shard met him halfway up the severed spacepost at a medical bay. Kwort rushed to the biobed. He wasn't through disconnecting the main power relays when Mote and Ash returned with a miniconverter and his bot pouch. As Kwort quickly connected the converter, he couldn't help remembering how he had become so familiar with these units. He had used one exactly like this to shock Kitarin and Murroom. Through long nights in his berth creating simulations of what must have happened, he had determined that a feedback loop had been caused by the catwalk that circled the engineering well. That had killed Horc and set off an explosion in engineering.

Kwort tried to concentrate and ignore their shrill voices. There were too many of them in the small room, but his only concern was getting the biobed running. Whit had already supervised inserting Nip into the bed. Now he checked the nutrient and medicinal reservoirs.

"It's full!" Rose insisted. "We already looked."

Dab was leaning into the biobed holding Nip's arm. Nip was moaning and jerking so the others pinned him down inside.

"What about his flightsuit?" Rose asked. It hung in tatters from one arm. "Will the biobed work with him in the forcefield?"

Kwort looked up, stymied for a moment. The flight-suit would have to be deactivated, but they couldn't do it before the biobed was shut because of the vacuum. "We need an empty cartridge."

"An empty one?" Ash asked. "Why?"

"Put it on Nip's belt. We'll take all the others off except the empty one. There will be enough charge for it to last a few moments longer, and that will give us time to shut the lid and pressurize the bed. After the forcefield dies, the bed can get to his arm."

They started working over Nip. Rose taped a handful of full cartridges to the inside of the lid so Nip would be able to activate his flightsuit before opening the biobed. There were various exclamations of: "Make sure it's empty." "Stop, don't take them all off!" "He's turning white." "Hurry!"

Kwort kept his eyes on his work. The bots quickly knit the power relays together. He ran a diagnostic to be sure the life support and medical scanners were working properly. The others were urging him on, but he was too scared to ignore procedure.

Someone warned, "Watch out, he's starting to convulse."

"The power's on," Kwort told them, moving to the controls. "I'll need to program it."

There were groans, but Rose cut through the mayhem. "Quiet, everyone!" She was holding on to one of Nip's legs but she managed to make it look as though she were on the command deck. "We'll need to time this right. When Kwort's ready, I'll give the signal. Mote, you pull the full cartridge on his belt, leaving the empty one. Everyone let go of Nip. I'll put the lid down."

They were watching her expectantly, a few of them nodding. Faces were flushed and anxious, but chaos had retreated. Dab glanced up from her grisly job as Mote positioned herself to grab the full cartridge. Whit, Shard, and Stub were also holding on to Nip, who continued to cry out and writhe in pain.

Kwort entered the last few commands. The biobed signaled that its prep was completed. He nodded to Rose. "Ready, Captain."

"Okay, everyone." She took a deep breath. "Go, Mote!"

Mote grabbed the last full cartridge, and the field faded visibly. Dab had to pull to get her hand out of the deep wound. Blood gushed under the forcefield. The rest of them let go of Nip who was shaking uncontrollably.

Rose was fast and had the top down as Nip cried out. The biobed cycled on with every light reassuringly in place.

Kwort leaned over the clear window, his stomach clenching. He might have done something wrong—

But the stasis field snapped on as Nip's blue forcefield weakened. The air inside quickly rose to full pressure. The cartridge took longer to fail than Kwort expected, and blood flowed out of the wound. But when the forcefield failed, Nip continued to breathe and his motions stilled. The bed had probably drugged him.

"Is he okay?" someone asked.

"He's breathing," Kwort said in relief. "He's alive."

"But what about his arm?" Rose asked. "Will he lose it?"

Kwort shook his head. "These things can stitch you back together as long as all the pieces are inside. I've been in enough bio-beds to know."

The others sighed, not quite sure that the crisis was over. They took turns looking through the window. Nip appeared to be sleeping, and they couldn't see what was happening to his arm under the rising gel that the biobots worked in. Mote attached the universal sign for vacuum in the clear pane so Nip would know he had to activate his flightsuit before the biobed could be opened.

Rose finally turned to Kwort, who was feeling a bit shocked. "Thanks, Kwort. Nip would be dead without you."

Kwort realized she meant it. None of the others could have jury-rigged a converter to power a biobed.

The others gathered around him saying their thanks. Kwort could hardly realize that he had saved Nip's life. But he looked at their faces, full of relief and even smiling down through the pane at Nip as he rested in stasis. Kwort felt an immense satisfaction.

But it made the pain and horror seem even more stark. He had saved one life, but he had destroyed dozens of others. How could he ever learn to deal with that?

Rose ordered one crew member to stay near the biobed with Nip at all times. The readout said it would take an estimated three more days for him to heal completely, but Rose wasn't taking any chances of the lid popping open before Nip had activated his flightsuit.

Kwort rigged a light so they could see in the medical bay. Then he unhooked the biobed from its stabilizers so it could be floated out of the medical bay. They would have to get it onto the *Purpose* to take Nip with them. Kwort was already planning to open up one of their retractable cargo containers on the ship. They would have to find jet harnesses so they could maneuver it through space to the ship.

After he was done with the biobed, Kwort returned to salvaging. Everyone was skipping sleep because time was their enemy. They couldn't afford to be seen by the Fleet or by raiders. Rose insisted that they stay only until they found jet harnesses, then they were packing up the stuff they had found and were leaving, biobed and all.

Kwort's partner this time was Clay. Kwort had gotten used to dealing with the silent bot tech. Clay was so expressive with his face and hands that it wasn't hard to communicate. He could also whistle. Clay did one whistle with a rising note at the end that Kwort especially liked.

"Let's go to the upper half of the cylinder," Kwort suggested. Clay nodded agreement.

Kwort wanted to search the commanders' quarters. Sometimes the smallest items were worth the most, as long as you knew where to look. He had seen a few personal safes back when he and Horc were exploring the spacepost. With that in mind, on their way to Sirius, Kwort had programmed a pouchful of bots that could trigger the locking mechanism on safes. They worked great on the safe in the captain's cabin on the *Purpose*, but that one was old.

He almost explained it to Clay, having no reason to hide anything. But Kwort was suddenly very uncomfortable and couldn't quite get the words out. It wasn't because Clay was withdrawn or threatening. He was nearly as short as Kwort, with large mild eyes and rich olive skin. Kwort's gaze rested on the curve of his jaw, and his black hair swaying softly at the back of his smooth neck. Kwort had seen some sex happening in odd places on board the *Purpose,* though the Solians usually tried to avoid him. But he hadn't ever seen Clay with anyone. He wondered if Clay would react with pleasure like others when he was having sex, or if he would remain a dark, limpid pool, letting him sink with no resistance into the depths . . .

Kwort abruptly realized he was in lust.

He felt like an idiot. He kept losing track, because the *Purpose* had a shorter day than everyone else in the Domain. He often ended up working two out of four shifts before going to sleep, then during his next "day" worked only one shift.

It was annoying enough when the lust came on him while he was on duty, but he could usually run back to his berth to satisfy himself. Sometimes it even woke him from sleep. Now it was excruciating. He was used to indulging his lust and had little practice in ignoring it.

Since there was nothing he could do, he clenched his teeth and tried to think about something else.

Clay didn't help. He glanced continually at Kwort, watching him as he watched everything so closely. Kwort wondered what it was like to be silent, to have to struggle to make your desires known. Clay didn't seem to be close to any of the other slaves. Perhaps he felt as isolated as Kwort.

Kwort tried breathing deep as his head swam and his lust pulled his hips forward. Visions of what he could do to that lithe young man filled his brain. He could hardly restrain himself from reaching out for Clay. The guy would probably be shocked. The only thing Kwort had ever talked to him about was bots.

Scratching his ridges furiously, Kwort tried to think about something, anything else. It wasn't his fault! He was constantly surrounded by pleasure slaves. They were born and bred for people like him to desire them. How could he resist?

Then he had a bright idea. Maybe Clay would want to give it a whirl? He wouldn't know until he asked.

"Uh, Clay. Uh, I don't suppose . . ." Kwort tried to get his tongue around his request, stumbling over himself in confusion.

Clay stopped and tilted his head at Kwort. That one gesture, his face so open and sincere, his virile body so tempting . . . and Kwort's lust abruptly peaked.

Kwort groaned, his face contorting.

Clay reached out in concern, not understanding.

Kwort waved him off and started walking. His legs could hardly work. He felt giddy with relief and humiliation. He hadn't had such a satisfying lust since . . . Horc.

Tears welled up and slid down his face, a release he couldn't stop after the tension of lust had flowed from his body.

Clay was watching him sympathetically.

Kwort finally stopped and turned around. He knew he owed Clay some explanation. "I was thinking of my friend, Horc. You reminded me of him."

Clay slowly nodded. He put out one hand and rested

it on Kwort's shoulder as they walked together. It felt good.

Kwort and Clay searched the highest-ranking offices and quarters they could find. Furniture and objects floated or were mangled together along with the wall panels. It was like sifting through a garbage pile, with the gems few and far between.

But Kwort found a few safes. The bots did the job, opening the locks more quickly than he had estimated they would. Perhaps he was finally tapping his full potential. Too bad it lay outside the law of the Domain.

Clay held onto the fine-mesh net that swelled with credit chips, ingots of rare metals, jewels, advanced technological devices, including a nifty cartridge belt that had a weapons shield. It was a treasure hunt with a real payoff.

Clay was as excited as Kwort. Though Kwort was the only one whooping and calling out at their finds, Clay was right there, nudging him and slapping his back at the wealth they were gathering.

"The captain will be pleased when she sees all this!" Kwort exclaimed.

Someone else might have tried to figure out how to conceal a few of the precious items, but he wasn't greedy. Yet when they opened the secured safe in a sub-commander's office in the administrative level, Kwort had a personal interest. There was a stack of identity chips and a programmer inside.

"I'm saved!" he cried out.

Clay shook his head, raising his shoulders.

The black box didn't look like much, and the programmer could have been an old-fashioned dataport.

But Kwort examined it and saw that a simple software bot could alter the units' internal stats, changing the date and location that was imprinted on the identity chip.

"This is exactly what I need," Kwort assured him. "Watch."

First he used his bot baton to program a bot, requesting a change in the settings to that of Deneb's starport with a date of about three cycles ago. There were plenty of ID readers in the mess of stuff, so it wasn't hard to find the codes for Deneb. He inserted the blank identity chip, a square smaller than his palm, to complete the preliminary imprinting. The programmer beeped confirmation as the chip popped out.

Kwort held the chip in front of himself, staring at the small silver square. With a slight tilt, it captured a tiny reflection of his face. He held still for a moment; then it flashed.

He pressed the dimpled edge of the chip against his wrist. He wasn't sure how bad it was going to hurt, but it was necessary.

A sharp ping rang through his arm as the correlating beacon shot through his skin and buried itself against his artery.

"Now it's got my image and the beacon is implanted. I can enter my new identity," Kwort told Clay. "I've never had a chip before. Denebs only get them when they leave the planet. But I joined the Fleet and was subject to eye scans."

Clay gestured with interest at the chip as Kwort inserted it in the programmer.

"Who am I going to be?" Kwort asked. "I'm Deneb, of course. But my new name will be . . . Cwart. That's close enough. I'll give them a different identity number.

There's millions of Denebs, and most don't ever leave the planet."

Kwort filled in the information, including occupation as bot tech. He listed his post as a commercial cargo transport that had been attacked and destroyed by raiders on the edge of the Sirius sector. The *Conviction* had responded and fought the raiders, but Kwort had missed it because he was lying in a biobed like the one Nip was in. He remembered watching the logs afterward, wishing he had been awake for his first space battle. The name of the freighter, *Duty*, and its designation number had stuck in his mind because of the unusual sequence.

For "training," he put down the name of the technical school on Deneb Prime near his old neighborhood. He had always wanted to go there but couldn't afford it. That's why he had worked so hard to be accepted by the Fleet. His age and other particulars he kept the same.

"Now I'm Cwart Deneb. My ID was most recently updated when I accepted a post on the freighter *Duty*. My ship was attacked by raiders and destroyed."

Clay was nodding and smiling. He gestured to himself and whistled.

Kwort agreed, "We could give all of you new identities. But you look Solian. You'd need some kind of physical alteration to pass as a Delta or Gamma. We should talk to the captain about it first. Once you're implanted with an ID chip, it's bloody hard to get rid of it."

Clay nodded in understanding. He carefully tucked the chips, the programmer, and a couple of readers into the net. Then he gestured downward.

"You want to get back to the *Purpose?*" Kwort asked. At Clay's nod, he agreed, "You're probably right. We should let the captain know what we found."

They were climbing through the wreckage of desks and floating terminals when the floor shifted under Kwort.

He flung his arms out, trying to catch his balance. Clay went crashing into a nearby wall. Everything moved on the spacepost, then settled again.

When Kwort regained his balance, he helped Clay up. "What was *that?*"

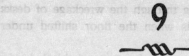

9

Dab heaved another heavy cargo barrel off the grav sled. She was sweating and her muscles ached, but she didn't stop unloading the sled. There was a ton of salvaged stuff stuck outside the airlock of the *Purpose*, and they had to get it in so they could leave this dangerous raider magnet.

As Dab worked, she thought a lot about Kwort. She had never trusted the Delta because she had suffered too much at their hands. Dab wasn't beautiful or unique like the others. She didn't have Shard's sensual perfection, or Rose's native beauty, or Jot's exotic innocence. She was an ordinary Solian and had sunk to the bottom of the slave trade. She had worked in public pleasure houses on constant rotation among space stations and planets. She serviced Deltas and Gammas, people like Kwort, who were enjoying their once-a-year bonus or their saved credit to act out their favorite fantasy. She had been used in the worst possible ways, and forced to do some things that she would never speak about. She knew the others understood. Only Kwort was an outsider.

"Need a hand?" Mote called through the door to the cargo container.

"Nope, go get another load from Rose." Rose was outside shuttling the stuff into the airlock. The rest of the crew were on the station looking for jet harnesses. Hopefully soon they would be able to move Nip's biobed onto the *Purpose*.

Grunting with the last toss, Dab grabbed the sled and shoved it out the door. She was in shape to do this work. After Rose had rescued them, Dab began to learn new things. She had trained on every duty station on the ship. And she had defiantly cut her black curls down to the nub. Shard said she liked it, and that was good enough for Dab. She also cared about Whit and Nip. They were the core four, the ones who had bonded in the cargo container before Rose broke them out. So when Kwort helped Nip, it was as if he had helped her . . . and Dab couldn't understand why. She had never seen a Delta do anything for a slave unless he expected something in return.

The sled tilted on its side for easier transport. Dab's muscles flexed under her flightsuit as she worked. After their escape, she had discovered that repetitive muscle movements actually made her stronger instead of weaker like the handlers claimed. The handlers wouldn't let them move around much in the barracks, but Dab had a nervous energy that had expended itself in eating as much as they would give her. But she had never been strong until now.

"Watch out!" Mote called. The tall, thin woman came to a stop, hardly able to control her full grav sled.

They were facing each other when the deck shifted slightly. They put out their arms to balance. Dab looked questioningly at Mote, who was also startled. Her shocking red hair flared as she turned back to the corridor.

Suddenly Dab went flying into the air along with everything on the full sled. A screech of metal shattered her ears and Mote screamed.

Dab ended up on the floor, her hands braced on either side of her. The floor was vibrating hard as if the converter were nearing overload. But the converter was off-line!

Mote was groaning, lying not far away. Dab crawled over, feeling her own bruises and pangs. "What happened? " Mote moaned.

"I'll find out."

Dab scrambled past Mote, who was shaking her head and trying to get up. She was heading through the corridor, when she looked through the airlock portal.

Stars!

"The airlock seal is broken!" Dab cried out. "We're drifting."

She rushed to the airlock. Instead of retracting, the locking mechanism was torn in half. "It's ruined!" she exclaimed as Mote joined her.

"What happened to Rose?"

"Who knows?" Dab didn't wait for Mote. She could fly this ship if she had to, and the command deck was where they needed to be.

Whit was calling out from command as she passed through engineering. "There's another ship! It's right off our bow—"

They were jolted again.

"They're on top of us!" Whit exclaimed from the comm.

Dab slid into the helm, seeing the position of the enemy ship in the navigational terminal. "How did it get so close without you seeing it?"

"Blindsided us." Whit sounded grim. "Probably pure luck. They were trying to slip into our spot."

Mote joined them, still holding her head. "What's going on?"

Dab was trying to move them with the thrusters, but it wasn't working. She also had the converter on auto-initiate, but that would take longer.

"They have us in an attractor field," Whit explained.

"Is it Fleet?" Mote asked.

Whit shook his head. "No Fleet designation. And no attempts to communicate. Fleet wouldn't jerk us off the station like that."

"Raiders?" Mote asked, clearly hoping to be contradicted.

"Looks that way." Dab slammed her fist down when the converter wouldn't cycle on-line while the attractor field surrounded them.

The three of them stared at each other. Dab almost couldn't breathe. All their effort, their pain, for nothing.

"It'll be slavery," Mote whispered. "Or worse."

"I'll ram them!" Dab activated the stabilizers. They were strong enough to toss the ship around. She would shove the *Purpose* into them. "I don't care if I destroy both ships—"

There was a scuffle as Whit grabbed Dab's arms to make her stop. Dab couldn't understand what he was doing. "Let me go! We don't have much time—"

"You could kill us!" Whit protested.

"I don't want to die," Mote agreed.

Whit's strong arms were around Dab, restraining her. It felt familiar, and calmed her down. Dab realized he meant what he said. "Okay, I won't ram them!"

"But what are we going to do?" Mote asked.

Whit let Dab's arms go and returned to his terminal. "They're moving into position to dock with us."

"How can we stop them?" Mote asked.

"The stabilizers!" Dab's hands touched the terminal. "I can use them to rock us. They won't be able to get a lock that way."

She deactivated all three port stabilizers, hoping to start a spin on the *Purpose*. That would give them time to come up with something else.

Mote pointed to the imager. "It's coming closer! Why aren't we moving?"

Dab was wondering that herself. "It must be that attractor field. I'll try jamming the stabilizers on and off."

Mote was checking the power readings on the ops terminal. Normally the three of them worked with the bots, but Rose had insisted that everyone train on the command deck.

"It's too much!" Mote cried out. "You're going to blow the main power relays."

"So what?" Dab demanded.

"Stop it!" Whit ordered.

Dab hesitated, but she had always listened to Whit and Mote before. They were smart. So Dab resynchronized the stabilizers again. The terminal indicated that there was going to be some damage to the field distortion amplifiers. Dab knew exactly which bot would fix it.

"What now?" Dab looked from Whit to Mote.

There was silence for a few moments; then finally Whit admitted, "I don't know."

"I don't either," Mote agreed.

Dab swore under her breath. "*Rose* would have a plan."

"Rose isn't here," Mote shot back.

"No, but *I* am," Dab retorted. She got up. "I'm going down to that airlock and I'll stop them with a laser welder if I have to."

Whit followed her to the top of the stairs. "You know raiders—it's surrender or die."

"I'm *not* going to surrender." Dab headed down. She knew where a primed laser welder was waiting for her. There was only one airlock the raiders could use, so that made the job easier.

"What if we'd rather surrender than die?" Mote called plaintively after her.

Dab hesitated for only a moment. "You can't make *me* surrender."

She headed down to engineering and Whit followed. Mote was calling out for her to stop. Dab knew it was what Rose would do if she were here. It was very possible Rose was dead right now, killed when the airlock tore in half.

The only thing that mattered to Dab was the curve of the welder grip under her hand.

Rose was near the open airlock when it happened. At the first jolt, the seal cracked and the airlock hatch slammed shut. Rose was lucky she wasn't in the way or inside with the salvaged stuff.

There was an explosion in the portal and the spacepost shifted around her, almost knocking her grav boots from the floor. Everything inside the airlock shredded in a hurricane of tiny bits as the docking joint ripped apart.

"Stop!" Rose yelled, jumping forward to pound on the portal.

Another ship wrenched the *Purpose* away from the

spacepost, holding it in an attractor field. The ship had a strange bulbous node on the underside of its hull.

Rose remembered when Captain L'ors had held the *Purpose* in an attractor field. The helm had been unresponsive under the field.

Stub joined her at the portal to the ruined airlock. "Hey, did you feel that? What happened?"

"Another ship has the *Purpose*."

Stub quickly looked through the portal. "That's a modified laser array," Stub said grimly. "It's a raider."

He looked as shocked as she felt. The raider used its thrusters to shift down to the port side of the *Purpose*, probably to dock. Rose knew it was over. Once they gained access to the *Purpose*, they owned it and everyone on it.

She had lost her ship and a good chunk of her crew.

Then again, she couldn't give up hope. Maybe they would dock with the spacepost to get the rest of the Solians. Maybe she could give them incentive. Then they would have a chance to get their ship back!

Rose triggered her comm. "Raider alert! Everyone, get back to the airlock now."

Stub shook his head at the loud announcement that came through his comm, then he switched back to their private channel. "What about Nip?"

"He's not going anywhere." Maybe she could lure the raiders onto the spacepost by offering herself as bait. Bait and trap . . . She tried to open the airlock but the damage must have permanently sealed it. "Let's go to the next airlock over."

"Aye, Captain," he said with perfect seriousness.

Rose didn't remind him that she had just lost her ship and no longer deserved that title. It probably made him feel better. She wouldn't feel better until she talked to Ash.

Rose bit her lip as they ran down the corridor to get to the next airlock. By the time she reached the portal in the hatch, she could see only the lower bulge of the raider that was nestled on the opposite side of the *Purpose*. The two ships floated very close to the damaged spacepost, with the raider clearly using it as cover.

"Let's get this open and try to signal them," Rose told Stub. Right now they needed those jet harnesses even more than before. She could envision herself motoring over to that raider and doing some damage of her own.

But there was no power to the airlock without a ship in dock. Even when Ash arrived, with a lot more experience as a bot tech, s/he had no suggestions. Jot appeared and started to cry.

Rose looked through the portal, wondering what was happening over there. Dab would fight the raiders. Could the three Solians on board beat them off? If anyone could do it, those three could.

Finally there was movement by the *Purpose*. It was the raider. "It's backing off!" Rose called out.

The raider pulled away from the *Purpose*. There was a pause, and then it began to leave, picking up speed as it cleared the station.

The *Purpose* turned and followed.

Rose cried out, "No!"

She pressed herself against the portal watching as the two ships dwindled to toys, then finally disappeared.

They were stranded on the derelict spacepost.

The Solians gathered in the landing disc to have one of their infamous conclaves—only this time there were no solutions. Rose had six crew members left. She had lost the others one by one. Obviously, in hindsight, coming to the spacepost had been a bad idea.

The one good thing about her dwindling crew was that Rose didn't have to listen to Chad gripe about how stupid she had been.

"That raider could come back for the rest of us," Rose warned them.

Stub was back near the original damaged airlock, trying to keep watch in the direction the raider had departed. "We won't be able to stop it if it does."

She shot him a look. "You never can tell."

"When raiders show up, they always get what they want."

Rose couldn't vent her frustration in a fight with Stub. She was their leader, or something like that. Anyway, the others were depending on her as they always did.

"Any ideas on how we can fight them if they do come back?" she asked.

Nobody had a suggestion. Not one. Usually she couldn't shut them up to save her life. Now the blue-tinged faces were mutely staring at her as if she could fix everything. Pull another miracle out of her butt . . . but she didn't feel a miracle coming on right now.

Even Ash silently shook hir head, looking scared.

"What was your backup plan?" Kwort finally asked.

"You mean in case the *Purpose* was ripped off the spacepost?" Rose countered sharply. "Somehow that one slipped my mind."

Jot glanced up from her belt. "My cartridges are almost empty."

Everyone looked down, suddenly very aware that their flightsuits were the only thing between them and vacuum.

"I'm almost empty, too," Shard said. "Did we take all the cartridges that we found onto the ship?"

"I hope not!" Kwort blurted out, a note of panic in his voice.

"No." Ash calmly looked through the anchored nets of goods in the corridor. "Here's a carton right here. We can last for decnights on these if we have to."

"Decnights!" Shard exclaimed. Jot was crying so hard she couldn't see. Clay was also alarmed.

For once Rose didn't think they were being ninnies.

Kwort let out a wail. "We're gonna die!"

Rose ordered, "Stop it, Kwort. We're not going to die—"

His eyes were wide, the whites showing all around. "We're gonna die! We're stuck here—"

Rose grabbed his arms and gave the little guy a shake. "Shut up! We'll figure something out. We always do."

"I don't want to die—"

Rose shook him again until he met her eyes. "I'm telling you, Kwort. You better shut up."

Slowly he nodded, hearing the real threat in her voice. She wouldn't have hesitated to knock him out if she had to. She couldn't afford to have him panicking out of control.

"Get hold of yourself," she warned him. She had to figure out something or the others would start following his lead. Jot was nearly there already.

Kwort nodded, scratching his ridges frantically, but he was listening again.

"Okay, let's figure out what we have to work with. We need weapons. And anything else we can use to get off this spacepost." Perhaps there was something they had overlooked. They hadn't searched either landing disc very well because there was so much wreckage strewn about.

"Let's go." Rose tried to sound confident, but for the first time she knew she was kidding herself. She didn't have a clue how to get them out of this.

Fairly quickly they discovered the lifepods. The pod would send out a distress ping that could reach ships twice as far as long-distance scanner range. They could even drag Nip's biobed inside the pod, though it would be a bit cramped. They could live in a lifepod with its own atmosphere for a long time.

They selected a lifepod near the medical bay that held Nip's biobed. Kwort managed to jury rig power to the lifepod-ejection system. He apologized repeatedly for suggesting they come to the spacepost. Rose didn't mind making Kwort feel guilty, because it made him work harder.

At least the lifepod option helped to banish their first terrifying fright at finding they were stranded on the derelict spacepost. They could always go into the lifepod and wait for someone to detect their emergency beacon.

But that was a passive course of action. Rose decided to keep looking for a better plan. They slept in shifts tied down, bumping softly into the wall. Rose didn't like sleeping in vacuum. Weightlessness was fine when her feet were firmly pulled to the deck by the grav boots, giving her an illusion of gravity. But when she lay down, everything was topsy-turvy. She had terrible nightmares during her short naps, involving people she knew back in Tijuana and the sick stuff that Jolene Alpha had forced her to do when she had first arrived on this spacepost. It made Rose furious to remember the way her body had reacted in pleasure at times, despite Jolene's hard, sadistic streak. But she'd had no choice, and had only gotten through it as best she could. That experience had started Rose on a downward slide into nothingness, but Ash had snapped her out of it with a few words.

They barely lasted a full day on the spacepost. Her crew ambushed Rose on the balcony outside the medical bay.

"We have to get into the lifepod," Stub told her. "We're dying like this."

"Not dying," Rose contradicted. "It's just uncomfortable."

Shard gestured to Jot, who was crumpled down around her boots. "She's throwing up blood now. She's too spacesick to stay here."

Rose lifted her hands, ready to give in. She would order them to move Nip's biobed into the lifepod. "Do you understand the risk? We'll be broadcasting we're here. We're bound to be picked up by the Fleet."

"Who cares?" Shard exclaimed. "Anything would be better than this!"

In the silence, Kwort hesitantly asked, "What about a patrolship?"

"Even a patrolship," Stub agreed with Shard.

"Well, there's one now," Kwort replied.

Rose whirled to look out the top of the truncated end of the spacepost. A Fleet patrolship hovered in the jagged hole.

They didn't panic as Rose expected. They went very still and quiet, staying in a group outside the door of the medical bay. Kwort stood to one side, and Rose couldn't blame him. He would probably try to pass as Cwart, according to his new identity chip. She hoped none of the others would rat on him. Rose had carefully drilled them on what to say in case they were captured, but it all depended on if they had the guts to stick to it.

Jot was down on her knees with her hands clasped in front of her. Rose reminded her a few times to not say anything. Clay's eyes burned as if the slender man wanted to go down fighting. Ash was stricken so pale and silent that s/he couldn't speak, like Clay.

When the big Delta enforcers appeared, Rose tried to show them into the bay where the biobed was located. She didn't want them to leave Nip behind.

But the Deltas thought she was trying to resist and one of them raised his stunwand. She saw the butt coming toward her head. That was the last thing Rose remembered.

10

Heloga Alpha activated the holo-monitors to watch her subordinates. Twelve images appeared in a half-circle around her desk. The administrative staff of Canopus didn't know she could see and hear every word they said.

Heloga switched among them to listen to anything that looked interesting. They were having a senior staff meeting today, and the commanders usually talked about things they were worried about with their staff while they downplayed their real concerns during their reports to her.

As she watched the monitors, Heloga absently stroked the skin next to her mouth until she abruptly realized what she was doing. No wonder her physique was prematurely stressed! She wasn't helping the efforts of her new biotech, Fanrique, by rubbing her face. She must have been doing things like that for years without realizing the consequences.

It reminded her of something she didn't want to think about. Her lust was approaching and she needed to prepare for it. Ever since the disastrous Renewal Festival when she realized she couldn't allow anyone close to her unless she had absolute control over them, her views toward Kristolas had changed. She couldn't afford to make up with him, not until she had her body restored to perfect condition.

But she needed someone for her lust. Since she couldn't risk any Alpha seeing her skin problems, she would have to make do with a Solian. That meant going to the slave barracks and choosing a male Solian to service her. The prospect was repugnant, but the alternative was the agony of an unrelieved lust.

Heloga irritably focused on the holo-monitors. Her own secretary, Waanip, never gave her a moment's worry. Heloga had almost stopped watching her, but spot checks were still prudent. Today Waanip was busy as usual, speaking to no one except when it directly pertained to her duties. Heloga liked it that way. The next holo showed the commander of her personal security enforcers. She trusted the highly conditioned Beta-commander with her life.

The other viewers were split into four smaller windows. She kept an eye on the senior commanders of each department: Fleet, planetary governors, commerce, industry, energy, labor, transportation, health, nourishment, and InSec. These Alphas controlled everything that happened in the Canopus region.

Today the computer analyzer indicated several of the departments were agitated: Fleet, transportation, and industry. That was not a good combination. Heloga removed the other departments from her monitors and split up the trouble spots to watch the subcommanders and administrative staff right down to the clerks. Often the lower level staff felt freer to discuss the problems than the senior Alphas. With a flick of her finger she could isolate and listen to any of them. She ordered the computer to analyze key words and phrases. She couldn't be bothered to listen to everything herself. She had only one pair of ears.

It took some time but there was plenty until the senior staff meeting. This was her job, and Heloga knew she did it well.

Finally her dataport chimed. Heloga ordered the tagged logs to be played.

The most informative was from the Fleet. Two under-secretaries were gleefully discussing whether their boss would be cashiered before or during the senior staff meeting. These two were regular, unwitting informants for Heloga, so she wasn't surprised to see them in the thick of it.

Then one of them added, "The Qin are mighty tough customers," while the other replied, "Yes, but an entire mining station! That's a sixth of our fuel-ore supply gone."

Heloga banged one fist down, as the two idiots chattered on. So, Fleet had lost one of their mining stations in Qin. No doubt those hairy barbarians were attacking the other three mining stations right now. *How?* Every bit of intelligence InSec had compiled couldn't explain how Qin warships could beat Fleet installations.

Heloga checked the InSec monitor again. Nothing appeared to be amiss. But InSec was good at hiding its own secrets. Perhaps they knew about the destruction of the mining station, but they were lying low so her wrath wouldn't fall on them.

She stood up and started pacing. At least she didn't have to worry about frowning. Her biotech had immobi-

lized certain muscle groups in her forehead and around
her eyes so she couldn't do more damage to herself. It
felt good to let go with her rage, kicking the ruffled train
of her skin suit out of the way as she turned.

What should she tell the regents? She had received a
report from Jolene Alpha on Starbase C-4 that Winstav
and Felenore had completed their investigation and were
proceeding directly to Qin territory. They would be responsible for retaliation, even though they couldn't
reach Qin for another decnight.

So far there was nothing from the *Conviction*. It
seemed to have disappeared without a trace somewhere
between the Domain and Qin. The Alpha commander in
Jenuar, the outer occupied system, reported rumors that
the battleship had been destroyed by Qin warships.

After that report had arrived, Heloga separated Rikev
from her entourage. She knew it would be better to completely disassociate herself from the Rikev line. She sent
Rikev into the field to gather the data from the investigations on Delta sabotages that recently occured in
Archernar. Removing Rikev also served as a precaution
to keep him from discovering her secret.

Besides, Heloga was tired of Rikev's indifferent manner. He did nothing she could fault him for, exactly like
the first Rikev. But she wasn't pleased with him because
he made no effort to pursue her. This time she wouldn't
trust him with one of her spaceposts. He would be lucky
to rise above the level of her lackey.

Waanip commed her from the outer office, *"Regional
Commander, Senior Alpha Yonith and Senior Alpha Gustance request permission to speak to you before the staff
meeting."*

Heloga stopped pacing and returned to her desk.

Commander Yonith was in charge of the Fleet, while Gustance controlled the vast industrial network with facilities spread throughout the region. She hesitated, knowing she would enjoy humiliating them in front of the other senior staff, but it would be better if they gave her the details in private.

She deactivated the viewers, and they disappeared. "Send them in."

Yonith was a fine physical specimen, and her brown Fleet flightsuit admirably set off her tan skin and bright green eyes. Gustance was heavy for an Alpha, with rounded cheeks, and a belly that pushed out his colorful layered outfit. They were an unlikely pair in temperament as well.

Gustance was breathing heavily as they approached. He was clearly waiting for Commander Yonith to take the lead, as was her right by seniority. Heloga simply sat there adjusting the thick ruffles around the wrists of her skinsuit, watching them expectantly.

Commander Yonith didn't try to soften her report, which Heloga had always appreciated about her. "We regret to inform you, Heloga Alpha, that Qin invaders disabled our mining station in Balanc and killed all Fleet personnel in the system."

Heloga tried to narrow her eyes, but the immobilizer wouldn't allow it. *"How?"*

"A patrolship entered the system not long after the attack. We've analyzed their scanner logs, and it appears that two Qin battleships attacked the station."

"Qin *battleships?*" Heloga demanded.

"Yes," Yonith agreed.

Heloga would have to do something about her incompetent InSec staff. For now she must deal with these two. "The regents don't take kindly to senior Fleet commanders losing their ships and stations."

Yonith didn't flinch. "Yes, Heloga Alpha."

"Consider yourself stripped of rank. Confine yourself to your quarters pending an investigation by the regents' strategists."

Yonith stood up and didn't meet Heloga's eyes. The commander nodded once, then turned smartly and left. Both she and her line would suffer terribly because of this blow.

"Waanip," Heloga said over the comm. "Contact the Fleet first subcommander and inform him of his promotion. Get him here immediately."

Gustance winced as Heloga turned to him. His eyes were almost round in alarm.

Heloga thought it was a disgusting display from an Alpha. "How does the loss of the mining ship affect our production quotas?"

"Exports will cease," Gustance said reluctantly. "Our reserves will easily help us meet the refueling requirements for the next two quarters in the outlying sectors of Sirius, Archernar, Procyon, Pyxis, and Capetta."

"Capetta is one sector away from Canopus," Heloga reminded him. Gustance withered under her intense gaze. It would have been a glare but she couldn't make her brows draw together anymore. But it was enough to demoralize the master of industry.

Heloga fired question after question at him based on the likelihood that all four of the mining stations in Qin had been attacked, leaving only two mining stations left in production. Gustance became quite agitated and pointed out that at least those two were safe inside the Canopus region. Clearly it was an economic disaster not only for her region, but nearby frontier regions would be impacted as well.

Gustance was still trying to answer her questions when the rest of the senior staff arrived, including the new commander of the Fleet in Canopus. Heloga focused on him and the other commanders, who clearly would do anything rather than head down Yonith's destructive path. Heloga even managed to make the Alpha in charge of medicine and health feel like he was responsible for the attacks by Qin.

But her most pointed barbs were for InSec. How could they miss the fact that battleships were being built in Qin? She didn't care that the Qin society was so interlocked in familial structures that it was difficult for operatives to infiltrate. Obviously the Qin were building up to an all-out offensive against the Domain.

Heloga picked at her ruffles, precisely settling them around her wrist while she picked apart her staff. By the time they left, they were desperate to keep their ranks. As long as she had that power, she could keep everyone in line. Now it was up to the strategists to take care of Qin.

Soon after the senior staff meeting, Heloga stepped into her aircar and ordered her driver to take her to the slave complex on Canopus Prime. The suspended mushroom-shaped building hung over the moon by antigrav, and had become a flashy symbol of the quality slaves Canopus had to offer.

Heloga was reluctant to take this step, but every Alpha used Solian pleasure slaves now and again. Most Alphas had one or two slaves of their own. Yet she prided herself on avoiding the use of a Solian for decades. Even her last few lusts had been covered by an

Alpha aspiring to replace Kristolas. He wasn't bad, but he was too deferential. She needed more passion and fire in her sex. Besides, she couldn't use him again because he might notice the slackness under her jaw or the tiny wrinkles around her eyes. A Solian was the only safe solution.

Heloga had called ahead to the slave compound, and her own enforcers had gone over the viewing suite. It had windows with a spectacular downward view of Canopus Prime, but she had ordered them to be blacked out. She didn't want anyone to see her choosing a slave. That would be high entertainment for some people in Canopus.

The viewing suite was a few steps away from the landing platform. Heloga merely nodded as she received a report from the Beta-commander of her personal enforcers that the suite was baffled and sealed. At a wave, everyone withdrew except for the Beta-commander and the slave master in charge of the compound, who launched into a flowery prepared speech: "Welcome, Regional Commander! Yes, it's this way. We are most pleased, Regional Commander, that you have graced us with your—"

"Silence," Heloga ordered. She seated herself on the cushioned chair placed for her. "Bring them in."

She had asked to see at least thirty male Solians who were tall, muscular, and clean of any trace of hair. The compound commander ushered twice that many past Heloga. They strolled and posed naked except for their collars so she could examine the entire package. Finally she chose ten who met her stringent physical requirements.

"You two leave," she told the slave master and her Beta-commander. "Seal the door."

They complied instantly.

Heloga stood up and looked at the ten acceptable specimens she had chosen. "If any one of you speaks about what happens here, I'll have you *all* killed."

That did it. Fear appeared on their faces. For that, she was half-tempted to kill them anyway. It depended on how pleased she was by their performance.

"I like my males to be sexually dominant." She looked at the first one in line and ordered, "Kiss me."

She waited expectantly. He hesitated before coming forward. Then he stood too far away and leaned in, giving her a respectful peck on her cheek.

"You call that dominant?" She waved the offender away and gestured for the next to take his place. "See if you can do any better."

It was horrible. She had to endure awkward grabs and mashed lips. Some were so scared they were shaking while others hardly touched her. She castigated them, cutting them down as the useless worms that they were.

Heloga was ready to quit in disgust when one of the last slaves stepped into place. He looked into her eyes, unlike the others.

"Let's see what you've got," Heloga told him.

He reached out and gently slipped his hand around her waist. Her eyes opened wider as he pulled her forward until her hips brushed his. She leaned back to look up at him, putting her hands on his chest. He felt warm and strong.

His mouth curved as he gazed down at her. His fingers brushed against her cheek, feeling how soft her skin was. Her eyes closed briefly in relief. He thought she was beautiful.

His hand curved around the back of her neck, holding her firmly, bringing his lips to hers. She opened her mouth under his, feeling his growing lust for her, his desire to take her.

When he let go of her and stepped back, he was smiling slightly. Heloga knew that this one understood. Desire would lead to complete surrender with him, or he would take her over and over again until she yielded. Letting herself go in this slave's hands would be excruciatingly demeaning . . . yet she was as eager as a slave to get started.

Heloga sank to her knees in front of him, offering herself to him in front of the rejected slaves. She leaned back her head, jerking open her skinsuit to expose her proud breasts. Heloga wanted to humiliate and debase herself, to cleanse her mind of everything else. When the slave's hand roughly grasped the back of her head, thrusting his hips toward her, her eyes closed in a burst of pleasure. *Yes,* she thought, *use me as you will.*

The other slaves shifted uneasily at first, but the sexual tension flared and burned hotter as she abandoned all restraint. They gathered around closely to watch. Some were touching their genitals and stimulating themselves as if expecting to join in. As they encircled her, Heloga threw herself into the pit of her corrupted pleasure. Later there would be enough time to think about killing them all for participating in her degradation.

Rikev Alpha had played Heloga's game well and escaped her deadly inner circle as he had planned. It was easy to see that Heloga destroyed anyone she became intimate with.

So he had ignored her hints and had avoided contact in every way. It was fortunate that their lusts had not coincided; if they had, she would have demanded that he pleasure her. He had evaded that trap, and now that they were no longer in each other's company day after day, their lusts would not shift toward each other.

Yet Rikev knew it came down to luck, not his own skill. A decnight ago Heloga inexplicably thrust her favorites away from her, including himself. Rikev had calmly accepted an insignificant assignment to fetch data from a series of investigations that were being conducted in Archernar. Several key facilities had been sabotaged. He was assigned to the courier *Rapture* and told to return the data to Canopus Regional Headquarters.

Rikev knew it might take years for him to gain Heloga Alpha's esteem. He had much to compensate for because of the last Rikev. So instead of simply acting as courier, Rikev took an active interest in the information he was gathering. If he could uncover something significant in the Delta uprisings, that could improve Heloga Alpha's opinion of him.

Archernar was literally on the edge of the Domain. First Rikev went to Hofsta to see the senior Alpha of the sector. That's where he hoped to find the best InSec analysts. He emphasized Heloga Alpha's concern about the ramifications of a Delta uprising until the Alpha-commander let him have access to every part of their investigations.

It was an interesting few days. Rikev even went down to the blindingly hot planet of Hofsta to inspect its irrigation system, which was almost repaired after decnights of hard labor with massive construction bots. Hofsta's solar system, with its two colonies, its manufacturing facilities, and a starbase, was having to rely on warehoused foodstuff to supply the transposers with raw material.

Local InSec had interrogated every Delta on the place, and informed Rikev on his arrival that they weren't responsible for the sabotage. Then they began interrogating the native Orlee slaves to find out if they had seen something.

Rikev went to watch an interrogation in the main station on the planet. The Orlee were a sorry lot. Rikev couldn't imagine them as a threat. But to his growing amazement, one slave after another admitted that the irrigation system had been destroyed by fellow slaves.

Rikev was intrigued because his research indicated that the Qin attack was the first time slaves had rebelled against the Domain since the native uprising on Picayute eight decades ago. Slaves rarely fought back once they were collared. But here was another recent example, if it was true. It seemed like a remarkable coincidence.

Another Orlee slave was dragged in, her purple-blotched skin hanging slackly from her face and body. She was slung into the mobile uninhibitor which immediately clamped around her arms and legs. When her head was raised to slip on the skullcap, Rikev realized she was worn almost to death. It was perhaps the most disgusting example of genetic mutation that he had ever seen in a humanoid.

Rikev held a breather over his face, inhaling the filtered air. The Orlee were toxic on the nose. This was the fifth one he had seen interrogated and she smelled worse than the others.

The slave fought the uninhibitor as the others had. But each time the InSec staff got a bit more out of them before they were turned into drooling idiots fit only for animal food.

This female spilled more than the others. Rikev was astonished when she confessed that the slaves had planned the attack on the irrigation system with some visiting aliens.

Instigated! thought Rikev. These stupid natives had been prodded to rebel against the Domain. The InSec staff were right on top of this new information, pressing the female and manipulating her with the uninhibitor to drag out every shred she knew. But names and descriptions were too self-protected to pull from her brain. After hours of effort, they only managed to get the location of the meeting—a regional municipal depot on Hofsta.

The InSec staff scrambled the slave's mind before they could get anything more useful. As they cheerfully dragged another slave in to mind-strip him, Rikev tightened his lips in annoyance. That female slave had known everything they were looking for, but these incompetents had botched the job. Now they would have to search to find another who possessed the same knowledge.

It wasn't worth wasting his time watching them plow through slaves until they amassed the information piece by piece. If Rikev were in charge, he would have made sure it was done correctly, but his suggestions were curtly turned down by the Insec Alphas. He decided to return to the courier and do his own bit of investigating while they flailed around on the planet.

Two days later, Rikev Alpha got the results directly from the InSec commander. Through interrogations and investigation into the groundport and municipal depot, they had narrowed it down to three Polinar suspects. The Polinar had landed and departed on the same night a decnight before the irrigation system was destroyed. The last time their shuttle had been used at the groundport had been two quarters ago, and then two quarters before that. Their stated occupations were "purveyors," but there was no record of them purchasing or selling any goods on Hofsta.

The three Polinar had been logged going into a storage facility. A number of Orlee slaves had also entered the structure. Later that night, the three Polinar left and returned directly to the groundport.

InSec offered a wide assortment of theories, and they were sending operatives to Polinar, two regions away, to investigate the data from their identity chips. They intended to determine who on Polinar was profiting from a famine in Hofsta. Rikev thought their logic was faulty, in part because every Alpha in Hofsta had the irritating habit of assuming that their system was of paramount importance because it was the home of the senior Alpha in the sector.

Rikev examined the images of the three Polinar who came through the starport. Two males and one female. The younger male caught Rikev's eye. Something about his neck, how long it was. Also the younger male looked different from the other two.

He checked, but no bioscan had been taken of the Polinar. Hofsta had been lax in their security and was paying for it.

When Rikev ran the suspect's specs against known parameters for Polinar aliens, they matched up fairly well. The younger male was slightly high or low in the relative proportions of every feature.

Yet Rikev doubted they were Polinar. That's what the Hofsta InSec believed and they weren't following any other leads. Whereas Rikev believed there was another connection: the Orlee slaves had sabotaged Hofsta after the Qin slaves had attacked Spacepost T-3.

Rikev requested three images of Qin to compare to the three Polinar.

When the row of images appeared above the Polinar, there was a distinct resemblance. Polinar had triangular faces with relatively small chins, exactly like the Qin. The Qin had manes of hair that thickened their heads, but when Rikev shifted the three Qin on top of the bald Polinar, they could have been the same people.

So Qin had instigated the slave revolt on Hofsta. He wouldn't have realized it if he hadn't been so personally focused on the Qin. But now it was clear as starlight.

He doubted that Hofsta InSec would make the same correlation. And it was not his job to inform them. Heloga Alpha would hear it from him and him alone. To convince her, he would connect Qin to the other sabotages in Archernar. That would reveal a conspiracy with serious implications for the Domain. Qin would be turned into rubble.

Rikev felt satisfaction at that thought. The Qin had damaged the reputation of his line. He would do anything to destroy them.

Rikev notified the captain of the *Rapture* to leave immediately for his next scheduled stop in Archernar. He would acquire all the evidence from the various sites that were sabotaged, and shift through it with an eye toward his new theory. Rikev knew his ultimate redemption lay in Qin.

11

—⁓—

The crew of the battleship *Defiance* tolerated E'ven only because he was the captain's clansman. E'ven knew it, but there was nothing he could do about it except train harder.

At least S'jen allowed him to watch their attack in Impelleneer from a jumpseat on the command deck. E'ven chewed on a ragged thumbnail, wishing he was allowed to do more than watch. But it had taken a while for him to regain his strength. S'jen kept reminding him to stand up straight, and when he did, he realized he was slightly taller than her. After years of stooping in front of the overseers to try to avoid their attention, it was hard to change. He was also awkward, bumping into other people and knocking things over. He knew the crew was sympathetic because he had been enslaved, but they dismissed him as some kind of mascot. S'jen's pet Huut . . .

"There's the Fleet!" S'jen announced. "Prepare to go through their patrolships."

E'ven felt a spike of fear. A defensive block of patrolships positioned themselves between the approaching

Qin battleships and the mining station. The Fleet knew they were coming and the Alphas were fighting back.

This was the third attack for S'jen's crew. After leaving Balanc, they had liberated Atalade, another Qin system that had been subjugated by the Domain. Now it was Impelleneer's turn.

There was a flurry of activity as S'jen drove the *Defiance* through the Fleet's defensive line. One patrolship went up in a fireball while the others tumbled out of their path. In the towering imager, the *Defiance* headed straight for the bulky mining station. Their Qin warships were avoiding missile strikes from the Fleet, and the shields on the *Defiance* and the *Endurance* easily deflected the explosions from the missiles.

E'ven chewed his thumbnail faster, hanging on to his chair. S'jen sounded so calm, as if nothing bothered her.

Admiral J'kart was even more reassuring. E'ven had never seen him smile, not even after they disabled the mining station in Atalade and destroyed every Fleet patrolship in the system. That was the first time E'ven had watched from the jumpseat as the Qin battleships ripped into the Fleet.

This time the mining station was maneuvering and picking up speed. Yet despite his fear, E'ven knew Qin would win. That feeling had been growing as he became stronger. He had never known it was possible to defy the Domain. Growing up on Balanc, all he had known was hiding and surviving in the ruins. When he was a child he had been caught and taken to work in the fields that supplied the local Fleet ships and mining station with raw foodstuffs. Years later, he had been sent to work on the mining station.

His lip lifted in a sneer, showing his fangs as S'jen gave the order to fire on the mining station. Red lasers crisscrossed in the imager. He wanted that bulbous mining station to pop like an overripe melon spewing its contents. He wanted the overseers to suffer and die.

E'ven had learned how to handle a laser rifle, and he practiced every day in the combat bay, hoping to join the raiding party on the mining station. Weapons training and hand-to-hand *kantara* practice were his focus, except for the time he spent with S'jen in simulations learning the ship's systems so he could staff the comm. He wanted to captain his own warship someday, and eventually a battleship like the *Defiance*.

In Atalade, S'jen had destroyed the command segment in one pass. This time, because of the active resistance, they had to swoop around the bulbous segment in a twisting evasive pattern. Their battleship was nimble and fast. Only one patrolship returned to try to protect the mining station, but it was quickly transformed into a puff of vaporized atoms. Most of the Qin's red laser strikes concentrated on the mining station.

"Forward weapons array destroyed," C'vid reported evenly.

"Targeting power nodes on the command segment," S'jen announced.

"Incoming laser fire from the aft weapons array," C'vid pointed out.

"Where's G'kaan?" B'hom asked in frustration. "He should be on it."

"He stayed to fight the patrolships!" C'vid was shaking her head at her terminal. "The *Endurance* is setting up its first attack run."

E'ven boiled over at the injustice. G'kaan always

made it tougher for S'jen! Admiral J'kart didn't move a muscle as he absorbed the information.

S'jen was busy with evasive maneuvers, but she got off a series of direct hits on the command segment.

"They're heading into the asteroid ring," C'vid said.

E'ven knew that meant trouble. When he was a slave, he went into a similar asteroid belt every day in a personal mining pod to drag ore-rich chunks of asteroid back to the mining ship at the end of the long shift. A battleship was too big to go in the belt. He didn't understand why it would try.

There were so many things he didn't know or understand. Half the stuff the crew said went right over his head. He always had a vague feeling that they were laughing at him because of his ignorance. Except for S'jen. She never laughed at anything.

"Aft weapons array destroyed by the *Endurance*," C'vid finally announced.

S'jen was frowning in concentration as the battleship gracefully skimmed around the command segment. With pinpoint precision, she blasted the inner curve of the command segment where the power nodes were located.

When the nodes went up in smoke, an explosion engulfed the entire imager from floor to ceiling in a rainbow of sparkles. The battleship shot into clear space. The imager tracked the mining station as the massive chain reaction rapidly dispersed.

E'ven shouted out in victory, his fist clenched. B'hom glanced over at him. S'jen and J'kart acted as though nothing had happened. The hush on the command deck resumed.

He realized they were still concentrating on the rapidly moving mining ship—now missing its forward segment. Propulsion systems were down because of the catastrophic damage, yet the ship had built up incredible momentum.

As the asteroids rapidly approached, E'ven realized why the overseers had aimed toward the belt. They intended to destroy the station and everyone on it, including the thousands of Qin slaves.

It was so cold-blooded that E'ven instantly knew it was true. The Domain was a juggernaut that rolled over everything in its path. Even in their own death they wrought utter devastation.

But S'jen would never let the Fleet beat her. "All power to the attractor field."

The crew leapt into action and applied a brilliant green attractor field to the milling segment on the station. They were joined by the *Endurance*, which placed an attractor field on the slave segment. E'ven could see the station slowing in the imager. The station finally came to a stop right on the edge of the asteroid belt.

E'ven was so impressed that he bounced up and down on his seat the entire time. The two battleships began pulling the mining station to a safe distance from the asteroids. But there was a desperate rush, because there was no telling what the overseers were doing over there.

E'ven couldn't help himself. When S'jen stood up from the helm, hurrying to get to her pinnace where the combat teams were waiting, he jumped in front of her. "Let me go with you, S'jen! I can fight. You know I'm good with the laser!"

S'jen turned to him, her eyes distant, hard stars.

E'ven stepped back. He had never seen her like this before.

But she nodded shortly. "Get a weapon and stay with me."

S'jen knew that E'ven was ready. He had trained every day for this mission. His heart was strong and his body was growing stronger. Now she needed to know if he could handle war. If he couldn't, he would be sent back to Balanc to infuse the Huut with his passion. She had no use for him if he was weak.

"You're taking *him?*" a combatant asked as E'ven clamored into the pinnace behind C'vid.

S'jen gave the combatant a look and he fell silent. C'vid slid in beside her as S'jen took the helm of the pinnace. She expertly lifted the *Wrath*, moving through the bay and out of the battleship.

The four surviving Qin warships were deployed near their battleships, protecting the mining station. G'kaan would doubtless complain that she had not remained with his battleship to fight the Fleet patrolships. One of their own warships had been destroyed. But the crews knew the risks they were taking. It was remarkable that they hadn't lost any Qin ships until today.

S'jen took the *Wrath* through the familiar bay doors of the mining station. The mining pods looked the same as those on Balanc and Atalade, with a glaring bubble shield over the top third of the pod.

Scanners picked up Fleet enforcers waiting on the platform at the back of the pod dock. S'jen increased speed and swooped to hover over them, blasting her thrusters as they let loose with two laser cannon. It wasn't the most precise attack, but it did the job. Cinders were left of the enforcers. The other pinnaces were blown back out of the bay by the explosion.

As S'jen landed the *Wrath,* her combat teams leaped out and began to batter the enforcers who had managed to retreat to the doors. S'jen locked down the pinnace as the other three pinnaces landed, one after the other. She grabbed E'ven on her way out. His flightsuit was already activated and he looked too excited to be scared, a good sign. C'vid followed with her headset camera to log the atrocities for the politicians on the Clan Council. S'jen had learned that it took graphic images to get them motivated to fight back against the Domain.

The all-clear signal sounded as S'jen stepped onto the platform. The combat teams were good at their jobs, though this was the fiercest resistance they had encountered. As they moved into the milling segment, the whine of lasers echoed constantly.

S'jen activated her headset so she could see the layout of the mining station. Small colored dots marked the position of the combat teams from both ships. G'kaan was leaving the *Pluck,* his own pinnace, but S'jen went the opposite direction. The less she had to do with G'kaan the better for everyone.

As she moved through the industrial machines that filled the milling segment, S'jen saw dozens of dead Qin. They had been butchered where they worked.

It was the same throughout the mining station. They found pockets of overseers and enforcers, but they were easily dispatched. Everywhere there were bodies of Qin who had been mowed down with lasers. C'vid walked behind S'jen, logging it all. E'ven didn't breathe a word through their common channel.

When they broke into the slave barracks segment, there were so many dead Qin that reddish black blood coated the walls and ceilings. The combat teams were covered in it, the blood of their own people.

S'jen knew it was a mere drop compared with the oceans of Qin blood the Domain had shed over the decades. It would never stop, not until the Fleet was gone from Qin forever. C'vid logged it for everyone to see. Qin would never be the same again.

Then S'jen found E'ven. She had lost sight of him as they had searched the barracks and found no remaining Qin alive. Now he stood over a pile of fellow Qin, almost as hollow-cheeked and skeletal as himself. His face was smeared with rusty black Qin blood. At first S'jen thought he was ruined.

But his eyes burned. "It could have been *me*."

He wanted to kill, she could tell by the way he held his laser rifle, as if it were an extension of himself. He was no longer a boy but a man with a man's passion for revenge.

Now she could use him.

12

Mote hated being in jail, but she was glad that raiders had picked them up instead of Fleet. At least for now.

When the raiders boarded the *Purpose,* she and Whit had somehow managed to restrain Dab. For one fleeting moment, when Dab picked up the laser welder and faced the airlock, Mote almost wanted her to try. But they knew the raiders would be armed with real weapons. They didn't have a chance against them.

The three Solians had surrendered, holding their hands up in the universal sign for compliance. Dab was nearly crying in frustration, but Mote wasn't about to die over an old freighter. The raiders could have it, as long as they were left alive.

Now the three of them were shut into a room with five double bunks. The walls, floor, and ceiling had been welded over with sheets of polytanium. Nothing was exposed except for the door and a half-round eye in the center of the ceiling that logged everything that happened. The door was locked on the outside. Apparently the raiders were used to dealing with hostages.

Mote felt reassured by their precautions. At least they

wouldn't be summarily killed. At worst, they would promptly end up back in the slave trade.

Dab was lying in one of the bunks. She wasn't exercising the way she used to, and she had hardly eaten for two days. Whit had also barely spoken a word since the raiders stuck them in their prison. But Whit would undoubtedly land on his feet. He was smart and knew how to please his sex partners. His winning ways would probably secure him a steady mistress.

Mote was most worried about Dab. Mote would be depressed, too, if she had to service Deltas. At least she was a gene job so she could command the highest bidder. Alphas weren't easy to deal with, but they tended to be possessive about their slaves. Since they were on a six-day cycle, that meant lots of downtime for her. She could only imagine what it was like to work in a public pleasure house, serving anyone at any time. She knew she would die if she had to do some of the disgusting things Dab had described.

But despairing wouldn't help anything. They were adults; they knew what life was like. They'd had a brief, heady vacation on the *Purpose*, a bit of freedom. Maybe it had been too much for some of them. Mote had always expected it to end someday, and her fears had been borne out.

One of the raiders opened the door. He brought in their evening rations while another one stood in the doorway with a stunwand. They both had small fleshy heads that were narrower than their necks. Their miniature features made Mote want to laugh whenever she saw them. But that wouldn't help the situation.

She jumped up to assist the raider in shifting the grav tray into place. She thanked him and tried to smile into his eyes. But he avoided her.

He got away so fast the door slammed shut behind him. She couldn't understand why he wasn't interested.

Dab suddenly asked, "Why are you fawning over him? Do you *want* him to use you?"

Mote looked up in surprise. She hadn't heard anything out of Dab for over a day. "If he wants me, then I can barter with him."

Dab snorted. "He'll take what he wants."

Mote went to sit down on the bunk next to her. She didn't care about Dab's sarcastic tone. It was good for her to talk. She was filled with too much nervous energy to shut down like this. "Maybe I can get something in return if he likes me."

Dab pushed up on her elbow. "Like what?"

Mote shrugged. "I don't know yet."

"Oh." Dab flopped back down. "I thought you had a plan."

"You mean like before?" Mote glanced up at the ceiling, knowing anyone who cared to could be listening right now.

"Sure, like Rose."

Mote sighed. "This is different, Dab."

"Then why mess with those Delts?"

"Wouldn't you like to have another blanket? Or some happy juice?" Exasperated, Mote wondered if she was going to have to spell out everything for the listening raiders.

"Okay." Dab shrugged. "They're Boscans. You're irritating them by getting in their face. They like really passive slaves. If you stand there with your eyes down, he'll look you over. If he likes what he sees, he'll let you know."

"Uh . . . thanks." Leave it to Dab to know the sexual practices of every Delta in this arm of the galaxy.

Whit finally rolled over and looked at Mote. She had thought he was sleeping, but he had heard everything. He didn't speak but he gave her the briefest nod to let her know he was with her. She smiled and looked away. Now she needed to figure out their next move.

The next day Mote was no closer to a solution. But things had picked up with her fellow hostages. Whit was talking to her again, while Dab had eaten a big meal earlier and was now doing her exercises. Mote fervently hoped they weren't expecting her to create a Rose-like miracle. But she figured keeping their spirits up was miraculous enough, so she didn't disillusion them.

Dab's black skin was glistening with sweat as she pumped herself up and down using only her arms. Mote was impressed. Dab's arms were much larger than her own slender limbs. She knew she couldn't do that more than a few times, but Dab counted up to one hundred with no problem.

Dab finally collapsed on the floor. Mote tossed down the towel so she could wipe her face. "You're getting strong, Dab."

Dab's expression changed, as if she was listening to something. "Hold on . . . I didn't notice that before."

"What?" Mote asked.

Dab glanced up to check the eye, blocking it with one arm. She mouthed quietly to Mote. "Vibration in the deck."

Mote raised her brows.

Dab nodded, placing her hand on the deck. One finger moved in time to the distinctive arrhythmic rattle.

"Injector sequencer," Mote mouthed back.

A faulty valve in the *Purpose*'s injector sequencer had

given them some trouble while they were still in Qin. It had caused a malfunction in their injector relays and a subsequent increase in fuel consumption from the waste. Kwort had finally discovered it, and as they changed out the sequencer, he had explained that this sort of problem was why they couldn't rely on bots alone. A good bot tech looked at the whole ship, not only the bots. The two bots that controlled the injector sequencer hadn't been able to detect the minute variation caused by a flaw inside the valve. It took a scanner diagnostic of the system to identify the uneven flow, and the only reason he knew to do that was the vibration in the engines.

"That's it," Mote agreed quietly. She looked over at Whit.

There were questions in their eyes, but they didn't want to blow her plan. Dab went back to her exercises with renewed determination. Whit joined her not long after that. Maybe they thought Mote was going to take over the raider so they could return for Rose and the others. But Mote had set her sights on a much more attainable goal.

Mote gestured for Whit and Dab to get into their bunks as if they were going to sleep not long before it was time for their next ration delivery. Things would go more smoothly if the Boscans were focused on her.

When the door seal popped, she stood next to the table where the tray would be placed. Her hands were clasped in front of her and her head was bent. Her bright red hair fell in front of her eyes so she could see them while seemingly avoiding their gaze.

The Boscan hurried in as usual, but this time Mote didn't fuss over the arrangements. She waited calmly next to the table as the raider took the old tray and set down the new one. He kept looking at her sideways. As he did, his hands slowed.

Dab's advice was dead on target. Now both Boscans were staring at her as if they couldn't get enough. Who could have guessed that ignoring them would draw their attention?

The Boscan finished unloading the grav sled, but this time instead of rushing away, he reached out his hand. She stayed very still as he touched her hair, stroking it gently. Most people couldn't get over how red it was, each shiny strand like translucent fire. He tugged on a few strands sharply, as if testing her quiescence. When she didn't glance up, his hand dropped to her breast, quickly squeezing and grasping her nipple tightly. In a flash, she was a slave again, unable to say what she wanted. Only his needs were important, and her ability to fulfill his desires would determine if she survived.

Mote winced as his rough and careless fingers man-handled her, but she kept her eyes down. "Your captain needs to know, your injector sequencer has a faulty valve. Your bots won't be able to detect it so you'll have to do a scanner diagnostic. You're losing fuel effi-ciency—"

The Boscans reacted quickly. Both retreated to the door, glancing from her up to the half-round eye in the middle of the room.

Mote changed tactics, turning to look directly up at the ceiling. "You're losing fuel efficiency. It's probably down at least seven percent. We know because we're trained bot technicians. We can fix it for you."

Dab was sitting up now staring at her. "What?" Whit shushed her with a quick gesture.

Mote ignored her. "It looks like your bot techs could use some help. This door also shouldn't make noise when it opens. The alignment must be off in the locking mechanism—"

The two Boscans backed out of the room and the door slammed shut.

Mote focused on the eye in the ceiling. "We're worth more to you as crew than the measly credit you'll get for us on the open market. You're burning up credit right now. We'd be glad to help you while we're on board."

There was no answer. The door remained shut.

Mote eventually went over to the table and opened up the tray.

"Is that it?" Dab asked. "That's your big plan?"

"Yes." Mote sat down. "It looks good tonight—"

Dab strode over, slapping the eating utensil out of her hand. "Don't give me that! You offered to help them."

"Of course I did," Mote said calmly. Actually it was good that this would be on the logs.

"But they stole our ship!" Dab protested.

Mote reached over and picked up her utensil. "That's a moot point now, Dab. Would you rather be a pleasure slave or a bot tech on a raider?"

Dab got a funny look on her face as she reluctantly sat down.

Whit was grinning as he joined them. "I'd rather be a bot tech, thank you. I think they could use help holding this bucket together. I know a few things I could do to speed up this cleaning bot in here if I had a diagnostic unit."

Mote dug into the lumpy grain dish that was usually served in the evening. "Dab, you've got to stop being stuck in the past. The *Purpose* is gone and so are our friends. Rose didn't rescue everyone by whining about things. She looked forward. Well, this is our future. We can help these people—who don't like Fleet any more than we do—or we can make a living on our backs. I choose bots."

Dab finally nodded. "I'm with you there. Do you really think they'll let us stay on as crew?"

"It depends on how badly they want to save seven percent on fuel costs. And how much they want a friendly pleasure slave on board their ship . . . I know how to treat people who treat me well. They're losing their profits right now, so I certainly hope they make the right choice."

Mote kept on calmly eating. She knew they had no hope of trying to escape. It was sad, because she would miss Rose, Ash, and the others. She had gotten close to them. But she was with two people she cared about, and she wasn't going to give up now. Dab and Whit would have an even harder time letting go of Shard and Nip, because they'd been such a tight foursome. But anything was better than slavery.

Mote intended to join the raiders any way she could. If they scanned the injector sequencer, they would find out she was right. Maybe she had made her offer tempting enough. Maybe . . .

13

Nip opened his eyes. He didn't know where he was. There was light shining in his face, making it hard to see.

He reached out and scrambled his fingernails on the close curving walls around him. It was a coffin—

His arm! He frantically checked it, but it was fine. The last time he had looked down it had been hanging in nearly two pieces, cut right through his biceps. He thought he was going to die.

This must be a biobed. He had never been inside one before. All the inductions slaves were forced to go through kept them healthy and squeaky clean. Sick slaves were taken away, and he had never seen one come back.

His hand found the release lever, and he almost pulled it.

Then he saw the sign for vacuum stuck on the window above him. He almost missed it because of the light shining in, but now his eyes were focusing better. Next to it was a smudged imprint from lips.

Nip got up on his elbows to see better. It was a kiss from Shard. He'd recognize those lips anywhere.

Whew! That was close. He had almost opened the biobed without activating his flightsuit. He pressed the switch on his cartridge belt.

Nothing happened. His fingers searched the belt, but there was only one cartridge on it. One empty cartridge with the orange seam showing.

They left him in here without air! Nip tried not to panic as he felt around inside the biobed, carefully avoiding the lever that must open the lid.

He breathed a heartfelt sigh of relief when he found another air cartridge, then another. There were five cartridges taped to the top curve of the biobed. He loaded his belt and activated his flightsuit. The familiar blue buzz engulfed him. Now he was safe.

The top of the biobed opened easily. The atmosphere inside propelled him out of the bed.

Nip pushed himself back down from the ceiling and grabbed hold of a railing, looking around as he floated. His flightsuit hung in tatters from one arm, but the forcefield was holding. The dangling rags were stiff and stained brown from blood and biogel.

Where was everyone? Because of the weightlessness and the crumpled walls, he knew he must still be on the spacepost. One lonely light in the corner illuminated the medical bay. The biobed was being powered by a mini-converter, and it was outfitted with antigrav units so the bed could be moved.

Nip suddenly felt much better. They had taken care of him and kept him from dying. He was lucky to have good friends.

He tried to call them through the comm around his neck, but there was only static. He wondered if it had been ruined by the gel or the stasis in the biobed.

So he pulled on his grav boots, tied handily to the rail. There was nobody in the nearby rooms. And there was no one in sight as he clumped down the cylinder to the bend that had nearly killed him.

It was weird. He had never been alone. He was always either serving someone or hanging out in the slave barracks. Even when he was in a cube, there were other slaves all around him.

When Nip reached the landing disc at the bottom, he had to push aside the netted bundles of salvaged goods that were near the airlock. A couple had been opened and were spilling their stuff. Some bot batons and hand scanners floated among the remains of the ceiling.

Nip rushed up to the airlock. There was nothing but stars on the other side. The *Purpose* was gone.

At first Nip thought they had abandoned him. But when he looked closer, he realized that the docking arm was in shreds. The seal must have blown.

Nip went into a frenzy searching the other airlocks in both landing discs, hoping to find the *Purpose*. He could hear his own panting, and he called repeatedly through the comm, but there was only silence. The *Purpose* was gone.

He clumped all the way back up the cylinder and into the medical bay where his biobed was tied down. There were several tethers in the room next door, where it looked like people had slept. There was also some netted garbage, mostly packages from meals, but it didn't amount to much.

Then Nip found the lifepod next to the medical bay. It had been rigged with another miniconverter so they could eject it. Inside were hundreds of packaged meals, and some of the benches had been removed. At first he couldn't figure it out, then he realized they had planned to shove his biobed inside to take him along.

So where did they go instead?

Nip searched the spacepost even more thoroughly. They could have gotten trapped behind some shifting wreckage. Or caught in a locked room.

But he found nothing but eerie, empty silence.

When Nip was finally worn out and shaking with nervous exhaustion, he stood in front of the lifepod. His arm ached and his fists were clenched in fear. He couldn't stay on the spacepost. He couldn't sleep or eat. It was too big and empty. He didn't know how to be alone. He couldn't die alone.

He got into the lifepod. If he ejected it, the beacon would send out a wide-ranging signal. Some ship would detect it and be bound by space law to rescue him. It could be raiders or a merchant ship or even a patrolship. Then he would be a slave again.

Nip hit the airlock. It clanked shut, sending a vibration through the floor. The others had decided the pod was a good idea. So it must be the right thing to do.

He pressed the ejector. The lifepod shot away from the spacepost. Soon he could hear the blowers as the lifepod repressurized. It wasn't long before he could switch off his flightsuit. He sat down, hoping he had done the right thing.

He was still alone.

Trace saw the indicator light up, and though she had never seen it on her terminal before, she knew what it was. "Scanners are picking up a distress beacon."

Gandre Li rolled her eyes. "I knew we should have avoided this pocket."

"It's the best route through lower Sirius," Trace reminded her.

They were the only two on the command deck. Trace transferred the data received from the beacon. Gandre Li put the star chart on the imager so they could both see. The orange flashing beacon floated near the bold red slash of the destroyed spacepost.

"There's a Fleet warning prohibiting ships within missile range of Spacepost T-3," Gandre Li pointed out.

Trace glanced at her in concern. Gandre Li had changed since she had been forced under the uninhibitor. Several decnights after they were finally allowed to leave Canopus Regional Headquarters, Gandre Li was still distant and nervous. Trace had tried to soothe her, and she appreciated that the rest of the crew had given them their space, staying out of the lounge when they were off duty.

"You know we have to respond," Trace said quietly.

"It could be a trap," Gandre Li pointed out. "A raider could be hiding behind the spacepost."

"You've never refused to help someone before," Trace pointed out. Gandre Li was usually generous to a fault.

"What's a lifepod doing near the spacepost anyway?" Gandre Li demanded. "Nobody's supposed to be there."

Trace shrugged silently.

"Fleet can take care of it. There must be a patrolship that keeps an eye on the spacepost."

Trace hesitated, but it had to be said. "I know you're scared because of what happened under the uninhibitor."

Gandre Li flexed her shoulders as if trying to shrug off a bad memory. Her smooth head was flushed.

"I'm afraid they changed you," Trace finally admitted. "You haven't been yourself since."

"It was a warning!" Gandre Li snapped. "It showed me that I can't stick my neck out."

"You were protecting me," Trace reminded her.

"No, it was those Solians. I almost confessed. It made me realize how stupid I was to risk everything for them."

Trace went to stand next to Gandre Li, putting her arms around her shoulders. "But that's the Gandre Li I love."

Gandre Li encircled Trace's waist with her arms, hugging her tight. Trace rocked her gently, hoping that her lover was finally responding.

"I know you," Trace whispered. "You wouldn't be able to live with yourself if you killed those Solians. Hundreds of them! You aren't that cold-blooded."

Gandre Li ruefully laughed, burying her face in Trace's stomach. "You're right!"

"And you'll be tortured by guilt if you don't respond to this beacon," Trace added. "You know what we have to do."

Trace watched as Jor and Takhan each held a stungun pointed at the airlock where the lifepod had been carefully docked. Danal was at the helm, retreating from the spacepost with all haste. But they had circled the spacepost carefully before picking up the lifepod, making sure there was still nothing within scanner range.

Trace saw movement in the portal as Gandre Li opened the hatch. It was one of those huge spacepost lifepods that could hold sixteen people. But there was only one life sign on board the pod.

"Get ready!" Gandre Li warned. "Trace, get back!"

Trace ducked further inside the doorway, but she wasn't going to miss it.

The hatch to the airlock lifted up.

"Help!" someone cried out inside the pod, leaping away from the stunguns.

Gandre Li held her own stungun ready as she edged around the airlock. "Come out of there."

"Please don't hurt me." A man's head appeared with his hands held out. "I'm just a slave."

Trace exclaimed, "He's Solian!"

Gandre Li took a closer look. With all that hair, it had to be a Solian. Her stungun fell slightly. "What are you doing in that lifepod?"

His hands were still held out. "I was trapped on the spacepost. I knew the lifepod beacon would bring a ship to save me."

Trace wasn't scared but her heart was pounding. She hadn't seen many Solians since she left the creche. She didn't ever talk to the slaves who were brought on board the *Solace* by Alphas and Betas. Gandre Li said it was safer for Trace to stay in the cabin and keep away from everyone.

This Solian was older than her, but not by much. His slender chest made him look more boyish than manly. His wild, curling brown hair formed a halo around his head, with corkscrews spiraling out in every direction. At first it looked funny; then she realized how frightened he was. He staggered out of the airlock, his blue eyes wide with fear. His flightsuit was ripped on one arm, and there was a livid red line running around his bicep.

"Don't come any closer!" Gandre Li ordered, raising her stungun.

Trace ran forward despite Gandre Li's yell. "Don't be afraid," she assured the Solian. "We won't hurt you."

Jor and Takhan finally lowered their stunguns. Gandre Li seemed reluctant to do so. "Doesn't look like he's any threat," Jor commented.

The Solian was staring at Gandre Li. "I know you. You helped us before."

Gandre Li looked confused for a moment; then it dawned on her. "You're one of those slaves who was with Rose!"

"I'm Nip," he quickly agreed. "You—"

"That's enough," Gandre Li ordered, silencing him. "We've got to get out of here before a patrolship arrives."

It dawned them at the same time. They were in serious danger if they were connected with the escaped slaves. Jor and Takhan didn't even know the whole story. Only Trace knew that Gandre Li had plotted the grav slips for the slaves so they could escape to Qin.

Jor and Takhan immediately left for their duty stations. Gandre Li paused only long enough to jettison the lifepod. Nip looked after it as it rapidly tumbled away.

"Take care of him," the captain ordered. Trace nodded, knowing that things had just gotten a lot worse for Gandre Li.

14

_____~m~_____

Kwort lay dozing on a narrow, hard bunk inside the mesh cell. He was in the brig of a patrolship, with his back to the Solians. Ever since their rescue from Spacepost T-3, he had studiously ignore the slaves. It was for his own safety. He had to play his part, because the enforcers were undoubtedly watching them.

A light flashed over the door to the brig.

Kwort rolled off the bunk and came to attention before he caught his Fleet-trained reaction. Quickly he stretched as if he were trying to work out the kinks in his muscles; then he slouched and scratched the ridges on his head.

The Solians stirred in their cells. Each one had a narrow space that was barely long enough to lie down and stand up in. The fine mesh barrier kept them apart from each other.

The enforcer came directly to Kwort's cell. "You, Deneb, come with me."

Kwort felt a leap of fear as he was taken from the dingy brig and down a short corridor. The patrolship felt smaller and older than the _Conviction_.

Kwort shook his head, trying to banish the memory

from his mind. He couldn't afford to think of that now! Not here. He couldn't make these enforcers suspicious. It would only take one retinal scan to identify him as Kwort Delta, Technician Fourth Grade, assigned to the *Conviction*.

The enforcer was a Delta, so Kwort figured some curiosity was expected from a fellow plebe who had nothing to hide. "Where are you taking me?"

The enforcer shoved the butt of his stunwand into Kwort's back, making him stumble forward. "Shut up, dwarf fish!"

Kwort regained his balance, frantically reminding himself that he wasn't Fleet anymore. Deltas who were in the Fleet were elevated above ordinary Deltas.

The enforcer took him into a small room that was divided by a low counter.

"Sit," the enforcer ordered.

Kwort sat down on the chair. The enforcer stood at the door, his arms crossed. He was twice as tall as Kwort and was intimidating enough without the stunwand slung over his shoulder. Kwort was too scared to rub his back where the Delta had butted him.

The other door opened and the captain stepped in. Kwort almost rose, but the enforcer ordered, "Sit!"

Kwort bounced down so hard his teeth snapped together.

The Beta-captain didn't look at Kwort. His face was concave with two round holes for a nose and prominent chin and forehead. He wasn't much taller than Kwort. But he was bald as an Alpha, and that counted for a lot in the Domain.

The enforcer was at attention. "The Delta prisoner as ordered, Captain Nijellan."

"ID." Captain Nijellan leaned back in his chair, holding a dataport near his face to read it.

The enforcer handed over the chip that matched the chip in Kwort's wrist. The captain waved at the enforcer to check it, so Kwort held out his wrist. The card lit up in confirmation.

Kwort sat back, as the enforcer handed the chip over to Nijellan.

The Beta-captain slipped it into his dataport and examined the screen. "Cwart Delta. According to your chip, your current contract is with a merchant freighter, the *Duty*."

"Yes." Kwort felt the stigma of belonging to the lowest of the low space professions, a mere freighter.

"Designation number?" the captain demanded.

Kwort's heart was racing. He hoped he had remembered the designation number correctly, but it was unusual. "L-33300333."

The captain checked his dataport. "How long were you assigned to the *Duty?*"

Kwort realized it was working. "Three years. It was my first space job. I hitched a ride out from Deneb to find work. Since I don't have experience, only the frontier ships would take me on." He hoped that would explain how a bot tech from Deneb got to Sirius without any record on his chip.

The captain slowly turned his concave face to look at Kwort. "Just answer the questions, Cwart Delta."

"Sorry." Kwort sat back in his chair, feeling very small.

"Classified Fleet records state the *Duty* was attacked by raiders and all hands were lost."

Kwort nodded. "I ejected in a lifepod. The raiders picked me up."

"What was the class of the raider?" the captain demanded.

"An G-class courier," Kwort replied, hoping Rose had correctly remembered the appearance of the raider she had seen. "With laser array modifications."

The captain made a note in his dataport. "And how exactly did you end up on the spacepost with six pleasure slaves?"

His tone was highly suspicious, so Kwort kept it simple, stamping down on his instinctive desire to puff up his own part in the fictional drama. "The slaves escaped from their room somehow, and they let me out of mine. I was kept in secured quarters, when the raiders weren't forcing me to fix their bots. I showed the slaves the way off the ship and used them for cover. There were a lot more when we started," he added honestly.

The captain leaned forward. "Why weren't the slaves wearing collars?"

Kwort shrugged, knowing that was the tough one. "I think they came from the Procyon sector." He hoped the Beta-captain would assume the raiders had a back door into the Sol system.

"Do you know anything about their trade route?"

"No, Captain, the raiders kept that information from me."

The captain looked disappointed. "Didn't the raiders try to stop you from leaving?"

"Yes, Captain," Kwort agreed. "The raiders had left a laser rifle near the airlock. I held them off from inside the spacepost. I thought they were going to swarm me, but then they suddenly withdrew."

"How long were you on the spacepost before we arrived?"

"Nearly a full day."

Kwort hoped he had stuck to the main points of the cover story Rose had outlined for them. She had insisted that everyone tell the truth about the details as much as possible because she said that was the only way to lie. She seemed to have a lot of experience, so Kwort did as he was told.

"Well, Cwart Delta, you're in luck," the captain said. "Four days ago we were in pursuit of an G-class courier inside Perspokesor. They won't trouble the Fleet anymore."

Perspokesor was the system adjoining the pocket that held Spacepost T-3. Kwort thought about Mote, Whit, and Dab, who had been on board the *Purpose* when the raider stole it. "What happened to them?"

Nijellan glanced over, his eyelids lowered as if to chastise Kwort for asking a question.

"They kept me captive for a quarter," Kwort hastened to explain. "I hope they got what was coming to them."

Nijellan seemed disposed to brag. "We drove them into the spiral nebula next to the O-class star. The radiation fried the crew and the silicates in the nebula clogged their external ports, choking the ship's systems."

"Oh." Kwort imagined the effects of severe radiation. He wasn't so sure about the silicates. He had programmed bots to clean the external flues, and they could be fairly efficient. "Good," he added more emphatically.

The captain stared at him for a few moments, disdain permanently etched in his dish face. Then he tapped his dataport rapidly. Kwort wondered if he had blown his cover somehow.

Finally, Captain Nijellan popped out the ID chip and slid it across the counter to the enforcer. "You have been charged with trespassing on Fleet property, Cwart Delta. See that it doesn't happen again."

Kwort nodded, his eyes huge. The ID chip worked!

"Don't bother appealing the decision," Nijellan told him sourly.

"Oh no!" Kwort assured him.

The captain lowered his lids skeptically. Kwort shut his mouth.

Nijellan stood up to leave. "You'll be released on the Archernar shipyard when we arrive, sentence served for mitigating circumstances."

Kwort gulped. "My deepest appreciation, Captain Nijellan—"

"Take him back to the brig," the captain ordered the enforcer.

Ash thought Kwort looked dazed but immensely relieved when he returned to the brig. He retreated to his bunk, refusing to look at them.

Ash didn't hold it against Kwort. They were all fighting for their lives. Ash's worst nightmare had come true, and s/he was stuck in it, unable to free hirself. It had been bad enough when S'jen had kidnapped hir. S/he knew from that particular experience that s/he would never be able to adjust to being a slave again. But somehow, with the other Solians in the cells around hir, even though they cried and despaired, Ash felt better knowing s/he wasn't alone this time.

S/he stuck hir fingertip through the narrow mesh so s/he could touch Shard. Shard's expression was sympathetic as they rubbed fingers. They were suffering their own private tortures, imagining what would happen to them. It was even worse for Ash, because s/he felt responsible for their recapture. If s/he hadn't brought Kwort on board, none of them would have thought of going to Spacepost T-3.

Soon the enforcer returned again. This time he came straight to Ash's cell. "You, the herme."

Ash stood up. "Yes?"

"Come with me."

So it was hir turn to be interrogated. The enforcers had done a genetic scan of each of them when they were captured. Ash knew that hir genetic code was logged at hir old creche, and since s/he was relatively unique, it was possible that the enforcers could correlate hir code with known hermes. But they would have to get the data from hir creche first.

The other slaves came to the doors of their cells to watch as the enforcer clamped shock restraints around hir wrists. The shock restraints were like mini-collars that sent an electrostatic jolt from one wrist to the other when the enforcer activated the shocker. The enforcer was also carrying a stunwand.

S/he saw Rose as s/he went out the door. Rose looked worried.

The enforcer took Ash to a day cabin. From the fine craftsmanship of the furnishings to the decorative statuettes that filled numerous niches in the walls, it was clearly the captain's cabin. Hir experienced eye told hir it belonged to a Beta-captain.

Ash stood in the center of the room while the enforcer stayed near the door, watching hir with his hand on his stungun.

The door opened and a Coomen Beta entered. The insignia on his Fleet uniform indicated that he was the captain. Like all Coomens, he was rather short and had a concave face. They were known to be stubborn and fiercely proud of their rank.

The Beta-captain was eating something as he came in, slipping the last morsel in his mouth and murmuring appreciatively. Ash didn't look directly at him, though s/he was hungry after their few meals of fiber-protein bars.

"You have the shocker?" the captain asked.

The enforcer handed it over. "Yes, Captain Nijellan."

"Wait outside the door."

The enforcer retreated, but Ash was puzzled. Why would the Beta-captain risk being alone with a slave who was known to have escaped from raiders?

"So you're a herme." The captain thoughtfully sat down on the edge of the desk facing Ash.

Hir instincts told hir this man was dangerous. S/he knew better than to say anything, but s/he had learned with Rose how to speak up for hirself. S/he was in conflict, not knowing what to do.

"Hermes are very rare," the captain continued.

Ash couldn't look up from the floor. Maybe he knew who s/he was. He could have checked local slave shipments and seen that there was a herme among the slaves sent from Spacepost T-3 in the *Purpose*. Not for the first time s/he wondered what the former crew of the *Purpose* had reported. Did they blame the loss of their ship on raiders? Or did they admit that the pleasure slaves had taken over their ship?

"I've always been curious," the captain said.

Ash's stomach clenched at his tone. Oh, no . . .

"Open your flightsuit."

Ash felt as if s/he were falling. No! Not this! S/he couldn't.

The captain twitched, lifting the shocker slightly.

A burning pain ran through hir arms into hir chest. Hir heart skipped a beat as hir lungs clamped shut. Ash dropped to hir knees, bending over, trying to breathe, trying to relax the clenched muscles in hir chest.

"I won't repeat myself."

Ash's hand went to the collar of hir flightsuit. Gasping, s/he ran hir thumb down the seal, opening it. The enforcers had already taken hir cartridge belt, so the flightsuit fell open.

"All the way down," the captain ordered. "Let me see everything."

Ash continued down the seal to hir crotch. The stars in hir vision caused by the shock restraints were fading. S/he could see his avid eyes locked on hir body.

"Stand up."

S/he almost couldn't. A roaring filled hir head, maybe because of the shock. S/he stumbled up and stood swaying.

He examined hir closely, running his hand over hir smooth flat chest and down to hir genitals. His palm was rough, searing hir skin with every touch. Ash flinched but tried not to pull away. The Beta-captain seemed to enjoy hir reaction.

Anything, s/he chanted to herself, *I can stand anything.* S/he thought of Rose and felt a strength from the thought of her friend's angry eyes.

"Very strange!" The captain sounded as though he had found an unusual and repellent insect. "You have both male and female genitals. Smaller than I expected. And no breasts to speak of." The captain sniffed. "I like breasts. But you'll do."

Do! The word screamed through Ash's foggy shock.

The captain told Ash what he wanted from hir. But

Ash couldn't understand; it was a garble of meaningless sounds.

S/he was shaking and folding up when the burning shock hit hir again. And again. S/he curled up, feeling choked and hir heart seizing until s/he thought s/he would die. But s/he couldn't move.

Something hit hir hard in the back and legs, boots maybe. Ash cried out, not caring. But s/he couldn't hear, couldn't move, couldn't resist the horror that had fallen on hir.

The enforcer eventually dragged hir back to the brig and dropped hir on the floor of hir cell. There were outcries from the other Solians, Rose's voice in particular. Ash raised hir head to see the enforcer taking Shard out of her cell.

"No— Sor-sorry—" Ash stuttered, feeling only worse to see her friend taken in hir place.

"Don't you worry, sweetie," Shard assured Ash, leaning down very close to the mesh. "I'll take care of this."

Ash watched her go, reaching out one hand. No, s/he couldn't inflict that on Shard! Not by hir own failure.

But Shard was gone with the enforcer to face the Beta-captain. The others started talking to hir, but Ash couldn't stand it. S/he curled up with hir arms clamped over hir head, unable to speak or think. S/he couldn't face what lay ahead.

It was a new low for Rose. She even wondered a few times whether Chad had been right. Maybe she should have listened to him and kept the *Purpose* out of the Domain. It was suicide to risk being enslaved again.

Then again, she thought—*nah* . . . There was no way

a bloated testosterone bag like Chad was smarter than she was.

The Domain was like the ocean: she would have to learn how to deal with it since it was right on Earth's doorstep. Back in Tijuana she had learned how to swim and pilot a boat on the ocean, here she would learn how to navigate as well.

Besides, she had escaped from these idiots once already. She could do it again.

They were in the cells on the patrolship for days on end, and then the enforcers came and put shock restraints on their wrists. They were walked through corridors, airlocks, and a round terminal filled with crisscrossing aliens. One of those awful induction centers directly adjoined the terminal.

A familiar blue Poid came forward holding several collars. Rose sneered at him. "I put two of your buddies down, and I'll do the same with you!"

The restraints were triggered and she cringed from the burning flash through her chest. But she managed not to fall.

The Poids seemed puzzled by their lack of collars when they obviously had translator implants, but they had extra ones on hand so they must occasionally malfunction. Rose jerked away, but the Poids managed to get one sealed on her. Then they ordered her to stand still.

Nothing happened. Rose hesitated when she realized the collar didn't shock her. When S'jen had broken the key component in the implant in her neck, it must have permanently disabled it. The handlers didn't know it didn't work.

Rose cringed, trying to remember how the shock

made her react. She stopped struggling so the handlers turned to the other slaves. She motioned to the Solians and pretended to react from a collar shock. Blank faces stared back at her, but she thought there was a spark of understanding in Clay's eyes.

She watched as collars were put on Shard and Stub. Neither of them seemed to mind. Rose figured those two could weather a nuclear storm and come out fine. It had made her horny seeing Stub in his cell, perched in the corner, whistling to himself and watching everything with accepting eyes. You had to love a man who had some bounce.

Jot cried as they put her collar on, as usual. The waterworks show was irritating in its predictability. Rose thought it was about time the girl grew up. But maybe she couldn't. Maybe those Alpha-geneticists had created her to be a helpless girl forever, just as they had made Clay a mute. She wondered what kind of sick Alpha enjoyed that in a pleasure slave.

Ash was dragged forward by a handler. Rose felt awful every time she looked at Ash. When the collar went around hir neck, there was such emptiness in hir eyes that Rose bit her lip to blood. Ash had experienced things as a slave that Rose couldn't imagine. No wonder s/he was immobilized with fear.

"Don't worry, Ash!" Rose called out, and was rewarded with another order from the handlers. Rose let her knees sag as if she had been shocked. She didn't fight back when the handlers started stripping off their now filthy flightsuits.

Rose had bitter memories of her first induction on Spacepost T-3, and she had taken great pleasure in trashing the place while they were salvaging. The delicate machinery that probed, irrigated, sucked, pulled, pricked, and flushed every part of her body had made a satisfying crunch when it was pounded flat.

Similar instruments were used on her by these bored Delta handlers. Rose was invaded in every orifice, scraped in every crevice, and came out pink and flushed and feeling every touch like fire. One of the Poids was enjoying it more than was necessary. She almost made a break for it then, but none of the Solians were paying attention. They didn't realize this was their best chance. She couldn't do it by herself, even with a malfunctioning collar.

Naked, they were marched into the storage bay, where two large blocks of cubes were stacked.

Rose knew once she was placed inside, any chance of escape was gone. She had to try to get away, even if she had to do it alone.

She made a break for what looked like the main door, but it was locked shut. The handlers yelled orders, then came after her. Rose didn't pretend she was being shocked, she only tried to get away. But the big handlers carried her back and stuffed her into a cube, sealing it shut with a bot.

Rose paced along the interior walls of the cube, feeling the smooth, clear surface. The slaves around her were staring, drawn away in horror because of her fight with the handlers. She could barely see Shard and Ash at the bottom of the block, five cubes square. Jot was up and over one, while Stub and Clay were out of sight behind glinting walls.

In a flash, she remembered how she lost Jac and Rowena. She would lose these people too. Only they were her crew.

Slowly she sat down in the middle of the cube. Her tender skin burned and throbbed from the thorough probing. She was a slave again.

When Kwort left the patrolship, he was shoved out the airlock by a silent enforcer. He was glad to get away.

"Make way!" an enforcer called behind him.

Kwort stood to one side as the Solians were brought down from the patrolship. They each wore the silver shock restraints on their wrists. Rose looked like a star ready to go nova. Her eyes flashed at everyone, unsettling the enforcers.

Kwort sadly watched as he followed along behind them. He would never have imagined he could feel so much for slaves. But they had been real decent to him. Other than Horc, few people had treated him with respect and kindness. And he had brought them to ruin by suggesting they go to Spacepost T-3!

Ash longingly glanced over hir shoulder at him. S/he looked awful. He gave hir a little wave. At the bottom of the docking arm, the slaves were marched into the adjoining cargo bays.

A wrinkled Umpqua enforcer was at the desk at the bottom of the docking arm. She gave him a bioscan and demanded his identity chip. Though she was tiny, barely reaching Kwort's shoulder, she radiated grim authority. He was reminded of First Tech Rekest from the *Conviction,* and he sadly realized that no matter how completely he changed his life, he would never be able to get away from his past. It would haunt him until his dying days.

"Baggage?" the Umpqua Delta demanded.

"Uh, I don't have any."

She didn't raise a brow. "Credit?"

Kwort handed over the chits the enforcer had shoved into his hands. He had stashed some credit in his flight-suit from the bundle he and Clay had salvaged. But the enforcers had scanned him and found every chit. They had returned only a tiny fraction, but Kwort was in no position to argue.

"Decnight pass," the Umpqua decided. She tagged his identity chip. "Find work or get off the shipyard before then."

And with that, Kwort was a free man. For at least the next decnight.

The Umpqua returned the chits and he stashed them in several sealed pockets in the arms and legs of his flightsuit. Space stations were notorious for pickpockets so he made sure they were closed tight.

The Umpqua barked, "Move along!"

Kwort jumped and scurried away. He couldn't risk upsetting anyone. The first time his eyes were scanned, he was lab meat.

Now the question was how to survive. He wandered through the terminal and into the Archernar shipyard, ogling the multilevels that intercepted each other at odd angles. It was an engineer's nightmare. It must have been built up gradually over the centuries, with new additions every time the shipyard was outgrown.

Kwort had trouble finding the night rentals, and then he had to search for one that wouldn't gouge an obviously new arrival. Finally he found a hostel that rented him a cheap cylindrical berth. His berth was on the bottom row, and as short as he was, he couldn't stand up in it. Clearly it was only for sleeping.

He started to crawl back out of the berth when someone pushed him in deeper.

"Hey!" he exclaimed.

The door clanged shut, and Kwort squealed in terror, thinking he was going to be robbed or killed. He scrambled to the rear of the berth.

"Take it!" he shrieked, tossing out a credit chit. "It's all I've got! I'm destitute—"

"I don't want your credit."

Kwort peeked out from behind his protecting arm and realized a female was crouching near the door. She checked through the peekhole. "I'm avoiding a few people. I'll be moving along in a moment."

"Oh." Kwort stared at her, feeling awkward. She was actually cute—a humanoid he had never seen before. Her round baby face had reddened cheeks and big gray eyes. She would be much shorter than he was when she stood up. Hardly the threatening type, and he had screamed like a child in front of her.

"It's not your creche nanny, is it?" he had to ask.

She giggled. "Hardly. Only a few enforcers I don't want to meet up with."

"Are you in trouble?"

She glanced back at him. "You almost sound concerned."

Kwort shrugged. "You did get into my berth. I feel a bit responsible."

"As long as you're not going to turn me in to the enforcers, I'm ahead of the game."

Kwort shook his head. He couldn't tell her that the last thing he would do was call attention to himself with the authorities.

She sat down, turning to him. "Maybe there is something you can do for me, chum."

Now he was wary. "What?"

She held out a tag. "This is for a locker on the B level. I need to get my stuff out, but I'm afraid they'll see me."

Kwort eyed the tag. "What if the enforcers stop me?"

"They don't know I left the case there. I did it a dec-night ago before they started to tail me." She slipped a credit chit from her pocket. "I'll make it worth your while."

Kwort tilted his head to see the numbers on the face of the chit. It was big. Enough to buy some essentials, including a bot baton so he could get freelance work.

"What's in the case?" he asked. "Anything illegal?"

"No! It's nothing to worry your head about." She grinned at him, looking like an innocent toddler. "I'll wait here."

Kwort was afraid that it was too risky, and halfway down the ramps to level B, he resolved to return and kick the cherubic alien out of his berth so he could get some sleep. But the lure of the credit was more than he could resist.

He wasn't stupid, so instead of going straight down to the locker, he spent a handful of his precious chits on a pillow and a foil blanket. That would be his cover.

He went down to level B and walked very slowly as if the carryall were heavy. It gave him time to unobtrusively search the numbers on the lockers. He found the one that matched the tag in his hand, and he went to the empty one beside it.

It opened, and he stuffed the voluminous carryall with the blanket and pillow inside. Then he shut the door and locked it. He chose the cheapest option—a one-day rental—and inserted a small chit. Then he was able to pull out the key. He hoped this worked, because he had just spent enough to pay for a day of food and board.

Turning, he didn't see anyone.

Kwort meandered out of the locker area and went to the nearest food kiosk. There he got a veggie-stuffed pocket, a hot meal in a hand. He ate it while watching the aliens go by. They were busy with their own tasks, and he had nothing to do. He had rarely ever felt this way. There was always something that had to be done and there were always responsibilities he couldn't avoid.

When he finished, he wiped his hands and realized that this was his last chance to give up this nonsense. But he was seemingly immune to the disasters he created. He had destroyed his own battleship, and he had convinced the slaves return to the spacepost to salvage. Apparently he wreaked havoc wherever he went and rose out of the ashes like some kind of mythic beast.

He tossed aside the degradable wrapper from his meal and marched back to the locker. This time he went to the one that matched the little girl's tag and opened it up. If anyone stopped him, he was prepared to swallow the tag and hold up the one for the adjoining locker. It would look like a fluke that this locker had opened.

The door swung open and nothing happened. He stared into the locker as if confused. Then he reached inside and pulled out the heavy cylindrical case. It scraped along the metal but nobody paid any attention.

He set it on the floor and looked at it some more. Still nothing happened. So he closed the locker.

With a quick twist, he opened his locker and got out

his bedding. The cylindrical case fit inside the carryall with the pillow over the top.

Kwort started off carrying the stuff, afraid that he would feel a hand on his shoulder and the dreaded words from an enforcer: "Stop right there!"

By the time Kwort returned to his berth he was feeling buzzed, as if he had taken lots of frenetic. Now that it was safely over, he was thoroughly enjoying himself.

The door to the berth popped open and the little girl was still there. "It's about time!" she exclaimed irritably.

Kwort squeezed inside and shut the door. "I didn't want to barge right up to it in case they were watching it."

Grudgingly she nodded. "But where's the case?"

Kwort pulled down the carryall, revealing the black cylindrical case.

"Smart!" Her high voice carried approval.

She tried to take it. Kwort held on. "You have something for me?"

She giggled and handed over the credit chit. "It's a pleasure doing business with you."

Kwort took the chit and confirmed that it held the sum he had been promised. "You, too."

He handed over the case. She quickly opened the lock and checked the contents, probably to be sure he hadn't stolen anything. It had never occurred to him even look at her stuff. He couldn't see what she was pawing through.

"So what's your name?" he finally thought to ask. "I'm Cwart from Deneb."

"I'm Taffle." She looked at him hard for a moment. "You a bot tech?"

"Yeah, how'd you know?"

"I can spot 'em a light-year away." Taffle began to smile. "Well, my young man, I think we can do some more business together."

Kwort's blood was singing, and he felt curiously alive. "Sure, why not?"

15

When Winstav Alpha saw the damaged mining station in the Balanc system, he knew their carefully crafted strategy for the Qin was worthless. Felenore was angry, with her ugly face twisted even more grotesquely than usual. But she was sharp, almost as sharp as Winstav, so she kept her mouth shut as her superb brain began to work on the implications of what they saw.

"Well, well," Winstav said quietly, for her ears only. "The Qin have apparently acquired a battleship or two."

"Two, from the pattern of attack," Felenore bit off.

Captain Shippanz of the *Persuasion* was blustering about making an example of "these barbarians." His crew were commenting freely, a lax environment that Winstav had already noted for censure by the regional Fleet commander, Alpha-Commander Yonith. Yonith was the same person, incidentally, who was ultimately responsible for this mess in front of him.

"I'm reading Qin on board the mining station!" the comm officer reported, igniting new comments from the officers in command. "Forty-two in the barracks and processing segment."

"We should finish them off," Captain Shippanz demanded, looking at Winstav and Felenore. "Our lasers can destroy what's left of the station."

Winstav let Felenore reply. Her sarcastic bite was needed right now.

She snapped, "Then you'll be brought up on charges for destroying Fleet property. Punch a few holes where the Qin are located and send in your enforcers. That should take care of them."

While the crew of the *Persuasion* carried out the order, Winstav and Felenore quietly discussed this disturbing development.

"Odd that the command staff in Jenuar hadn't heard about this," Winstav pointed out. "Their patrols must not be as integrated as they claim."

"I trust nothing we were told in Jenuar." Felenore was controlled as always, not even allowing Winstav to see her dismay.

Neither of them had been impressed by their first stop in Qin. In the Jenuar system, they had heard glorious accounts of the victory that awaited them. The Alpha-commander of the Jenuar mining station had boasted that their battleship would smash the Qin civilization, and he was envious that he couldn't go along. The Alpha-commander had also laughed at the rumors that the *Conviction* had been destroyed by two Qin warships. But every freighter captain Winstav had interviewed repeated that a new debris field had appeared in an outer grav pocket near Balanc. Independently Felenore had reached the same conclusion that the battleship had been destroyed. They had not determined whether Rikev 5G had sabotaged the ship.

The best thing about stopping in Jenuar before going

to Balanc was that Winstav had been able to exchange his pleasure slave for a new model. Winstav valued novelty over every other characteristic in a slave. Felenore, ever the stolid plodder, kept her old slave, saying she was satisfied with his services. During the long journey to Qin, Winstav had managed to use every other slave on board the *Persuasion*, including the Alpha-captain's, but Felenore refused to allow him access to hers. It simply added to Winstav's respect for Felenore for not giving in.

From Jenuar, the strategists had ordered the *Persuasion* to skip the systems that lay between. They went straight to Balanc, the innermost system that was held by Fleet, to get the latest data on the Qin. Instead of finding patrolships in Balanc, however, they had been attacked by several Qin warships. Even though the warships had been easily destroyed, it was a clear indication that the situation in Qin had changed.

Winstav consulted his dataport as it correlated the scans of the scarred mining station with his own database implant. "The damage is at least four decnights old."

"The battleships are no longer in Balanc," Felenore agreed. "Atalade has already been hit."

"Impelleneer, as well," Winstav agreed, glad that Felenore could keep up with him. It made things so much easier.

"We have only one choice for our destination," Felenore said.

Winstav smiled, knowing she wouldn't suggest they return to Jenuar. Not yet. That system along with its overconfident Alpha-commander were doomed. The two Qin battleships were probably in Jenuar right now.

"Captain Shippanz, set course for the planet Balanc."

Winstav smiled. "The Qin will have a surprise when they return."

Chad drove his crude spear into the water. The shaft jerked from his hand and leaped forward. His bare feet were braced, so when the line to his wrist went taut, it didn't pull him off balance.

The shaft of the spear began thrashing in the water at the end of the fishing line. Chad grabbed the shaft and came up with a fat water creature that looked like it had a head at both ends. It was slippery and an unappetizing shade of yellow-green, but he and Newt had learned that it made a good meal when rolled in mud and roasted on the fire.

As Chad trudged back to their rough camp, he was glad he could provide food for Newt after dragging her down to this awful place. Balanc was not anything like he had expected. The Qin were half a step up from the stone age. The only place with any mechanization was the central depot for the vast farms.

They had lived there at first, in a nice enough room with running water and decent food. But it wasn't long before the authorities took away his sled-piloting job and gave it to a qualified Qin. No one wanted them around, because they weren't Qin.

"That's a nice fat one!" Newt exclaimed, running up to him. Her silvery blond hair reminded him of Shard, but Newt was uncomplicated and innocent. He loved that about her. There was a sweet, devoted tenderness in her touch and in her eyes that made their sexual encounters more than physical. Chad felt like he and Newt fused together into one when they coupled. That was something Shard had never given him in spite of her innumerable talents.

"I'll cook it up for us now," he assured her. "This is what food was meant to be."

Her smile made it worth it, as always. She was frightened a lot, but she had stopped complaining when they both realized they had lost everything. He knew she was happier now that they had left the Qin and struck out on their own. They had hitched a ride on a supply run down to the ruins of an equatorial compound. There they managed to scratch out a place for themselves on the outskirts of a small Qin settlement, which reluctantly tolerated them.

A sonic boom hit, making them both flinch.

"What's that?" Newt asked, looking around.

There was another boom, even louder.

Newt cringed and covered her ears. "What is it?" she cried.

Chad ran along the bluff out to the point where he could see the ruins of the compound that a few hundred Qin salvaged from in order to survive. He thought at first it was a ship entering the atmosphere at too sharp an angle. But there was nothing in the brilliant sky but dark purple clouds massing on the southern horizon.

Then a light flashed that was too bright to bear. An explosion lifted an enormous pillar of rubble into the air, churning up a boiling mass of rock and debris.

Chad was flung off the bluff by the shock wave. He ended up in the water, gasping and unable to see because of the white-hot light that seared into his eyes.

He bobbed up and down, trying to stay afloat in the violent waves. They had been mirror-smooth a moment ago when he was fishing. Frantically he tried to get away from the crash of the water against the rocks.

Everything was burning. He could hear the crackling

and rushing wind as brilliant spots formed and shifted in his vision. The overgrown foliage that lined the shore was mostly succulents, and from his experience, it didn't burn easily. But the heat that raced over the water made him duck under again and again to avoid being burned.

He swam away from the bluff, thinking, *Newt!*

"First pass completed," Captain Shippanz announced.

Winstav downloaded the scanner readings directly into his dataport; 93.4 percent of the humanoid lifeforms had been destroyed, while another 6.3 percent had moderate to serious damage to their biosystems. A 99.7 percent casualty rate for over one hundred thousand scattered humanoids was fairly impressive for a man of Shippanz's abilities.

"Prepare for a second pass," Shippanz ordered.

"Aye, Captain," the comm and helm acknowledged at once.

"Countermand," Windstav ordered. "There will be no second pass."

Shipopanz looked askance at the strategists. "I thought we were going to clean them out. You made sure they were all dead on the mining ship."

"That was to prevent them from effecting repairs," Felenore sneered.

"We must leave survivors to report to their leaders," Winstav explained. "They value their kinsmen, so they loathe to see them suffer."

Captain Shippanz looked confused, as did the other officers. They were primed to obliterate the Qin from the face of the galaxy.

Winstav sighed. "The Qin form tight family bonds. They even raise their own children."

Shippanz shook his head. "That's impossible! That would destroy productivity."

"Why do you think they're savages?" Felenore retorted.

"If we allow the remaining Qin on the planet to tell the others what happened to them, it will spread fear and panic," Winstav explained. "That was the first strategic mistake when we invaded this territory. Some Qin should have been allowed to return to the general population to bear witness to the power of the Domain. They wouldn't have dared to strike us."

Felenore was nodding in agreement. Heloga Alpha had been remiss in not requesting strategists to evaluate the efficiency of the Fleet occupation of Qin territory. It was highly negligent considering that Heloga Alpha had authorized the placement of the first mining station nearly three decades ago. Any strategist could have told her that a few hundred Qin released from the stations and decimated planets would spread the terror, resulting in a mass migration of Qin away from the Domain, opening up more systems they could easily pluck as needed.

As the *Persuasion* made another scanner pass over Balanc, the numbers jumped to 95.8 percent dead. "Excellent," Winstav said, satisfied. "This colony won't recover."

"Slaves will have to be imported from elsewhere if the mining is continued," Felenore pointed out.

"Unfortunately there are plenty of Qin," Winstav sighed. They were savages indeed, breeding indiscriminately and spreading over these planets like an infestation.

"What are your orders?" Captain Shippanz asked, looking from Winstav to Felenore.

As one, they said, "Jenuar."

The captain lifted his hands in agreement and began inputting the course change.

Winstav raised one brow as he glanced at Felenore. "You're ready for two against one?"

She briefly stretched her lips. "I like those odds."

Winstav chuckled low. "I should have known."

Chad crawled out of the surf, hardly able to support himself with his weakened arms. His hair was half burned off. His head flared with pain every time he turned.

His fingers dug in the sand, so familiar. He kept seeing bright red, yellow, and purple spots that faded in and out of view. It smelled burnt and bad, like the garbage they threw in the fire.

He couldn't recognize the niche in the bluff where he and Newt had set up their camp. It was completely black. He climbed a few terraced levels, searching. Straight blackened trunks stuck up from the side of the bluff, but the enveloping vines and leaves were stripped off. The ground was a mass of cindered succulents crunching hot under his bare soles.

He shuffled his feet, trying to figure out where their camp had been. There by the curve of the wall that protected them from the wind at night. And there—

Newt's charred body lay on the ground next to the burned roof of the shelter they had created from the foliage. He couldn't go closer. The outline of her body was smaller, as if she had never been as big as she seemed. Everything was black, a vaguely Newt-shaped mound of soot, half-buried with one skinny foot kicked up.

"Newt!" he cried out, falling on his knees. *"Newt . . ."*

*   *   *

Eventually Chad climbed the bluff and headed toward what was left of the ruined compound. A brand-new, nearly round bay had formed in the coastline, far too symmetrical to be natural.

It felt like a hallucination. The once-green landscape was twisted and charred a uniform blackish gray. The sky had gone leaden and the air was filled with ash and falling bits of debris.

There were dead Qin bobbing in the blackened, foamy water. The shores were littered with people and body parts that had washed up or been blown away from the initial impact. They all looked the same, indistinguishable blackened lumps like Newt.

Chad skirted the newly formed bay, heading inland. It was unbelievable how big a chunk of the planet had been vaporized. It hung in the air, falling in a thick layer on his raw, burned head, filling his eyes and mouth, choking him with every breath.

It didn't seem possible that the world could be changed in one instant. But that was how it had happened. Newt used to be alive, and now, because he had run out on the point but she hadn't, she was dead. When choices as simple as that could make a difference of life or death, how could anyone choose correctly?

Chad wondered if he was the only one alive on the planet. What if every settlement had suffered the same cataclysmic fate? It must have come from space. Only lasers could have packed this much punch. Apparently the Fleet had sent in a battleship to avenge the loss of their mining station. He couldn't understand how they got to Qin so quickly, though.

Then he found someone who was alive, if only barely. Chad stayed with her until she died.

Chad almost sat down next to the dead Qin after she went limp. He almost gave up. But his own pain drove him on. If he could drink some water, he would feel better. If he could wash his burning eyes and head, he would feel better.

When he reached the river that now let into the new bay, he found several other people gathered on the shore. They were silent and numb, with some nearly dead. Chad was accepted among them at once. They didn't know he wasn't Qin until he dunked his head repeatedly in the water. Even then, they didn't seem to care.

Chad wondered dimly at that. Did it take the end of the world to make people tolerate those who were different?

One of the men muttered continuously, "A thousand deaths to those who did this deed . . . A thousand deaths to the ancestors of those who did this deed . . . A thousand deaths to the children of those who did this deed . . ."

Chad took him some muddy water, but the man barely drank it. His staring eyes focused on nothing as he chanted, "A thousand deaths to those who did this!"

Heloga Alpha paused under the rosy spotlight, waving to the lesser Alphas and Betas as she strolled through the new merchants' promenade on Canopus. She was making it a fad to be followed by a lighting enhancer who created unique and beautiful displays around her. It ensured that she was seen in only the most flattering light even when she was outside.

Thus far there wasn't a hint of a rumor about her looks. She intended to weather this unusual skin reaction to recent stressful events, and return to her immaculate self. Her biotech Fanrique seemed confident that he could restore her complexion to perfection. The immobilization of the muscle groups throughout her face had done wonders for her already.

Heloga waved one last time, then turned down the corridor after her Beta assistant. The lighting enhancer followed, switching to a more muted palette. Two Alphas who were her current favorites followed while the rest of her entourage fanned out to cover her at the grand opening. As part of her restoration cure, she went out less and spent large blocks of time listening to calming music while immersed in soothing baths.

Suddenly there was a cry in the narrow corridor as a hulking humanoid burst through a door. Heloga screamed as he grabbed on to her, pushing her back into the lighting enhancer.

"Stop!" someone yelled out.

His hands got caught in the filmy stuff Heloga was wearing. His nose was long, hanging over his mouth, and it was wet with slimly drool at the end.

A nasty, disgusting Delta! Touching her! Daring to hang on to her, imploring her with misty frantic eyes.

"Get it off me!" Heloga cried.

Her own Beta-commander grabbed the Delta, and two local enforcers snapped wrist restraints on as they removed him.

Heloga furiously patted at her soiled and torn garment. "I thought you cleared this corridor!"

The commander of the local enforcers was bowing and scraping, trying to withdraw. "Our apologies, Regional Commander. We were chasing him down. A *frenetic* overdose—"

"Destroy it immediately," she ordered.

"As you wish, Regional Commander," replied her own Beta-commander. He would see to it.

Shaken, Heloga hurried to the platform where her aircars waited. "Follow me home," she told her lighting enhancer and Beta personal assistant. She ignored the two Alphas. They certainly weren't accompanying her home now.

Heloga settled into the 'car. Her chest had several reddened marks where the Delta had grabbed at her, trying to support his weight against her. She shuddered at the memory. She would have those substandard enforcers shipped off Canopus tomorrow. They obviously weren't competent enough to remain at Regional Headquarters.

As the aircar lifted and headed rapidly toward her home, she raised the mirror in the side window. With a sigh, she adjusted her tousled hair. It was a good thing the Alphas hadn't come with her. She would soon be going into lust, and she wanted to prepare herself for her new pleasure slave.

She had ordered the death of all the slaves who had participated in her lust at the slave compound, except for the prime stud who had performed so well. Her long-standing prejudice against slaves was gone, but she was still surprised at how well it was working out. Her Solian certainly knew how to use a woman. She had to shock him occasionally during lust when his eagerness caused him hurt her. The man had a dominant streak that almost wasn't good for him, but she didn't mind. Her ultimate control inflamed him even more, forcing him to ride that line in subduing her. It was exhilarating to be able to completely let go and not be concerned about revealing her desire for shameful things involving body fluids or humiliation. She had never allowed herself that ultimate freedom with Kristolas or any other Alpha—she couldn't have borne the knowledge in their eyes afterward. Thinking about her impending lust and the depths that she would wallow in sent a tingle of anticipation through her . . .

Leaning closer to the mirror, her eye caught by something. A tiny Y-shaped crack next to the corner of her mouth.

Heloga kept very still so as to not flex the muscles. She had screamed back there when that nasty Delta had surprised her. Maybe if she let it rest, it would heal.

"Magnify mirror," she said softly.

The crack grew to enormous proportions, widened by her speaking. She lifted one polished fingernail and flicked at the edge. Several flakes of skin broke off. Underneath was raw red.

Heloga pressed the comm button direct to her biotech, and cried, *"Fanrique!"*

16

—ᘁᘁ—

Nip lay back on the bed in the main day cabin of the *Solace*, bouncing a ball the size of his palm against the wall. It hit with a satisfying thwack and rebounded into his hand.

They were docked at Starbase M-7 in the Triella sector. Nip and Trace were holed up in Gandre Li's cabin with the Alpha-grade baffler going. The Beta-captain was concerned that InSec or station officials would scan the *Solace* and discover an unregistered Solian on board. That would be disastrous. If it was discovered that Nip was an escaped slave, everyone on the *Solace* would be in big trouble. So he stayed hidden behind the baffler whenever they docked somewhere.

Trace stayed in the cabin with him, apparently out of boredom. She had complained that she rarely left the *Solace*. Now she turned to Nip. "I want you to kiss me."

He missed the ball. It bounced against the wall at his head, then ricocheted off. "What?"

"I want you to kiss me." Her fair face reddened slightly as she shook back her shiny bronze hair.

"Are you sure?" Nip didn't know Trace was interested

in him that way. She seemed so wrapped up in Gandre Li.

"Yes," Trace replied. "I want to know if it feels different kissing another Solian."

Nip sat up, uncertain of what to do. He was grateful to Beta-Captain Gandre Li for keeping him on board instead of turning him over to Domain enforcers or a Fleet facility. It was the luckiest break of his life. So he didn't want to offend the captain, who clearly treasured Trace to a degree he had never seen in a master.

But Trace was the only one on board who paid any attention to him. The others were afraid of what would happen if he was discovered. Takhan Delta was openly hostile, and refused to allow him to touch the bots despite his offers. So he spent a lot of time hanging out with Trace in the lounge. She was the most curious slave he had ever met, and she soon got the entire story out of him about their life onboard the *Purpose.*

Trace was particularly interested in Kwort. It didn't take long for them to put it together that Kwort was the one who had saved her from the predatory Deltas on Archernar shipyard. Trace was fascinated by anything Nip could remember about Kwort, but he hadn't tried to get to know the little Deneb. He was ashamed, because it must have been Kwort who had rigged the biobed for him.

But aside from talking, nothing had happened between Nip and Trace. There were no side-long looks, no casual touching, and she never leaned against him when they reclined on the same couch. So when Trace asked for a kiss, he was surprised.

"What about Gandre Li?" he asked, stalling for time.

"I don't think Gandre Li would mind if I kissed you." Trace smiled, her dimple showing.

Nip felt a tug of desire for her. She was good-natured and smarter than he was in many ways. He wondered what it would be like to have sex with someone who was that forthright—probably a lot like being with Shard. He felt a pang at the memory of his friends. He missed them terribly, and he had a bad feeling they hadn't been as lucky as him.

He awkwardly smoothed back his curls, grown almost down to his shoulders. Dab liked him all "wild and woolly," as she called it, though her own hair was cut microshort.

"Okay," Nip finally agreed.

He leaned closer to Trace. She puckered her lips and lifted her face to him. He brushed his mouth against hers and pulled back.

She opened her eyes. "Is that it?"

"I don't want to rush it," he protested. "Have you ever kissed a man before?"

"Well, I've been kissed, but I didn't want it." Trace shuddered. "I've been used by two male Alphas since I was given to Gandre Li. I didn't like either of them."

"Okay, hopefully you'll like this better. Ready for another one?" He was feeling very interested now. She was so ripe and tempting.

"Sure!"

Their lips met again, and this time Nip pulled her shoulders closer to him, feeling her chest brush against his. She made murmuring sounds as she kissed him. He opened his mouth as hers opened. When he finally pulled back, they were both breathing heavily and Nip was ready to find out how much further she wanted to go.

"*That* was a kiss!" Trace exclaimed.

"Is it different with a Solian?" he asked.

"Yes, for some reason it is." A troubled expression flashed across her face.

"Do you like it?"

She grinned at him. "Yes."

They kissed again, and rubbed up against each other like kids in the creche. It took Nip back to those happy days when they had created their own little society and protected each other from the handlers and sex instructors. They laughed and kissed and rolled around on the big bed together. Nip fondled her tempting yet fully clothed body, ready and willing to keep going.

But Trace pushed him away, standing up and straightening her bright red flightsuit. "I've got to stop! Or I won't be able to stop."

Nip liked the sound of that. He reached out one hand, trying to draw her back into bed. "Would that be so bad?"

She shook her head playfully at him. "Behave!"

There was a sound at the door and it opened. The Beta-captain in her immaculate white flightsuit filled the doorway. She frowned when she saw Nip sprawling across her rumpled bed.

Nip quickly got up, feeling incredibly guilty. He knew he couldn't hide it.

Trace quickly went to Gandre Li. Her welcoming smile had no trace of uneasiness. "How was it?"

"No problem," Gandre Li said absently. "I got an earlier departure. The crew is reporting back now."

"Do you need me on the command deck?"

The Beta-captain ignored Nip. "Yes, let's prepare to depart. The quicker we're out of here the less chance of anyone scanning an extra slave on board."

They left, with Trace giving Nip a smile and a reassuring wave on the way out. He nodded back, but he didn't feel very good.

Things were getting complicated. He couldn't stay on the courier, but it was difficult finding a place where he could go without landing immediately back in the slave trade. Trace had told him that the Beta-captain had located two small settlements across the border from the Archernar sector that might take him in. Only people who wanted to avoid the Fleet would scrape a living from a backwater system outside of the Domain. It would be a dangerous place for him with no one to protect him, so he wasn't looking forward to it.

But if the Beta-captain got mad at him, she could shove him out an airlock. Nip knew that was always top on her list of options, and by fooling around with Trace, he had made it a choice Gandre Li might feel forced to take.

Nip grabbed his ball and began tossing it against the wall again. He didn't have much faith that he could stay away from Trace. He always got sex wherever he was. He even managed it in the slave barracks with other Solians, right under the eyes of the handlers. Besides, Trace was so delectable, how could he resist? Wearing her tight, colorful flightsuits with those perky breasts and dimples . . . he knew if she spread her legs, he would be on her in a flash.

As the ball went thwack! then thud into his hand, he wondered what would happen to him then.

Gandre Li knew something was up, but she answered Trace's questions about the latest InSec pickup. They were being sent to Starbase C-4 in the Archernar sector.

"There's a settlement on a moon outside that sector," Gandre Li reminded Trace. "Maybe we can leave Nip there."

"I hope he'll be okay," Trace agreed readily enough. But Gandre Li was irked by that new word that had crept into Trace's vocabulary: *"okay."* That was what Nip always said.

After they reached the command deck and settled into their departure routine, Gandre Li asked, "What did you and Nip do while I was gone?"

Trace hesitated. "The usual—we talked and looked at a viewer. He likes bouncing that stupid ball." She glanced at Gandre Li. "Then we kissed for a while."

"Kissed?" She had known something was happening between them today when she found them on her bed. But it sent a weird pang through her chest. "You made out with Nip?"

"I wanted to see what it was like to kiss a Solian. I never have, you know."

Gandre Li felt so immensely threatened she couldn't figure out what to say. The depth of her instinctive reaction stunned her. She couldn't show it to Trace, who was being deliberately nonchalant about it.

"What was it like?" Gandre Li asked in a tight voice.

"Not bad," Trace admitted. She got up to put her arms around Gandre Li's neck. "It's not nearly as nice as kissing you, though."

Gandre Li hugged her but she felt strange giving her a brief kiss. She kept thinking about Nip touching Trace, his lips on hers . . . She knew her expression was not quite right as Trace gently shook her. "Are you okay with this?"

Gandre Li took a deep breath. "I'm fine. It's natural to

be curious. You've been with me since you left the creche."

"I knew you'd understand."

They worked together for a while, undocking and departing the station. Gandre Li tried to let that distract her, but Nip's goofy face and corkscrew hair kept popping into her mind. Why did Trace want to kiss him? Just because he was Solian? Trace must like him, because she was spending most of her free time with him.

"Are you going to kiss Nip again?" Gandre Li finally had to ask.

Trace cocked her head. "I don't know. Would you be upset if I did?"

There was a pain in her chest again. "I have to admit, it does bother me."

"Oh." Trace's happy expression fell. "I was sort of hoping the three of us could have sex together."

Gandre Li knew the horror showed on her face. "What?!"

"We've talked about having a triad," Trace reminded her. "You said we could rent a pleasure slave at any port. But we didn't want to force someone to do it." She smiled. "I'm sure Nip would be willing."

"I'm sure," Gandre Li agreed, for want of anything better to say. "But I'm not interested in having sex with Nip."

"Why not? He's nice and he kisses really good."

"I was thinking the third would be another woman."

"Oh." Trace thought about that. "Does that make a difference?"

"To me it does. Maybe not to you."

"I never thought about it," Trace admitted with a sigh. "I thought it would be perfect, exactly what we wanted."

Exactly what you wanted, Gandre Li thought. She couldn't understand why Trace had any interest in being intimate with Nip. Until Gandre Li had walked in on them today, she hadn't considered that Trace could be attracted to him. Maybe she shouldn't have let them spend so much time together.

But that brought her back to the Big Question that had haunted her ever since she had helped the Solians escape from the Domain. Was Trace her lover or her slave? If she kept Trace locked in her cabin or used the collar to control her, that would be enslaving her. Trace had so few choices in her life.

"If it's really what you want," Gandre Li finally said. "I won't stop you. I don't like it, but it's your decision."

Trace stood up and came over to Gandre Li again, leaning her cheek against hers. "I don't ever want to hurt you, Gandi. I love you so much."

"I love you, too, Trace."

Gandre Li hugged Trace for a while. She tried to say something a few times, but there was nothing else she could say. She held on to Trace's waist tightly, hoping she would understand how much she was needed.

When Danal arrived to take over on the command deck, Trace went down to their cabin to have a fresher wash. Gandre Li finished compiling the logs and was leaving when Jor and Takhan arrived in command. "Can we speak to you for a moment, Captain?" Jor asked.

Gandre Li knew it was important from the way they were looking at her. Danal was at the helm with Takhan and Jor standing next to him. Takhan had a hostile expression and Jor was worried.

"What's wrong?" Gandre Li asked.

"We don't want to be lied to anymore," Takhan said flatly. Her stance was aggressive, with her fists on her hips. Her spiky blond hair stuck straight up over her icy blue eyes. "It's bad enough you let that slave stay on board—"

Jor gently shushed her, holding out his hand. "Let me handle this, Takhan."

"Is this about Nip?" Gandre Li demanded. She stood facing them.

"No, we want to know why you always go to InSec," Jor told her.

"What?" Gandre Li retorted, getting flushed. This was not happening! How did they find out?

"If this ship is engaged in InSec business," Jor said reasonably, "we have the right to know. If anything goes wrong, we would be held accountable along with you."

Gandre Li hesitated. "The only reason I keep things from you is to protect you."

"Do you really think you could protect us if InSec decides to investigate?"

Gandre Li had to admit, "No. But the less you know the better for you."

"But we found out about it," Jor said. "Now we have to go from here."

Gandre Li didn't like being put on the spot. She went over to the wall and glared at the ornamental plaque engraved with the name *Solace*. "Why bother asking when you already know? Did you follow me?"

With a quick look, she ascertained that Jor was guilty and Takhan defiant. Danal was impassive as usual, his yellow skin kicking back a glare from the command lights.

"What's more to tell? I'm a courier. I take messages and information where I'm told to go."

"You're not a spy?" Jor asked in surprise.

"Me?" Her voice sounded harsher than she expected. "Only a courier. At first I had to do it to survive. Now I can't get out."

"You don't like it?" Jor asked.

Gandre Li rolled her eyes. "What do you think?"

"We don't know, that's why we're asking," Jor said. Danal and Takhan also looked curious.

Gandre Li held up her hands. "Do you see? There's blood on these hands."

The others looked from her palms to her angry eyes.

"You think I like being responsible for death and destruction?" she demanded. "Do you think I like being InSec's slave?"

"No," Jor said softly.

"Good, then you three have a decision to make." Gandre Li stalked to the door. "Let me know if you're leaving by the time we reach Starbase C-4. I may be able to find a crew there. I'll let you out of your contracts and give you each a recommendation."

On the way back down to her cabin, Gandre Li wasn't sure which bothered her more, the imminent loss of a top-grade crew or Trace's unsettling experimentation with Nip. The crew was much more important, but she realized she was more concerned about Trace. What if she was with Nip right now?

Gandre Li rushed into her cabin. In the doorway, she heard the fresher going and Trace singing in a high voice. Nip had returned to his own small berth next to the lounge.

Gandre Li sighed and leaned against the doorway. What was she going to do?

* * *

Trace was confused. Her mind was telling her one thing—she had to respect Gandi's wishes and help her through this rough period. The loss of their crew would be horrible! Takhan, Jor, and Danal accepted her status on the *Solace*, and it would be difficult to befriend new people. Anyone who came on board would see her as a mere slave; someone to be ignored or tolerated. They would also have to hide Nip, an uncollared and undesignated slave, from any new crew members. It would be a real mess.

Meanwhile she was obsessed with the thought of having sex with Nip. Her body was urging her to touch Nip and let him inside her; it was the right thing to do, a good thing, exactly what she needed and craved. She couldn't look at him without feeling a tug of desire that shot right to her core.

It made no sense, because, while she liked Nip, she loved Gandre Li. She had none of those tender, cherishing feelings for Nip that she had for Gandi. It was pure lust, like none she had ever felt before. It went far beyond rational thought, and she actually began avoiding Nip rather than have to fight herself.

A few days after her first kiss with Nip, Trace left Gandre Li on the command deck and headed down for her nap. Nip had described how Rose shortened their day on board the *Purpose*, and it made them all feel much better. It was funny to think of something so normal, like taking her daily nap, and realize she was tired because she was out of her native environment.

Trace knew she had to stop thinking about Nip. At least until everything was settled with the crew.

Suddenly she decided to take matters into her own hands with the crew. They must be in their quarters—they didn't like to relax up in the lounge with Nip.

Trace pressed the light that would announce her presence and waited. She was almost ready to leave when the door finally opened.

"I thought it might be you," Jor said, pulling back. Takhan was sitting on their couch.

"Where's Danal?"

"In the fresher," Takhan replied. She didn't meet Trace's eyes.

"You've all been avoiding me," Trace said sadly. "I wanted to talk to you."

"Gandre Li told you?"

"Yes, she said you might leave us."

Jor and Takhan exchanged wary looks. "Did she tell you why?"

"You're upset because Gandre Li works for InSec."

Jor's eyes opened wide. "You know about that?"

Trace went to sit on the stool next to the low table. "Of course. InSec gave me to Gandi."

Jor came over next to Takhan, who was looking at Trace. "How long have you known?"

"I found out a few years after I was given to Gandi." She raised her brows in appeal. "I'm sorry I didn't tell you. We thought it was safer if you didn't know anything. That way, if something happened, they wouldn't be concerned with you because you don't know any details of what we do. Gandre Li worries all the time about it."

Jor blew out his breath. "We weren't sure if we should tell you or not."

"Did you think I was too stupid to notice?" Trace asked, frowning a bit. "I'm the one who keeps the accounts."

They exchanged looks again, and Takhan started to

smile. "I should have known! You know everything that happens on board."

"That's because I can't leave," Trace pointed out.

Jor patted her arm. "I'm sorry. We should have asked you instead of following the captain around."

Trace smiled at them, feeling somewhat better. "You can't leave us. We need you."

Takhan had a strange expression on her face. She looked at Jor for a long time. "I don't know."

"We have to talk to Danal," Jor agreed.

Trace jumped up and gave them a hug. "We're family. We can't lose you now. It's tearing Gandi up inside."

Takhan and Jor hugged her back, but Trace sensed they wanted to be alone. She couldn't push them too hard. But after the door closed behind her, she let out a little whoop of joy. Surely they wouldn't leave now that they understood that Gandre Li had been trying to protect them.

It was a huge weight off her mind.

But almost immediately, the void was filled by thoughts of Nip.

Trace was supposed to go to the cabin for her nap, but her feet carried her past the door. She scolded herself for her weak will. She should got to the command deck and tell Gandre Li that the crew probably weren't leaving. But she didn't want to say anything until it was certain.

Trace climbed the spiral steps up to the lounge. But Nip wasn't in sight. He must be in the narrow berth that was often used by slaves who traveled with their masters.

She told herself to go back downstairs. Nothing could be gained by coming here. But she opened the door to the berth.

Nip looked up from the viewer. "Hi!"

There he sat on the bunk—gawky, with food stains on an old flightsuit, and hair that was really too much. But he smelled irresistible and there was a genuine kindness in his expression. She knew he had been through some awful things in the slave trade, but he had sweet disposition that was endearing.

Trace sat down next to him. He stiffened, then leaned closer to her. She put her hands on his face and brought it to hers so she could kiss him.

Soon they were tangled in a clench on the bunk, breathing hard and straining against each other. When her hand went to the neck of her flightsuit and she unsealed it down to her stomach, his eyes grew wide.

"What about the captain?" he asked.

"I told her I wanted to have sex with you."

"You didn't!"

"She said it was my decision." Trace had to admit, "I don't think she'll like it. But we can do it."

Nip was shaking his head as if he couldn't believe any master giving their slave that much freedom. "We better not."

Trace reached up and pulled him back down on her, tightening her fingers in his wild curls. "You have to. I can't stand it anymore. I have to have you."

He couldn't resist either. He ripped his own flightsuit off and more carefully unsealed hers down to the inseam. Then she urged him on in guttural tones. She had never wanted anything so badly as him. As he finally took her, she cried out in complete pleasure.

Afterward, they lay entwined together on the bunk. Trace was a bit worried that someone would come up to the lounge, even though she wasn't doing anything wrong. Still, she felt guilty about Gandre Li.

Her finger traced his shoulders where the collar had left darker calluses on his pale skin. "How does it feel to have the collar gone?"

"Good," he said drowsily. "Real good."

She touched her own slender, silver collar. Other Alphas had used it on her, and she hated it. Gandre Li had also inadvertently shocked her with it when Trace didn't do exactly what she said. That's why she had become very good at listening. That ring around her neck was a constant warning that she was a slave.

"I bet it's nice," she agreed.

Nip lifted his head to look at her. "I could take yours off. Rose made sure we all knew how to do it."

Trace tensed. "You can?"

"Sure. I watched Rose do it with lots of the slaves. It's connected to your translator implant. All I have to do is crush the little red cylinder, and the collar is deactivated. We could saw it off in a jiffy."

Her hand touched her collar again. "It would be too dangerous if anyone saw me without a collar."

Nip shrugged. "I can deactivate it and leave the collar on. That way you won't get shocked."

She was shaking at the idea. Suddenly she wanted to do it. The thought of never having to endure another shock was enough to make her dizzy with relief.

"I have to ask Gandre Li."

Nip's expression fell. "That's true. You have to do what she says."

Trace nodded uncertainly as she lay back down. She put her head on Nip's smooth chest, snuggling into his arms. It was funny but she had never felt more like a slave than now, when she had freely chosen to be intimate with someone she liked. But the collar around her neck was a reminder. She could be taken away from Gandre Li at any time if a powerful Alpha got a craving for her. And there was nothing she could do about it.

17

From his place in the cube stack, Stub could talk to Jot and Clay. Clay couldn't talk back but he could whistle and wave. Ash didn't try to talk at all.

Rose was at the top of the stack and she didn't try to communicate with Stub. Maybe she couldn't see him. The stack was tricky that way. He also couldn't hear her, though he watched her talking through the tubes quite a bit.

Shard and Jot could hear Rose. Jot passed on that Rose had warned "don't tell anyone." Stub knew Rose was talking about their collars, which no longer worked. Jot seemed confused by the cryptic message, and Stub wasn't about to explain to the little idiot when other slaves could hear. It didn't really matter because Jot had probably never disobeyed an order in her life. The girl probably wouldn't even realize her collar didn't work.

Stub did pass the message on to Clay, who touched his own collar and signaled agreement.

They were warehoused in the cubes for two long days. Stub spent his time whistling with Clay. The guy could make a lot of beautiful sounds. Stub made stumbling efforts to echo him, playing back and forth.

The handlers eventually returned to unstack the cubes. These handlers were the long-nosed Swarks, Stub's least favorite Deltas. They kept slaves tightly in line. Poids and Bratamas were much more easygoing.

The handlers unloaded them from the cubes. Stub knew the drill. They were going to the slave barracks. Anyone who had enough credit could use the slaves in the barracks.

They had to stand in parallel lines, facing forward. Stub gave Rose a quick grin, but she frowned back at him, her beautiful face twisted in fury. She acted out—snarling at the handlers and trying to talk to the other slaves. She would have been brain-dazed from the shocks if her collar weren't deactivated.

That girl runs on a constant boil, he thought. It made for great sex, but Stub didn't need that much drama to entertain him. Usually he laughed at her when she got this way. Right now, it would only infuriate her more, so he restrained himself.

They were expertly cut into two groups by the handlers. Stub noticed that he was included among the two dozen most desirable slaves. They didn't know his training record, which was recorded on his old collar, but these handlers could spot a prime stud without it. They were destined for Alphas and Betas. The other group was three times as large, and those slaves would serve the more numerous Gammas and Deltas who worked at the shipyard.

All of the former crew of the *Purpose* were in the same lineup. It didn't surprise Stub. Each one was unique in some way: Shard for her dual heritage, which made her hypersensual, Rose because she was clearly a native Solian, Ash for hir unique physical characteristics,

Jot because she was so young and pretty, and Clay because he was silenced. Stub figured they had been put together in the same cargo container on the *Purpose* to keep the treasures together. Dab didn't fit that mold, but she had probably been filler.

Stub grinned at Shard as they were marched into the tubes of the shipyard. Shard knew the score, too. At least they would have a few more decnights together before they were scattered throughout the Canopus region. They might get lucky and tour together for a while as their shipment was passed from station to station. Even if they were separated, he often met up with slaves he had known years before in different barracks. It was the life of a slave.

He got a good look at the busy Archernar shipyard as they went up the ramps and through the levels. There wasn't another maintenance yard for sectors out on the frontier, so lots of ships put in here for repairs. The industrial complex featured bare bulkheads filled with rooms interspersed with crude public spaces. It was crowded with off-duty crews filling the mezzanines, with merchants standing on every protruding beam, hawking their wares to the crew members and shipyard workers.

Stub had been here once before, so he knew the slave barracks. It was a dull, functional place with a small viewing center opening onto a long narrow room filled with bunks. The baths were barely adequate, but there was a nice strand of reeds at the end that towered to the ceiling and were as thick around as his ankle. They had slender leaves that rustled under the air ducts.

Stub snagged a bunk near Rose, hoping he could help her adjust. She tried to talk to him, but the handlers were hovering over her after the way she had acted out. She had even tried to make a break for it, and only a quick grab by a Swark kept her from getting away. After that, a Swark had marched next to her with one hand on her collar. Swarks weren't the brightest Deltas in the Domain, which was probably the only reason they didn't see that Rose's collar wasn't working.

He lay down on his bunk, motioning covertly for Rose to do the same. She would have to learn quickly or somebody would figure out about her collar. She copied him, feigning sleep to get the Deltas off her back. The Swarks retreated to the door to the viewing room, then eventually left.

Rose lifted her head to look through the archway.

"Don't," Stub warned. "Stay still or they'll come back."

Rose relaxed back as if she were settling in. "They're watching us?"

"Move your lips as little as possible," he added. It was second nature to the slaves to speak in a murmuring undertone.

"They won' le' us talk?" she slurred through barely parted lips.

"They're keeping an eye on you now. Rose, you have to play along or they'll figure out your collar isn't working."

"I'll get away 'fore they fin' out."

Stub knew he would have to stretch the truth a bit for her own good. "What if they start asking questions? Like: why don't you have a collar even though you have a translator? Where did you come from? What were you doing on Spacepost T-3?"

She was tensed, ready to spring off the bunk, as if she wanted to start kicking and screaming.

"You know I'm right," Stub urged. *He* knew they would sooner toss her into an incinerator than ask a pleasure slave any questions. "If they find out you escaped, they'll mind-suck you and they'll track down the rest of us."

"I can' le' hem push me aroun'," Rose slurred.

"You have to," Stub said flatly. "Unless you want to kill us all."

Rose blew out her breath, caught.

"Relax," Stub told her soothingly. "It's not that bad."

Rose tightened up, rolling onto her back and letting out a strangled cry of protest.

One of the Swarks appeared in the archway and stared for a moment. Rose didn't move and her eyes stayed closed. The handler disappeared again.

Rose didn't speak again. Stub knew she would learn. Rose wouldn't do anything to hurt them.

Shard was glad to get a decent bath. The cubes were uncomfortable and never very clean, and the brig of that patrolship had been disgraceful. So she luxuriated in a hot bath for a long time, washing herself carefully and using the lotions in the cupboards to soothe her skin and hair. She hadn't had a decent wash up since before Spacepost T-3 was attacked by the Qin. The *Purpose* had inadequate freshers that barely provided any water, relying on ion attractors to lift the dirt off. She never felt clean after a fresher the way she did after a bath.

When the viewing bell rang, her hair was still wet and slicked back in a fall of shining white strands to just below her shoulders. She didn't bother putting on a tunic. She strolled naked into the viewing room and took one of the small round pedestals.

The other Solians hurried in, prodded forward by the handlers. Stub snagged the pedestal next to hers and gave her a wink. Rose was glowering on the other side, her arms crossed and her body language defiantly unsexy. The handlers had to rip the tunic off her. She feigned a shock from the collar, and pretended to subside.

Shard shook her head at Rose. There was nothing to be gained from her rebellion. It would only focus the handlers' attention on her. And she was ruining it for everyone. The handlers were watching them all too closely because of her. Rose needed to calm down so they could enjoy themselves while they had the chance.

In some ways being in the barracks was better than serving one master. At least Shard got variety and she had a chance to relax with other Solians when she was not working.

The doors opened and the handlers rushed to the front of the viewing room, ready to prod the slaves into their best presentation.

Shard had placed herself in the back corner, where she could judge the three prospective masters before they reached her. One was an Alpha who was primarily looking at males. He was in a rush and took the big ebony slave that Shard had been eyeing herself.

The two Betas took their time. The female Bariss wore a Fleet uniform with an officer's insignia and the seal of a ship. It was probably in dock and she was spending some of her quarterly credit on a pleasure slave. This Beta wasn't high enough in rank to have a pleasure slave of her own.

The other was a Novamdil Beta merchant. It was a male and had a rather long, downturned mouth.

The Bariss stopped to check Ash. She reached out to

examine hir genitals. Ash was frozen, hunching in on hirself, unable to move. S/he stared at the floor with a stricken expression. Shard had been glad to service that Beta-captain on the patrolship for Ash. It had been ridiculously easy to satisfy his mammalian urges. And she had gotten a quick hop in the fresher in the bargain.

The Bariss poked at Ash but s/he didn't respond. The Beta lost interest and focused on the males. She seemed torn between Stub and another superior male who worked for it. Stub was too easy going to make an effort at anything, even for some pleasant diversion.

The Bariss chose the other male and Stub gave Shard a small shrug. He didn't care.

The Novamdil merchant was moving slowly from slave to slave on his thick legs and feet. His flat face was notable for its mouth—a perfect half-circle curving downward. It made him look mean, but Shard knew a thing or two about Novamdils. They were gentle and considerate. And they knew how to enjoy themselves. This one was probably a regular customer so he wouldn't expect too much like that Fleet officer who was on leave after decnights of space patrol. That Bariss would probably work the poor slave all night to get her credit's worth out of him.

The Novamdil paused to admire Shard. He seemed undecided between her and Jot. Shard was amused to see that Jot watching the Beta with eager eyes. That girl was a slave through and through. She lived to serve.

Shard gave the Beta a knowing smile, letting her lips part and moving her hips slightly. Jot didn't have a chance. The Novamdil couldn't take his eyes away from Shard as he handed over his credit chit and helped her off the pedestal.

Shard kept her attention on the Beta as she accepted a tunic from the handler. The Swark recorded the transaction on her collar. If she worked this right, he wouldn't return her until the end of the shift. Since Novamdils enjoyed their food, she also would get at least two excellent meals. Maybe she could convince him to play some music or even give her some happy juice. They might go out for dancing or entertainment. The Archernar shipyard was as good a place as any in the Canopus region to have fun.

Jot stayed close to Ash as they settled into a routine in the slave barracks. Ash wasn't responding to anyone, not even Rose. They could hardly get hir to eat. It frightened Jot, who was used to looking up to Ash.

Otherwise, Jot felt better now that the worst had happened and they had been caught. It wasn't as bad as she had feared. She had heard some of the others speculating while they were still on the *Purpose* that they might be incinerated if they were discovered to be escaped slaves.

It had kept her awake at nights wondering what she would do if she was asked, "Did you help hijack the *Purpose?*" She couldn't lie. She had helped, and she deserved to die for it.

But nobody asked.

So gradually she relaxed in the barracks, enjoying the fact that a whole ship wasn't relying on her while she was at the comm. It had been hard for her to concentrate for that long every day. Now she didn't have to get scared whenever the scanners picked up another ship. She didn't have to decide things for herself. It was a lot harder being free, even though some of it was nice.

The bell rang again, as it did frequently in these slave barracks. Most Alphas and many Betas had their own pleasure slaves, but the shipyard got an enormous amount of traffic and there were plenty of opportunities for each of them to be selected.

Jot helped Ash get up and guided hir into the viewing room. Ash was fading every day, slipping into catatonia. Rose, who should have been the one vulnerable to that malady since she was a native, was still causing too many problems with the handlers. The other slaves who didn't know Rose were starting to turn on her; leaving the bathing room when she was there, or taking rations that were meant for her. Jot didn't like it when it got ugly among the slaves. She wished Rose would behave, but she could never tell her captain that.

Jot took her place on a pedestal, glad that Shard was already occupied. Anyone who was interested in a feminine woman inevitably took Shard. She was gone all the time.

Two Betas came into the viewing room. They were wearing the regulation blue shipyard flightsuit, so that meant they were overseers of lower-ranked technicians. They were plump with ashen rubbery skin that hung in folds on their face and hands. There wasn't a trace of hair on them.

The Betas went around the room together examining the slaves, turning them around to inspect every bump and crevice. They discussed each one in undertones, their fat mouths opening only slightly. Jot made an effort to not listen since clearly they wanted privacy.

When they reached Ash, s/he was apathetic, sagging where s/he stood on hir pedestal. They quickly moved on to Jot. She lowered her gaze obediently, aware of their probing eyes and their fingers exploring her body. She tried to stifle her gasps as they pinched her in delicate places, quivering under their hands. They seemed to like her response.

When they began dickering with the handlers over her price, she realized that they wanted to use her together. That cost more credit.

Jot was glad they had chosen her. It wouldn't look good on her collar if she wasn't picked very often. She had served only a few masters since she had arrived on the shipyard.

The handler recorded the transaction on her collar and gave her a tunic. Stub waved at her as she left, and she felt better. She hoped someone remembered to watch over Ash while she was gone.

The two Betas walked her through the station and she scurried after them with her eyes lowered. She got the feeling they were showing her off, because they paraded through several levels and sections where shipyard workers lived and relaxed when they were off duty. Maybe she was a bonus for them because of a job well done. Her shoulders straightened so that she presented herself well. She was glad her hair was finally getting silky, the way it was before. It hung to her waist, but it was frizzed because of the breakage from tying it back so she could look at the comm terminal. It would take a while to get it back into shape.

When they reached the quarters, Jot realized that the Betas lived together. She was their plaything for the night. They ordered her to get down and crawl around as she fetched things for them and served their meal. To decorate her, they tied brightly-colored cords around her body, knotting them strategically. They used the harness to lift her up and move her around like she was a toy, displaying her in various poses while they enjoyed their meal. Later, she realized how easily they could access her.

Jot happily did everything they wanted, glad to be doing what she was born and trained for.

Clay could see truth behind the lies the other slaves were fooling themselves with. Maybe because he couldn't speak, he could see better than them.

More than a hundred Betas had come through the viewing room, and a handful of Alphas came every day. Shard was gone a lot, sometimes returning for a few minutes only to be chosen again. But she seemed to enjoy it.

All three—Shard, Stub, and Jot—were trying to forget the *Purpose*. Clay knew they had been happier on board the ship because they could choose for themselves who they served. Even Jot had set limits for herself on the *Purpose*, and had been healthier because of it. Clay was sure Shard would rather sleep sometimes than be called to duty so constantly. And Stub preferred women though he sometimes was chosen by males. Yet there was nothing they could do about it, so they acted as if they didn't care.

Clay didn't have the luxury of self-deception. He had never liked what the higher ranks wanted him to do sexually. Maybe because he was silenced, he was often ordered to perform the most disgusting services, things nobody wanted to speak of. He had already been chosen by five Alphas and two Betas, but that was a fraction of how many Shard and Jot had done.

Clay splashed to the end of the deep pool where a

short fall of water poured over the edge from the sitting pool. He put his head under the falling water to try to scrub himself clean. Like everyone else, he was glad to be able to bathe.

But unlike them, Clay couldn't convince himself that bathing was an acceptable trade-off for freedom. He had never been so happy as he was on the *Purpose*. He had been isolated from his earliest years in the creche because he couldn't speak. For that reason people assumed he was feeble-witted and not worth bothering with. Other slaves usually ignored him. That had changed when they escaped and needed every pair of hands to run the *Purpose*.

Rose swam up to also let the water fall on her head. She was not handling slavery very well, but she was doing better than Ash. Jot and Stub were washing Ash in the warm sitting pool, talking to her without eliciting a response.

As Rose lay back in the water to rinse her hair, Clay noticed that the slashes across her stomach were healing well. When Rose had been returned to the slave barracks after her last brutal session, she had been snarling and covered in bloody sweat. She had refused to tell the others what happened after the male Alpha had selected her. Some of it was written clear on her skin, and in the rope burns on her wrists from her struggling. Only the cruelest Alphas chose rebellious slaves and enjoyed subduing them. But at least the marks had kept Rose from being selected again for the past few days. Most Alphas preferred their slaves in pristine condition.

Rose snorted and wiped the water from her face. "Nothing like a little water to make everything all right," she drawled sarcastically.

It was so close to what Clay had been thinking that he silently laughed.

She noticed and gave a wry smile. "So bathing isn't your favorite thing either?"

Clay shook his head.

"I'd take the freshers on the *Purpose* any day," Rose sighed.

Clay nodded vigorously, though he knew what Shard and Jot would say to that. Shard was a creature of her senses, while Jot was a baby without an original thought in her head. Clay sometimes wondered what it would take to make Jot think for herself.

Rose caught the direction he was looking and sighed. "Poor Ash, s/he won't talk to me anymore."

Clay nodded sympathetically. Rose and Ash had been a team ever since Rose escaped from the cargo container. It must be hard for her to deal with Ash's reaction. He had seen Solians slipping into catatonia before, but never someone he knew.

"They should all drop dead!" Rose's voice raised as he glanced around. "Usually those slave-drivers are on my back if I talk to anyone."

Clay gestured to the falling water and made the descending whistle that he used for "water."

Rose glanced at the waterfall. "You mean they can't hear us because of the splashing water?"

Clay nodded and made the same whistle, moving his fingers to imitate the falling water.

"Of course!" Rose rolled her eyes. "You can't speak and you're the one who tells me this is where I can talk." She began looking around for one of the slaves she could drag over to the waterfall.

Clay shrugged at that. He whistled again in that descending note, patting the water. He tried again, because it was second nature for him to attempt to communicate with other slaves even though no one ever listened to him.

Rose's head swiveled. "I've heard you make that sound before."

Clay raised his brows. He whistled the notes for water again then made a motion for drinking.

"That means water," she realized.

He nodded again, patting the water with his hand as he whistled the falling note.

"That whistling . . . you've been trying to talk to us, haven't you?"

Clay began to breathe faster. Only a few slaves had ever understood that he was trying to talk with his whistles. He felt a real connection with Rose as she started to grin. She understood! She wasn't looking through him because he didn't mean anything without a voice. She understood him.

Rose leaned closer. "What's your whistle for the Deltas?"

Clay made the low cautious whistle that was his sign for the handlers.

Rose imitated it, trying a few times before she caught the tone.

"Teach me more," Rose demanded. "If we learn, we can talk this way. The Deltas won't know what we're doing."

Clay nodded eagerly and began giving Rose the different whistles he had come up with to represent different words she said—go, come, give, bath, viewing room, slaves, Alphas, foodbars . . . it went on and on until the handlers came in and forced them to leave the bathing room.

Clay walked out of the bathing room with Rose and returned to the barracks, still exchanging whistles. He felt a deep sense of gratitude.

So he tried a new whistle he had recently created. It started low and went high at the end. He made a motion with his hands of something flying through the air, and he pointed up.

"Ship?" Rose asked.

Clay gestured to her and himself, then up.

"Escape?" she asked.

Clay nodded and blew the swooping whistle again.

Rose leaned closer, her voice lowered so the handlers wouldn't notice. "Clay, you can bet we're going to escape. You don't think I'm going to live like this, do you?"

Clay felt an immense relief. The others were too busy denying what they had lost. And he knew his own limitations. But if Rose was committed to getting them out of here, she would do it.

18

The *Endurance* was in orbit around the Jenuar colony, having liberated the last Ωin system from the Domain. Captain G'kaan was at the helm when a gravity burst came through the remote comms they had planted from the intrasolar slip that led to the planet.

The two remote comms relayed the alert perfectly. The signature indicated that it was a very large ship, most likely a battleship. Their time had finally run out—the Fleet had arrived.

G'kaan met M'ke's eyes. "Get the *Defiance*."

M'ke knew what that signature meant. "Hailing them."

L'pash shifted uneasily when she realized what was happening. They had been waiting for this moment. They knew the Fleet would come; it was only a matter of when.

E'ven's surly, dark gray face appeared in the imager. "*Defiance here.*"

"Get me Captain S'jen." G'kaan didn't like dealing with S'jen's young clansman.

The youngster had no education or training, so

G'kaan had successfully pushed for S'jen to delay E'ven's apprenticeship until after their liberation mission was completed. But the moment Jenuar had been freed, E'ven suddenly began appearing on the comm. Since it was the admiral's decision, G'kaan had to ignore it. It was understandable why S'jen would want to keep her clansman close to her. After all, he relied on M'ke. But now was not the time to break in an ignorant boy.

"The captain is busy. What do you want?" E'ven knew that G'kaan had interfered in his apprenticeship and he didn't try to hide his resentment.

L'pash was frowning as if about to say something.

But G'kaan glared at the young man. "Battle alert! Get S'jen on the command deck *now.*"

The young man looked flustered as he worked his terminal. The imager abruptly switched back to the starscape.

G'kaan shook his head. "Let's hope S'jen has the sense to replace him before we take on the Fleet."

E'ven winced as he accidentally closed the comm channel. He wondered if G'kaan would call back, but the channel remained dead.

S'jen's second-in-command blinked at him, then reached over and tapped the internal comm. "Battle alert!" A'gith announced.

E'ven wished he could have done that. He would have been fine if they hadn't rushed him. That G'kaan was so arrogant. It wasn't right. The *Endurance* was second to S'jen's flagship.

S'jen arrived in command looking exactly as she always did: unsmiling and focused, without a bit of downy fur mussed. E'ven watched her closely, as he always did, to try to catch the secret of her power. Even with a Fleet battleship bearing down on them, she was serene.

She took the helm from A'gith, and gestured with one hand. "You're relieved, E'ven."

He got up immediately, even though he desperately wanted to work by her side. C'vid didn't glance at him as she slid into his seat. E'ven retreated to his usual post at the auxiliary comm. At least he had graduated from the jumpseat. S'jen let him handle the auxiliary comm whenever he wanted to.

Admiral J'kart appeared, looking unhurried. "Status?"

J'kart listened to S'jen's concise summation of the situation, as E'ven read the scanners on his terminal. It was a Fleet battleship! They would finally get a real fight after cutting through the paltry patrolships.

E'ven shifted his feet to plant them firmly on the deck, just like S'jen. She looked ready to destroy the Fleet.

But he should be by her side! It was his birthright as a Huut to assist S'jen in vanquishing their enemies!

The admiral's strategy conference had dragged out as they covered all contingencies. Thanks to the remote comms, they had six hours to prepare their attack before the Fleet battleship arrived from the intrasolar gravity slip.

G'kaan was assigned to take the point. That was his preferred position, with the cool-headed S'jen waiting in the ambush spot. When G'kaan had commanded their warship squadron, they had successfully bagged three ore freighters with their tactics. Since assuming command of their battleships, the admiral had regularly tested them with intensive simulations of various Fleet-attack scenarios. By now it felt like business as usual.

"We've reached the agreed-upon coordinates," M'ke announced, checking G'kaan's navigational sensors against the star chart. "The Fleet battleship isn't in range of our scanners."

"Location of the *Defiance?*" G'kaan requested.

M'ke put the star chart on the imager. After their strategy conference with the *Defiance*, the *Endurance* had moved to the outside of the asteroid belt to take a position on the far curve. In the imager, the *Defiance* was represented by a blue icon, bracketing the assumed trajectory of the Fleet ship from the interstellar gravity slip to the Jenuar mining station.

"The *Defiance* is in position," M'ke confirmed.

As G'kaan watched, the blue icon for the *Defiance* began to blink. They were in stealth mode to await the arrival of the Fleet battleship.

Since there had been one gravity burst, there was only one battleship. That was their best-case scenario. However, the planet Jenuar was too close for comfort, hardly three hours directly behind them. There was nothing they could do about that accident of orbital patterns. But G'kaan wished the planet was safely on the other side of the sun.

"Duty stations report all systems shut down," L'pash said. "Stealth mode operational."

"Switching to passive scanners," M'ke announced.

G'kaan smiled. "Now we wait."

L'pash admired G'kaan. In spite of having to defer to S'jen on the admiral's flagship, he had handled his duties with grace and dignity. S'jen was as vile as possible to him. L'pash was glad, because it seemed to finally be the end of their relationship. And slowly, ever so slowly, G'kaan was warming to L'pash. She could feel his interest grow every day.

After many long hours on the command deck, the expectant silence was broken by M'ke. "On scanners! Battleship approaching."

He sent the coordinates to G'kaan, who triangulated the position on the star chart. The battleship appeared on the imager as the computers analyzed trajectory and speed. A dotted line sprang up that would take the battleship past the asteroid belt. "They're heading to the planet," G'kaan said flatly. "Not the mining station."

"Coming from that slip, they could have seen what we did in Impelleneer or Balanc," M'ke pointed out.

The element of surprise had been an asset while it lasted. Before they saw the trajectory, L'pash had ventured to hope that the Fleet ship was taking a roundabout approach to avoid Qin warship patrols.

"We're in a good position to drive them into the *Defiance*," G'kaan said with satisfaction.

"They won't know there's two battleships," L'pash added.

G'kaan looked at the projected trajectory. "Don't count on it."

"I've triggered their identity beacon," M'ke said. "It's the battleship *Persuasion*, captained by Shippanz Alpha. Home port is Canopus Regional Headquarters."

"As we expected," G'kaan replied calmly.

L'pash nodded, checking the ship's systems one last time. With her cousin at auxiliary ops, her post was secure. With G'kaan at the helm, she felt even better. He would get them through this. He always did.

* * *

"The *Endurance* is powering up!" C'vid cried out.

S'jen kept her eyes on the imager as the *Endurance* suddenly appeared in the starscape and accelerated out of the asteroid ring. Finally the battle was engaged! Qin would wipe out this Fleet battleship and every one that dared to follow.

The *Persuasion* turned to engage. The *Endurance* passed, exchanging laser blasts. The deep purple lasers of the Fleet ship were wider and more diffuse than the new tertiary-focus lasers the Qin scientists had developed. The sharp red lasers from the *Endurance* repeatedly struck the shields of the Fleet battleship, leaving afterimages in her eyes.

Her crew cried out at the sight. S'jen stayed absolutely focused on the imager. She felt none of the jubilation of the crew. She longed to act.

After the first hard clash, both battleships were relatively unharmed. They engaged in evasive maneuvers as they exchanged a few more rounds. As soon as the *Persuasion* took the offensive, G'kaan began the process of pushing the battle in the direction of the *Defiance*.

S'jen was waiting for the optimum moment to attack. She followed every twist and turn of the Fleet ship, knowing it would help when the time came for her attack. G'kaan was doing an adequate job of drawing out the captain's moves. She had been studying the specs since their scanners had discovered that the *Persuasion* was an H-class battleship, one of the older Fleet models, and had found there was a weak band across the aft burners. She intended to primarily target that area.

"They're nearing optimum coordinates," C'vid warned.

In spite of the fact that Qin had the advantage, two to

one, S'jen felt strange. Something was wrong. It didn't have anything to do with her ship or the crew. But usually when she had attacked the Fleet, the will of her ancestors carried her along. Now their presence was silenced. She felt alone and plagued by a nameless dread.

Then, from across the command deck, E'ven hit his chest with his closed fist three times in the sacred pledge. "In the name of our ancestors, Clan of Huut!"

The crew instantly echoed him with their own clan alliances. Their voices rang through the battleship. Even J'kard nodded in approval and gave the dedication in his serious bass voice.

"In the name of Huut!" S'jen repeated, looking straight at E'ven, her clansman, the living link to her past.

The target in the imager began to flash, indicating that it was retreating from their ambush location.

"Initiating the converter," S'jen ordered.

"There's the other one," Winstav murmured as a second Qin battleship appeared from the asteroid belt.

Captain Shippanz glanced at the strategists. "Exactly as you predicted."

"Now that the vermin are flushed out, let's finish this job," Winstav ordered.

"On your orders, Alpha strategists," Shippanz said formally.

Felenore's mouth was twisted in distaste, but Winstav was enjoying the show. The captain was engaging in maneuvers to tease out the Qin responses. Every bit of data they were gathering would be used by the Fleet to crush these upstarts. Winstav had no fear that two Qin battleships could beat the *Persuasion*, as old as the ship was. Minds won battles, not ships.

Damage reports swirled around command, both their own and their hits on the Qin battleships. Captain Shippanz was doing a good job. Winstav had trained him well in the simulation runs. He had expected the battleships to ambush them—that was the sneaky Qin way. Which in turn meant they would have to hide behind something. The asteroid belt was the obvious choice.

"Initiate sling maneuver," Winstav ordered.

The captain announced a change in course. The crew acknowledged their readiness.

Winstav pushed the grav button, locking himself down in the seat. He had used a sling maneuver a few times in the Kund war, but Felenore had been doubtful of its success. This was where the respect he had garnered from her in the past paid off. Felenore had agreed to do it his way.

The Qin were caught by surprise when the *Persuasion* abruptly shifted directions. The Fleet battleship dived toward the asteroid belt. Captain Shippanz had carefully positioned his ship for the maneuver during the exchange of laser strikes.

The imager showed the two Qin battleships following closely behind. Winstav tapped his dataport, which was keyed to the ship's scanners. The Qin ships were closer to the asteroid belt than the *Persuasion* was. That could prove to be a fatal mistake.

Winstav checked the navigational computations. If they were a thousandth of a degree off, they would hit the asteroids with disastrous consequences. The ship's data matched his own calculations exactly.

"Initiating dive," Shippanz intoned.

Winstav let a smile tug at his lips.

*   *   *

The *Persuasion* suddenly increased speed and headed toward directly toward the asteroid ring.

"Follow them!" Admiral J'kart ordered.

S'jen was fighting the helm against the intense gravity pull of the asteroids. They were already too close, and they couldn't speed up fast enough to cut off the Fleet battleship.

She rode the roughness as G'kaan's ship shot up and away from the ring, abandoning the effort. S'jen clenched her teeth, refusing to give up.

Her crew cried out that the systems were overloading, but S'jen ignored them, focused on the *Persuasion*.

Suddenly the proximity warnings flashed on the command deck and the automated safeties kicked in. She felt the helm give under her hands; then she had to struggle to regain control of the *Defiance*. The aft swerved and they almost tumbled among the asteroids.

The battleship was bigger than she was accustomed to, but it handled like a dream. S'jen pulled the *Defiance* away from the asteroid ring, deflecting off into space.

The Fleet battleship disappeared around the outer curve of the asteroids.

"Where are they?" G'kaan shouted. His crew was trying to repair systems damaged in the battle and were all talking at once.

"The *Persuasion* went around the asteroids," M'ke replied.

G'kaan returned to the asteroid ring, then followed the shifting outer edge. S'jen was also tracking the Fleet battleship.

There was nothing but large tumbling rocks on the imager. The ships picked up speed.

"Did they dodge into the asteroids?" G'kaan asked.

"Full scanner sweeps indicate nothing inside. Yet they could be hiding behind a large planetoid."

"We were only off them for a moment," G'kaan murmured. He continued taking them around the asteroids. The loose debris formed a cylindrical swath that was much larger than a planet.

Then the end was in sight. "Clearing the asteroid belt," he announced.

"Scanners at maximum range," M'ke confirmed.

There was a few tense moments, then M'ke lit up an indicator on the imager. "There they are!"

"Are you sure?" L'pash demanded, leaning forward. "How'd they get that far away?"

"They must have used the gravitational pull of the asteroid ring to give them extra momentum," M'ke declared.

G'kaan set course after them, pushing their engines to the limit of their capability. When the trajectory came up on his navigational terminal, he felt a cold wash of foreboding.

He looked up. "They're heading to the planet Jenuar."

S'jen ran numerous simulations as they neared the colony planet. The Fleet battleship would have time for only one pass around Jenuar, then they would have to maneuver to meet the attacking Qin. The crew tried to assure themselves that the attack wouldn't result in a large loss of life.

S'jen was concerned for her people, but that was the cost of war. If colonists had to die in order to give them time to destroy the Fleet battleship, then that was what the Qin would pay.

Admiral J'kart was equally stoic. He didn't engage in false assurances. He merely ordered the crew to cease their speculations and run additional simulations on the most likely scenarios.

But as the Fleet battleship neared the planet, C'vid finally spoke up. "They aren't decelerating. I don't understand it. They'll shoot right by if they don't . . ."

S'jen saw it at the same time on her navigational scanners. The *Persuasion* was curving inward toward the planet. According to the computer, the Fleet battleship would skim through the atmosphere of the planet. At their rate of speed—

She quickly ran the calculations and the result was clear. She looked up as the battleship streaked toward the thermosphere at full speed.

The first sling maneuver had been rougher than Winstav had anticipated. The battleship had vibrated as if it were going to rip apart. His teeth had rattled in his head and Felenore looked distinctly unhappy as she clung to her seat despite the grav lock.

But after that they had a straight shot at the planet. The Qin were so slow in responding that Winstav gave Captain Shippanz approach coordinates that would optimize their devastating path. Winstav believed that severe retaliation would be the key to controlling the Qin. His attack on the planet would likely make the Qin overreact and become even more reckless. Then he could exploit their weaknesses.

"Prepare for second sling maneuver," Captain Shippanz announced grimly.

Winstav locked down the grav on his chair as the ship entered the upper atmosphere. This maneuver would probably be even more turbulent. The planet had a much stronger gravity well, and the ship had to be deep in the atmosphere for the chain reaction to work. It would take expert handling to bring their battleship safely around.

"Approaching mesosphere," the comm reported.

Shippanz was concentrating on the helm, ready to guide the computer navigational systems. Winstav trusted his calculations, but this old battleship was not like the new T-class models he was accustomed to.

Winstav knew he would upgrade from the *Persuasion* soon enough. He intended to finish off these Qin savages and return to his former glory because of them. It had been fortunate for him that the Qin had acquired battleships and then did so much damage to Fleet facilities. One lost spacepost could be a fluke or the fault of a defective commander. But now the flow of fuel ore in Canopus would be cut drastically because of the four damaged mining stations. He wouldn't need to exaggerate anything in his reports—the Qin were a serious threat to the Domain.

Winstav knew he couldn't annihilate the Qin too quickly. He needed to call maximum attention to his deed. Issues crawled to the surface very slowly on the regency planets. He wanted his name on the regents' tongues while the Qin grew to significantly threatening proportions, an enemy fit only for a hero to destroy. He would save the Domain from this incursion and would be honored for it.

The battleship began to vibrate.

"Entering the upper atmosphere of the planet," Captain Shippanz called out.

The clattering and sounds of emergency alarms filled the air while Winstav tried to ride it out as nonchalantly as possible. Felenore had her hands over her face, and was hunching down in her chair. But Winstav wouldn't greet death, if that's what happened, with his eyes closed.

He leaned forward to see the imager, but it was difficult to focus because of the jolting. It sprang into high magnification as their ship skimmed through the atmosphere. The icon of their ship looked tiny against the massive bulk of the planet, but their speed would more than compensate for their size.

It was Winstav's idea. His attention to detail had paid off, as usual. During their first visit to Jenuar, he had noted the heavy concentration of sodium and calcium particles in the mesosphere. Balanc had similar conditions, and analysis revealed that it was related to the high levels of volatile metals, including cesium, found in Qin territory. Matter was unstable out here.

Their battleship caused a rapid series of explosions as it seared through the atmosphere. The imager relayed the effect as a wave of red spreading from their path across the planet. The progressive acceleration of the reaction gave rise to a shock wave, which rapidly radiated from the red in a purple stain. The increase in temperature due to compression in the shock wave was resulting in the self-ignition of the atmosphere.

"It's working," Winstav muttered gleefully.

Down below them, every living thing was being engulfed in a thermal firestorm. The chain reaction eventually petered out, leaving a wide band of utter ruin behind them.

Winstav laughed out loud as they passed the ninety-degree mark. They had turned the corner and were slinging around the planet. Two down, two to go. Their next target was Impelleneer.

*   *   *

"No!" G'kaan shouted out as the Fleet battleship tore through the atmosphere of Jenuar.

The *Endurance* was close enough to see the life signs plunge.

M'ke was stricken, while L'pash mechanically continued working to keep the ship operational despite being pushed past its performance levels.

G'kaan couldn't believe it. Even liberating the tortured and starved Qin couldn't prepare him for this mass slaughter. It was a level of brutality that he had never imagined existed, and his mind recoiled.

Their scanners revealed a lethal shock wave had ripped across the most populated part of the planet. When they had liberated Jenuar a few days ago, there were over a hundred thousand Qin on the surface.

Incredibly, the Fleet battleship appeared on the opposite side of the planet, heading off at an angle.

"I'm receiving a coded message from the *Defiance*," M'ke said.

G'kaan could see on his navigational scanners that the *Defiance* was turning after the Fleet battleship.

"Admiral J'kart ordered us to rescue and evacuate the survivors to Balanc," M'ke reported. "They will continue pursuit in the *Defiance*."

G'kaan nodded. He had always expected to split away from the *Endurance* once all four systems had been liberated. Now he could make his own decisions. He no longer had to watch S'jen mold that young man into a ferocious replica of herself. And he could rest easy knowing that Admiral J'kart was looking over S'jen's shoulder.

"Let's see what's left of Jenuar," G'kaan told his crew.

19

—≈—

Rikev Alpha arrived at the Archernar shipyard feeling confident in his theory that the Qin were responsible for the sabotages in Archernar. He had found additional evidence at the Desmintary starbase, in orbit around the popular pleasure planet. Desmintary had a crude InSec department, but the commander had pushed his staff to compile thorough files on every Delta who had been implicated in the environmental shutdown that had paralyzed the orbital starbase for several days.

Desmintary had no industry or economic value, but it was the only planet in the Achernar sector blessed with a balmy climate. Fleet personnel and merchant shipping crews on the frontier often took their leaves on Desmintary, and everyone on this edge of Canopus gravitated toward it as a vacation spot. The sabotage on the environmental systems had inconvenienced thousands of travelers.

It took some time for Rikev to work his way into the staff of Desmintary station. But once he had access to the port records, he had found the three Polinar purveyors who he believed to be Qin. He had combed through the data provided by local InSec, but couldn't locate any evidence to link them to the slave population or to the regular cycle of imported pleasure slaves. It would be serious if the Qin had managed to corrupt Deltas, so he had alerted the InSec officers about the "Polinar" and sat back to wait for more data to accrue.

InSec compiled a complete dossier on the Polinar. They had arrived at Desmintary two decnights before the sabotage. Rikev now had new images of the trio, including one that showed a height comparison. That convinced Rikev they were indeed Qin, though he hadn't mentioned his suspicion to the InSec officers. They never noticed that Polinar were typically much shorter than these three suspects. In the end, there was no evidence that Deltas had been involved in the sabotage of the environmental system. Rikev believed the Qin had instigated the malfunction themselves.

Which brought him to the Archernar shipyard. His first interview with the shipyard Alpha-commander had gone well, and he was referred directly to the commander of InSec.

"Rutith Alpha will see you now," a Beta assistant informed Rikev.

Rikev walked through the arched door behind the assistant. But he found himself in an open room rather than an office, with a few draped benches and stools. The brightest spot was the wall opposite him, showing a sweeping view of turquoise mountains rising up from a river gorge. The sky was filled with floating masses of yellow-green condensed fluorine.

"You like my view?"

Rutith Alpha appeared from behind an intricate iron screen in a vine-and-leaf pattern. Instead of a Fleet flightsuit, she wore a black embroidered bodice and gray leggings. Her head was perfectly formed and balanced.

Rikev took her in with one glance. He knew the InSec type—crafty, cautious, intuitive, and dangerous. This one apparently liked theatrics.

"I don't tend to like poisonous environments."

Rutith clasped her hands together, changing the subject. "So you're a Rikev."

Almost every Alpha he had met since coming to Canopus had managed to comment about the spectacular failure of his predecessor. It was tasteless, in his opinion, so he didn't bother to respond.

Rutith tucked her chin down, looking at him from the tops of her eyes. She gave him a coy smile. "Oh, the things I've heard about your line . . ."

Rikev handed over a datarod with the orders from Heloga Alpha. "I have been charged with collecting evidence regarding the sabotage on your shipyard production lines."

"It wasn't sabotage, merely incompetence." Rutith accepted the datarod, still smiling. "You know, people usually lie when I ask them about my views."

Rikev didn't glance at the wall. "Will you provide the evidence your investigation has gathered? Or shall I return to the regional commander empty-handed?"

Rutith pouted and stepped closer. "A request like that takes time. Would you like quarters here on the station?"

"I intend to begin at once."

"But you didn't answer my question."

Rikev met her eyes. They were flat green, as if there were nothing behind them. But she was clearly trying to manipulate him. "I will remain on board the *Rapture*."

Rutith wasn't displeased. "If that's what you wish. But

later, I insist on taking you to dinner, then showing you the shipyard."

There was a note in her voice that he couldn't ignore. Rutith was commander of InSec on this station and she had seniority over him. He needed for her to cooperate so he could get supporting evidence about the Qin. Yet he would have to do so without arousing her suspicions. This Alpha could very well try to win points for herself with Heloga by claiming credit for his theory.

"Very well," Rikev agreed, letting his eyes linger on hers.

That tiny indication of interest caused her to lift her head. Her mouth opened slightly.

Before she could say anything, Rikev gestured to the door. "Shall we begin?" he asked.

"Why not?" Rutith agreed, walking with him toward the arched doorway.

Rikev accepted Rutith's perks when she offered them. Rutith Alpha impressed him as being very sharp, and she was aware of everything he was doing at all times. It was an impressive feat, but then again she had been in command of InSec on the busy shipyard for several decades, so she knew her job well.

Rikev agreed with Rutith that the sabotage had been caused by the incompetent Baast slaves rather than the Deltas on the production lines. However, Rikev believed the Baast had done it deliberately, though he didn't tell Rutith that.

Rikev concealed from Rutith exactly which information he was most interested in. When he did find a log of the Polinar trio arriving on the Archernar shipyard, he didn't pause. He simply continued correlating. Later he issued a request for images of hundreds of aliens who had flowed through the Archernar shipyard during the last quarter to avoid drawing Rutith's attention to the Polinar.

To help distract Rutith from his investigation, Rikev continued sparring with her during their evening meals. Yet he didn't let his guard down for a moment. She seemed fascinated to find an Alpha who could parry her every thrust.

One day she arrived unannounced in the office he had appropriated for his use. She carefully closed the door behind her, as if the room weren't scanned for every whisper.

"Here's something for you," Rutith said, slipping a credit chit across the desk.

Rikev Alpha looked down. It was set very high. "What is this?"

"A gift from the shipyard." Rutith dipped her head with a sly smile. "The slave barracks are near the top level, in section G-7."

Then she was gone. Rikev looked at the credit chit, carefully considering the consequences. Apparently Rutith knew that his lust would come tonight. She was giving him the use of a pleasure slave.

Rikev was particular about his slaves. He would rather tough it through a lust than make do with a substandard product. Canopus Regional Headquarters was blessed to have an abundance of raw slaves, but that was not his style. He liked breeding and superior training which one could only get in the inner regions of the Domain. Since he had left Canopus Regional Headquarters, he had found few quality slaves on the frontier.

He decided to accept Rutith's offer in his own way. If there was nothing that met his standards, he would reject them all. That would be a subtle affront to Rutith for her presumption.

If he found a suitable slave, so much the better. He had gathered the information he needed at the shipyard. Rikev now had logs that documented the Polinar in the corridors near the Baast slave barracks. The Baast slaves were used for the more dangerous jobs in new-ship production, such as administering the coat of magnetic fluid on the new hulls to aid in structural integrity. They had access to the sabotaged production lines.

Rutith Alpha didn't suspect a thing. She still believed it was the result of incompetence. Rikev knew his investigation into the production line sabotage on the shipyard would be completed in a few more days. Then he had one more outpost in Archernar to visit, in the Picast system, before returning to Heloga Alpha. He was certain he would find images of the fake Polinar in Picast that would prove the string of sabotages in Archernar had been instigated by Qin.

Heloga Alpha would be very pleased with his work.

Rikev Alpha stepped into the viewing room of the slave barracks. He slowly surveyed the slaves on their round platforms. Some preened and posed, while others gave him sidelong looks and smiles. Rikev wasn't interested in any of them.

"Exotics?" Rikev asked the Swark handlers.

"Yes, very good exotics," the senior handler assured him. "Two, we have available now."

The long-nosed handler scuttled over to gesture to a curvaceous female with silvery white hair. But she met his eyes before glancing down. That was too bold for Rikev's taste. "No."

"The other one, there," the handler suggested. He ran over to prod the slightly hunched slave. The slave hardly reacted.

Rikev felt the first stirrings of lust. "What's wrong with it? Is it sick?"

"No, no, not sick. Lazy!" The handler prodded the slave harder. It flinched and tried to hunch into itself deeper.

The handler gestured to the genitals. "It's a herme," the Swark said proudly. "Both sexes!"

Rikev reached out to feel for himself. A herme . . . he had never tried one. Imagine finding a prime slave on the edge of the frontier. It must be worth a fortune. But it looked as if it was sliding into catatonia—maybe it was a native Solian.

Rikev made up his mind. "Deliver it to the *Rapture* immediately."

Ash went wherever s/he was led. The handlers had rougher hands than hir fellow slaves, but s/he hardly noticed that anymore.

But the sound of the space station filtered through. S/he was walking down a corridor with a handler. His hand was around hir arm.

Was s/he going to the incinerator? Wasn't that where Rikev Alpha was sending hir before the mad dream of freedom began? Ash didn't mind if s/he was going to die. It was a long time coming, so s/he couldn't complain. Then the pain would stop.

Vaguely s/he realized the handler was taking hir onto a ship. Visions of decompression vied with the incinerator in hir mind. It was so long since any thought had penetrated that s/he couldn't stop thinking of hir own death.

S/he was marched down a short corridor and into a cabin. Finally it was quiet and s/he was standing alone.

"Kneel," a male voice ordered.

S/he instantly responded, kneeling down and sitting back on hir heels. It was a habit drilled into hir by Rikev Alpha . . .

Hands touched hir shoulders and the panels of hir tunic fell down to hir hips.

Suddenly s/he realized what was happening. S/he could barely think, having shut down to keep from seeing anything outside of hirself.

"A perfect blend of male and female," the voice said.

His voice sounded terribly familiar, evoking long conditioned responses in hir. Ash felt the fog shifting in front of hir eyes. S/he looked up, trying to focus as hir instinct cried out *danger*.

It was Rikev Alpha!

"So you *are* aware," Rikev said, amusement in his voice. "This won't be as challenging as I had hoped."

Ash lurched back to get away.

But Rikev easily caught hir shoulder. S/he was so weak from hir long inactivity, s/he could hardly hold hirself up at his command.

His hands went to his cartridge belt, slowly unhooking each cartridge. The belt came off and he doubled it into a wide strap. Ash watched with dull, helpless eyes as Rikev stepped closer to hir.

"You're trembling," Rikev told hir. "And I haven't begun yet."

* * *

Kwort saw Ash being taken through the shipyard by a Delta handler. S/he looked haggard and awful, as if s/he were walking in a trance.

Kwort had seen Jot a few days after he arrived as she was paraded through the Delta section by two of the overseers on the production line. Jot preened in her near-naked state, enjoying the attention of all the workers and the lust in their eyes. But Ash . . . Kwort had talked to hir about being a slave, and it wasn't pretty. Ash must be in serious trouble. He wished he could help hir as s/he had helped him. If it weren't for Ash, he wouldn't have gotten out of Qin alive.

It made him feel even more lucky to have his new little friend Taffle teaching him the ways of the shipyard. It had turned out to be impossible to get a job on new-ship construction because of the delays last quarter. Without Taffle's help, Kwort would have been kicked off the Archernar shipyard as an indigent.

But Taffle had introduced him to one of the overseers of maintenance and repair work for the shipyard. Kwort didn't realize until after he got his first job that Taffle wanted her operatives to have access to goods and information left behind on the older ships while the repair crews worked on the systems. So far Kwort had worked on several ships, doing routine maintenance.

Taffle knew everything about the shipyard. As far as Kwort could tell, her smuggling network was far-flung and very effective. He saw her talking to everyone on the shipyard, so there was no telling who was working for her and who was buying from her.

Kwort knew he would see Taffle as he returned to his berth from his current job, rebuilding the scanner system on a Fleet patrolship. Taffle had gotten him into a cheap residence, so now he had a berth he could stand up in. The bunk was folded to the wall when not in use, but at least he had private facilities.

Taffle was waiting for him inside the berth. She was seated on the bunk with her short, fat legs swinging far above the floor. He had never given her the door code, but he had already discovered that Taffle went anywhere she wanted.

"You got it for me?" she demanded, as soon as the door was closed.

"Yep, three more left to go." Kwort leaned over and pulled up the leg of his flightsuit. He had taped a bottle of Sinubian vitae to his shin.

Taffle watched him pull off the tape. "Remember, Cwart, I don't have contracts with the others on your repair team."

"I'm the only one who goes into the small access tubes," Kwort assured her. "The other two Delts are bigger than me."

He got the bottle loose and handed it over. Taffle gave him a credit chit. Kwort knew he was taking a huge risk for little credit, but Taffle was responsible for him working and she was introducing him to other people on the shipyard. The more he became known as "Cwart the freelance bot tech" the safer he would be.

Taffle checked the seal to see if it was broken. "These babies are in high demand right now. Make sure you bring me another one tomorrow."

"I won't be able to take another case," Kwort warned. "The stack wasn't that high, and they'll know when they take inventory that it's missing."

Taffle shrugged as she tucked the bottle into a bag that was nearly as big as herself. "They'll blame the crew. They always do. No one thinks the safety hatches can be opened without setting off the alarms."

Kwort had to agree to that. Every tube had safety hatches for easy access in case of emergency, and Kwort had learned in the Fleet that it was impossible for them to be opened without alerting the ship's systems and notifying the logs. But Taffle had given him a thin piece of metal that somehow interrupted the beam that latched the safety hatches closed. It looked exactly like a bottle opener, so it wouldn't raise any suspicions with enforcers if it was discovered. Using the hatch key, he had stolen a case of Sinubian vitae from the ship's stores and hid the bottles in a tube to await slow and unobtrusive transport back to Taffle.

"One case will be enough for this job," Taffle assured him, slipping the bottle into her copious bag.

Kwort felt awkward, but he couldn't forget about Ash. Taffle would know the answer to the question on his mind. "What if someone wanted to talk to a Solian slave? How would you go about it?"

She shrugged. "Get enough credit, Cwart, and you can do whatever you want with one."

"How much credit would it cost?" he asked.

"It depends. A lot more than you've got, I can say that."

"Oh." Kwort felt bad about Ash. "I only want to talk to hir. I saw hir passing through the station today, and s/he didn't look good."

Taffle looked mildly interested. "Never heard that one before. You only want to *talk* to a pleasure slave."

Kwort knew he shouldn't have asked. He wasn't in any position to indulge his curiosity. "Well, it's really no big deal."

Taffle nodded with the air of a competent child. "You work well, Kwort. If you want to get into higher-stakes games, let me know. You could buy any Solian you want."

He smiled noncommittally. He couldn't afford to take that risk. Stealing a bottle of Sinubian vitae was one thing, but he had heard rumors that Taffle could get anything for anyone, including death hits.

But after Taffle was gone with a wave of her chubby hand, Kwort couldn't stop thinking about Ash. In Qin, he had been alone and despised. If he had stayed, someone would have rounded up a lynch mob against him. He was Fleet, and that meant he was the enemy. So when Ash asked him to help them on the *Purpose*, it was his only hope to survive. If that wasn't enough, Ash had gone out of hir way to be friends with him, despite the fact that s/he had probably suffered more than anyone in the hands of the Alpha masters and the Delta handlers.

Now that Kwort wasn't Fleet anymore, his status had sunk to the lowest of the low. Some food kiosks refused to serve him, and there were levels on the shipyard where he wasn't allowed to go. He was already having trouble with the transient Fleet Deltas who put it to the station for ship repairs. The crews were always looking to let off steam. So he usually stuck close to the section for the maintenance and production Deltas, where they had strength in numbers. Apparently Kitarin and Murroom weren't that unusual in the Fleet.

Kwort had a feeling that if he hadn't been picked up by Taffle, he could have gotten into deep trouble at the shipyard. With such tight security in place, getting a job was difficult at best. But his gratitude didn't extend to doing serious work for Taffle. He would have to reach Ash another way.

Kwort pulled the hatch key out of his boot. The station had access tubes exactly like ships. But if he suddenly appeared inside the slave barracks, he was going to have a lot of explaining to do.

He put the hatch key back in the lining of his boot and washed up to go out to eat.

The map Kwort accessed at one of the tourist booths showed that there were several pleasure-slave barracks on the station. One was for Alphas and Betas, and the others were for Gammas and Deltas. Kwort figured that Ash would be at the upper-rank barracks, since s/he was unique.

The map didn't show access tubes, of course, but his trained eye would be able to spot the hatches. The problem was getting in without attracting attention from people in the corridors. He was wearing his regulation blue flightsuit with his bot baton in the cartridge belt loop, so he could pose as a station tech. But other station techs would realize he was an impostor if he was seen in the tubes.

As Kwort ate his meal, he wandered up the levels. He thought he was being unobtrusive, but as he sauntered down the corridor toward the entrance to the slave barracks—he saw Taffle.

Taffle walked right up to him. "You're about as subtle as a nova, Cwart."

"Huh?" he asked.

Taffle grabbed his arm and kept him walking. Under her breath, she asked, "What's the first rule I gave you with the key?"

Kwort stiffened. "Don't use the key on the station."

"Right . . . 'cause I'll kill you if you try." Kwort gulped, as she asked, "You know why?"

He shook his head.

"Because Rutith Alpha has this station logged down to the molecule. They'll see you go in and you're in the brig. Before you know it, you're incriminating *me*."

Kwort wondered if he should deny it, but Taffle laughed at him. "Don't go stupid on me now, Cwart," she told him. "You were such a promising find."

They headed down a level and Taffle ducked into an entertainment arcade with him. "I've got an appointment, so you don't have much time. Tell me why I shouldn't take back that key and boot you off the pay-roll."

"I won't use it," Kwort promised. "Believe me, I don't want to get caught by enforcers."

She cocked her head, her pixie face too lovable to be that ruthless. "I hear a 'but' coming."

Kwort realized she was right. "I can't explain it. I'm worried about hir. I need to find out if s/he's okay."

"And if she's not?" Taffle demanded. "You won't be able to do anything about it."

Kwort hesitated. "Maybe it would help if s/he knew how much I care about hir. Sometimes that's the most important thing, having someone care enough to try, even if they can't help."

"I see you have this all figured out." Taffle appraised him for a few moments, much to his discomfort. "You're too good to lose, so I won't take back the key. But you're too smart, so I know you won't give up."

Kwort didn't know what to say.

Taffle sighed. "I'll have to help you. But you're going to pay for it."

*   *   *

Kwort promised to wait until Taffle got him a real map of the tubes around the barracks, marked where he could safely access them. In return, he agreed to steal some information out of the patrolship's database while he was running the diagnostic bots on the passive neutrino imaging scanner. Even though he risked being caught, he realized he had to do it to get to Ash. He couldn't explain it to Taffle or anyone—maybe Horc would have understood. Horc had reached out to him in the same way Ash had done.

Taffle wouldn't let him keep the map, so he memorized the three available hatches and the best route inside. First he went to the level above the barracks, hoping to survey the rooms from the ceiling hatches. The floor hatches would be the best way to talk to Ash, but he needed a wide view first so he could see what he was getting into.

As soon as Taffle left, Kwort casually strolled down the corridor until he reached the door that had been marked on the map. He turned as if going inside. Within the recessed doorway, he was off the logs according to Taffle's map.

Kwort quickly bent down and used the key to open the hatch in the floor. He slipped in with practiced ease and lowered the hatch over his head. When it clicked shut, the sounds echoing down the corridor were cut off.

He thumbed on his bot baton, and a pool of light sprang up around him. It swung from his belt, casting shadows around the tube.

It was a quick crawl to the slave barracks. He could tell where the room started because of the wider cross-tube over the corridor. He looked carefully to be sure there weren't any other bot techs in the area.

The first hatch he reached, he pulled out the key and slid it into the latch.

The hatch popped open, but Kwort caught it before it could swing down. He widened the crack and peered through.

He couldn't see anything. There was something in the way that looked like leaves. And he could hear water. He panicked, wondering if he was in the right place. Maybe he went in the wrong direction.

But no, he went over the map in his mind and this should to be the barracks. He carefully closed the hatch and crawled on to the next one.

The key slid in quietly, doing its work. Kwort held on to the edge of the hatch, supporting it as he looked through. This time there was a long row of bunks below with people lying on them.

He recognized Rose right away. And Stub next to her with his bright orange-red hair.

Kwort closed the hatch, afraid that the other slaves would see him. He was near the back of a room that had a door at the front. He needed to go down a level and open the hatch directly below his current position.

20

Rose was boiling mad when Ash was dragged back from hir session with the golden Alpha. When he took Ash, Rose had to be restrained by Stub and Clay from fighting the handlers. Rose's fears were borne out when Ash was returned with hir skin marred by hundreds of welts and bruises. Rose had suffered her own hell at the hands of a few Betas and Alphas who had chosen her despite her defiant attitude, and she still had the scars to prove it. But what Ash had gone through was horrible. Ash kept stuttering "Rikev" as if trapped in a vivid flashback of hir dead master.

Eventually Ash fell asleep, tended by Shard and Jot. Rose feared for hir sanity. She was afraid for them all. According to Stub, in a few days they would be exchanged with fresh slaves for the barracks. They would be locked in the cubes and scattered throughout the region.

Rose was sitting on the floor leaning against the end of her bed, her head in her hands. She was wondering what she could possibly do to escape.

Suddenly the floor seemed to move. Under the bunk next to her, one square tile slowly lifted up.

The top of a bald head and eyes peered through. When the eyes saw Rose, the tile abruptly dropped back down.

Rose scooted across to the next bunk to get closer. When the tile lifted again, her head bent low. She recognized those concentric ridges and that bulbous nose. She couldn't see the rest of his face, but a few fingers waved and his eyes crinkled in recognition.

"Kwort!" she murmured through tight lips. "How'd you get in here?"

"I have a key," he whispered. "Can anyone else see the hatch?"

"No." Rose sat against the bed where she could see him, so it wouldn't look suspicious to the handlers. "Don't lift it too high."

Kwort's eyes shifted. "How's Ash? I saw hir yesterday and s/he didn't look good."

"S/he's in bad shape. That torturer almost killed hir."

His brows drew together.

"Can you get us out through there?" Rose demanded.

"No!" Kwort almost closed the hatch. "You'd have to leave through the corridor, and they'll see you before you reach the first corner. InSec has this station logged from end to end."

Rose figured Kwort was too afraid to try. But she couldn't scare him away. This was her first break since raiders had stolen the *Purpose*. "We have to get out. They'll be shipping us off soon."

"How can you get out?" Kwort asked.

"I'll think of something," Rose assured him. "Can you come back this time tomorrow?"

Kwort drew down so only his eyes showed. "It's dangerous."

"Do it for Ash." Rose remembered how Ash had been nice to him on the *Purpose*. "S/he needs to get out of here or s/he'll die."

"I can't risk it," Kwort reminded her. "If they find out about me, I'm a goner."

"You can't stay here on the shipyard," Rose told him. "How long do you think you can go without getting into trouble? As soon as you sneeze wrong, the enforcers will scan you and realize who you are."

Now Kwort looked alarmed. "I'm doing fine!"

"Your luck always runs out," Rose hissed. "You know you can't stay."

The hatch lowered until only the top of his head showed.

"Come back tomorrow," Rose whispered urgently. "I'll wake Ash so you can talk to hir."

The hatch closed with a quiet click.

Rose scooted over and tried to pry it open. But once it was closed, it fit as tightly as the rest of the flooring tiles. She couldn't get her fingernails into the crack. But somehow Kwort had managed to get it open, so it could be done.

She thoughtfully stood up and surveyed the room. Nobody had noticed what had happened. Clay was on a bunk next to the door, keeping an eye out for the handlers. He gave a low "all clear" whistle. She nodded and whistled back.

That's when Rose realized the key to beating the Domain. If she could get the others to help, then she would succeed.

Rose reminded herself not to forget that important point the next time she had to escape.

*   *   *

While Ash slept, Rose talked to the others about breaking out. Shard, Jot, and Stub refused to listen. Rose reminded them of the *Purpose*, but they thought it was impossible. It boggled her mind. It was as though they were brainwashed into being slaves.

Clay was another story. He understood immediately. Rose found herself telling the silent man about Kwort's appearance. His black eyes were serious. He made a swooping motion with his hand a few times until Rose realized he was saying they needed a ship.

"You're way ahead of me." Rose pretended to wash her hair in the waterfall. "I'm still trying to figure out how to break out of here."

Clay winced and made the whistle that stood for the watching eyes that recorded the logs.

"There has to be a way," Rose insisted.

Clay whistled, trying to communicate something. But she couldn't understand him. It was something to do with the slaves and the handlers. Frustrated, they both finally had to give up when the handler came into the baths.

She needed Ash.

Rose was by Ash's side when s/he finally woke up. S/he opened hir eyes but nothing was there. Hir face was a blank.

Rose tried to talk to hir, but Ash didn't react. It was as if s/he couldn't hear anything. Rose tried to tell hir that Kwort had come and they would be escaping soon. She called hir name, and said her own. "It's Rose, Ash. I'm here, listen to me."

But Ash didn't respond. Eventually Shard brought some water and food, and Jot helped feed Ash. S/he chewed if a small bite was put in hir mouth. Then they took hir into the bathing room to wash hir terrible wounds.

Rose watched the entire time, trying to see a spark of awareness in Ash's eyes. But s/he was gone. This wasn't the Ash she knew. This was an empty shell that didn't even look like Ash. This poor creature was near death.

At the end of the bath, Rose finally stepped forward. She took Ash's arm from Jot and murmured sternly, "Don't interfere."

Shard and Stub were drying off on the other side of the room, smoothing sweet-smelling cream on each other. They looked like they wanted to have sex, but the handlers would be on them in an instant if they tried. A few of the other slaves were also taking the opportunity while the handlers were both in the viewing room to fondle each other.

Rose seized the moment. She dragged Ash over the edge into the deep water beneath the waterfall. Ash was unresisting, floating in the water.

Rose pushed Ash's head under the waterfall.

Ash gasped and spat out water, shaking hir head to try to breathe. Rose pulled hir back out and hissed, "Snap out of it, Ash!"

Ash was coughing, hir head lolling to one side.

Rose knew she had only an instant. She pushed hir back under the waterfall. "You're killing yourself for nothing, you idiot! I'm trying to get us out of here!"

Ash started to fight to get air, hir survival reflex kicking in. Rose hauled hir back out, spitting and choking as Jot appeared at her shoulder.

"Rose, stop," the girl cried.

Rose kept her voice low. "Get away!"

Jot leaped back as if she had been shocked by her collar. She hung on the side of the pool, anxiously looking toward the other slaves, but they were busy rubbing each other.

Rose shook Ash hard, but hir head didn't roll this time. "Snap out of it, Ash! I need your help. Or you'll kill me along with yourself."

Ash was suddenly looking back. S/he seemed confused.

"Ash?" Rose asked. "It's Rose. Can you hear me?"

Ash hesitantly nodded.

"Good," Rose told her. "I'm going to break us out of here. I already talked to Kwort. You can help me. You did it last time."

Ash's expression was oddly blank, but hir eyes were intent on Rose. Almost desperate. S/he slowly nodded again.

Rose put her arm around Ash to help hir to the steps. "Just stay with me, Ash. I'll take care of everything."

Ash felt as if s/he were sleepwalking, but somehow s/he was awake. S/he was weak and could hardly hold hirself up. But Rose was there, helping hir.

Everything else was gone behind a fuzzy blank wall in hir mind.

The other slaves were familiar, and s/he had vague harmless images of a life lived in metal rooms like this one, but no details. S/he felt safe with the wall in hir mind. S/he also felt safe with Rose. Rose would take care of hir; she always did.

When the handlers weren't around, Rose spoke to hir. She talked fast and moved quick, so it was difficult to understand. Someone named Kwort had magically appeared through the floor. Apparently the Delta was supposed to return any moment to speak to Ash.

Ash didn't know who Kwort was, but that didn't matter.

Eventually, Rose took hir to a bunk and lay down on the one next to it. "Clay had an idea," Rose murmured, "but I can't understand him. Something about all the slaves and the handlers."

"How did we get here?" Ash asked, unsure of anything.

"We walked here from the induction center," Rose said thoughtfully. "Maybe Clay meant we should escape when they take us back. We're supposed to be exchanged soon for new merchandise." Rose glanced admiringly at hir. "That's why I need you, Ash, to help me figure these things out."

Ash glanced around the room. There was a word for where s/he was, but s/he couldn't remember it. "What is this place called?"

"Archernar shipyard," Rose said. "Don't you remember?"

Ash shook hir head. The word was a meaningless jumble of sounds. "This room?"

"It's the slave barracks."

"Yes." S/he felt relief. Those words were familiar. "Slave barracks."

"Are you all right?" Rose asked in concern.

"Yes," Ash said simply. S/he felt nothing, no pain, no worry.

A young woman walked by and smiled at Ash. She had a sweet face and long black hair.

"I know her," Ash said.

Rose's gaze was fixed on hir. "That's Jot."

"Yes, Jot." Ash remembered the girl crying, maybe because Rose's eyes seemed filled with tears.

"Don't worry," Rose told hir. "I'll get us out of here."

Ash smiled slightly. "I know."

It was heartbreaking for Rose to see Ash as tender as a young child, looking around as if everything was new to hir. But s/he seemed more at peace than Rose had ever seen hir. In this case, amnesia seemed almost like a blessing.

Ash seemed to vaguely recognize the Solians who had been on the *Purpose*, though s/he couldn't remember their names. All of the slaves were amazed that Rose had managed to bring Ash back from the brink of catatonia.

When Kwort finally reappeared, Rose let Ash speak to him. Rose kept an eye on the door where Clay was on watch. When Ash crawled back to hir bunk, Rose slipped down and took hir place.

"You see what they did to Ash?" she demanded.

"S/he doesn't remember anything?" Kwort was appalled.

"No. And if s/he gets tortured by another Alpha, it'll kill hir." Rose stared into his eyes. "You have to help us escape."

"There's no way you can get through the corridors without being spotted," Kwort protested. "And these maintenance tubes don't link up, I checked. So you can't come through here."

"We've got that part solved. We'll make our move when the handlers take us back to the slave cubes." Rose grinned. "All we need is a ship."

"You need a lot more than that," Kwort protested. "One order and you'll all be on the floor."

Rose ran her thumb under the collar. "These don't work on my crew."

Kwort's forehead ridges creased. "You'll be outnumbered. The cargo docks are busy! And there's too many enforcers."

"Then we need weapons," Rose said.

"What?"

"You're the one who blew up a battleship with a practical joke," she reminded him.

"Don't say that!" Kwort glanced from side to side. "Don't ever say that. Someone could be listening."

"If anyone's listening, you're in deep trouble anyway."

Kwort looked trapped.

"Weapons waiting in the cargo terminal and a ship." Rose made her tone wheedling. "That's not too much to ask."

"Not too much!" Kwort snorted.

"You'll save your own life, too."

Kwort sighed. "I think I know a patrolship you can take."

Rose talked to Ash near the waterfall. "Kwort's doing maintenance on a patrolship that's two docking arms away from the slave cubes. All we have to do is get there."

Ash nodded slowly. "How?"

"I told him we need weapons." Rose wasn't sure how much of this was reaching Ash. "I need your help. To pull this off, we'll need more than six people to run a patrolship. We'll have to convince the other slaves to come with us."

Ash looked around. Two of the other slaves were sitting on the edge of the bath watching them. Rose had gained a new respect from them after reviving Ash, but they still weren't listening to her.

"They think I'm nuts, frankly," Rose admitted. "I don't know how I can convince them to help us. Even Shard and Jot refuse to help."

Ash seemed to have difficulty understanding.

"We broke out of the cargo container on the *Purpose*," Rose reminded hir. "The odds aren't any worse now. Why won't they try?"

Ash looked at Rose expectantly. "Why?"

"I don't know!" Rose exclaimed. "What made you agree last time?"

"I trust you."

"You didn't even know me," Rose protested.

Ash considered it for a long time. Rose was almost ready to give up, thinking that Ash was too far gone to help her.

Then Ash said, "You're from Earth."

Rose met hir eyes. "Earth?"

"Yes."

"That's right!" Rose exclaimed. "I said I was going back to Earth! But Gandre Li convinced us to go to Qin instead." She snorted. "Look how good that turned out."

Ash furrowed hir brow, but Rose hastily assured hir, "It doesn't matter. Now I understand."

"Understand?" Ash asked.

"Yes, we're going back to Earth."

21

Several days after the aerial attack, Chad and the Qin survivors were picked up and taken into orbit to dock with an old interstellar transport. It had been used by the Fleet to convey fresh food and goods produced by the Qin slaves to the mining station. Chad didn't care about the crude accommodations; he was grateful to get off that hellhole of a planet.

He had known he was making a mistake when he left the *Purpose*, but he had been too proud and stubborn to admit it. That was why he had rushed through his good-byes with the crew, hardly looking anyone in the eye. It was ironic and humiliating to remember his last words: "You'll all die if you go back!" Because his decision to stay had killed Newt. That was all Chad could think about, sitting among the pitiful remains of the Qin.

Then slowly he realized that someone was trying to address them from the main doors of the cargo bay. Other Qin realized as well, just as the ship's comm switched on, amplifying his voice.

"—take care of you. Those of you who have chosen to be evacuated from Balanc will be transported to the Endunara colony for the duration of our battle with the Domain. Balanc and the other three planets we've liberated are no longer safe for Qin."

Chad wondered who in their right mind would volunteer to stay on this decimated planet. Fleet battleships were sure to come back. The Domain didn't ever roll over and give up on anything. He should have known that.

The Qin captain continued giving instructions on how to receive medical attention and nourishment. Chad thought there was something familiar about the voice. He got up and weaved his way through the Qin who were lying and sitting on the floor, filling every bit of space in the bay.

"We will never stop fighting!" the Qin captain finished. "We will protect Qin territory. You will return to your homes to rebuild your clans."

Some of the Qin looked vaguely encouraged by that, but most had been through too much to care about words.

Chad reached the front of the room and saw it was G'kaan.

"Captain!" Chad cried out, waving his hand. There were other Qin around him, and they tried to ward him off. "Captain G'kaan! Have you seen Rose?"

That caught his attention. The black Qin pushed through his people and with three steps was in front of Chad. "You were with Rose? Where's the *Purpose?*"

"Gone," Chad replied bitterly. "When you wouldn't work with us, Rose took them into the Domain. They went to salvage from Spacepost T-3."

G'kaan's brow furrowed, and for a moment he looked very different from the other dispassionate Qin. "That was foolish!"

"They had no other choice," Chad reminded him. "I stayed here, and look what happened! Newt is dead—"

He broke off, unable to do anything more than glare at G'kaan. The other Qin were trying to draw their captain away from him. A female Qin with a white blaze down her nose said urgently, "we must return to the battleship, Captain."

"Take me with you," Chad demanded.

The female Qin retorted, "Solians don't belong on Qin ships."

G'kaan frowned at her vehemence.

Chad ignored her, looking at G'kaan. "You have to let me help. You said you needed Solians to infiltrate the Domain. I can do it for you."

"You understand the risk of returning to the Domain?" G'kaan asked. "You could be enslaved or killed."

Chad met his eyes, refusing to withdraw. Rose was right. They couldn't turn their backs on the Domain. It was too big, too powerful. They had to find a way to beat them at their own game. "I'm not going to roll over and die."

G'kaan gestured for Chad to follow. "Then you're with me."

Chad tightened his fist, glad that he would get a chance to avenge Newt. He would make the Domain pay for what they had done to him and those he loved.

From Balanc, G'kaan took his battleship to the border of Qin territory to get a report from the warships on patrol. They would know if the Fleet battleship had left Qin.

He hoped the *Persuasion* hadn't attacked Impelleneer, but that was the direction they were heading after their sling maneuver around Jenuar. However, since the

Defiance would remain on their tail, G'kaan could afford to strategize. G'kaan doubted the battleship would penetrate deeper into Qin territory, since Fleet patrolships hadn't been allowed to gather intelligence within Qin. They wouldn't know if there were more Qin battleships waiting inside. But the Fleet battleship might go from Impelleneer to Atalade.

Only another few decnights and Qin would have two new battleships ready for flight testing. That would give them more freedom, because the new battleships could remain inside Qin for homeland defense.

G'kaan performed the pre-slip maneuvers and braced himself as the *Endurance* slid through the next gravity slip. The inevitable disorientation wasn't enough to shake him from his main concern: Were there any Fleet ships in this perimeter pocket?

M'ke quickly reported, "Scanners indicate nothing within long range."

G'kaan checked with his navigational scanners as well. He hadn't met up with a warship yet to get a report. He set course for the inner slip that would take him through the perimeter pockets, intending to strip the beacon on the way through. The warships had left reports of exactly when the Fleet battleship had penetrated Qin, but there were no other sightings.

G'kaan felt confident. As they circled the border, they were also heading toward Impelleneer and Atalade.

"Setting course," he told the others. The star chart on the imager shifted to show their targeted slip.

They had traveled a few standard hours when a large gravity burst appeared on the scanners.

"A ship!" M'ke announced. "By the size, it must a battleship."

"Which slip did it come through?"

M'ke worked over his terminal. "From the degradation of the signature, it appears to have come from Qin."

G'kaan altered course to intercept the battleship, assuming it was heading for the slip to the Domain. They would intercept in approximately ten hours. G'kaan grinned. "We may get another crack at that Fleet ship sooner rather than later."

The emergency lights were glowing near the ceiling. When Chad heard the battle alert, he couldn't resist going to the command deck. He stood just outside the doorway. The captain might have brought him on board, but Chad definitely wasn't one of the crew. The Creb wouldn't let him set foot inside engineering, and nobody seemed happy to see him eating in the galley.

The only good part about being on board the *Endurance* was his training with G'kaan. They worked out in the bay where the combat teams practiced, and G'kaan taught Chad skills he could use during his covert missions—from climbing a slick wall to knocking out a Poid or a Swark with his bare hands. G'kaan also gave Chad information about the Domain. Chat had spent much of the decnight since he came on board in his own berth looking at the viewer.

Chad wasn't standing there long before L'pash saw him. She turned to the captain. "That Solian is lurking around."

G'kaan turned his head to look at Chad. "Don't block the door." Chad was ready to protest when the captain added, "You can sit in the jumpseat."

Surprised, Chad stepped onto the enormous command deck. The fold-down seat G'kaan indicated was to one side.

L'pash snapped, "Don't touch anything!"

Chad sat down, turning so he could see the towering imager. He knew from commanding the *Purpose* that the red indicator represented the *Endurance*. On the opposite side of the imager was another ship. Its icon indicated that it was an unidentified battleship.

Chad had been hoping a few Fleet ships would get what they deserved at the hands of the Qin. It wouldn't be enough to pay them back for Newt's death, but it would be a start. He wasn't afraid. Everything he had seen about the Qin showed that they could beat the Fleet—if they arrived in time.

Now it looked like the *Endurance* was aimed directly at a Fleet battleship. Maybe it was the one that had killed Newt.

In spite of the imminent danger, L'pash kept glancing at Chad as if his presence irritated her. She wasn't alone. The other Qin on the command deck gave him narrow looks as well. It reminded Chad all too unpleasantly of living on Balanc. He shouldn't have left the *Purpose*. That was where he belonged.

"Captain, according to the energy-output readings," M'ke exclaimed, "it's the *Defiance!*"

G'kaan analyzed the distortion field created by the converter. "You're right, that ship is Qin. It must be the *Defiance*."

"Then where's the Fleet battleship?" L'pash asked.

Chad thought that was a good question. "Did you lose it?"

L'pash glared at him. "Stay out of this!"

G'kaan raised his hand. "Stop."

Chad wasn't sure if G'kaan was irritated at him or at L'pash. According to the talk he'd overheard, L'pash was encouraging a closer relationship with her captain. Chad hadn't seen any evidence of that, but the Qin were very cagey about their personal lives. It was nothing like the *Purpose* where Solians were coupling in every off-duty area. But apparently Qin courtship was conducted through glances and subtle words. Chad had heard enough to know that the legendary Qin lust was approaching. He wondered if he would still be here to see it happen. He couldn't imagine the stodgy Qin loosening up enough to have a three day orgy.

The captain turned to M'ke. "Send them an encoded message with our coordinates."

"Aye, Captain."

They watched as M'ke completed and sent the message. It was only a short wait, but Chad held his breath, hoping it would turn out to be a Fleet battleship.

"We're receiving a message from the *Defiance*," M'ke finally said. "I'm decoding it now."

Chad sagged in his seat. So the nearby ship wasn't Fleet.

M'ke reported, "Admiral J'kart says that the battleship *Persuasion* is heading to the innermost slip and is approximately eight hours ahead of their position. We're ordered to pursue."

"Changing course," G'kaan announced, inputting the new coordinates.

Their new trajectory sprung up on the imager. M'ke input the data from the *Defiance* and a target icon appeared more than halfway across the pocket.

"At our current speed, we are approximately five hours behind the Fleet battleship," G'kaan informed them.

"They must have seen our grav burst," L'pash said. "So they know both our battleships are in pursuit—"

"I'm receiving another message from the admiral," M'ke interrupted. "The Fleet battleship destroyed the colonies on Impelleneer and Atalade using the same tactic that incinerated Jenuar."

There was silence as the crew on the command deck exchanged glances. Chad noticed that G'kaan stared down at his terminal, his jaw clenched.

"Qin has more than this one battleship to worry about," G'kaan finally said.

Chad silently agreed. With no fuel ore flowing out of Qin, soon enough the Domain would send a whole squad of battleships to fix everything. He wasn't sure he wanted to be on the *Endurance* during that particular fight.

M'ke looked up. "Should I tell the *Defiance* about Balanc?"

There was a charged silence, though Chad didn't know why. Finally, G'kaan shook his head. "We'll wait until we're close enough to open a channel. It would be too cruel to tell them by coded text message."

Chad refused to budge from his spot until at long last there was a gravity burst that indicated a ship had passed through the gravity slip ahead of them. M'ke announced that it correlated with the parameters of the Fleet battleship *Persuasion*. Right on schedule to be heading back to the Domain. With two Qin battleships on its heels.

Admiral J'kart left command, and S'jen was preparing to go off duty after the *Persuasion*'s gravity burst. She was glad now that G'kaan's battleship had rejoined them; they might be able to force the battleship to turn and fight. Domain territory was a decnight away, and it was packed with planets and stations worth defending.

C'vid raised one hand to stop her. "We're being hailed by the *Endurance*."

S'jen sat back down. "On imager."

E'ven grunted in disdain. He was still seated at the auxiliary comm. S'jen usually had to pry him loose for sleep and food. The young man was determined to learn everything as fast as he could. She understood his resentment towards G'kaan after he had insisted that normal training rules be suspended for the duration of their war with the Domain. But J'kart had the sense to see that training must continue in order to staff the new ships being commissioned. She intended to release one of her experienced corpsmen to serve on a new battleship while E'ven could take his rightful place on the command deck of the *Defiance*.

But at this moment, S'jen simply ignored E'ven. He had the enthusiasm of youth and would soon enough settle into maturity.

S'jen faced the imager as G'kaan appeared. His expression was overly concerned. She felt nothing but distaste at his typical display of emotion.

"S'jen, I'm glad you're still in command." G'kaan glanced to one side, hesitating.

"What is it, G'kaan?"

"We evacuated the Qin from Jenuar to Balanc before proceeding here. But Balanc had already been attacked by the Persuasion. *Pinpoint laser strikes took out most of the populace and destroyed their settlements."*

C'vid and B'hom gasped, and E'ven cried out in disbelief.

S'jen felt herself go colder and more unfeeling as if defying G'kaan's emotional tone. "And the clans?"

"Hardly a thousand people survived. Only seventy-four

Huut are accounted for, including you and E'ven." G'kaan's voice cracked. *"I'm sorry, S'jen—"*

"Where are the survivors?" she interrupted.

"A cargo transport is taking everyone from Jenuar and Balanc to the Endunara system. They have extensive cave systems the populace can take refuge in if the Fleet returns. The clans of Endunara will each take responsibility for one of the refugee clans."

G'kaan stared at her through the imager, his blue eyes disconcerting. S'jen could see through the transparent image to B'hom, who had his head in his hands. They had just found their clans again, and now they were truly lost.

S'jen realized G'kaan was watching their misery. "Is there anything else?"

"No. I thought you'd want to know—"

S'jen hit the control terminating the transmission. She didn't want to see his face anymore. She would have preferred a simple text message rather hearing about the extinction of her home world from G'kaan's mouth.

"He's lying!" E'ven exclaimed, standing up with his fists clenched.

"You saw what happened on Jenuar," S'jen calmly reminded him. "And Impelleneer and Atalade. Why should Balanc be any different?"

"But Huut . . ." E'ven protested. "They can't be . . ."

S'jen went over and placed her hands on his shoulders. "I lost Huut half a lifetime ago. The Domain took them from me, and I thought I would never see another clansman. Then I found you."

E'ven slowly nodded, his own hands clinging to her shoulders. "We *are* Huut now."

S'jen glanced over her shoulder at B'hom and C'vid.

They stood up and joined her and E'ven, their arms intermingling.

"We have the *Defiance*," C'vid murmured.

"Yes," S'jen agreed, her eyes burning. "And we will wreak vengeance on the Domain in the name of Qin!"

The Qin battleships fell farther behind as they chased the Fleet battleship. Twice they headed to the wrong slip and had to backtrack as the *Persuasion* took an unusual route to return to the Domain. It was apparent they were going to lose the battleship.

G'kaan knew they had a problem as soon as they entered the gravity pocket near the border of the Domain. According to their database, this pocket had two slips equidistant from the one they had entered through. The midway slip led back to Qin, while the innermost slip led toward the Domain.

G'kaan figured that the Fleet captain was trying to lose them while taking a route that would avoid population centers in the Domain. But this pocket offered them the perfect opportunity to double back to Qin, unbeknownst to them, and renew their attack.

G'kaan waited with his crew to hear Admiral J'kart's orders. The options must be clear to the admiral. G'kaan had gained new respect for J'kart's mental agility during the past decnight as his crew ran the daily simulations the admiral created. G'kaan saw a similarity in the solo simulations for the *Endurance*. J'kart's selected targets were in the Domain and were nearly impossible for the *Endurance* to defeat alone. One simulation called for them to attack Canopus Regional Headquarters. As hard as they tried, his crew was defeated in every run.

Clearly the admiral wasn't interested in targeting a

multitude of smaller objectives. G'kaan could see that would make the Qin too much of a general threat. The admiral was trying to find a way to hit them so hard the Domain would think twice about going into Qin again.

Unfortunately, none of the simulations called for the subtlety requiring G'kaan's underground slave network. But G'kaan created his own simulations for the Solian on board. He didn't remember Chad, but the man had been Rose's third-in-command. He trusted Rose's judgment, and Chad turned out to be an eager pupil. G'kaan was pleased by the Solian's progress, and less happy about the xenophobic reactions from his crew—including L'pash.

"Admiral J'kart is hailing us," M'ke finally announced.

G'kaan faced the imager as the dour face of Admiral J'kart appeared. He looked worn and haggard. They had successfully liberated the Qin, only to lose every colony in the first Fleet counterattack. It was taking a toll on the older man.

"Captain G'kaan, you are to proceed through the innermost slip toward the Domain. Maintain pursuit of target."

"Acknowledged," G'kaan agreed.

"The Defiance *will take the midway slip. We will be returning to Qin."*

So G'kaan would be going into the Domain instead of S'jen. J'kart must intend to return to Armada Central to consult with the advisors. They had gathered a wealth of information on their mission and subsequent engagement with the Fleet battleship. G'kaan had coded his own logs and sent them over days ago for the admiral to analyze.

"What are my orders?" G'kaan hoped the admiral

wouldn't tell him to follow the *Persuasion* all the way back to Canopus Regional Headquarters. That simulation had been disastrous.

"Engage the Persuasion, *if possible. Then distract the Fleet as per your simulations. Locate a single prime target that will require Fleet intervention. You must buy us some time again, G'kaan."*

In amazement, G'kaan realized that Admiral J'kart was smiling slightly. The admiral trusted G'kaan's crew with the most delicate task of provoking the Domain into aiming their Fleet away from Qin.

G'kaan nodded back. "We'll do our best, Admiral."

The admiral's image faded, and G'kaan was left smiling across at M'ke. "And I thought S'jen was his favorite."

M'ke agreed, "The admiral is placing a great deal of confidence in our judgment."

"Let's not disappoint him."

G'kaan maintained their course toward the innermost slip, where he was sure the battleship was heading. Regardless of what happened with the *Persuasion*, they would see more action yet.

One thing was certain: S'jen must be furious that G'kaan would get to attack the Domain instead of her.

Days after the two battleships split up, Chad realized that there was a lot of waiting between battles. But his training continued at a rapid pace. He had consented to comm implants, and body pockets were inserted into his shins that could hold a stunwand and laser knife. While he recovered, he had to miss the workout routines he and Dab had developed together. Instead he concentrated on the simulation runs with G'kaan—basically elaborate infiltration games.

Chad looked up from his dataport. "Are you sure we lost the *Persuasion?* They could have shut their systems down and are waiting until we leave this pocket."

G'kaan sighed and put down the dataport. "The battleship isn't our ultimate target."

"Any progress on that?" Chad asked with interest. He had also been thinking about which Fleet facility it would be best for the Qin to target.

"No, I'm loath to do anything in Archernar since we already activated the slave network in this sector."

"Then where to?" They were currently near the Picast-Yliandor gravity slip. The pulsar of Yliandor was the brightest star visible from the pocket that ran along the edge of the gravity well of the system.

"We're in a sparsely settled area. Volans sector is not far away, but it has nothing worth targeting."

Chad leaned forward. "I know you want to avoid Archernar, but what about the shipyard on the other side of the sector? You gave me a couple of simulations for it. It's one of the biggest facilities in this part of the region."

"Over half of our simulated attacks on the shipyard result in the destruction of our battleship."

"That's not good enough," Chad had to agree. 'What about—"

He broke off as the battleship shifted abruptly. Chad had to brace himself in the chair. The emergency battle-alert lights immediately flashed on.

G'kaan swiftly left for the command deck. Chad followed, trailing behind the taller Qin.

The comm corpsman was shouting as Chad entered the command deck. "It's an unknown ship, Captain! They appeared out of nowhere and fired on us. We were scanning the debris cloud for the battleship—"

G'kaan had already slid into his seat, replacing R'yeb, his frazzled second-in-command. "Lasers locked on."

Chad reached the jumpseat in time to activate the grab restraint. The imager showed a hostile target, but it wasn't the big icon that represented a battleship. This ship was much smaller.

"Firing!" G'kaan announced.

"Missiles incoming," the comm reported.

The ship was jolted again, harder this time.

"Damage to the aft burners," L'pash reported, taking the place of her cousin at ops. "They're at point-blank range!"

The Qin lasers shot out and struck the smaller ship repeatedly. The red beams seemed to tear through the shields as if they were tissue paper.

The ship exploded, ballooning into a cloud of sparkling debris.

By the time M'ke arrived on the command deck, the battle was over. "What was it?" he asked over the damage-control reports.

"A Fleet courier," G'kaan informed him.

"I don't understand," L'pash said, drawing G'kaan's attention back to herself. "A courier would have no chance against a battleship. Why did they attack?"

"I think we caught them by surprise," a relieved R'yeb suggested. "The pulsar is interfering in our scanner readings. It was refracting signals through the debris field. The courier came around it as we were pulling away."

G'kaan shook his head. "Any sign of the battleship in the debris field?

"Negative, Captain."

"Then there's no reason to stay—"

"Captain!" M'ke said. "I'm picking up the emergency beacon from a lifepod."

"Someone will rescue it," L'pash replied dismissively.

Chad knew that if this was a simulation, he would definitely pick up that pod. "Maybe they know something."

L'pash glared over her shoulder at him, but G'kaan had taken Chad's side enough times that she didn't try to order him silent.

"How many are inside?" G'kaan asked.

"Life signs indicate it's one humanoid," M'ke replied.

Rikev Alpha positioned himself in front of the portal of the small lifepod. An oddly shaped vessel as big as a battleship floated in front of the debris that was once the courier *Rapture*. With its bloated, round form, the ship looked Qin. Undoubtedly they were performing hostile acts against the Domain.

Now Rikev could only wait to see what the Qin would do. One touch of their lasers would vaporize his lifepod and the last witness to their attack.

Rikev had already gathered everything he needed to prove that the Qin, masquerading as Polinar, were at the scene of every sabotage in Archernar. His last stop in Picast had garnered more images of the three Polinar purveyors visiting the colony before the two weather satellites fell from orbit. His courier, the *Rapture*, had been on course for Regional Headquarters to take the news to Heloga Alpha.

When Rikev had heard the battle alert and saw the size of the ship the courier was firing on, he had darted into a lifepod. It was automatically ejected when the shields fell, right before the courier was blown to bits by the Qin battleship.

The pod shifted and Rikev caught hold of the bulkhead. The Qin had seized his lifepod with an attractor field. They were taking him prisoner.

Quickly, Rikev pulled from his sleeve pocket the two datarods that were filled with his investigation. He dropped them on the floor and carefully crushed them into small crystals. Now his job was to keep the Qin from finding out that he knew about their sabotages.

As the lifepod was drawn closer to the massive ship, Rikev tightened his lips. He had been on the verge of repairing some of the damage done to his line by the G-series Rikev. But the Qin had interfered again.

Yet Rikev remained resolute about making this opportunity work for him. To personally defeat the Qin would be an accomplishment worthy of a regent.

Rikev passed through the airlock into the Qin battleship. He kept his arms down and didn't make any quick gestures, behaving as one would around a wild animal. Anything could set these beasts off.

"So . . . It's an Alpha." A tall, black Qin stood in the corridor, his arms crossed. "I'm Captain G'kaan, of the battleship *Endurance*."

Rikev nodded his head, but declined to return the introduction. He tried to imagine this furry brute shaved like a Polinar. There was a remarkable resemblance to the younger male in the images he had seen.

The Qin stepped closer, opening his mouth to reveal sharpened fangs. "You will tell us who you are."

Rikev calmly returned his gaze. The Qin was taller

than him, which was unusual. Most aliens were shorter than Alphas.

The Qin captain poked Rikev in the shoulder with a broad finger. "You will talk soon enough."

When Rikev refused to react, the captain ordered over his shoulder, "Take him to the brig. Tell the bio-tech to prepare the serneo-inhibitor."

As Rikev was marched off, his confidence remained unshaken. He would be able to keep these barbarians out of the secrets of his mind. If he had to die protecting the Domain, that was his duty.

22

Trace was in Gandre Li's day cabin, lying on the couch
with Nip. In one of Gandre Li's rare, uncomfortable interactions with Nip, she had asked him to stay off her bed.

The *Solace* was docked at the Archernar shipyard.
They were watching the activity on the station through
the monitor because Trace expected the crew to return
soon with fresh supplies. She could see through the eye
over the airlock, or switch to the long docking arm, or
even the remote eye that overlooked the mid-sized circular terminal. The terminal had airlocks leading to two
other docking arms, with a handful of ships docked on
each arm. The docking arm designated for repairs had
an enforcer posted at the airlock to keep people out of
the empty ships.

Trace had never set foot off the docking arm of the
Archernar shipyard. Last quarter, she had discovered
that venturing even that far wasn't safe. It was here that
the two Deltas had attacked her, and Kwort had saved
her from being raped by fighting them off.

She had never seen beyond the terminal into the shipyard's legendary maze of corridors and levels. The best

she ever got was watching the different aliens as they passed through the docking terminal.

"There's another Bariss, like Gandi," Trace called out, pointing. Her voice fell as she thought about Gandre Li's expression as she left the two Solians alone in the day cabin, hidden behind the baffler. Gandi was very jealous but she refused to talk about it. Instead she had closed down completely. She wouldn't even hug Trace when they slept at night.

Nip wouldn't meet Trace's eyes. She had confided everything in him, but he wasn't much help when it came to interpersonal relationships. He only shrugged and said they could stop having sex if she wanted to.

Trace had never made such a big decision before. Her mind was conflicted while her physical urges won out despite Gandre Li's unhappiness. Trace had sex with Nip at least once a day, trying every position they could from an old Solian book on pleasure. It was considered to be the classic sex manual for humanoids, but Trace found they laughed almost as much as they strained together in lust. She liked to play sex games with Gandi, too, and she knew her lover would be even more upset to know how much she enjoyed her intimacy with Nip.

"Hey!" Nip exclaimed, sitting up abruptly. "That's Kwort! I swear, that's got to be him!"

Trace sat up too. "Where?"

"Right there," Nip pointed to the lower part of the holo. "He just came out of that airlock."

Trace magnified the image. Across the terminal, a short Deneb with a ridged skull was talking to the enforcer posted in front of the airlock at the base of the docking arm. The Deneb wore a blue maintenance flightsuit like the other techs employed by the shipyard.

"That's him!" Nip exclaimed.

"Are you sure?" Trace knew how vague Nip could be sometimes.

"Yes! Run after him!" Nip pulled her up and toward the door. "Tell him I'm here. Bring him back!"

Trace went along reluctantly. "That might not be a good idea. Gandre Li may not—"

Nip rounded on her. "You owe Kwort! He saved you from those two Deltas!"

Trace had never seen Nip this way. She glanced back at the holo. Kwort was waving good-bye to the enforcer. She did owe him for keeping those two slobbering hulks off her.

Without another word, Trace ran out of the cabin to the airlock. She cycled through using the ship's code. As she darted down the corridor, she knew Nip would be watching her in the monitor.

When Trace passed through the airlock at the bottom of the docking arm, she had to pause to reorient herself. She had never been this far before. Then she saw the enforcer stanchion. She ran toward it, only to realize that Kwort wasn't there anymore.

The noise and the crush were overwhelming. People were filling nearly a third of the terminal, queuing up at the other docking arm to get onto a spaceliner.

Looking around frantically, she wondered if she had missed her chance because she had hesitated. Then she saw the main entrance to the terminal. She hurried over to it, weaving her way through the crowd. She felt exposed, feeling as if anyone could grab her and carry her off.

Trace almost turned and fled back to the safety of the *Solace*. But she couldn't, knowing that Nip was watching her. Instead, she went along with the stream of people leaving the terminal until she caught a glimpse of a short bald head ahead. She tried not to touch anyone as she rushed forward.

"Kwort!" she called out.

His ridged head ducked and swiveled.

Trace ran, shoving past the people who were trying to get into the terminal, ignoring their turned faces.

She finally caught the sleeve of his flightsuit. "Kwort! Nip sent me!"

Kwort was shaking his head. "I'm Cwart—" Then his ears caught up. "Wait, did you say Nip?"

Trace was breathing hard, nodding her head. "We picked him up from the spacepost."

Kwort's eyes widened. He was as short as she was, so she didn't miss a thing. It felt weird after looking up to people all her life. Passengers for the liner were bumping by them, starting to stare.

She pulled his arm. "Come on, let's get to the ship."

"What ship?" Kwort asked, but he went with her.

"The *Solace*." Trace was feeling scared now. Aliens were looking at her as if she were a juicy tidbit they wanted to snap up. She had caused quite a scene trying to catch up with Kwort.

He also seemed to want to avoid attention. He bent his head down and drew her into a flow of passengers who carried them through the terminal.

"It's this docking arm," she said, as they almost went by.

"This is dangerous," he muttered as they went through the airlock.

Trace agreed, and she hoped they wouldn't suffer for it. But it was the only thing Nip had ever asked of her.

They hurried up the long docking arm into the airlock to the *Solace*. Trace input the code, and they cycled through the lock.

Inside, she sealed it shut again. Kwort was watching her warily. "Who are you?"

"You helped me," Trace said impulsively. "You stopped two Deltas who were trying to rape me."

"You!?" Kwort exclaimed. "That was you?"

Trace nodded eagerly. "I never got to thank you. I'm Trace."

Kwort was shaking his head. He looked upset.

"I'm sorry it caused problems for you," Trace said hesitantly. "Nip told me your battleship was destroyed."

Kwort blew out his breath. "That's a secret! He's not supposed to tell anyone."

"I won't say anything." Trace wanted to cry at the way he looked. It was her fault. If she hadn't gone into the docking arm to wait for Gandre Li, none of it would have happened. Kwort's friend would still be alive.

But then again, according to Nip, the battleship would have invaded Qin and destroyed their civilization. So maybe fate had drawn her into the docking arm that day.

"Nip's in here," she finally said, showing the Delta into the day cabin.

Kwort was feeling stunned. He had gotten off his duty shift and was supposed to take another crawl through the access tubes to see Rose. She had asked for a station map that showed the automated runways between the terminals. Her ill-fated scheme to escape with the slaves was looking more and more disastrous, but Kwort had no other choice.

He was living on borrowed time. Several of his fellow bot techs had been put through a retinal scan this morning. They were assigned jobs on a battleship that had docked on the same repair arm as his patrolship. Kwort shuddered when he realized that he could have been picked for that assignment. It would be highly suspicious if he refused a job that required a security clearance.

"In here," Trace said, gesturing through a door. "We have the baffler going to prevent scans."

Kwort slipped through the doorway and was immediately jumped by someone yelling out his name in greeting. Kwort was almost smothered, but when he looked up and saw the grin on Nip's face, he was amazed. Nip had never liked him on the *Purpose*.

"Kwort! It's good to see you—"

"Nip, your arm!" Kwort grabbed his upper arm, glad to find it whole again. "You got out of the biobed all right?"

"Yeah, what happened?" Nip demanded, smacking him heartily on the back. "How'd you get here?"

"We were caught by enforcers," Kwort replied.

Nip's smile faded. "You mean . . ."

Kwort told him as gently as possible that raiders had stolen the *Purpose*, with Mote, Whit, and Dab onboard. Nip took that hard, especially after Kwort added that the Beta-captain of the patrolship had confirmed a kill on the raider.

"But the others are here on the shipyard, including Shard," Kwort added hastily. Nip had been especially close to Shard, along with Dab and Whit. "Rose had some wild idea of stealing a patrolship so we can escape."

Trace exclaimed inarticulately, putting her hand over her mouth.

"That's impossible!" Nip declared.

"That's what I keep telling her," Kwort agreed. "But the handlers will be taking them back to the cube stack tomorrow. She says this is their last chance before they're sent to the opposite ends of the Domain."

"They'll be killed!" Nip insisted.

"You know Rose." Kwort shook his head. "You can't say no to her. Besides, Ash is doing really bad. S/he can't remember a thing anymore."

"What about the others?" Nip asked doubtfully.

"They're going along with it. Rose keeps talking about Earth. She says they're going to kick out the Fleet once and for all."

Both Nip and Trace opened their mouths and didn't close them. Kwort realized that that was how Rose had convinced the slaves . . . she had mesmerized them with the mere thought of returning to Earth.

They both asked lots of questions about Rose's demented plan. Kwort explained everything, including the fact that Rose not only was going to rescue the remnants of her crew, she intended to take along every Solian in the slave barracks. According to the shipyard's schedule, the handlers would be moving the slaves out of the barracks tomorrow and bringing in fresh stock.

"What can we do to help?" Nip asked.

Kwort scratched one of his ridges. "They'll have to make it past the enforcers with their stunwands. For that they need weapons."

Kwort had gently hinted his need to Taffle, only to be rebuffed instantly. He had backpedaled, knowing he couldn't afford to alienate Taffle, but it was clear how weak his position was with her.

Nip was looking at Trace.

Trace cleared her throat. "I know where we can get weapons."

She went over to the locked cabinet under the baffler. She pressed her palm on the sensor until the door opened. Pulling out a case, she lifted the lid to reveal four handheld weapons. "Stunguns. Gandre Li got them in case her ship was ever boarded by raiders. She used them once to take care of a berserk crew member, right before I came on board."

Kwort's future suddenly looked brighter. "That's perfect! They've got a good range, and they won't kill anyone."

Nip picked up one to examine it. "Fully charged and ready to go."

"Give them to me—" Kwort started to say.

Trace held on to the case. "I have to ask Gandre Li if we can use them."

Kwort shook his head. "We can't risk it. What if she turns us in?"

"She wouldn't do that!" Trace protested indignantly. "She's been hiding Nip for decnights, port after port, even though it's a huge risk for us."

Nip sheepishly nodded, nudging Kwort. "Trace is right. We have to ask the captain. If the stunguns are traced back to the *Solace*, the crew would be in big trouble."

Kwort reached out, but Trace tried to close the lid. "Can I see one? I'm not going to run away with it."

Trace reluctantly opened the case and let Kwort pick

up a stungun. He examined it carefully. "The identity code has to be chipped out."

"How?" Trace asked.

"You have to gouge out this ridge." Kwort showed her the place where the ID code was buried. "And they would have to be thoroughly sterilized to disintegrate any particles that may have gotten inside. It wouldn't do for a bit of your genetic code to get picked up by the enforcers."

Nip turned to Trace. "Do you really think you can convince Gandre Li to lend them to us? She hasn't been happy with you lately."

"I hope I can," Trace replied doubtfully.

"Should I talk to her?" Nip asked.

"No!" Trace grimaced. "I'll have to do it alone. She'll stop listening as soon as she sees you."

Kwort was surprised by the intimate tone they used with each other. He appraised the two Solians again. Trace's shoulder was touching Nip's arm, and the way they looked at each other—

"You're fooling around with the captain's slave?" Kwort asked Nip in exasperation. "Even *I'm* not that self-destructive."

"It just . . . happened," Nip replied with a shrug. "We couldn't help it."

"Well stop it!" Kwort ordered.

"It's not your concern," Trace told him, her voice going higher.

Kwort leaned closer. "It's *my* head on the line, Trace, not yours. This has to work, and I'm not going to die because you two can't keep your suits on!"

He glared at both of them until they dropped their eyes in guilt. "We're all relying on you," he added urgently.

"I know," Nip assured him, stepping slightly away from Trace. She nodded, trying to hide the stricken look on her face.

"Do whatever it takes," Kwort told them. He quickly described the waste receptacle where they could place the stunguns, in the center of the cargo terminal next to the slave-cube bay. Then he downloaded the map into Trace's dataport with the location marked so there was no confusion. "You have to leave the stunguns there before second shift starts. They should be coming through right after that."

Trace and Nip nodded solemnly. "We'll make sure it happens," Nip assured him.

Kwort would have felt better if Trace had said it. "You better make sure it does," he insisted, looking at Nip, hoping his meaning was clear. If Trace didn't convince Gandre Li, then Nip would have to persuade Trace to steal the stunguns. It was a slender thread to hang his life on, but Kwort didn't have any choice. His heart had almost seized this morning when the enforcer at the airlock pulled out the retinal scanner. He might as well beat himself to death with his own bot baton rather than put his eyes to that thing. But the enforcer had waved him through to the patrolship before he could bolt.

It had been a very close call, and Kwort knew he couldn't risk another one. He had to trust Nip and Trace to do the right thing. Rose would take care of the rest.

Gandre Li lived in agonized confusion for decnights. Trace had confessed about her sexual explorations with Nip right away, of course. Her emotions played in full view of everyone on the ship. No one could miss that she was entranced by Nip and sought out his company and his bunk every chance she could get.

Trace probably thought she was keeping it low-key, but she was so delighted with Nip that joy flowed out of her. Except for when she saw Gandre Li; then guilt clouded her face and her mouth turned downward. Even her shiny hair seemed less bouncy, as if a black cloud descended when Gandre Li was around.

In a very bad mood, Gandre Li reported to Rutith Alpha and received her new courier assignments, which would surely spread more death and destruction. Rutith seemed to like her better when she was depressed. After that, Gandre Li checked on their refueling schedule. There were unusual delays caused by a severe drop in the fuel supply, and her ship would have to stay for at least another two shifts, possibly three before it was released.

Gandre Li was in no hurry to do InSec's dirty work. She wandered around the Archernar shipyard for a long time. She dreaded returning to the *Solace*, where Trace and Nip were probably in each other's arms. Part of her wanted to rush back to separate them, but she couldn't force Trace to love her. Her dignity was all she had left. That, and knowing that she didn't stop Trace from doing whatever she wanted.

But eventually Gandre Li had to return to her ship. As she walked through the airlock, she hated the sight of the delicately swirled marble that lined the walls. Trace had been playing with the lighting, casting colorful spots here and there, reflecting her buoyant mood. Gandre Li wanted to change them to something darker like red or purple. Her own mood should be reflected in her ship.

But Trace had chosen the yellow, blue, and green spots, so they would stay.

A the door to her day cabin, Gandre Li hesitated. Trace was smart enough to watch the decking arm and would know Gandre Li had returned. But she dreaded what she might see. Every memory of Trace and Nip together tore a bulkhead from her heart.

Gandre Li opened the door to the low hum of the baffler. With a quick look around, she saw that Nip wasn't there. "Where is he?"

"He's in there," Trace said quickly, pointing to the shut door of the bedroom. "He wanted to apologize himself, but I told him I wanted to see you privately."

Gandre Li stiffened. "What did he do now?"

"Nothing," Trace assured her. "We're sorry for how we've been acting, Gandi. We've—I've been very selfish. I shouldn't have hurt you."

Gandre Li hadn't expected this. When she had left Trace and Nip, they were acting like kids who couldn't wait for the creche nanny to turn her back. She was sure they would have sex while she was gone, maybe twice. Apparently Nip was insatiable. His fingers left small round bruises on Trace's arms and legs where he griped her so tightly.

Trace got up to approach her. But Gandre Li backed away a step.

"You're still angry," Trace said. "I am sorry, Gandi. It was purely physical. I wish I had restrained myself. I hate hurting you."

Gandre Li tried not to breathe. She used to take deep breaths of Trace's hair and neck, and in those private parts that smelled so sweet. Her sense of smell was not keen, but she thought she could detect Nip's musky scent on her. It was awful.

"You're not really giving him up?" Gandre Li asked flatly.

"Yes, it's over." Trace lifted her chin.

Gandre Li saw that Trace was conflicted over it. "Why? I didn't ask you to stop."

"I know. That's why. I didn't realize it would hurt you so badly. I don't want it if it causes you this much pain." Trace sighed. "It's not worth it."

It was such a sudden reversal, it was hard to believe. But Gandre Li's heart was starting to sing inside her chest, and her arms wanted to reach out to hug Trace close. She steeled herself and turned away, pacing over to the portal. The intersecting bulkheads of the shipyard with its distinctive pronged docking arms made it look like a bristly bush.

"We have to get Nip off this ship," Gandre Li said quietly. "It's too dangerous for us to keep him here."

"I know." Trace's voice caught, but she quickly went on. "He has to leave."

"We'll delay my assignments in order to divert down to that settlement outside of Archernar," Gandre Li suggested.

Trace looked more eager than Gandre Li expected. "There may be another way that's faster."

"What's that?"

"Kwort is here on the Archernar shipyard." Trace paused but Gandre Li shook her head. "You know, Kwort, the Deneb who saved me from those Deltas last quarter. Only he's in big trouble, and I have to help him."

"You've seen him?" Gandre Li asked incredulously.

"He was here—"

"Here! You let him on board?"

"Yes." Trace went on bravely. "He's in touch with Rose and the other Solians who are in the slave barracks. They're escaping from the shipyard tomorrow on a patrolship—"

"What!"

"They did it once before," Trace pointed out.

"They'll get caught! They'll tell the enforcers everything." Gandre Li sank down on the couch with her head in her hands. "We're doomed! Those dimwitted Solians . . ."

Trace sat down next to her. "They'll get away, I'm sure. We can meet up with them in the Mahrashatra or Triella sector, then transfer Nip to them. That gets him off our ship."

Gandre Li was appalled. "I never should have helped them! I'm doomed to be haunted by Solians forever."

Trace hesitantly twisted the cartridge belt of her flight-suit.

Gandre Li stopped wringing her hands. "What is it?"

"They need our help again, so they won't get caught."

"You've got to be kidding!"

Trace got up and went to the cabinet. The door was open, though Gandre Li hadn't noticed it. Trace pulled out the case with the stunguns in it. "They need weapons. Kwort showed me how to get rid of the ID code and we can plant them in a trash receptacle tomor—"

"Are you out of your mind!?" Gandre Li exclaimed. "You want me to give my *stunguns* to a bunch of slaves?"

"They can escape," Trace insisted. "Rose can do anything. They're going to Earth and they're going to kick the Fleet out forever."

Abruptly, Gandre Li realized what it meant. "That's it!

That's why you said you would give up Nip. To convince me to help them."

"No, Gandi—"

"Don't call me that!"

Trace shut her mouth, looking startled.

"You want to go to Earth," Gandre Li said quietly. "I could hear it in your voice."

Trace seemed caught off guard. "I guess in some way, yes, I do. But I don't want to leave you, Ga—" she broke off without finishing the nickname.

"No, you only expect me to risk everything to help your lover."

"I have to help Kwort," Trace pleaded. "Those Deltas could have killed me or sold me or done something awful. He lost everything because of it."

Gandre Li started to the door. "You didn't have to pretend to give up Nip. I would have agreed, and you know it. I don't have any choice. I can't afford to let them get caught and spill everything. You've already endangered us by letting that Delta on board."

Trace was crying. "I didn't mean—"

Gandre Li shut the door behind her. She couldn't bear to hear Trace lie.

She strode down the corridor and went up the spiral stairs to the lounge. The crew was out enjoying their leave. At least someone was happy.

Gandre Li went into the empty guest room that was reserved for Alphas or Betas who traveled on board the *Solace*. She sealed the door and began pacing, knowing that she had no choice. She must help the slaves escape. If they were caught and interrogated, they could implicate her in their first escape. She would have to let them use her stunguns in spite of her worst fears.

After that, if she got away from the shipyard alive, she would have to make another serious decision. She had always told herself that Trace wasn't a slave. If Trace wasn't her slave, then she should be allowed to choose where she wanted to go.

It was heartbreaking how Trace had tried to bribe her by pretending to give up her lover. Gandre Li wished she hadn't done that. But it didn't make any difference in her decision.

If Trace chose to be with Nip, Gandre Li would have to let her go.

Takhan had just returned to their room with Jor and Danal when Gandre Li pressed the admittance light. They had stayed out very late on the shipyard and were getting ready for bed.

Gandre Li glanced in. "I'm sorry, but I must speak to you."

Takhan thought the captain looked terrible. Her clear peach skin was blotched and her eyes were puffy. For the first time since Takhan had joined the crew, she felt sorry for the captain. She was naturally suspicious about any Beta, but watching Gandre Li deal with the loss of the affections of her beloved slave had made her think differently about her. Takhan knew that if someone had come on board the *Solace* and took her place with Jor and Danal, she wouldn't have been so quiet about it. She would have made everyone hate her.

Jor looked uncomfortable in his scanty sleepwear. "Is something wrong, Captain?"

"Yes." Gandre Li came in and sat down.

"Is it about InSec?" Takhan asked, her wariness returning. She thought they had settled all that. The crew had decided to stay on board the *Solace*.

"No." Gandre Li passed a hand over her eyes. "It's about those Solian slaves who kidnapped me in the Capetta sector last quarter."

Takhan sat down, glancing at the others. They had talked about that, and Takhan had always been dubious about the captain's motives. Jor and Danal tended to believe she didn't destroy the slaves because of Trace. But Takhan thought it was because Gandre Li didn't want to call attention to the *Solace*. If InSec had discovered that the captain had been taken captive by Solian slaves, she might have been mind-stripped for more information. Takhan believed Gandre Li had ignored the slaves because it was the easiest thing to do.

"Did someone find out about that?" Jor asked, his dark eyes serious.

"Some of those slaves are here, on the shipyard, and they're planning to make another escape attempt. If they're caught . . ." Gandre Li shrugged.

"Can't you stop them?" Takhan demanded.

Gandre Li said, "It's their choice if they want to die rather than be slaves."

Takhan wanted to insist that it wasn't right, but she couldn't. She knew her own place in the Domain and resentment burned inside of her because of it. Also, she had seen Trace go through some awful things because she was a slave. Perhaps Trace would rather die than be the slave of a different master.

"I'm giving you the opportunity to break your contracts with me right now," Gandre Li quietly told them. "I'll give you excellent recommendations so you can find another post. You'll have to leave tonight."

Takhan exchanged incredulous looks with Danal and Jor. "You're firing us?"

"No, but I have to give you the option of leaving."

"We already agreed to take this risk," Takhan said sharply. "If we're asked about the slaves, we'll say we thought you reported it."

Jor looked worried. 'Yes, we knew this could happen."

Gandre Li prepared herself. "But there's more. Trace has asked me to loan the slaves my stunguns so they can escape."

"You can't do that!" Takhan exclaimed. "Ignoring that you saw them is one thing. Helping them is another."

"I helped them already," Gandre Li replied. "I gave them the grav plot to Qin."

Takhan opened her mouth to exclaim again, but Jor beat her to it. "I thought so."

Takhan turned on him. "You did? Why didn't you tell us?"

"It was safer for you not to know," he reminded her.

"Well now I know!"

Jor put his hand on top of hers. "It's done."

Takhan took a deep breath, trying to focus on the problem. "So we're in deep trouble if those slaves are caught. Right?"

"Yes, unless you leave the *Solace* now," Gandre Li agreed. "You could always say I started acting erratically and you feared for your lives."

They looked at each other, knowing they would never find another ship that would take on all three of them. They would be split up, perhaps forever.

"Are you really going to give them the stunguns, Captain?" Jor asked.

"Yes." Gandre Li lifted her chin. "I don't think Solians should be slaves."

None of them knew what to say. Takhan thought that Trace didn't deserve to be a slave. Takhan also wasn't sure she deserved to be a Delta, which was nearly as low in the grand scheme of things.

Gandre Li stood up, going to the door. "You have until second shift tomorrow to decide. The *Solace* will be departing soon after that."

Takhan watched openmouthed as Gandre Li walked through the door. As soon as it closed, she leaped to her feet and let out a frustrated cry.

Jor said, "Calm down, Takhan."

She pointed at the door. "Do you realize the ultimatum she's given us? We're either complicit in a crime of treason or we're split up forever!"

Jor's brow was furrowed and his dark hands rubbed together. "Perhaps two of us could find work together. But it's not likely."

Danal finally spoke up. "Then we stay on the *Solace*."

Jor and Takhan stared at him. "Don't you realize how dangerous it is?" Takhan demanded.

"Every day is risky," Jor qualified. "The captain's association with InSec is already bad enough."

"That's why we can't stay," Takhan insisted. "We'll be separated and miserable, but we'll be alive."

Danal said flatly, "I don't want to live like that."

"You mean you'd take that kind of risk to keep us together?" Jor asked.

Danal nodded, actually smiling a bit.

"He would," Takhan breathed, not sure she believed it. "Our . . . family is that important."

"Our family," Jor repeated thoughtfully.

Takhan took hold of his hand and Danal's. They

stood looking at each other. Perhaps it was worth it. She had lost everything when she left her Aborandeen ship. This was her family now. Could she give up and walk away from everyone she loved again?

No. She would do anything it took to keep them together.

23

To Earth! That was Rose's rallying cry. And it worked. Even the most skeptical Solians agreed to follow her lead. They had heard too many stories about the wonders of Earth, where freedom reigned, to be able to resist.

Rose had to talk to them one at a time because of the handlers. It took some effort to convince everyone that Earth was an attainable goal and then brief them on her escape plan. Next she discreetly worked with them, sorting them into groups of three. They learned to quickly lock their arms around each other's waists and walk along the pool together, breaking off at the end of the room so as to not attract the attention of the handlers.

Within a day, they could group together in threes at a whistle from her or Clay. It wasn't much, but hopefully it would give them something to concentrate on instead of panicking while she did the tough work of breaking them out.

Clay was a pillar of strength for Rose. Clay would take one stungun, while Shard and Stub would take the other two—*if* Gandre Li came through for them.

That was a big "if." Their escape depended on getting

those weapons. After examining the map on Kwort's
dataport, Rose had realized that the two automated runways that carried cargo and people between the terminals were much longer than she imagined. Even though
the runways were fast-moving, enforcers would have
time to respond. But that wasn't anything she shared
with the others.

At long last, a staccato whistle from Clay signaled
the alert. Their departure from the slave barracks was
according to the schedule Kwort had managed to get
hold of.

The Swark handlers hustled everyone into the viewing room. The Solians shifted into position as agreed,
with Rose and her three chosen gunmen up front while
Jot and Ash brought up the rear. Rose was glad to see
that Jot was serious about her job of watching over Ash.
Ash was in a sad state, as compliant and defenseless as a
baby. Rose had tried to explain to hir what would happen. Ash was confused but s/he readily agreed to do
whatever Jot said.

The other Solians looked worried. They had never
seen her in action. Just wait till they did! She was raring
to go. She had surprise on her side, and that counted for
a lot. These people had no idea that slaves would dare to
defy the Domain.

It was time they learned a different tune.

Clay kept glancing back on the other slaves as they were
marched through the shipyard. One long-nosed Swark
handler was in the lead, the other guarded the back, and
one was in the middle. The Archernar shipyard was
known for its network of intersecting levels and ramps,
and he knew he couldn't have found his way alone.

Everyone watched as their slave convoy went by, their eyes eager, as if they were thinking about their next lust.

Clay walked next to Rose in the front. He had seen it once before, but it still amazed him how Rose bewitched everyone. Shard's eyes were sparkling at the excitement they would cause, and the usually easygoing Stub looked like a commando ready for action. Fragile Jot had turned into a ferocious sprite hovering protectively next to Ash. Apparently all those quiet, preparatory pep-talks were working.

In between, walking in pairs, were the clueless slaves, sixteen in all. Clay wasn't sure if they really believed they could escape, or if the thought of going to Earth had so scrambled their brains that Rose could make them do anything.

Even his own planned part in the escape somehow seemed reasonable, though he had never touched a stungun before. It was true that Rose had explained to them via Kwort how to operate the stungun, but Clay wasn't certain that information would stick in their minds in the heat of the action.

As their convoy entered the cargo terminal, Clay tensed. It seemed impossible.

But his job was to wait for Rose's signal. He could do that much.

Rose caught sight of the square trash receptacle in the center of the terminal. It was bigger than she thought. What if she couldn't get into it? What if the stunguns weren't inside?

Then her second escape attempt would end before it began. She would be killed after she was interrogated into revealing everything. But she refused to think about that as the handler led them across the terminal toward the cargo bays. According to the map, she wouldn't get closer than halfway to the trash receptacle.

There were lots of cargo handlers going through the terminal at the end of the long row of bays. Two blue Poids were pushing a grav truck nearby, but they weren't close enough to use as cover. The other Deltas avoided their convoy, but their eyes followed the slaves every step. Probably thinking of how they would use such prime flesh if they had the chance.

That was the final spur. Rose gave two low whistles.

She darted toward the trash receptacle. Clay was right behind her. She didn't glance back to see if Shard or Stub were following.

"Stop! Sit!" the handler yelled behind her.

Rose hit the receptacle at full speed. It leaned up from the bottom, then abruptly slammed back down. Brackets on the floor kept it from sliding.

"Sit!" the handlers were yelling uselessly.

People were turning to look as two of the Swarks ponderously started toward them. The other slaves had dropped to the ground to avoid being shocked.

Rose lifted the bottom of the receptacle, flipping it over on its side. The top broke open spilling trash across the floor.

Clay scrambled through the trash with her, and Rose came up with a stungun at the same time he did.

"This is it!" Rose cried.

Trace nervously waited in the corridor by the airlock. Gandre Li was pacing back and forth. They hadn't spoken much, even though Trace tried to thank her. Gandre Li ignored everything she said.

The airlock dinged. Gandre Li hit the cycle button, opening the door.

Takhan appeared in the doorway holding a small carryall.

When the airlock closed behind her, Takhan said, "I did it. Dropped them in the receptacle in the cargo terminal." She opened the bag to show the distinctive Aborandeen flightsuit with its green hood. "I changed before I came back. I went through so many levels of the station, they won't be able to track me here."

Gandre Li nodded at her, and for the first time ever, reached out to touch Takhan's arm. "I don't know how to thank you."

Takhan jerked her chin to one side. "I was the best one to plant the stunguns. Every eye in the place would have been trained on a Beta-captain. Who's looking at a simple Aborandeen? No one cares what rubbish I toss in the trash."

Trace stepped forward, her hands over her heart. "Thank you. You've saved their lives."

Gandre Li's expression hardened and she turned away. "Enough of this. We have to get out of here now."

She stalked through doorway toward the command deck, giving orders over the comm to Danal and Jor. Trace sighed, unable to meet Takhan's eyes. She felt so guilty. How could she have hurt Gandre Li? Trace wished she could explain that her feelings for Nip were nothing more than lust and curiosity. It had nothing to do with her love for Gandre Li.

There was a jolt through the floor as the *Solace* undocked. Trace went to the airlock portal and looked out. The station was huge around them. There were two patrolships on a nearby docking arm, flanking the menacing bulk of a Fleet battleship. She wondered which patrolship the Solians intended to take. Then she hurried back to the day cabin to tell Nip it was done. Now it was up to Rose.

Rose grabbed an extra stungun and looked up as Shard skidded over. Shard snatched it from Rose and turned, priming the stungun as if she had been doing it her entire life. She let out a screech that pierced the ears as she dropped the Swarks like rocks. Rose wasn't surprised to see an untapped core of anger inside that fiery woman.

"Don't hit the Solians!" Rose rolled and aimed in the other direction, spraying the terminal with the stungun. Aliens fell around them and grav sleds were shoved out of control.

When Rose got up, there was nobody moving but her other three gunmen. The Solians were still huddled in a tight group.

Rose let out a piercing whistle. It was the signal for "Follow Clay!"

She ran toward the main entrance to cover them, while Clay gave the same piercing whistle.

The slaves jumped up so fast it might as well have been an order from an Alpha. Rose glanced their way as she rushed by. Jot had hold of Ash with a grim grip, and for once she wasn't crying under pressure. The others were in tight groups and moving fast. So much for small wonders.

They were heading toward the automated runway after Clay. Shard covered the rear of the slaves, while Stub hung back in the terminal, stunning anyone who came from the cargo bays or docking arms.

Rose waited a few moments in the entrance, stunning

another trio of enforcers arriving on the scene. Then she gave the whistle for her armed crew to fall back. She retreated to the runway the slaves were getting on. Hopefully it would take time for the enforcers to recover their wits and turn off the runways.

She jumped on last, running as she looked over her shoulder to stun anyone who followed. Now every second counted.

Kwort wasn't sure when the Solians would arrive at his terminal, so he lingered inside the main entrance eating his breakfast. No one paid attention. Second shift had already started, but he couldn't go to his airlock until the Solians appeared. His fellow bot techs were already on board the patrolship, probably laughing at the credit he would be docked for being late.

If the Solians didn't come, Kwort didn't know what to do. Trying to hide in plain sight would get him caught. It was only a matter of time before he was scanned and discovered.

"So what's up, Cwart?" Taffle asked, sliding in next to him.

"Taffle!" He was so surprised he stopped chewing. "What are you doing here?"

"Close your mouth, Cwart." Taffle laughed. "I'm finding out what you're doing. You know—with that pleasure slave. The one you were stranded on the spacepost with."

Kwort stared at her. "How did you find out about that?"

Taffle just gave him a look.

"It's nothing." Kwort swallowed. "Maybe you should leave, Taffle. You really don't want to be here."

She cocked her head at his urgent tone.

From the runway came shouts and the distinctive echo of a stun reverberation.

Taffle glanced back at him. "Maybe you're right."

Kwort didn't spare her another look as he ran the opposite direction, across the terminal toward his usual airlock. As he approached the enforcer, he hoped his lateness would cover his agitation. "I'm late! I know."

The enforcer didn't care. He dilated the airlock. Kwort started past him.

But the enforcer's attention turned to the sounds coming from the entrance. His hand went to his stunwand. "What's going on?"

Kwort stepped through the airlock, putting his hand on the edge to hold the hatch open. The safeties on the dilator wouldn't let it close if anything was in the way.

Suddenly Clay appeared in the entrance of the terminal, his knees bent as he swept his stungun in front of him. People collapsed like dropped bots.

Kwort waved at Clay, trying to draw his attention.

"Stop!" the enforcer shouted. Nobody was afraid of pleasure slaves.

Suddenly the emergency lights flashed and a warning came over the internal comm. *"Fugitives armed and dangerous approaching Passenger Terminal 14! Secondary enforcer squads report immediately!"*

Kwort cringed against the blaring sound. But he was still holding on to the airlock. "Clay!" he shouted, as chaos erupted.

People were running in every direction while Clay and Shard mowed them down. The busy passenger terminal was stopped in its tracks.

Then Clay caught sight of someone across the terminal waving an arm. It was Kwort. He whistled the commanding come-along signal to the others and went forward.

Rose moved up from the rear to cover the main entrance, as the Solians ran toward the airlock after Clay. Nearly every alien in the terminal was down. Clay fired on the last enforcer, stunning him before they reached the airlock. Rose caught up from behind.

They still had everyone.

"Inside!" Rose shouted, waving the Solians through the airlock.

Kwort went ahead with Clay and Shard to lead them to the patrolship. They were assigned to take care of the Delta bot techs onboard.

Rose guarded the Solians as the last ones slipped through the airlock. There were several enforcers running across the terminal toward her. She stayed just behind the airlock as it shut, stunning the enforcers before it sealed.

Then she went to the control pad on her side and smashed the butt of the stungun into it repeatedly. The metal bent and crystals shattered. Optical fibers spilled out and she fried it with several close-range shots.

"Come on!" Stub shouted at her.

Rose withdrew, still looking backward to watch for anyone following.

Halfway up the docking arm, Kwort was waving people through the airlock. "Hurry, they'll depressurize this arm!"

"We caught 'em with their pants down!" Rose cried gleefully. "They didn't even get an alert out in time!"

"Get in!" Kwort insisted frantically, shoving her through.

They tumbled through the airlock together. Rose came out grinning.

Stub cycled the lock closed. Most of the others were milling around in the corridors. They avoided the Delta who was lying stunned on the floor.

Shard appeared breathless along with Clay. "We've taken care of both bot techs."

"Good. Clay, recruit some help and lock these techs into a lifepod. You know the drill. Kwort, Stub, and Shard, you're with me in command." She glanced at Jot, who was still by Ash's side. "Take the others into the galley and keep them calmed down."

"Aye, Captain!" Jot said with obvious pride.

Rose kept grinning as she ran after Kwort to the command deck.

But she stopped short in the doorway to command. It was a place of technical beauty. This was no cargo ship, it was the newest hardware available in the Domain. Her hand ran across the glossy navigation terminal. Weapons keys were clearly marked down the left.

Rose laughed. "We've come up in the world!"

"Get us out of here!" Kwort demanded. "Or we're dead meat in a fancy can—"

"Shut up and sit down somewhere, little man." Rose took the helm and activated the navigational computer. She started the sequence to initiate the converter and the weapons systems. "We'll be out of here in two shakes."

Stub had the ops terminal up and running, his hands flying across the surface. "It's a lot more complicated than the *Purpose,* but we only need the basics for now."

Shard read the information on her terminal. "This ship is called the *Relevance.*"

"Get the imager activated," Rose ordered.

"Activating imager," Shard acknowledged.

A miniaturized version of the star system appeared in the imager. Archernar shipyard loomed in the foreground, in the grav pocket. In the distance was a brilliant blue-green star, surrounded by a fuzzy red ring.

"I'm disengaging umbilicals," Stub reported.

Rose activated the thrusters. All systems read go. "Stub, blow the airlock."

There was a jolt as their patrolship detached. They lurched sideways.

Kwort screamed as he was thrown from his jumpseat.

Rose held on along with Stub and Shard. "Stabilizers on!"

"You should have done that first!" Kwort cried, gasping out in pain. "You don't know what you're doing. You're going to kill us—"

"Shut up!" Stub snapped over his shoulder. "Or I'll toss you off the command deck."

Rose ignored Kwort, busy flying the unfamiliar ship. It was much more responsive than the *Purpose*. She tried to manually operate the thrusters and almost rammed them into the adjacent docking arm.

"Whoa, steady there, girl," she said under her breath. She switched to auto-pilot and input her request.

The ship pulled back, giving her a good view of the station. That fat battleship was a tempting target. As if on cue, weapons came up on the helm.

"Targeting the battleship," Rose announced.

"No!" Kwort started to exclaim, "I know people working on that ship—"

"Rose is captain of this ship," Stub interrupted, "and don't you forget it!" Even Shard glared at him.

The battleship was dead center in the imager.

"We were too quiet last time," Rose said flatly. "This time they'll remember us."

The battleship icon blinked with a red X.

"Target locked." Rose pressed the button. "Firing missiles."

Four blinking lights flashed onto the imager and into the battleship one after the other. At this close range, inside the shipyard's deflectors, the missiles tore into the unshielded battleship. Explosions ripped out from each entry point. As the internal atmosphere decompressed, the sparks were swallowed by larger explosions taking out huge chunks of the hull.

As the battleship lurched, the end of the docking arm bent. It moved slowly, collapsing under the tension. The other patrolship was dragged into the flaming battleship. Another explosion billowed out.

The docking arm fell slowly toward the next arm. Several docked ships were crushed in the fiery inferno.

Rose got the *Relevance* away as fast as possible using thrusters, silently urging the converter to cycle on already. They needed their legs.

Kwort groaned at the destruction she had wrought. "I'm done for! Every beacon in the Domain will have my face plastered on it!"

Rose knew she had used Kwort, but it had been necessary to save everyone. She would do it again in a heartbeat. "As long as the Domain enslaves Solians, we have to fight with everything we've got."

Nods of agreement came from Shard and Stub. She had her crew back.

The converter light came on. "Power up!" Rose announced. "Let's see what this baby's got!"

24

G'kaan was on the command deck of the *Endurance* when their scanners picked up the first ship. They had detected four gravity bursts, which meant there were three more ships following several hours behind this one. The *Endurance* was two pockets away from the Archernar shipyard, taking a little-used route through the outer Domain, so he had not expected to find this much traffic.

It didn't matter. Ships had been scattering before them as they plowed through the Archernar sector. Any ship that got within long-distance scanner range saw a battleship and assumed they were Fleet.

"According to our scanners, that's a Fleet patrolship," M'ke informed them.

"From the size of the gravity bursts," G'kaan agreed, "the other three are also patrolships."

"Perhaps they were alerted to us," L'pash suggested.

"Possible." G'kaan didn't think the Fleet would send four patrolships after a battleship. Not unless they severely underestimated the Qin's capabilities.

Soon the lead patrolship would be able to scan them.

It would be interesting to see if the ship turned away. The admiral's strategy prohibited striking planets and merchant shipping. But if a Fleet ship came within weapons range, they were free to attack.

The sector beacons were already buzzing with reports about the severe fuel rationing in the outer sectors of Canopus. Typically, nothing official was said. However, ships were having to venture to the inner sectors to refuel. Liberating Qin territory and stopping the flow of fuel ore had been an offensive as well as defensive strike against the Domain.

"If the first patrolship enters ID range, we'll take them out," G'kaan said quietly.

"And the other three?" M'ke asked.

"The same with them."

Everyone in command was silent as they watched their terminals and the imager as the patrolship came closer. Their course slowly neared the Fleet ship on a direct approach. No other ships were in long-distance scanner range. But they knew there were three more out there, likely on the same course.

"The patrolship is holding steady," M'ke finally said. "We are within range of their scanners."

"Battle alert," G'kaan announced. The lights flashed their warning as his order was carried through the ship. They were on ready status at all times, so his crew leaped instantly into action. They were eager to fight the Fleet, and this looked like the perfect opportunity to take out an entire squad in one stroke.

The command deck grew busy as the secondary stations were staffed. Chad arrived on the command deck as usual when there was an alert. He nodded to G'kaan and slid into his usual jumpseat.

Weapons were primed. The crew was ready. G'kaan intended to pursue even if the patrolship realized what it was facing and tried to run.

"Captain! I'm receiving a message from the patrolship," M'ke exclaimed.

G'kaan hesitated. He had never been hailed by a ship he was about to attack. But there was nothing to lose. Soon enough they would know his battleship was Qin.

"On imager," he ordered.

The starscape disappeared. The last person in the galaxy G'kaan expected to see appeared.

"Surprise!" Rose grinned at him merrily.

"Rose!" G'kaan stared at her. "What are you doing here?"

"What's a girl like me doing in a sector like this?" she retorted with a laugh.

Rose was wearing a brown Fleet flightsuit. It was too incongruous.

G'kaan looked at M'ke, who was checking his terminal. "She's in a Fleet patrolship, Captain."

Chad was laughing helplessly on one side of the command deck, shouting out his glee.

G'kaan ignored him. "What are you doing in a patrolship, Rose?" At the same moment, he saw the collar around her neck. "You were recaptured!"

"We needed to upgrade." She proudly patted the helm in front of her. *"Seventy-missile capacity with plenty of spares in storage. Long-range scanners are having some trouble, but Kwort says he can finish the repairs. This ship was in dock at the Archernar shipyard when we hijacked her."*

"Well done!" G'kaan exclaimed.

"We also blew up a battleship and some other ships along with a couple of docking arms on the shipyard,"

Rose added. *"So there's a few patrolships following us. You think you can help out with that?"*

"We're on it!" G'kaan bared his fangs. "We'll go into stealth mode and ambush them when they're too close to evade. Stay on course and continue past us."

"Good hunting," Rose acknowledged.

G'kaan nodded back, terminating the image. "Power down!"

The crew were already implementing his orders. This was their first real-time test of their stealthing ability without the benefit of any distracting mass nearby. The converter cycled off and shields were lowered. The barest essential systems were left running. Then he put his ship into a slow spin and drift. With the scanner jammers on, and the converter signature from Rose's ship between them and the patrolships, that should offer the energy-baffling they needed to make the *Endurance* look like nothing more than a large, free-range asteroid.

M'ke switched to passive scans as the command deck darkened, leaving a pool of light from the imager in the center of the room. It showed the *Endurance* and the approaching *Relevance,* Rose's new ship.

Since the battleship could only use passive scanners while in stealth, the other three patrolships wouldn't appear on the imager until they were practically within weapons range. If their stealth was as good as it was supposed to be, the *Endurance* would continue to look like a harmless chunk of rock and metal until then.

For once G'kaan agreed with his crew. He was more than ready for a fight.

Chad held tightly on to his seat during the long, tense, mostly silent wait. Rose's captured patrolship increasingly filled the imager, bearing down on their battleship. As the *Relevance* passed, they could see every seam of its shiny new hull. Rose's patrolship continued on and eventually disappeared out of their passive-scanner range.

In one moment, everything had changed for Chad. There was hope, more than hope, there was proven success. Rose had gotten them out again, and had acquired an even more powerful ship. The Domain could be beaten.

Captain G'kaan seemed confident about the approaching Fleet patrolships. But Chad felt exposed as they waited with no shields, as vulnerable as in a lifepod.

"Patrolship entering passive scanner range," M'ke announced. "And closing."

On the imager, a tiny ship appeared instead of an icon. It was much closer to the battleship than Chad had expected.

He leaned forward as another patrolship popped onto the imager.

"Prepare to drop stealth," G'kaan said calmly.

A chorus of ayes replied. They waited, as the patrolships swiftly came closer. Soon they would be in visual sight—

"Activate systems," the captain ordered.

Chad slapped the grav button on his seat. He didn't have anything to do except watch the crew. They worked together raising shields and powering up the ship.

"Targeting lasers," G'kaan announced.

Hardly a moment later, bright red lasers leapt from the *Endurance* and hit the lead incoming patrolship. It repeated again and again before the patrolships could react to evade.

At close range, the power of the battleship was too

great for their shields. It looked like the hull buckled under the pressure of dozens of hits, and the front end of the patrolship collapsed in on itself. The ship was engulfed in white-hot sparkles.

"Got him!" Chad exclaimed. He ignored L'pash's scowl in his direction.

Now that the scanners were activated, the other patrolships appeared in the imager. They changed course to escape.

G'kaan was already moving to intercept. Their battleship was faster than the patrolships so even from a dead stop, they gained on the first one quickly.

Command was practically swimming in blood lust. *No mercy!* was the silent cry. Chad remembered the colonists on Balanc, his sweet Newt, and he wanted them *all* dead.

"Targeting lasers," G'kaan repeated.

The second patrolship was pounded by the red beams. This time it was the fuel cells that ruptured first, blowing up the ship.

"Second target destroyed," M'ke confirmed.

G'kaan turned the *Endurance* and they pursued the third patrolship, now heading back to the grav slip as fast as it could.

The desire for revenge seemed to quickly carry them into weapons range.

"Targeting lasers," the captain said one final time.

Murmurs of agreement and encouragement rose in command. Chad joined in.

Their lasers struck the fleeing patrolship. G'kaan's expression was grim as he continued firing. It was ceaseless.

When the patrolship exploded, cheers erupted from

the crew. The captain concentrated on maneuvering to avoid the debris.

The outcry continued from the crew. Even L'pash was grinning, glancing at her cousin at auxiliary ops.

Then M'ke broke through. "I'm reading two lifepods!"

The imager focused in. Two lifepods were stabilizing their tumble.

"Lifesigns?" G'kaan asked.

"Four humanoids."

A long silence drew out. Chad knew how important stealth was to the Qin. It would be necessary to fire on those lifepods to silence the witnesses. Besides, none of them deserved to live.

He thought G'kaan would do it. He wanted the captain to do it. The others were leaning forward eagerly. L'pash was showing her fangs.

G'kaan entered commands into the terminal. The battleship slowly turned away from the debris, curving back around to head toward the distant *Relevance*.

The corpsmen cooled off slowly, realizing what they had been thinking. Chad noticed that the crew didn't look at each other, as if ashamed of themselves. Killing people in a lifepod was a violation of the most fundamental space law. But only G'kaan had been able to restrain himself.

"I'm receiving a message from the *Relevance*," M'ke said quietly.

"On the imager." G'kaan's voice was rough. Chad wondered how difficult it had been for him.

Rose appeared on the imager, her grin wider than ever. *"Good going, Captain!"*

G'kaan hardly responded; his gravity at killing so many people was clear. "It had to be done."

"And you always do it," Rose agreed.

"We'll rendezvous near the outer slip," G'kaan suggested. He gave Chad a glance. "I have one of your crew members, who would like to return to your ship."

Chad was starting to shake his head. Rose wouldn't care about him. He had run away from them. But G'kaan turned the eye in Chad's direction.

Rose's image faced him. *"Chad!"*

He cleared his throat. "Balanc was destroyed by a Fleet battleship. Newt was killed."

"Oh." Rose frowned a bit. *"So you want to rejoin my crew?"*

"If you'll have me, Captain."

She shrugged. *"We need experienced hands. You're welcome on board the* Relevance, *Chad."*

As G'kaan turned the viewer and made the arrangements to meet the patrolship, Chad felt an immense relief. He would work with Rose and her crew, teaching them everything G'kaan had taught him. Together they would be able to handle the Domain.

The captain signed off, then came over to Chad. "It was good having you on board, Chad. But you belong with Rose."

"I owe you, Captain." Chad clasped forearms. "If you ever need a Solian infiltrator, I'm your man."

"I'm sure we'll work together," G'kaan agreed.

Rose was glad to see that by the time they reached the outer slip, Kwort had finally gotten the long-range scanners working properly. She didn't like having to depend on the battleship to see what was around them.

It felt good to be back in command of her own ship again. And she was a beauty! Unlike the old *Purpose,* the *Relevance* was newly commissioned and had the latest technology. Their scanner range turned out to be as far as the *Endurance*'s. And the database was filled with information about Fleet protocols and patrol patterns. She used the encryption nodule to read secured Fleet messages left on the beacon, and sent everything to G'kaan. She trusted he would ransack the Domain and wanted him to have every tool he could use.

So she handled the airlock herself when they docked with the *Endurance*, hidden in the lee of the gravity slip. They had encountered no other ships during their voyage through the obscure pocket, but G'kaan had insisted on taking no chances.

Shard and Jot were waiting behind Rose, eager to see Chad.

As the hatch opened, Rose stepped forward. "Welcome aboard, G'kaan." Without waiting for any greeting, she prompted, "What do you think of my new ship?"

"Impressive." G'kaan came through the airlock and stood next to her, towering in the tall corridor. She grinned up at him. But there was a new, grim expression on his face. "You have a powerful weapon in your hands, Captain."

"I intend to use it," Rose assured him.

Chad appeared in the airlock behind G'kaan. He looked thinner and there was a reddish scar across the left side of his face and shaved head. Yet he met her eyes frankly, quite unlike his former surly self. "I'm glad to see you, Captain."

"Chad, welcome back." She had never liked him and he had bucked her authority at every turn. But he was one of her crew. He was also a helmsman and capable of commanding this ship, which was something she desperately needed right now.

Shard and Jot moved in to greet Chad with noisy kisses and hugs. Rose knew their meeting would be hard with Dab, Whit, and Mote presumed dead. Hopefully Kwort had gotten the rendezvous coordinates in the Mahrashatra sector right so they could pick up Nip.

Rose led G'kaan up to command, showing off the *Relevance*. From his sly references to her abilities and her Fleet uniform, she was sure he was also getting a kick out of seeing her in command of a patrolship.

They had already given each other a detailed report, but after the tour, there were a few things Rose wanted to clarify. "You said you captured Rikev Alpha, and he's on your ship right now."

They were standing over the engineering well, an immaculate white-plasteel edifice. Kwort was tweaking some of the main bots and giving a workshop to a handful of the new crew. Rose wasn't sure how to shake them down yet. They were dazed from their astonishing escape, but she needed them to run the ship.

"Yes, near the Picast system on the outer edge of Archernar."

Rose shook her head. "So Rikev wasn't on the *Conviction* when it blew up?"

"Yes, he was. That was Rikev 5G-177. We caught Rikev 6J-151."

"So it's not the same person."

G'kaan shook his head. "Depends on what you mean by that. The Rikev in my brig is a later cloned version of the Rikev series."

"Cloned?" Rose felt a deep repulsion at the idea. "How many Rikevs are there?"

"As far as we can tell, the regents don't assign more than one clone to a region. So there could be over a hundred Rikevs out there. Depending on how well they perform, their entire line can be considered for promotion or eventual extinction."

"That's—that's just wrong!"

"It's been their way for thousands of years." G'kaan realized he hadn't been as thorough in her training. "Ask Chad for some background information. He's pulled together some valuable research on the Domain."

Rose thought Chad must have changed to impress G'kaan. "So none of the Alphas are unique. They're only copies of each other?"

"The Alphas are trying to improve their race. Their offspring are made by geneticists who provide the creches with new citizens."

'I everyone cloned?" She glanced uneasily down at engineering. "Is Kwort a clone?"

"No, only the Alphas. Other humanoids are left to random chance and mutations. The Alphas think the lower ranks are genetically impure."

Rose didn't like it. On a gut level it felt wrong. She remembered those unpleasant sessions with the Alphas who had chosen her on the shipyard despite her contempt. They had violated her! And to think they were really automatons, an identical, unnatural army enslaving humans.

"I'm going to stop them," Rose declared flatly.

Amused, G'kaan glanced down. "How are you going to do that?"

She turned to face him, her thumbs hooked on her cartridge belt. "We're going to liberate Earth. We're going to kick the Fleet so far out of the Sol system that they'll think twice about ever coming back."

She expected him to scoff the way Gandre Li had.

Rose didn't care. She wasn't abandoning their goal again.

But G'kaan began to smile, the line in his forehead easing. "That's it! You're brilliant, Rose!"

"You like my plan?" she countered. "That's a first."

"It's exactly what we've been looking for. I've been ordered to distract the Domain from Qin. What better way than by cutting off their pipeline of pleasure slaves?"

It was her turn to be surprised. "You mean you'll help us?"

"We can do it!" G'kaan was practically laughing. "With your patrolship and our battleship, we can do it."

Rose let out a whoop that frightened everyone in engineering. She didn't care. "Then let's get started planning our attack!"

25

Ash didn't have anything to do on board the *Relevance*, and that seemed only right. It was strange to hear from Jot that s/he had once been the second-in-command of the *Purpose*. It didn't make sense that s/he had helped Rose run the ship. Ash trusted Rose implicitly. Sometimes Rose talked to Ash, but not often. She was too busy. Instead, Ash spent hir time with Jot and Shard, or watching the others play in the lounge and have sex in the day cabin.

It took many days to reach the place where they were supposed to wait for another ship. Shard was happy because Nip was returning. Ash didn't remember Nip, or the new arrival, Chad. Chad seemed upset about it, but it didn't really affect hir.

Meanwhile there was a lot of excitement going on, with Rose talking to the Qin battleship all the time. Ash wasn't interested in any of it. The one thing that lodged in hir mind was something Jot had innocently dropped: Rikev Alpha was a prisoner on the battleship. The name didn't mean anything to Ash, but Jot told hir that Rikev had been hir last master and he had sent hir to be incinerated. But S'jen's attack on the spacepost had saved hir life.

Ash had been told a lot of things about hir past, but this one bothered hir the most. It felt like it touched on something s/he almost remembered. Maybe it was supposed to stay forgotten. It was easy drifting in a pleasant fog with no worries and no pain.

Yet s/he couldn't stop thinking about Rikev Alpha, a faceless person who had dominated hir life. S/he couldn't remember him.

Finally one day, Ash asked Jot, "Can I see Rikev Alpha?"

Jot's eyes got very wide. "You don't want to do that!"

"Why not?"

"He did horrible things to you."

Ash tried to think, but it was a mist. "I don't remember."

"You still have the marks on you," Jot told hir.

Surprised, Ash glanced down at hirself. Hir body was covered by the brown flightsuit, but at night s/he saw the ridges and scars, some of them recent. Even hir hands were marked, a deep trough down one slender palm, and a crooked third finger on the other.

Ash was breathing harder, and Jot tried to calm hir down. "You can't see Rikev, so stop thinking about it. He's on the battleship."

After a while Jot left, but Ash kept thinking about it.

Eventually s/he got up from aimlessly flipping through the viewer and left the lounge. S/he knew the command deck was somewhere nearby.

Ash checked every door until s/he found the command deck on the upper level. Terminals formed a circular room with the imager and main stations in the center. It gleamed with intimidating complexity.

Rose stood up and came over to hir. "Ash, are you lost?"

"Yes," s/he said, realizing it was true. "I wanted to talk to you."

Rose smiled, putting her hands on her hips. It looked right now that she was wearing a flightsuit instead of a slave tunic. Even though Ash didn't like the color brown.

"Sure," Rose said. "We're drifting in the lee, waiting for Gandre Li to arrive. They must have taken a longer route than us."

None of that made sense to Ash. S/he wished Rose would go back to asking hir if s/he was lost.

Rose looked instantly at hir. "Is something wrong, Ash?"

"Yes!" S/he grabbed on to that. "I've been thinking about seeing Rikev Alpha. I want to, that is I think I want to see him."

"You think?" Rose asked with a laugh. "Okay, why not? We might as well dock now while we're waiting."

"I can see him?" Ash asked.

"Sure," Rose agreed, and she went into a flurry of activity.

Before Ash knew it, they were going down to the airlock. S/he felt hir stomach lurch. "Do I want to do this?" s/he asked Rose at the airlock.

"You said you did," Rose pointed out.

"Jot thought it wasn't a good idea."

Rose took hir arm. "Then that's the best reason I know for doing it. Jot is a sweet girl, but she's not fit to guide anyone's life."

Ash thought about that, and realized s/he did prefer to put hirself in Rose's hands. Rose had taken responsibility for them many times before. "Okay, I want to see Rikev Alpha."

Rose popped the hatch. "One Alpha coming up."

If Ash thought the *Relevance* was bewildering, the Qin battleship was more so. The scale and proportions were bigger, along with the number of people. The colors, the lighting, and the feel of the decks were different on the battleship. It was a marvel to hir tender senses.

A tall Qin greeted hir, and s/he saw the familiar distress pass over his dark face when s/he didn't recognize him. He spoke to Rose. "What can we do to help hir?"

"There's not much in the medical database." Rose sounded angry. "If you've got any ideas, G'kaan, we'd be glad to try anything."

"I'll let you know." G'kaan turned to Ash. "Rose said you wanted to see Rikev Alpha. Are you sure about this?"

Ash felt the formality of the question. "Yes."

G'kaan gestured for hir to follow. "We're holding him in the brig. He is weakened now by the serneo-inhibitor. We're piecing together what he's been doing here in Archernar. We don't want to rush our investigation."

"What've you got so far?" Rose asked.

"He's visited every Fleet station except for Starbase C-4 in the Archernar sector. And he was sent by Heloga Alpha, the regional commander of Canopus."

G'kaan opened a door next to another complex terminal, staffed by an enormous female Qin who stood as G'kaan approached. Ash followed them into a long room lined on one side by cells. G'kaan gestured to one in the middle.

Rose and Ash went closer. S/he could see that there was a shimmer between them and the man inside. It was a screen made of finely crossed wires.

"Don't touch the barrier," G'kaan warned hir. "It will give you a shock. Not lethal, but it is painful."

The man inside stood in the center of the cell, his hands behind his back. He had a distinctive Alphan head, with a strong-boned face and a high forehead. His skin was a rich gold, and his eyes were large and black.

"I've seen him before!" Rose exclaimed, pushing up next to the mesh. "That's the Alpha who took you at the shipyard. He tortured you, Ash!"

Rikev's expression hardly shifted, but Ash could tell he knew hir. S/he had become adept at reading it in people's eyes.

S/he searched his face and hands. Were those hands familiar? Yes, more so than any other part of him.

And yet . . . "I don't remember," Ash confessed.

"You don't remember him?" Rose demanded. "It happened."

The Alpha lifted one corner of his mouth, a self-satisfied smirk. Something inside of Ash shifted, but s/he felt a great weight supporting hir. It was impenetrable.

"No," s/he said sadly. "I don't remember."

"It was something *he* did to you," Rose told hir. "It was his fault."

G'kaan said, "He's paying for it, I assure you. We'll wring him dry before we're through."

Rikev Alpha was back to his bland self, seemingly undisturbed by his situation. Ash saw his implacable sense of rightness.

The comm beeped, and there was an announcement. *"Command deck to captain."*

G'kaan acknowledged, "Captain here."

"Our remote comm is picking up a ship approaching."

G'kaan acknowledged, as Rose said, "We've got to get back, Ash. We need to undock."

Ash looked into Rikev's eyes, but they were telling hir nothing. Empty of all meaning. But it was an illusion. He had the answers if only he would speak.

But the lights were flashing and people were rushing, so Ash followed Rose out of the brig. Rose was disappointed, but Ash didn't know what to feel.

Yet as s/he passed through the airlock back to the *Relevance*, Ash knew s/he had gained one thing from seeing Rikev. S/he wanted to know *why*. Why did this happen to hir?

Back on board the *Relevance*, Rose ran off to tend to everything that was important, and Ash realized that s/he would have to find hir way back to hir berth. It was frustrating wandering through corridors, so s/he decided to find and memorize a map of the *Relevance* as soon as s/he reached the lounge. Even if s/he couldn't remember the past, s/he could remember things that had happened since Rose had shoved hir under the waterfall.

It would have to be a start. S/he had to start living again.

Gandre Li slowed the *Solace* when they picked up the innermost gravity slip on her long-range scanners. Trace had given her the coordinates deep inside the Mahrashatra sector where they had arranged to meet Rose. A decnight had passed since they left the Archernar shipyard.

During the drop-off in the Carlidse system, Gandre Li had heard lurid reports of the attack on the Archernar shipyard. Since then, the beacons had been filled with unsubstantiated sightings of a Qin battleship. Rumor said the Qin had attacked the shipyard.

Gandre Li had talked to Jor about it, feeling strange
that she couldn't discuss it with Trace. Jor wasn't sure
what to make of it either. Had Rose and the other slaves
escaped from the shipyard? Or had something entirely
different happened after the *Solace* left?

As they approached the slip, Gandre Li told Danal,
"Open a channel."

"Ready," Danal replied.

"Ship in the lee!" Gandre Li announced, even though
their scanners couldn't see inside. "Come out or I'll assume
you're a hostile raider. I am prepared to fire missiles."

She cut the comm and nodded to Danal. He sent it.
To make sure her threat was backed up, she activated
weapons. The distinctive yellow lights on the helm
began to flash.

Jor quickly came onto the command deck and took
the seat at ops. They knew how dangerous this was. A
Fleet patrolship could be waiting inside the lee for them.

Gandre Li knew it the instant Trace entered the command deck. She was distracted by the diminutive Solian,
standing quietly to the side. Gandre Li could see her
from the corner of her eye.

"There's movement in the lee," Danal reported. "A
ship is emerging."

Gandre Li focused on her navigational scanners to
confirm. On the imager, a midsized ship appeared.

"It's the *Relevance*," Danal added.

"That's a Fleet patrolship." Gandre Li prepared to
panic. But its ID correlated with one of the two patrolships that had flanked the battleship at the shipyard.

"We're being hailed on an encrypted channel."

Gandre Li took a deep breath and looked at the imager, making sure the viewer could see only her. "Put 'em on."

A woman in a brown Fleet uniform appeared. But it was all wrong.

Gandre Li abruptly realized it was Rose, with her tousled brown hair and laughing black eyes. *"Scared you for a second, didn't I?"*

"You escaped," Gandre Li said flatly.

"You bet, and we have four stunguns to return to you," Rose agreed. *"They came in handy."*

"Well, forget it, would you? I mean really." Gandre Li was even more irritated now that she knew the Solians had succeeded. "Stop dragging me into your revolts!"

"You can always come to Earth if you change your mind," Rose taunted.

"Don't tell me anything!" Gandre Li protested. "I don't want to know. Let's get this over with."

"Fine, I think you have a crew member of mine."

"Yes," Gandre Li said flatly. "And Trace will be joining you, too."

Trace gasped behind her. Jor turned to look at her, and even Danal seemed startled.

"I did ask Trace once before," Rose agreed. *"We'd be glad to have her."*

"Let's move into the lee," Gandre Li suggested.

"It's too full," Rose equivocated.

Gandre Li didn't want to know what was in there. "Fine! I'll handle the docking." She had visions of Rose ramming that armored ship into her courier. She wasn't going to take any chances. "You hold still."

"In spite of everything, you don't think much of us Solians, do you?"

Gandre Li couldn't begin to answer that. "Prepare to dock."

She cut off the channel, and Rose's defiant face disappeared. She said to Trace over her shoulder, "Get Nip and go to the port airlock."

Trace came forward, her voice choked with tears. "You're throwing me off the ship?"

Gandre Li almost said yes to end the torment, but she couldn't lie. Not with those pleading eyes looking at her. "You don't have to be a slave anymore. I want you to be free. Now go, so I can dock us before we're seen."

Trace shook her head silently and ran out of command.

Gandre Li didn't look at Danal or Jor. She concentrated on doing what she did best, maneuvering her graceful ship into position next to the powerful *Relevance*. She had to admit that seeing Rose in command of a patrolship was frightening. Gandre Li was not happy with what she had unleashed on the Domain. She had been led far from what she had been taught, all because of her feelings for Trace.

When Gandre Li clamped the docking arm in place, she rose to go down to the airlock. She would have to see Nip one more time. And she would have to say her final good-bye to Trace.

"Captain," Jor said. "Are you sure you want to let Trace go? I know how much you care about her."

"She doesn't have to be a slave anymore," Gandre Li doggedly repeated.

Jor and Danal exchanged looks. Maybe they didn't understand how she felt about Trace. If she treated Trace like a slave now, it would negate everything they'd had together. Gandre Li would have to admit she had been fooling herself for years, and that Trace loved her only because she had to. Trace had replaced her bio-family after she had lost them. She knew what love was, and she couldn't allow her feelings for Trace to be less than real.

Gandre Li walked through the corridors without seeing anything. She felt far removed from herself. She was firmly on the wrong side of justice by helping these pleasure slaves escape. Surely that would catch up to her someday. It was only a matter of time before disaster struck.

This was her first and worst punishment—losing Trace.

Gandre Li pressurized the airlock to prepare it to open. Technically the patrolship was the larger and more powerful ship, so Rose should open her airlock first. She could see someone on the other side and hoped they knew what they were doing.

Voices carried as Nip and Trace approached. Trace was carrying a small bag. Nip was as empty-handed as when he came onto the ship.

Gandre Li swallowed hard and turned away. She popped open the hatch on their side.

The hatch on the patrolship was open, and voices called out Nip's name. He hesitated in front of Gandre Li, then ducked his head. "Thank you for everything, Captain. You saved my life."

"Yes," she managed to reply.

Nip turned to Trace and grinned. "Sure you don't want to come with me?"

"No, I love Gandre Li too much to leave." Trace held out the bag. "Don't forget your things."

"This is mine?" he asked.

"It's your ball and some other stuff. And there's a holo of me, too." She gave him a hug. "I've enjoyed our time together, Nip. You've shown me a lot about what it means to be human."

Nip hugged her back, seemingly unconcerned about Trace's refusal. A grin split his face as he turned to the airlock. "Shard! *Chad!* What are you doing here?"

As Nip went through the airlock, Trace watched with watery eyes, smiling sadly.

Gandre Li couldn't believe it. "Aren't you going with them? They're your people."

Trace put an arm around her waist. "I belong here with you."

Gandre Li didn't believe it. But Rose was handing a netted bag with the four stunguns through the airlock. "Thanks for the help!" Rose tossed off nonchalantly.

Gandre Li automatically took them, still looking at Trace.

"I'm not coming," Trace told Rose.

"Your choice," Rose said with a shrug.

"Yes, it is my choice," Trace agreed.

Rose gave an airy wave. Then the airlock on the other side was closing, and it only remained for Gandre Li to close her hatch.

Gandre Li hit the pad to seal the airlock and turned to Trace. "You're staying with me?"

"I'm here," Trace agreed, watching for her reaction.

Gandre Li couldn't help it. "I don't think you realize what you're giving up, Trace. You have your freedom now. You should go with the Solians."

"I choose to stay with you, if you'll have me."

It was too good to be true. But Gandre Li knew that Trace had been conditioned from childhood to serve.

How could Trace really know what she wanted? She wanted to comm Rose and order her to open that airlock again so Trace could go where she belonged.

But Trace's eyes filled with tears. "Don't you love me anymore?"

"Yes! Yes, that's not the question, Trace." She struggled to say it. "You had to . . . care about me because you were my slave. I never realized how wrong it was to . . . force you to be mine. I can't do that to you anymore."

Trace came closer, lifting her freckled face. "Oh, Gandi! That's not what we have. I love you. Of my own free will. I always have."

Gandre Li slowly realized that her dream of living her life with Trace wasn't dead as she had thought. The future which had seemed so bleak and lonely without her lover was transformed with dizzying speed. The *Solace* wouldn't be empty and bereft, it would once again be their private refuge from the galaxy. Trace wanted to be with her.

Gandre Li pulled Trace to her, hugging her tight. Her relief and pent-up frustration made her tremble. "You want to be with me!"

Trace nestled in her arms. "I couldn't be anywhere else."

26

~~~

Heloga let out a piercing scream when Winstav and Felenore told her what happened in Qin. "You led their battleships back to the Domain?"

"They know where the Domain is, Regional Commander," Winstav said dryly. "The point is, at least one Qin battleship has invaded your region."

"You didn't stop them!" she screeched, unable to control herself. At least they could hardly see her in the shadows carefully crafted around her desk.

Felenore cleared her throat. "We destroyed four of their planets with maximum casualties."

"The natives on those planets processed the ore on the mining stations!" Heloga tried not to wring her hands. The skin was so fragile. "The fuel supply has dried up while you've been roaming around out there, running away from the Qin—"

Winstav abruptly stood up. "We're here on regents' business, Heloga Alpha. It is our task to judge you and how *you* have handled this situation. Currently, your region has been invaded by hostile aliens. Unless you cooperate with us, our report to the regents on this situation will not be favorable to you."

Heloga sat very still. "What do you want?"

Winstav lifted one corner of his mouth. "We'll let you know. You'll give us whatever we need to destroy the Qin. And you will cooperate with our strategy. Understood?"

She almost couldn't say it, but it was clear. She was in their hands. "Agreed."

Felenore followed Winstav out as Heloga didn't move. She had to ally with them, but she could control the situation at the same time. She would figure out a way.

"Lights up," she said absently.

The lights brightened and she turned to look in the mirror she had mounted under her desk. Her bio tech was brilliant, though most of the muscles in her face were now immobilized. Fanrique had argued that if the foundation were firm, the surface would be. Heloga had to agree that it was rejuvenating her porcelain skin, even though it was impossible for her to frown or smile or make much of any expression. She had kept barely enough mobility to speak—

Heloga took one look and let out another shriek.

It happened in front of her eyes. As her mouth opened, it stretched the skin on either side.

Instantly she stopped, letting her lips go slack. Two deep troughs split open the skin by her mouth, from her nose to her chin. Bits of skin were flaking off, widening the cracks with every breath.

She stared, but there was nothing to be done. She couldn't hide this. It couldn't be repaired. Her skin was turning to dust in front of her eyes.

Tomorrow everyone would know. They would know that she was dying. And they would know that her region had been invaded.

Heloga flung the mirror into the wall, watching it shatter.

She wasn't going to be overrun by rapid hordes trying to bury her before she was dead. She would fight them every step of the way. She would make them rue the day they crossed Heloga Alpha!

About the Author

Susan Wright grew up mostly in Arizona and has lived in New York City for fifteen years. She has written nine Star Trek novels: *Dark Passions* 1 & 2, *Gateways: One Small Step*, *Badlands* 1 & 2, *The Best and the Brightest*, *The Tempest*, *Violations*, and *Sins of Commission*. Susan also writes nonfiction books on art and popular culture, including: *New York in Old Photographs*, *UFO Headquarters: Area 51*, and *Destination Mars*. Susan received her masters in Art History from New York University in 1989. Her Web site is: www.susanwright.info